Harsh Lessons

L. J. Kendall

The Leeth Dossier Vol.2

**For Patricia Mary Buttel (Patsy), 1928 – 2016.
Self-effacing world traveler, and deeply loving
and loved aunt**

National Library of Australia Cataloguing-in-Publication entry (paperback : A-format edition)

Creator: Kendall, L. J., author.

Title: Harsh lessons / by L. J. Kendall.

ISBN: 9781925430073 (paperback : A-format edition)

Series: Kendall, L. J. Leeth dossier ; Vol 2.

Subjects: Magic--Fiction.
 Fantasy fiction.
 Science fiction.

Dewey Number: A823.4

Story length: 90,000 words
Typeface: Georgia 9pt

This book is available as an A or B-format paperback, and in ebook formats.

Original release: Oct 2017. (First A-format edition.)
Release version: 9. Sep 2024. (Fixed some tiny typos)

Found the take on magic ability appealingly different and couldn't put these books down! Hurry up 2017 for the next one."

"While I quite liked the first book I thought this one was better. It was strong in many of the places where the first book was weak. [...]At risk of additional spoilers, Leeth FINALLY starts to come into her own and standing up to Harmon. But not before she has to suffer yet more abuse. [...] I'd actually recommend somebody jumping straight into this book as you are more likely to enjoy it, and then if you like it and want the background try reading the first."

"Much better then the first book which was also very good. I highly recommend this series."

"A sequel as good as the original. Great premise, great characters, good character development and well done action scenes. I found myself putting off things that needed doing to continue reading. It's a grabber of a book. I am eagerly awaiting the next book in the series."

"Not what I was expecting but even better! I am sucked in and can't wait for more! There are a lot of characters developing. I can envision great things from the Author. This book series could make a good TV series but definitely too long for movies."

"I am not one to read dark, mind twisted stories. [...]At the same time the message I received and got was there is always hope. [...] Yet I still read the book and will continue to read the books in this series because for me the author is just that good. [...] This not for everyone and the story is hard to read a times. I will say at one point I actually laughed out loud, and with the way the story is I did not think I would. [...] I am so torn with this book and the series and I hope the author does not disappoint because everyone one needs a hero, and everyone wants to be one, and everyone wants the bad guys to get what's coming to them."

*(As of October 2017, **Harsh Lessons** averaged 4.31 stars out of 5 on Goodreads, and 4.6 out of 5 on Amazon)*

ACKNOWLEDGMENTS

I want to thank my wife, Dr Stella St. Clair-Kendall, for her love and encouragement over the years. Missing you, darling.

An ongoing thanks to Jon Marshall for his insight, support, and help in shaping Leeth over two decades.

Sincere thanks also to http://www.ThEditors.com for Dave's insights and advice. Here's hoping the next book won't need cutting in half! (And thanks for the Superman bit.) If you see a problem, you've probably found a spot where I ignored his advice.

Special thanks again to Mirella de Santana, the artist who designs my covers. Check out more of her fantastic art at http://www.mirellasantana.com.br/

Thanks, too, to the Online Writing Workshop for Science Fiction, Fantasy and Horror, and the writers who reviewed a good number of these chapters at https://sff.onlinewritingworkshop.com/, more than a few years ago.

Thank you, all.

PS: I don't think you *need* to have read vol 1 to enjoy this!

Note: there's a special offer if you're 1st to inform me of an error in the text – see the Afterword for details.

Novels by L. J. Kendall

The Leeth Dossier:

> *Wild Thing*
>
> *Harsh Lessons*
>
> *Shadow Hunt*
>
> *Violent Causes*

The Leeth Dossier:

> *Lost Girl*
>
> *(Cold Heart?*
>
> *...)*

PROLOGUE

"She's a monster."

The older man did not reply. Ensconced in his white leather chair behind the expanse of gleaming white desk, 'Eagle' waited, studying him. Receding gray hair, strong jaw, and *intense* hazel eyes burned beneath heavy salt-and-pepper eyebrows. It was the eyes that had earned him his codename. The eyes, and his unique position.

Garland leaned forward, avoiding the empty vase to rest his knuckles on the polished surface. His own eyes narrowed to meet that unsettling stare. "A homicidal maniac in a girl's body."

He glared at the seated man, dismissing his cybernetic system's helpful offer to initiate combat mode. "Her so-called uncle may be worse. Yet *you* want them both."

Eagle ignored his anger; just as he'd ignored his pacing, his refusal to take a seat – and his destructive capacity. Garland fought the urge to clench his fists.

"What makes you think I want them, Detective Garland?" The deep voice was mellow, quiet. So very sure of itself.

Garland frowned, resisting the impression that Eagle could read his thoughts. He forced himself to relax. "Get real. You had my team and I bring them here before they'd even been processed. It's pretty fucking obvious. Sir."

"Good."

Garland scowled. This whole situation stank. He was glad he had his team tapping his audio stream: just in case. But something *right now* was screaming at him; demanding his attention....

His eyes fell to the sculpted glass vase.

The flowers were gone.

Only the stalks remained; with a faint scent of charring in the air, and a dusting of ash around the slender, aquamarine-tinted swirls of glass on the otherwise bare desk.

At the spike in adrenaline his augments went straight to combat mode. Neural parsers and additional electronic sensors powered up, all feeding data to the emergency threat-response system.

The two empty seats facing the lustrous desk were still warm – vacated less than ninety seconds before, the combat-comp told him. The charcoal smell: combustion of organic plant matter, probability 95%. Also detected: ozone. Analysis: laser cannon, 1.5-2kW, fired 5-10 mins ago. Active electrical current flows: nil.

Eagle simply sat, watching him. Apparently untroubled by seeing the heavily-cybered head of New Francisco's PASWAT team humming at full combat readiness.

Garland allowed himself the briefest of smiles. With a two kilowatt laser cannon in here? *Shit. No wonder he's calm!* He pinged his team, acknowledging their response even as he thought. *He wants me to know he wanted them.* "Why do you care what a mere detective thinks? Sir." *Does he want a hostile assessment?*

"Because I reviewed the report on your team's detection and apprehension, two years ago, of 'The God of 34th Street'." Eagle smiled. "It impressed me. You're an insightful man, Detective Garland."

"What makes you think that was my thinking alone? My team-"

Eagle cut him off. "Yes, yes. Let's skip ahead." The eyes locked on his. "The return of magic was a game changer. Tell me, Garland: do you want to see our nation return to its former role of the world's pre-eminent superpower?"

The large man snorted. "Do we even *deserve* to?"

For the first time, Eagle looked annoyed. "You'd prefer to trust China as the steward of humanity's best interests? Or *Newtopia?*"

Garland scowled. "I'm just a cop. World politics...." Staring at Eagle, he fitted two facts together: the Bureau's goal of restoring US influence, and a killer who looked like butter wouldn't melt in her mouth. "No fucking way. The United States does not use goddamned assassins! That's insane!"

Eagle looked simultaneously annoyed, surprised, and pleased. "Really? *You* know power corrupts, Garland. And magic changed the game for the worse. How do you think living 'gods' feel about democracy?

"But take a moment to consider the sensitivity of the information you've just deduced; the consequences should it become public."

Fuck! I'm transmitting this to my team. He stopped streaming, sent a signal to them – and received no response.

Holy Hannah! He'd been sequestered from the net. How was that even possible? He met Eagle's gaze.

Eagle watched, something in his eyes too knowing, as if somehow aware of exactly what Garland was feeling. As if he had... Garland wanted to groan: *of course* he'd have a whole array of bio-monitors measuring the stress levels of his 'guests'.

And as he realized that, Eagle nodded, microscopically. "Yes, Garland. Now send me the decryption key."

To the audio stream. Garland's face, although still expressionless, had paled.

"You'll want to take that seat now, Adam."

He did. Eagle accepted the short personal-range transmission with an inclination of his head, then shut his eyes for several seconds to examine the results.

Garland's weapons-comp was having a small meltdown, spamming his visuals with possible sight-lines for the laser cannon while simultaneously trying and failing to re-establish a net link. He sat, ignoring it. Certain that if Eagle didn't want him to leave the room, he never would.

Scant seconds later, Eagle opened his eyes again, pinning Garland to the chair. "Good: the decrypted contents confirm the stream destination was your own team, not some more *external* party."

Garland felt dazed.

"Let me welcome you to the Bureau of Internal Development." Eagle's smile was merciless.

"It was that, or have you killed." Eagle allowed him a full three seconds to absorb the bombshell. "Before you relax too far, though, let me make one thing clear: the Bureau's operations require the highest security we can achieve. You have no idea of the forces aligned against us.

Would you care to guess the penalty for your attempted transmission of our conversation?"

Garland straightened. "I accept full responsibility, sir. The secure channel was set up at my request. Not my team's."

"Very well. In view of your exemplary record, and upon my own authority, we can let the matter end here. Especially as you'll find your team received not one byte.

"But you need to re-evaluate your attitude, Garland. Do you have any concerns about trusting the Bureau, or my own capabilities?"

"No, sir. No concerns."

Eagle looked at him, then sighed. "Very well. I've read your report, and I'm happy to hear the mages were able to revive your colleagues, Berlusconi and Irons. I also know you're annoyed by my transfer of the offenders to the Bureau. Let me reassure you there is good reason for that."

"Yes, sir." Anyone who knew Garland would have known the flat response meant he was far from reassured.

Eagle waited.

Garland said nothing.

Eagle's expression changed. "I must say, reading your report, I was surprised how poorly the much-vaunted lead PASWAT team of New Francisco fared in the execution of its duty this evening. You were given every co-operation at the Institute. You were directed to the private rooms of Dr Harmon. There, you found his young charge bound and helpless.

"Yet you and four of your best – a team of six, counting my own agent, 'Stark' – was almost taken down by an unarmed teenage girl. Within sixty seconds of her release."

Garland's expression seemed to close in even further. "Yes, sir." His gaze was now as friendly as that of a Colt Terminator.

"Would you care to expand on your report?"

"It's all there."

Eagle simply looked at him for long seconds. "No. Not for my purposes. It covers just the bald facts. And for me to do *my* job, in our *nation's* service, today I need you to trust me enough to share your frank *impressions* of the two offenders."

One thing Garland knew about the coyly-named 'Bureau of Internal Development' – the secretive agency created, it was said, by the man now questioning him – everyone knew: Eagle always won. Never even made mistakes. Or if he did, always managed to make them look like pre-planned moves that won even bigger in the end.

The fact was, the more he thought about it, the surer he was that the whole thing had been orchestrated. Orchestrated, by the man in front of him.

As he remembered how his team had become involved at all, Garland's suspicions finally gelled. *To hell with this*, he decided. Their gazes locked, and Garland rose to his feet again.

"My *impression* is that my team was set up: that you specifically wanted a PASWAT team to attempt to bring those two in; that your own agent Stark was used to feed my team *mis*-information. My *impression* is that this was a test. Of me, maybe, or..."

Eagle watched.

"No, it wasn't me, or my team; or her magician 'uncle'. It was the girl, wasn't it? This was all a test of the fucking *girl!*"

He bent back down, putting his fists on the desk. "And maybe you do it with your own people, but I don't like people playing games with the lives of *my* team." Garland's look openly challenged.

"Better." Eagle laced his fingers together. "What makes you think Stark fed you false information?"

It was not the response Garland had expected, and he hesitated a moment. "He'd been there undercover for over a week. He was friendly with 'Sara' and, I assume, properly trained. Yet he gave us *no* indication we should expect any trouble from her." For a moment, Garland thought perhaps Eagle was smiling. The impression was fleeting.

"Consider – your own report clearly shows the *girl* was the real threat, not the magician. Could Stark have simply demonstrated a spectacular lack of perception?"

Garland scowled. "Are you saying he wasn't there to smoke us?"

"Correct. How did Stark seem afterward to you? It's not in your report."

"Well... I'd have to say it was like he was in shock."

"And how did he seem today? I hear you called in on him."

Did you, now, Garland thought, somehow not surprised. "Still seemed pretty out of phase," he admitted. He mulled over the implications. "You were testing the girl, Sara. Twice. First, you wanted to see what she could do to an agent sent in unaware, with no preconceptions: Stark. Then, to a group who were prepared, but not for anything specific."

Eagle ignored the remarks. "And your assessment of her?"

It was all the confirmation he was going to get, Garland realized. He considered the question. "Surprising. Dangerous." His eyes narrowed. "Unnaturally strong, and apparently aware of us outside the room-"

"Not the facts, Garland. I have those. Your *impressions.*"

"Unpredictable. A killer – as I said at the start of our meeting, probably a psychopath."

"And the mage?"

Garland raised one eyebrow. "I suspect *you* know better than I do. I only caught him in the middle of molesting a teenager. For all I know, that's exactly what you need!"

Eagle sighed, more tiredly. "Very well, Garland, thank you for your frank opinions. But at the Bureau for Internal Development you will need to work on keeping your emotions in check. We swim with sharks; and they *do* enjoy the scent of blood."

Garland's eyes narrowed.

"And don't worry, I won't ask you to work with the girl or her guardian."

Garland saw the unspoken rider: *Not ever.*

He frowned.

CHAPTER 1

Agent Emma Salt, her slim figure hugged by the white, zip-fastened cat-suit, followed the maze of underground corridors leading to the Department's private dojo and gymnasium. The new inductee would be there, having her first session with Paul Kawatsu. *A first session with Dojo in the dojo.* She shook her head. Why did Paul's unimaginative code name bother her so much? The wrongness of it was like an itch she couldn't quite reach. Maybe the *other* new inductee could tell her – he was a trained psychologist, Mother had said. She wondered what he'd be like. And the girl, too. Young, they'd said.

Gods! She was actually excited by the prospect of a new face. *I've been between missions too long.* She wished James were back. But a new face would do as well, for a while.

Of course, each person joined the Bureau with a clean slate and no obligation to discuss their past. *Thank god!* Although in practice – with sympathetic listeners who were sworn to secrecy – well, things came out in their own time. Meanwhile, though, there was the opportunity to penetrate a pleasant little mystery from whatever inadvertent clues were dropped.

Sometimes it wasn't hard, sometimes it was. Take Paul, for instance. With his Japanese background and knowledge of that country's criminal underground, it had suggested Yakuza membership – except for the lack of tattoos. The truth, in the end, had turned out to be stranger.

Of the new pair's history, she gathered even Father and Mother, the nominal Heads of the Department, knew little. Less, even, than Eagle normally passed along with one of his 'finds.' They'd told her the man, the girl's legal guardian, was a mage – *about time we had one again, too* – and a researcher in magical theory, which was impressive. He was to be called simply the Doctor. The girl's name was 'Leeth,' and apparently there was something strange about that, from the look Father and Mother had exchanged. Father had stressed her youth, and that she would receive special mental training from 'the Doctor' and intense martial arts training from Dojo. They'd also asked Emma to be friendly, but to avoid any philosophical discussions of the ethics of combat, or morals in general.

Emma considered those last points, recalling the look on Mother's face – she'd *not* been happy. Emma wasn't at all sure she herself liked the direction the clues were leading – martial arts training, immorality, and a strange name that suggested the word 'lethal.'

Most disquieting, though, were the final, casual instructions. "Oh, and in the interest of clear communication, use plain English with our new colleagues. We don't want to burden them with learning our technical jargon." *So they were disposables?* Perhaps that explained Mother's unhappiness. Perhaps.

Her mood lightened as she turned the corner into the final stretch of corridor, the overhead lighting tuned to match the leafy woodland scene displayed on the corridor walls. On her left, a swallow dipped low under a branch, reappearing on the wall to her right before disappearing in amongst the trees, heading deeper into the forest. Sometimes she wished she could step into that landscape and follow them. She sighed in appreciation. If they did have to spend so much of their time buried in these deep concrete corridors, at least the Department went to the trouble of brightening them up. She wondered what Checkbook had thought of the expense. No doubt Eagle had simply overridden his objections.

She was near the dojo now, and a thump from beyond the double swing doors recalled her own introduction to Paul's teaching techniques. She smiled wryly. It had been an ego-battering experience. She'd been glad James and Preacher had been there to share the suffering. Even Father had trained with Paul, bearing the punishment without complaint: the old man was tougher than you'd guess. She wondered how the new recruit would handle it, alone.

The sound of bare feet slapping the floor at a running pace met her as Emma reached the doors. Looking through the small perspex window into the room beyond, she was just in time to see a young woman's body arc gracefully into the air and land with a bone-jarring slam on the blue mats on the floor. Emma winced in sympathy, but watched with interest.

Paul, of course, looked completely fresh, and completely in control. The girl lay stunned, briefly, before rolling to one side and pushing herself up onto hands and knees, breathing hard.

"Never lose your temper," Paul admonished. "Head and heart must balance. When the animal dominates, judgment vanishes – strength undirected is easily deflected."

Ahh. They're at that *stage.* So 'Leeth' must have some degree of skill. And a temper, too, since this *was* her very first session.

The girl didn't respond, merely stayed on all fours, her sides heaving, drenched in sweat. Her hands were bunching up the material of the mat she crouched on. Emma frowned. From memory, that stuff was really quite tough, you couldn't-

The muscles of the girl's legs were subtly tightening, her weight shifting microscopically. Then she was up, flying toward Paul even as she spun into a flashing crescent kick. She was fast!

But Paul was ready, of course. Swaying aside, he pivoted then chopped down and back – a powerful elbow-strike into her side which the girl absorbed without a sound. Emma winced again, then more so as the girl landed hard, rolling, and struggled to come to her feet. She failed, clutching her side instead.

Emma replayed the engagement. *That had* not *been a very elegant attack.* She looked the girl over more carefully. Quite young, despite the womanly curves; and now huddled into herself, obviously in pain. Paul's blow must have been harder than it looked. Emma felt sorry for the girl as, head bowed, she rose clumsily to her feet, hugging herself to relieve the pain.

The tableau stretched out, neither person moving. And at last Emma realized something was wrong. Paul hadn't moved forward to assist her in any way: in fact, he kept his distance. Looking as if he expected another attack. And more than that: he seemed tense. Far more tense than she'd ever seen him.

The girl seemed to shrink slightly, a breath sobbing out. Still Paul didn't move – except for a minute rising and falling of his shoulders. *Wait* – *Paul's breathing hard?* Then Emma's eyes widened in surprise as the revelation hit her – the girl was trying to *lure him closer!*

What the devil was going on? This looked far too serious for a training session.

The girl seemed to realize her trap hadn't worked, slowly unwrapping her arms from her waist, raising her face to meet Paul's cold gaze. *He's angry.* And then she looked at the girl's face. *Quite pretty*, she started to think, just as it transformed into a mask of focused hatred.

Emma stood transfixed as the girl raised her hands before her in the Mantis position, and moved slowly toward Paul. The Mantis position? Did she think this was some silly movie? Just *who* had trained her?

Paul took a defensive posture. The girl, Leeth, moved determinedly closer. Emma watched, and saw that Paul had decided to let her try her attack, simply waiting.

Leeth feinted: Paul read it as such, counter-moved to take advantage of it, and parried the real strike that followed. Surprisingly, her blow nearly landed, *and* was forceful enough to jar Paul's counter strike off-line. And instead of moving away as his elbow hammered into her ribs, jolting her backwards with a gasp of expelled air, she turned in closer to lash out with her foot. Paul responded too fast for Emma to see properly, striking down at the leg, blocking another attack from a slashing arm and answering with a blow to the head before dancing back.

The sequence of attacks had been so fast they'd triggered Emma's own combat augmentations while she'd strained to follow the exchange.

The girl collapsed when her weight came down on the leg she'd just kicked with as she'd tried to follow him. Again, Emma winced. She saw Leeth press her hand, briefly, to her eye and cheek, where Dojo had struck. It'd turn into a *lovely* shiner, if she'd read it correctly. She frowned, though. There was something wrong here. Something wrong with the whole atmosphere. This should have been a simple sparring session, but instead it seemed like a serious fight.

Paul stared down at the girl – from a surprisingly-generous distance. In fact... *why* was Paul, of all people, standing so far back? Did he think she could *leap* at him from two meters away, on the ground? And though it was often hard to tell what he was really thinking, she sensed he was as mad as she'd ever seen him.

And cautious. He hadn't spared even a fraction of his attention to acknowledge her presence, outside the doors. Emma felt a shiver run through her.

What had the girl done? And something else, too. Emma herself had been on the receiving end of Paul's punishing blows, when things got hard and fast. And they *hurt*. Yet the girl had scarcely made a sound.

Paul was speaking again.

"I said you must not lose your temper. Yet you have. Very well. Now you must lose your *anger*. I cannot teach you if you will not think. And we are here so I may teach you."

The girl massaged feeling back into her left knee while he spoke. She didn't answer, though. Merely forced herself back to her feet. She looked tired, and hurt. But still angry, very angry.

Emma watched in disbelief as the girl moved in as the aggressor, *again*. Even Paul seemed surprised as he took the amateurish attack apart, this time with three perfectly-executed but intensely *painful* nerve strikes, Emma knew from experience. Apparently, Paul had decided to make a point.

Two lightning blows to the girl's radial nerves, briefly paralyzing both arms, and a powerful blow to her right leg's peroneal nerve, just above the knee. Emma saw the leg fail – but instead of collapsing, Leeth instantly shifted, somehow staying upright.

Still utterly silent, barely on her feet, and her head down. But not in submission, *that* much was obvious. Rather, so he couldn't see the look in her eyes.

In tones of disgust, he spoke again, words Emma had never heard him say.

"I cannot teach you. You refuse to learn." He pointed to the doors. "Go. You have failed."

The girl looked up, suddenly dismayed. She shook her head. Wordlessly. And then at last, spoke. "No!" Now, finally, at the point of tears.

Paul pointed to the doors, eyes never leaving the girl's face. Even now.

"No," she grated out, her jaw clenching tight. Her head went down slightly. Then she rolled it, very deliberately, from one side, to the other. Emma's eyes widened at the sound of the rippling crackle of muscles popping. Unbelievably, the girl flung herself through the air, attacking again.

For Paul, it was like being attacked by a whirlwind. One knee, and a second, smashed at his sides with astonishing force, barely deflectable; a palm strike simultaneously with an upward elbow blow, all while she was in mid-air. And the palm strike flowed into a hammer-blow from the following elbow. Twisting and bending just enough to parry the onslaught, as her hands crashed back down sooner than was possible, his eyes met Leeth's.

And there he read something strange. A look on her face as if she had something *more* in her arsenal, in reserve. Something which she held back.

As her feet touched the ground, relying on their contact to keep her upright and balanced, he swayed back, denying her that support, sliding around her. Efficiently, while positioning himself for his own attack.

They hammered at one another, then – Dojo, with minimal expenditure of energy; the girl, attacking with shocking speed and force. It continued far longer than Emma could believe, on and on; until finally the girl's head smashed back, Dojo's forearm a club, and Leeth flew from him unconscious, to the mats.

Emma watched, holding her breath.

Paul Kawatsu swayed, then folded forward, arms resting on thighs, his shoulders heaving as he sucked in breath after breath.

In a daze, Emma pushed through the swing doors. She stepped in and around Paul, who met her eyes. His blazed with anger – yet behind that, a strange delight. And the anger was not, she saw, at *Leeth*. He continued resting, his breathing now under control, and Emma waited. Finally, gathering his reserves, he stood, then crouched down and with an effort, lifted the girl.

Paul looked at Emma across the inert burden cradled in his arms. "You saw?"

"Yes, I saw." She shook her head. "I didn't understand, but I saw. How- what? What is she? Is she *augmented*?"

Paul shook his head. "No. Father and Mother say she is not. And it is so. She does not move in that way." He frowned. "I do not understand... all she did."

Emma opened the doors for him, and they moved off down the corridor, by unspoken agreement heading to the infirmary.

"What happens now?"

"I do not know. Her style is poor, but she is remarkably fast, and strong, and..." he grasped for the right word

– "hard. She has great potential. But her spirit...." He grimaced.

"What do you mean? I thought she seemed *too* spirited, if anything. I couldn't believe *she* kept attacking *you*."

He shook his head. "We came very quickly to the barrier of her pride." He looked sideways at Emma. "Which is common. But there was more. It was as if she thought I attacked *her*. Her *self*, not her body. As if she thought I attacked her spirit."

They walked on in silence for a while.

"And that made a barrier to my teaching I could not penetrate."

"So what happens now?"

He shrugged slightly. "Something changed, at the end. She heard me. But though she had lost the fight, and she knew it, *still* she attacked. And despite her speed and ferocity, tired and injured as she was, her attacks were easy to counter. Except at the very end." He paused, clearly savoring the memory. "But in the field, or in battle, I fear for her. Were she wounded or outmatched, I think she would attack, ready to die foolishly rather than retreat, regroup and rethink." He shook his head again. "She needs much instruction."

He looked with distinct satisfaction down at Leeth then back to Emma, and nodded. "*Hai*, shame of failure will unlock this oyster." The delight returned to his expression. "This one, I will *teach*. I will speak to Father."

They walked on. "I do *not* wish to speak to her guardian."

Emma looked at the cold anger on his face; then down to the young, bruised girl in his arms. Bruises which in a way he had been *forced* to inflict.

An unpleasant shiver ran up her spine.

Dojo left Emma in the infirmary preparing the medical scanner, signaling to Father that he wished to report face to face. The carved wood-paneled door whisked aside at his approach.

"Dojo. How did the first training session go?" The man behind the desk sat with military correctness, brushing the holo-display out of existence with a curt gesture. Although in his fifties, he adhered to a sensible exercise regime. Blue eyes in an austere face focused alertly on him. Then narrowed, noting Dojo's sweat, and disheveled look.

"Ah, a little bit strange. She will be... a challenge to teach."

Father looked intrigued. "Why? She was extremely keen to be given martial arts training. What happened?"

"You informed her of my abilities in this area?"

Father frowned. "Yes. I stressed you were a true Master of the Art. Pre-eminent. She was, as I said, *very* keen for you to teach her. She literally bounced from the room, she was so eager." His voice hardened. "What *happened*, Dojo?"

"You warned me not to underestimate her." Dojo paused. "The warning was necessary. She is as dangerous as you say. And when I have finished teaching her...."

He bared his teeth, but in something darker than a smile, and for some reason Father felt the man was *warning* him. Dojo's gaze went distant, and hungry, as if a long-held promise lay now in reach. And his next words confirmed that.

"When I have finished teaching her, we may have the weapon we need against *him*."

Father blinked.

"But there is something... wrong with the girl," Dojo continued. "She may not be completely sane. She has some basic skill, and you told her what to expect. Yet still, *she* launched the first attack on *me*." Dojo shrugged. "Much spirit, not so much sense. And she is as fast as you said. Faster.

"So. At first she listened to my words, and improved. But soon grew frustrated when she could not penetrate my defenses. Her attacks became more determined. She lost her temper. I explained to her she should not. I showed her, anger was senseless. She regained control. From then until the end, she sought only to kill me. But at that end... it was *glorious*." Dojo's delight was palpable. "And what she did..." He shook his head. "She is wildly unpredictable. She controls her center of gravity. You understand? *Magic*. Finally, you bring me the student you promised."

"And Leeth herself?"

"She is now unconscious in the infirmary."

Father waited, but did not see the embarrassment he expected. "Yet you are not," he prodded.

Dojo, remembering the fleeting expression on the girl's face at the height of their battle, smiled. "Of course. Yet, she held something back."

Father looked surprised.

Dojo shrugged. "I do not know what, yet. But after I have taught her...."

His smile turned wolfish. "Today, it was as if I fought a wild animal. She did not reason, reacting purely on instinct. And I think maybe she is not a complete person – she cannot deal with failure, except by a direct attack on its source." The smile vanished. "As I said: maybe not so sane. She may be impossible to teach."

"Impossible? Or just very difficult?" Father asked. At Dojo's angled head, he continued. "An agent who can barely tolerate failure will be useful, you must agree. Stubbornness can be a desirable attribute."

For a while, both men thought, before Father spoke again. "Her training will not follow the same path you've used for your other students, will it?"

"Not so much."

"Very well. You and I both know that to master the Art, you must master yourself. You say she is incomplete? Complete her."

"Ah. So simple."

Father frowned, unaccustomed to sarcasm from the warrior. Then saw that the man's anger had returned.

"You said the mage, 'the Doctor,' had raised her. Her incompleteness is his work, then. Did he know what he did?"

Father's expression went a little cold. "He is a trained psychologist. Yes, I would say he knew what he was doing. I will review this incident with him, immediately." Father's eyes returned to Dojo. "Eagle says the Doctor has laid the groundwork for a most useful agent. He wants us to 'round her out.' She is to become an assassin. She herself *wants* that."

Both men frowned at the implications. Dojo shook his head.

"You don't think she will make a good assassin?" Father asked.

"No," he responded without hesitation. "You will see when you review the session. Maybe she will be too good."

Father saw the hunger return to Dojo's expression. "But we can't let that long term goal ruin her *medium* term usefulness, Dojo. We need to be able to control her."

Dojo inclined his head. "Until we unleash her."

Both men shared a look, hoping Eagle knew what he was doing.

CHAPTER 2

Harmon went from Father's office to the infirmary. The female agent, Emma, was there. She appeared perfectly normal. Observing her movements and micro-expressions, he could see no outward signs of the agents' advanced neural circuitry. Their 'headware.' He shuddered at the thought of implants like that in Leeth. It would destroy her unique magic.

Stepping into the room he smiled at the smartly-dressed woman. "Thank you – Emma? – for watching Leeth. I'm Dr Harmon."

She turned, but despite his smile, he saw she stepped back, to the impressive automated medical scanner. Putting distance between them. Taking the unit's diagnostic sheet, she held it out to him. He waved it away and crossed instead to Leeth's cot.

Sketching a brief gesture in the air, he brought his hand to the purpling cheek, and concentrated. *Within* her. In seconds the contusions faded, the cut over her eye sealing and vanishing. *No internal bleeding, either.*

Looking up, he caught the shocked expression on Agent Emma's face at the speed of the healing. *Ah.* No doubt wondering whether he were so powerful a mage, or simply so accustomed to healing Leeth.

While matter-of-factly checking his patient for broken bones, he probed at 'Emma' Imaginally. Her aura showed she was offended by the way he touched his ward.

He met her frown with a friendly expression. "You would not believe how often I've had to do this." He looked down at Leeth, careful to smile fondly at her. "She doesn't know her own limits." As he gently cupped her cheek, she stirred, but didn't wake.

Returning all his senses to Leeth, he *probed* for further injuries. Echoes of violence laced her body: from her brain, shaken to the point of concussion, to bruises, torn muscles, pulled and stretched ligaments, and fading stresses in her strong bones. As well as a dramatic loss of body fat. *In just one hour? Fascinating.* A new ability, or a new situation?

Closing his eyes, he concentrated, encouraging the disrupted cells to knit back into the proper patterns, moving surely from each injury to the next.

Several minutes passed before he opened his eyes. "Could you fetch me a stimpatch, Emma?"

From the medicine cabinet, she peeled one open. Smiling his thanks, he applied it to Leeth's upper arm and waited.

She moaned. Raising a hand to her head, her eyes opened to focus on him.

Her face tightened, no doubt remembering her failure. Avoiding his gaze, her eyes then fell on Emma, and she blinked in surprise at the stranger's presence. Harmon, watching them, saw Emma's look soften into pity. Unsurprisingly, Leeth clenched her teeth and looked away.

"We haven't been introduced, Leeth, but my name is Emma." She approached, reaching out a comforting hand to the girl's brow. She stopped when Leeth flinched from the contact. Naturally. And of course, then sat up.

"Thank you, Emma, but my ward and I have something we need to discuss."

Emma looked at them both, apparently reluctant to leave Leeth alone with him.

"In private. Of course you understand. I'm sure you and I will have a chance to become acquainted properly, soon. I look forward to it."

Emma didn't seem at all sure *she* did. He kept smiling patiently, until she looked away. With one last glance at Leeth, who still avoided her gaze, Emma left the room.

He opened his mouth, but Leeth shook her head, and jabbed a finger at the doorway. Harmon got up noisily from the cot, then stepped loudly toward the opening, watching Leeth until she nodded.

He turned back to her, but she refused to look at him. Sighing, mulling over what 'Father' had said, and what they wanted of her, he sat on the end of the cot.

"So, Leeth. Tell me what happened."

Her fists clenched. Still not looking at him, she spoke in a tight voice, facing the wall. "I failed. Dojo says I can't learn. He won't teach me."

"What made him think you couldn't learn?"

"I... I lost my temper. I wouldn't do what I was supposed to."

"Why did you lose your temper?"

She still spoke to the wall. "I... He.... It started *out* okay. But I couldn't get to him at all! I kept trying, and trying, but all that happened was I kept getting knocked down, or thrown down, or knocked aside; but he could hit *me* whenever he tried, and I couldn't stop him, and I couldn't hurt him, and even at the end-"

"Don't *whine*," he sneered.

The tirade ended. She turned toward him, an angry denial on her face. But her mouth clamped shut on the words. For a moment he felt sorry for her, though he took care not to let that show. He saw Father's point. She never *had* been able to deal with failure.

Well. It was long past time she learned. "Leeth. Are you telling me he was a better fighter than you?"

She looked sullen, but nodded.

"But everyone knew that. That's *why* he is your teacher. You must have realized he would be more skilled than you."

"Yeah," she said in a small voice. "I just didn't think he'd be *so much* better than me."

"And you lost your temper."

"Yes."

"But you regained control, later, toward the end. Then what did you do?"

"I tried again, of course. But he beat me again. Then said I'd failed, and he wouldn't teach me."

There was a pause.

"Then you attacked him *again*, when you were near exhaustion. And almost succeeded." He struggled to understand: she was not behaving as expected. "Why didn't you try that hard from the beginning, when you were fresher?"

At that she finally looked directly at him, her words grating out with burning intensity. "Cause I didn't know *how*, at the start. But I learn fast."

Ahh. But she was no longer talking about 'Dojo.' She was adapting even faster than he had expected.

Assuming listening devices, however, he set that issue aside, and simply smiled. "Well, you and I both know you can lose without giving in. But Dojo wasn't looking at it that way at all." He shook his head. "He wasn't trying to make you submit, Leeth. He was trying to make you learn."

She glared at him. He could imagine the bitter words crowding her mind at the word 'submit.' Then saw the expected look of confusion flood in behind the glare.

He watched her pull herself back from that brink, and again pretended not to notice. "His job is to teach you.

And your job is to learn from him. The only one making the lesson into a contest was you. If you control that temper, and try to think about it, surely you can see that?"

"He won't teach me. He says I can't learn."

"Dojo has been told to try again. You have one last chance to prove to him you *can* learn. You were eager to, before. And now that you know just how good he is, imagine what you could become if you combined your strengths and abilities with the skills he can teach you." He knew her childish dreams of being a super-heroine, or a spy. His Huntress. "The girl I knew would be thirsty to acquire some of those skills for herself. I'm sure you could find a use for them. Don't you *want* them?"

"Oh, yes," she breathed, staring at him hungrily; and then past him.

He didn't need magic to know what she was thinking, seeing herself as a super-spy. Still, it would be advisable to distract her; and make her grateful for his part in their changed circumstances.

"I thought so – back at the Institute, you pestered me endlessly to find you a teacher. I'm sure you did well, in your first real lesson."

She giggled!

He stared at her, nonplussed; and her grin grew wider. "You just gave me a pep talk, Keepie! I can't remember you *ever* giving me a pep talk before!"

He felt an eyebrow lift. It was true. In the ten years he had cared for her, he had never felt the need. Oh, except for the second day, when she'd thought she was going to be sent back to the orphanage.

He felt warm for some reason, remembering the eight year old with the quivering lip and the determination not to cry.

Facing the echo of that happy child now, and considering what he had turned that girl into, he felt a disturbing mix of loss and guilt. He remembered her leap into his arms from the trampoline; her *Pouncing* him; her explosive arrival through the ceiling outside Godsson's cell....

Her *death*, as she slew Melisande's creation.

She truly was remarkable. He shook his head, allowing some of that genuine warmth to flow into his expression.

The depth of joy in her answering smile struck with the impact of an arrow to the heart. He had to look away.

Checking his watch, he used the time to catch his breath. "This little fiasco has wasted half an hour now; and Dojo has been told to be waiting in the same place for your next lesson, in a further half hour." He didn't mention that her instructor had needed that time to recover, himself. He had half hoped she might have injured the fellow, but of course it had been too much to expect him to be incompetent. "Will you be ready by then?"

"Sure."

"Good. I want your best effort, Leeth. Nothing less will suffice. Just remember, it has taken Dojo all his life to acquire the skills he possesses. To reach his standard in less time than that would be... remarkable." He watched as her expression settled into one of determination.

He got up from the cot. In the doorway, he turned to face her again. "One last thing, Leeth. When an *intelligent* person sees she is losing a contest, she tries to change the contest. Or looks at winning in the longer term. The *last thing* she does is stubbornly continue on a sure path to defeat. Blindly persisting down a dead end – that's merely a childish way of giving in, of giving up. Surrendering.

"And you are supposed to be sparring, not fighting. You're there to learn, not to win. The only way you can fail is by not learning, not listening. Your mind is a weapon, too, girl – use it."

She looked thoughtful as he left.

CHAPTER 3

Stretching on the cot, Leeth allowed herself the pleasure of feeling her body moving uninjured and pain-free. Even the acid burn from the earlier workout seemed less. *Keepie sure is good at Healing me.* That thought led to another. *And hurting me.* She remembered holding herself still while he beat her. Just before the police had burst in and shot him, making her think they'd killed him.

She felt confused. Could their 'sessions' really be for her own good? Look at the trouble she'd got Mr Shanahan into, after all.

Does he love me, or not?

He must *do. I'm* sure *he does.*

Forcing the doubts aside, she stood, then realized she was *dying* of thirst. She poured herself a glass of water, fretting at the slow stream, then gulped it down. Then another. She was supposed to wait thirty minutes, he'd said. From the bowl on her table, she took an apple in each hand. Biting alternately into one, then the other, she wolfed them down. Then followed up with a protein bar. And another.

She forced herself to wait for another five minutes, after that, before finally deciding it'd be better to be early than late. She shrugged. She could do some exercises if Dojo wasn't there yet.

Leaving her room, she stood frowning in the empty passageway that looked like a path through the countryside.

"Dojo," she said aloud, then began following the helpful arrows that appeared on the long corridor walls. For a while she walked, just appreciating the scenery, while concealed speakers projected bird calls, and the rush of wind, and the whispers of leaves.

But like all recorded sounds, it didn't sound real: none of the ultra-squeaky insect sounds, and no really deep rumbles, either. All a bit flat. She sighed.

This place is like a maze. I wonder how big it is?

She was taking too long.

She began jogging, which seemed to take the direction arrows by surprise: at the next junction she had to glance back to check which way she should be going. But instead of slowing down, she pushed on faster. The arrows started appearing faster, too.

She ran harder still. *Come on, arrows, see if you can keep up!*

At the T junction ahead, pointing to the right, an arrow flashed triumphantly green. Braking to a halt, she turned the corner and saw the double doors at the end.

Will he mind that I'm puffed? Or will he be pleased that I hurried?

Will he really *give me another chance? Really?* Pushing through the swing doors, she kept her eyes down until she'd crossed the room to where she sensed Dojo stood, waiting.

She looked up, meeting his gaze.

"My-"

Oh! This time, he wore no shirt. *Fitness* radiated from him. The taut skin, the firm muscles....

Suddenly she was sure: *this* was the teacher she'd always dreamed of. She'd never been so certain of anything. He *had* to teach her! She felt oddly off-balance, as if his presence alone somehow tugged her closer. She wondered how old he was. Much older than her; but much younger than Uncle. And well muscled....

"Miss Leeth."

She dragged her attention back from *him*, to his words. "Uncle said you'd give me a second chance."

She saw his eyes narrow.

Really? I have to apologize, *too? For what; getting beaten up?* "Please...." She wanted to look away, to look down, but she forced herself to stare straight back at him. Lifted her chin. "*Please* will you teach me?"

He said nothing, just stared at her, and her face went hot, then cold. But after long seconds, he nodded, as if deciding not to force her to say the 'S' word.

"Do you know the Japanese word for *teacher*?" he finally asked.

She shook her head.

"It is *sensei*. While I teach you, you will call me sensei, hai?"

"Sensay." She *wanted* to jump in the air and scream for joy; but she kept still. Studied him, all serious. "I'll remember." *I'll make you proud.*

"Then we shall start."

-

Paul watched her thud into the mat again, heavily, this time failing even to roll properly to absorb the impact. Clearly, she grew tired. *Finally.*

She had taxed his own reserves, despite him taking numerous rest breaks while directing her in solo exercises.

He checked his Link: two hours and forty minutes had passed. Astonishing. No other student had ever managed much more than an hour of this. His eyes narrowed. She looked... thinner. More of her magic?

He watched while she collected first her wits, then her breath, then forced herself up onto her knees. Then paused, gathering the strength to stand again.

She must have had a very bad teacher. One of those many flawed pretenders. She had known none of the basics; had mastered only a few superficial moves. She had not even known how to fall properly. It made no sense, considering her earlier performance. She was learning now, though. Quite well. Especially given her exhaustion.

Her balance was beyond exceptional: supernatural. She had also grasped the key concepts very quickly; like that of the three gates: hand, elbow/forearm, sides; the need to protect her center. What a difference the change in attitude had wrought. Before, she had not listened; now, she soaked up all he could show her, like parched soil absorbing rain. She had instantly grasped the idea of making and keeping contact, forming a bridge to your opponent to feel your enemy's intended moves.

Something about the speed at which she'd learned *that* lesson was faintly disturbing. She showed an eagerness to touch, to embrace – a hunger to make and keep contact – that was almost sexual. *Does she desire me?* He shook his head. He would deal with that if it arose.

She had made good progress in learning the eight basic moves, and the concept of combination attacks: although as often as not her offensives fell apart just planning two moves ahead while trying to remember the forms and defend herself. Unlike her glorious performance at the end of their first session, when she had attacked purely instinctively. He smiled, remembering.

She would be formidable indeed, once her body had learned the patterns. He felt a frisson of anticipation as he considered their future bouts. Already, he could see she would make a fearsome opponent, especially for someone who had not fought her. *Often.* With her unexpected responses, the speed of her blistering, un-telegraphed attacks, her uncanny intuition....

The lesson continued now only while he waited for her to ask for it to end.

While she moved on the floor, he massaged his elbow. It would bruise, he knew. He was still uncertain how she had landed that blow. It should have been impossible, yet the evidence was there – in the injury, and in the girl struggling to her feet before him.

And the uncertainty – that itself was a delight, something he had not expected to feel again. Certainly not from a badly-taught child. By his own dispassionate reckoning, he was one of the top three martial artists alive today.

Her magic still eluded his analysis. He felt sure she *had* magic, yet equally sure she herself was unaware she used it.

Shaking his head, he focused on the matter at hand. He had wanted to find her limits, and he had – mostly. He now knew the limits of her physical attributes – her remarkable strength, and speed, and stamina. He knew how hard to push to make her angry, and from their earlier session he thought he knew the point at which she would lose control of her anger. But as he watched her drag herself to her feet through pure nervous energy, he realized he had not yet found the limits of her stubbornness.

So there she stood, quietly panting, before once more adopting the defensive posture he had shown her: knees bent, feet turned in, arms held up – barely – and crossed at her center. But she was clearly exhausted. Again, he shook his head. The Department's accountant, or even Nelson, the skinny hacker boy, could take her in the state she was in now. *Probably.* Still, her attitude was completely different from the undisciplined chaos of their first meeting. This had been most rewarding.

"Miss Leeth, you are tired." *As am I.*

She nodded.

"Miss Leeth, if we continue, you will be unfit for days. I fear that even now, I may have pressed you too hard. Tomorrow, you will ache badly."

She simply shook her head. He waited for her to speak. Eventually, she seemed to realize that.

"Sensei. Did I... did I pass? Will you teach me?"

The eyes were big, earnest – entreating. He looked at her in surprise.

"Why yes, Miss Leeth, you performed... well. I will, I think, be most happy to teach you."

"Oh!"

Her face lit with joy. Suddenly, and with more energy than he thought remained to her, she leapt across the short distance separating them, arms spread wide. For a moment he misread her intent, and barely restrained himself from knocking her down. Then she was clinging to him, hugging fiercely. *Desperately.*

He was more than a little nonplussed. Perhaps she sensed it, for she suddenly released him and stepped back. And gave a little bow. "Thank you, Sensei."

"You have earned it, Miss Leeth."

A slight frown crossed her face. "Can I ask a favor, Sensei?"

"You may *ask*," he responded, warily.

"Could you please not call me 'Miss Leeth?' It makes me feel funny. Can't you call me by my proper name?"

He frowned at her. "The rules are strict. We are to refer to one another by the new names we have taken – never by our real names." *Surely the girl knew that?*

"But Leeth *is* my real name. My codename isn't '*Miss* Leeth,' so couldn't you leave it off?"

"Very well. That is the end of today's lesson – Leeth."

She smiled.

"You will be very sore tomorrow, but do not let the Doctor heal that 'injury': it will prevent the building of new muscle. So I do not expect you for a lesson tomorrow. You will ache too much." As her jaw set in a stubborn line, he added, "but I will let you be the judge of that."

She smiled again, and again they exchanged formal bows. As she was about to push through the doors to the gym, he called after her.

"Leeth?"

She turned.

"I am curious. Where did you acquire your, ah, style?"

"Mostly from trids."

He blinked slowly, in disbelief. "You cannot learn the Art by watching movies! One must fight!"

She shrugged. "Well, *mainly* from trids: I'd try out bits of it in the gym back at the Institute. Plus, Uncle took me to a real competition once. Oh, and when I killed; I fought then."

He could only stare at her, dumbfounded. She seemed not to notice: just waited to see if he wanted to say anything else, then ducked her head in a tiny bow and left the room.

The doors swung shut behind her and he stood staring at them unseeingly. Now he understood why she seemed so badly trained. The mystery of her appalling teacher had been solved – she'd had none. That she showed the skill she did was astonishing.

And whatever strange magic she held.... Recalling how he had exploited a sloppy and unbalanced stance, he visualized her recovery, once again feeling she had violated a law of physics. And that look, at the climax of their first encounter, when he sensed she held something back.

Together, the memories made the skin on the back of his neck prickle, and he smiled.

But the matter of killing. "*When I killed,*" he muttered under his breath, then pulled himself together. Once again, it seemed Eagle had good reasons for the role he had chosen for an agent.

He wondered, though, whether even Eagle knew what lay beyond the door he had opened, this time.

She would *be the one.* He just hoped she would be enough.

CHAPTER 4

Although the Bureau of Internal Development itself was of reasonable size, the *Accounts Department* – the ultra-secret agency concealed within it – consisted of just ten people. Of these, only three were on full-time active status: Preacher, Emma, and the third agent, James, who didn't meet Leeth until the following week.

Emma had helped him complete his recent mission, and both now enjoyed a quiet moment in the rec room. Gazing through the currently one-way translucent wall, they watched the figure swimming and diving – *playing* – in the pool beyond.

James and Emma sat together in the wood-paneled room, with its large billiard table and wall of books. The rich aroma of real coffee hung in the air.

James's eyes kept drifting back to the nymph undulating through the water. *Men*, thought Emma, shaking her head. "So, have you met her yet? What do you think?"

"We have been introduced, yes." James's voice was deep, the tones so rich that Emma felt somehow nourished just listening to it.

Emma had both hands round her coffee mug as she held it close to her face, her dark eyes shining mischievously over its rim. James could sense the dimpled smile concealed behind the mug. Relaxing back in his chair, he ran his fingers briefly through his short dark-brown hair. "She arrived last week, didn't she?"

"Mm-hmm," Emma agreed.

"Before you joined me in Seattle," he prompted.

"Mm-hmm."

"So *you've* seen her more than I." His eyes drifted back to the girl in the pool.

"Mmm. Though you seem to be doing your best to reverse the balance. But I'm asking *you*." Emma lowered the mug, flicking the fringe out of her eyes with a short toss of her head. "So?"

The girl emerged from the water at last. Something about the movement struck James as odd, but then he saw she was completely naked. Eyebrows raised, he watched her padding swiftly toward the diving board.

"Ahem."

He dragged his attention back to Emma, who watched him with a knowing smile.

"Ah." James had the grace to look faintly embarrassed. "Does she know that one can see into the pool from here?"

From up on the diving board, the figure waved to them.

Both stared in surprise, then shared a look, at the odd timing.

"I *think* she does," said Emma.

Unsettled, they turned back to watch as the girl bounced high off the board, spun twice in a somersault, unfolding just as she met the water. Emma and James winced in unison at the painful-looking impact.

"Well," Emma demanded, "what do you think?"

"Needs more practice?"

Emma pursed her lips, and James shrugged, relenting. "Well, my first thought was that the Old Man was losing his grip – she's absurdly young." He looked over in the direction of the concealed recording device, wondering when or if this conversation would be reviewed. Not that it worried him.

"It wasn't Father – it was Eagle who had her brought in."

James looked surprised. "Really? *Eagle* found her? *That's* interesting. Father also specifically instructed me not to do or say anything that might 'affect her unusual psychological orientation.' He said you'd fill me in?"

"Father and Mother told *me* not to discuss the ethics of combat, or sexual morals. Nor offer her any stimsense."

James frowned while he considered the girl's casual nudity. She reached the edge of the pool and pulled herself up out of the water, straight to a standing position in a single flowing motion, before padding back to the diving board again.

"And to avoid the use of in-house jargon."

At that he turned back to Emma, and they exchanged unhappy looks. "Expendable, then."

"Have you met 'the Doctor'?" Emma asked.

"Her guardian, the mage? No, not yet."

Preacher, the oldest of the Department's three agents, stalked in like a dark shadow. Dressed in his usual black synth-leather gear, he favored them with a brief sneer on his way to the coffee brewing in the corner. Judging by his self-assured swagger, he must be jacked-in to his neural enhancer chip, James decided. A shame the skill-set it provided wasn't packaged up with a more pleasant persona. The dark-haired man filled a mug before moving over to the wall to stare out into the pool area.

All now watched as the girl spun in the air. Preacher chuckled at her awkward entry into the water.

Not as bad as last time, though, James thought.

"She's doing a lot of work with Dojo," Emma continued. "They had a sort of, um, argument in her first session. But it was all straightened out the same day."

She desperately wanted to share her recording of that first, astonishing encounter – but Mother and Father had sealed it. "She's quite something."

James looked back at her, picking up the message. Emma widened her eyes and nodded, once. James pushed out his lips, and raised his eyebrows. Emma nodded, again.

"I've got her this afternoon on the weapons range. Teaching her to shoot," Preacher offered unexpectedly, not turning around.

"And I'm helping her dress for dinner tomorrow tonight – for a date with you, I believe, James?" Emma offered.

James frowned slightly. "Yes. And I have tickets for the opera, after dinner at the Muses, three weeks from now. I gather she needs practice, first."

"Ahh," Emma nodded. "Should I be offering to come along too, as a chaperon?"

"I don't think that will be necessary, old girl. I gather that I, too, am training her."

Emma arched one eyebrow.

"Slotting typical!" Preacher turned to glare at James. "*I* teach her to shoot, you teach her to screw."

James smiled. "I don't have any *firm* instructions on the subject."

Preacher scowled, then stalked off. With something like relief, the other two watched him leave.

Entering the adjacent room, he ordered Leeth from the water. For a moment it looked like she was going to refuse.

But she got out of the pool with that same fluid movement, and padded over to her towel. Patting herself dry, she followed Preacher to the door. Where she stopped, before darting back to the bench to snatch up her clothes.

CHAPTER 5

That night, Leeth lay on her bed, holding up the smartsheet with her 'timetable' before her, trying to work out whether she liked it or not.

It seemed very... organize-y.

	Sun	Mon	Tue	Wed	Thu	Fri	Sat
8:00		MA, Dojo	MA, Dojo	MA, Dojo	MA, Dojo	MA, Dojo	
10:00		GS, self	GS, self	GS, self	GS, self	GS, self	GS, self
11:00		PhysEd, self	PhysEd, self	Phys Ed, *	PhysEd self	Phys Ed, *	PhysEd self
12:00	Lunch						
13:00		Weap-ons, *	Weap-ons, *	Weap-ons, *	Weap-ons, *	Weap-ons, *	
14:00		MA, Dojo	MA, Dojo	MA, Dojo	MA, Dojo	MA, Dojo	
15:00		GS, self	GS, self	GS, self	GS, self	GS, self	GS, self
16:00		Hist, Dr	Fash, E	Etiq, M	Mil Tac, F	Sec Sys, *	
17:00		Comp, N	Fin, C	St. Cult., P	Soc sk-ills, M	Prac Psy, Dr	
18:00		Pol Sci, M	Pol Sci, M	Pol Sci, M	Pol Sci, M	Pol Sci, M	

I guess Dojo has other things to do besides training me. But still... only three hours a day? And she wasn't sure what 'Political Science' was, but it sounded boring.

Weapons sounded fun; and '*' meant the instructor would vary. But two hours of General Studies each day, on her own? It'd be like being back at the Institute. Though the auto-teacher software looked kind of interesting: better than the quizzes she was used to. But why were Saturdays and Sundays mostly empty?

Sighing, she put the timetable down. Tired, excited, and a little hungry, too. Flipping herself up off the bed she considered what to do now, stretching and feeling the aches and strains, replaying some of Dojo's moves and re-trying a few herself. Dojo was *amazing*.

But she should go to sleep soon, to make sure she'd be fresh in the morning, for her next session with him.

All her clothes had finally been delivered from the Institute, so she'd have something nice to wear for him. *I wonder what Faith's doing tonight?* The thought made her blink, rapidly. Normally, they'd have finished their patrol by now. Unless she'd managed to sneak out so they could have an extra loping run through the night-time woods. She missed Faith: missed cuddling her, wrestling her; missed her doggy-electric smells. And those dopey, wolfish grins.

She wiped at her eyes with her knuckles. *One day I'll go back.*

And what about poor Godsson? She wondered if anyone here knew about him? Surely they would, since they all worked for Eagle? Maybe she'd ask Emma.

Emma was nice. And despite dressing in really *covering* clothes, she somehow managed to look classy and sexy and elegant. She liked Emma best of everyone here; but James, the other male agent she'd met briefly today, was *cute*, in a rugged way. Much nicer than grumpy old *Preacher*.

She'd be eighteen, soon. She wondered if they'd told James she wasn't exactly eighteen yet: would *he* say she was 'too young?' She giggled: something told her she'd be finding out soon.

Preacher, though, seemed... mean. *Grubby.* And he sneered a lot, and his eyes looked kind of hungry. He'd be teaching her Street Culture.

The creepiest one of all, though, was 'Checkbook.' She didn't understand him *at all*. He hadn't smiled once while he'd been explaining to her about 'purchase orders' and 'justifying expenses.' She had *no* idea what he thought of her. If she hadn't heard his heart beating, by listening in her special way, she could have believed he was some kind of super-smart android.

She shuddered.

'Father' was nice, if a bit gruff. Really old – older than Keepie! – but very fit-looking. Very erect and unbending. *I wonder if I'll be able to make* him *bend a bit?*

Plus the two younger men, only one of whom she'd met. She guessed there was something odd about the one they hadn't introduced her to yet: Nelson. When Mother and Father had been describing her colleagues to her, they'd exchanged weird looks about *him*. Nelson was their 'information specialist,' they'd said; 'talented' with electronics. And then they'd stopped, each of them looking kind of constipated.

From his picture, Nelson looked a bit... pasty. But intelligent, and maybe excitable.

She'd examined his picture, hmm-ing while wondering whether she could convince him to exercise with her: build him up a little. He didn't seem that much older than her, so he *should* be fun. But when she'd looked up, Mother had been staring at her chest in disapproval, like there was something wrong with her nipples, and Father was easing back in his chair with his eyes narrowed and sucking in a long breath.

"What?" she'd demanded. But he'd simply shaken his head, and Mother's dark magenta lips had clamped tightly shut.

The one she *had* met, briefly, was called 'Little Brother' – which was a pretty lame code-name. He was a general assistant, earnest-looking in a wishy-washy sort of way. It'd been him who'd brought her and Uncle inside the Department when they'd first arrived....

When she and Uncle had been offered their chance, back in Eagle's office, to work for the Government a door had slid open and two matte black drones had appeared, buzzing powerfully, escorting them down into a maze of tunnels. She'd tried to remove the special hood and cuffs from her uncle, but they were sealed snugly shut, with no obvious unlocking mechanism. She'd gotten frustrated, then angry, hurrying sideways through passages trying to keep up with the watching drones. In the end, with the *slicey* feeling tingling through her fingertips, she'd slashed his bonds free. Deadly-looking tubes had sprung from the hovering black bots, and for a full minute no one had moved.

But in the end, when neither she nor Uncle had done anything else, the drones had bracketed them again. One had pincered up the pieces of her uncle's restraints, while the other had begun humming much more loudly, making aggressive little darting motions to herd them on. It'd made her want to punch it.

They'd led them on through more automatic doors, tunnels, and stairs – mostly down – and finally along a cold, damp stretch of passageway cut through stone and smelling of earth.

The drones had paused at a metal wall at the end, where a door had opened onto a bare concrete room. Inside, four sleek black arthrobots the size of dogs had faced them, bulging with energy pods and weapons. Behind them, an apologetic young man introduced himself as 'Little Brother.' He'd blushed as he'd urged them not to upset the anti-personnel bots.

His eyes had lit up when the flying drone had dropped the sliced-up hood and cuffs into his hands. It had been like she and her uncle had vanished, as far as he was concerned. After examining their damage, he finally seemed to remember they were there. He looked at her with such fascination she'd felt somehow embarrassed.

But he'd just welcomed them to the Accounts Department's 'back entrance' and then led them inside to a first meeting with Mother and Father. One at a time.

Finally, Father had handed her her timetable, and she'd studied it for a minute. "Why aren't there any actual *spy* lessons?"

Mother had pursed her lips. Mother pursed her lips *a lot*, actually – almost every time she'd asked her something, in fact. Like Mother thought she was just a child.

"Oh, you mean the bomb defusing courses, do you? And jet piloting? The nerve pinches, no doubt; and how to guess passwords in three tries?"

Leeth had nodded, excited, only realizing Mother had been making fun of her by Father's reaction. She felt her face heat, just at the memory.

Standing up, she crossed to her dressing table, taking up the old padlock she'd found all those years ago at the Institute. She smiled, remembering her eight-year-old self's plan to learn to pick locks, to recover the evidence of her sneaking around in the ceiling spaces. Except she never had worked out how to pick it. *At least here, I'm sure to be taught how to do that.*

She put it back down, still smiling, then lifted the heavy wooden block she'd started carving, mainly just to enjoy the *sharp* feeling always waiting at her fingertips.

She turned it over. She wasn't sure what it was going to be, yet. Something with swooping lines. Maybe a dolphin. Something simple; her invisible claws seemed better at killing things than cutting things.

But she didn't feel like practicing her control right now; practicing how to keep the... desire to *cut*, shivering at her fingertips. She put the hardwood back down beside her deadly black PowerShot, and started pacing her room, feeling cooped up all of a sudden. She wanted out.

She poured herself a glass of filtered, chilled water. Gulping it down, her stomach growled. There was a food dispenser in the Recreation Room. And she was a member of the Department now. So they could hardly object if she looked around.

Oh! I can go exploring!

They'd already explained that only doors she was allowed to go through would open for her.

So I'm totally allowed to explore! I wonder how hard it'll be to sneak past their security? She chewed her lip. *Probably even worse than Jax's upgrades at the Institute, that'd ruined years of work.*

But that thought only depressed her: made her remember Jax's betrayal. Of her, and Uncle. Getting them arrested.

She missed Faith. Who was still back there, missing *her*. Which in turn made her think about Godsson again and the problem of how to convince people they really ought to let him go. That was gonna be tough. Everyone thought he was mad. Which he was; kind of. Just not *that* mad. He wouldn't hurt people. At least, not good people.

She sighed, putting the memories of the Institute behind her as she cracked open her door. But the moment she stepped from her room, an arrow with a red question-mark appeared beneath a dark tree in the night-time forest scene on the wall opposite her door. She sighed. *Yeah, things here work at a whole 'nother level.*

"I don't want any stupid help!" she told the stupid arrow.

It hung there; paled to pink; then started flashing.

"No! I don't want directions."

The pink shape brightened to a golden glow, then morphed into a picture of Sleena, the pixie gladiator in Subworld, and she smiled.

But when Sleena's sword, Dragon Fang, twisted into a question mark, Leeth flushed. *How did they know I liked Sleena? When I was a child*, she amended.

"No directions! Go away!"

With a sad expression that made her feel guilty, the false Sleena faded out. It left just the moonlit woodland scene illuminating the corridor, and Leeth feeling somehow mean. She wished she could go *up*, aboveground. Out into a real forest. To run, dodging and weaving through real trees, under real moonlight.

Clenching her fists, she stalked off in the direction of the Rec room. Which wasn't too hard to find; from memory, and from the smell of chlorine seeping from the large indoor pool in the room next to it.

The Rec room seemed strangely empty and lonely. She wandered by the large 'billiards' table with its green felt inlay. Trailing her fingertips over the smoothly-polished wood grain, her gaze skipped from the couch, to the kitchen and its specialized appliances, to the wall of physical books and the weird wooden 'games' below them. She'd been hoping someone else would be awake to talk to, she realized.

Setting the wall to transparent, she stood looking at the pool, which glowed dark and mysterious and beautiful with just the underwater lights. She sighed, feeling tired all at once. *Something to eat, then a swim before bedtime.* Moving to the food dispenser, a section of pre-packaged snacks caught her eye.

Black Magic Bars.

She felt her eyes widen, and she looked around, biting her fingers. *Surely they wouldn't* really *be magic?* You couldn't put magic into food. Could you? And why would they put *black* magic into food? That'd be stupid and dangerous.

Unless it was some kind of test?

She pressed the code for the bar, and watched it drop down into the slot below. Hesitating, she reached in cautiously, and plucked it out. Then sniffed the shiny black and gold package, with its picture of a dark molten liquid pouring itself into a gleaming row of almost-black buttons.

Peeling it open, an unfamiliar aroma wafted out.

She picked free one heavy lozenge, alert for magic; for any tingle of unease; any kind of invisible attack... but nothing happened. It just smelled... real good.

Making her decision, she bit into it, the dark substance crunching satisfyingly between her teeth and melting onto her tongue-

Oh.

Ohhh!

Her eyes closed as she ravaged it; plunging through the powerful bitter-sweet taste, churning it to paste while her tongue dived and swam through paradise, her hand clenched tightly on the packet.

As she hunted down the last smears and licked her lips, her eyes re-opened, and she stared at the packet in shock.

*That was a-*mazing*!*

It tasted like... magic. So good! *But it's black magic.* She had to stop. *It's probably a trap!* She put the bar down, and backed away; watching the packet, alert; knowing there were two more equally delicious pieces inside. And more in the machine...

How could *anything* taste so good? She'd never tasted *anything* like that before, not in her whole life!

She listened, wondering if it would call to her, try to tempt her, like *She* had. But seconds passed; a minute... and nothing changed. Except her mouth watered. Turning away abruptly, she stripped off her clothes and pushed through the doors into the pool room, then dived from the edge, plunging deep.

But even as she held her breath, stroking through the caressing and enveloping water... from the next room, the Black Magic Bar called to her.

CHAPTER 6

A week later, Emma tossed her hand luggage onto the bed in her rooms in the Department, un-kinking her tense shoulder muscles. Successes like today's were to be savored: Mother and Father had reserved ten days to complete the infiltration of Newtopia's Brazilian embassy, and she'd managed it in less than one. She allowed herself a small smile. *Not bad, if I do say so myself.* And yes, the size of Newtopia's investment in the Antarctica project was simply mind-boggling: far beyond what the consortium had needed for re-icing the continent. She wondered what Eagle suspected.

A shower and then dinner called, in that order. Undressing, she dug her toes luxuriously into the soft carpet. *«Shower»*, she ordered via her link, then stretched and stood, padding into her en-suite and considering dinner as she went.

Inlays of mother-of-pearl winked at her through the steam as she slid the glass door aside and stepped under the welcoming, cleansing stream with a sigh. *«Pulse surge»*, she ordered, turning her back for the massaging spray to ease a tension knot.

She wondered how the new recruit was going. Perhaps Leeth might enjoy sharing dinner with her? Some female company would be nice. A smile quirked her lips: it would also be a chance to discuss the disappearing chocolate.

A little later, she left her rooms, accessing the security cameras until she spotted someone underwater in the pool, long black hair fanned out around a slim body. Wearing no swimming costume. And no one pulled her up for it. *Poor kid.* Emma didn't even want to *imagine* the sort of mission they were obviously grooming the child for. The depressing thought only reinforced her decision to invite her to dinner.

Leeth surfaced with a splash, lungs bursting, holding dice aloft triumphantly. Five! She'd been lucky, though: they'd landed in reverse order, so there'd been no need to retrace her route.

As she shook the water from her eyes she saw Emma standing at the poolside. She swam over, propping her forearms on the cool tiles, panting.

"Diving for pearls, Leeth?" Emma asked with a smile, brushing a lock of auburn hair back under a little black beret.

The girl grinned back. "Kind of. It's a game I invented. You toss in a bunch of dice, and collect as many as you can in one breath. But you have to pick them up in the right order. It's fun – do you want to try?"

"Another time. I actually stopped by to ask if you'd like to join me for dinner. Unless you've already eaten?"

"I'd love to! I did eat, but it was a couple of hours ago. What time is it now, ten o'clock?"

"Nine thirty eight, actually."

Emma saw Leeth's eyes dart to each of her bare wrists as if looking for a net-link, before frowning and pursing her lips determinedly. *Trying to work out how most of us are always so certain of the time?* Emma had the distinct impression Leeth didn't know they were augmented.

Almost, she considered letting her in on the small secret. But what'd be the fun in that?

Leeth shook water from her face. "Sure, that'd be great! Now?"

Emma shrugged elegantly, pleased if a little surprised by the eager response. "I'm starving. Can you be ready in fifteen minutes?"

Leeth tilted her head to one side as if puzzled by the question. Instead of answering, she opened one fist, dropping a small handful of translucent red dice to clatter on the stone tiling by Emma's feet, then diving to the bottom at the pool's edge. Swimming a few meters along the wall, she turned, then launched herself up and out, landing on her feet; water cascading from her skin. The whole thing had been a single flowing movement, and Emma stepped back, stunned. Surely it wasn't possible for someone to simply *jump* out of a pool? She re-cued her visual input, watching in slow motion as Leeth emerged from the water. This time she saw the hands slap down *hard* on the tiles for extra lift.

"Actually, I'll be ready as soon as I dry myself."

"How did you-? That was amazing!"

Leeth's face lit up. "Really? I've been practicing and practicing. You know, in case I need to overpower a guard one day by a billionaire's pool. I copied it from Black Mambo in *Sweet Revenge*."

While Emma stood, blinking, mouth open, Leeth picked up her dice and darted to the bench where she'd put her bathrobe, shrugging into it and patting herself dry.

"Okay, let's go!"

Emma collected herself. "Ah, Leeth, you don't think you'll be cold?"

"Nah, I'm pretty hot blooded. What'll we have for dinner?" she asked, linking her arm in Emma's and tugging her toward the exit.

"Do you like seafood?"

Leeth tilted her head. "You mean fish?"

Emma paused. "Ah, maybe. Look, why not let me choose? How hungry are you – would you like a starter as well as a main?"

Leeth looked at her blankly. "Uh, sure, that sounds fine."

"Wait, why don't we dress up, too? We can pretend we're having a girls' night out!"

A little later, in Leeth's rooms, Emma helped her choose an outfit. Strangely, apart from a few uniformly-tight items of gym wear, and a small selection of sensible shoes, there were *only* outfits suitable for clubbing.

"I take it you like the corseted look? I don't know why you bother – I'd kill for your figure," she said. "You even have a faint six-pack!"

The girl froze. Emma turned, and met a deadly serious expression: there in Leeth's walk-in wardrobe, still naked, the girl was ready to fight.

Then, just as suddenly, Leeth's posture relaxed. "That's just an expression, right? You couldn't get my figure by killing me."

Hoo, boy! "That's right." With a conscious effort, Emma smiled. "Why don't we go for the classic LBDs, and do your makeup? I haven't seen you dolled up yet."

Leeth's expression chilled.

Now what did I say wrong, Emma wondered?

Little Brother had organized and delivered their order with his usual efficiency. Emma watched now with enjoyment as Leeth cracked the last claw, extracting a final mouthful of lobster, her eyes screwed shut in pleasure. "*Mmm*, that was amazing! The best dinner I've *ever* had. I think I ate too much! Can you show me the combination for lobster mornay? Uncle will be *so* impressed!"

Emma blinked. "The combination?"

"Sure, the texture and flavor settings."

"Flavor settings?"

"Emma, don't be mean! For the T.V.P unit in the canteen," she explained.

"TVP?"

The girl scowled. "All right, be like that. See if I care. I'll work it out for myself. I reckon it's chewy-3, bite-3, water-4, maybe salt-2, cheese-6, lots of 621 to enhance the flavors-"

"Wait, stop. There's a textured vegetable protein dispenser in the canteen?"

Leeth's eyes narrowed, her head tilting to one side.

"And you've been using that to prepare meals for yourself and the Doctor since you've been here?"

A slow nod.

Emma covered her mouth with one hand. "How did you, um, find it?"

"The third day after we got here, I scouted around. It was pretty easy – all the places you're not allowed to go won't unlock, so anything that does unlock means you're allowed in. And I recognized the food machine since it was like the one we had at the Institute."

"The institute?"

"The Institute for Paranormal Dysfunction. That's where Uncle and me came from."

Emma *stilled*. "That's... interesting. What – ah, what sort of things did you both do there?"

Leeth frowned. "Uncle researched stuff. I used to just hunt things in the woods, mainly, and do lessons and train. Faith and I patrolled each night – she was a robodog – and sometimes I'd talk to Godsson. It was-"

She stopped, remembering they weren't supposed to talk about what had happened there, to people who didn't already know about it. On the other hand, she did need to find people who knew about Godsson, so she could convince people to let him free.

"Ah, did you talk to God's Son a lot?"

Leeth nodded eagerly. "Oh! You know about him?"

"Ye-es, Leeth. Most people have at least heard of him."

"They have? That's great! Are they *all* scared of him? Do they know where...?" She paused, then continued more quietly. "Um, do they know where he lives?"

Emma frowned. *Was this what Mother and Father had meant, when they'd warned her not to discuss morals, or ethics?* That didn't seem to quite fit, though. She probed, carefully.

"Do *you* know where he lives, Leeth?"

Leeth started to nod, then stopped herself. "I asked you first."

"The Institute for Paranormal Dysfunction, yes?" Emma called up the sketchy data she'd found online, much earlier. The material appeared in small panes around Leeth's face, so she could scan it again as they spoke. "Were there many other... famous people there, besides Jesus?"

Leeth frowned. "Who?"

Ahh, Emma thought. "Leeth, surely you know the Institute holds, um, people who are a little divorced from reality, yes?"

Leeth threw herself back in her seat, angry and disappointed. "Never mind. You don't know." *Which means I can't talk about him.* "You were going to tell me the combination for lobster mornay."

"Combination?"

"Yeah. On the meal dispenser."

Emma didn't answer straight away, then shook her head slowly, and braced herself. "Um, Leeth, I don't know how to tell you this, but if you'd read all the familiarization literature, in the section under 'Dining' you would have seen a link address for ordering meals. Little Brother takes the deliveries. Real food, not reconstituted and flavored soy products. Have you been selecting meals from the food dispenser every night since you've been here?"

Leeth nodded, slowly. "Not just at night. And not just for me, for Uncle too."

They stared at one another, and the corners of Emma's mouth began to twitch as she struggled not to laugh.

Leeth looked puzzled, then annoyed. "Do you mean I could've – we could've been having lobster mornay any time we wanted?"

Emma didn't trust herself to speak, just nodded, as she pictured the two sawing into plates full of chemically flavored fodder. A small snigger escaped, and she had to clamp one hand over her mouth.

It was the look of injured confusion that finally cracked Emma's control, and she snorted.

Leeth's offended look deepened, which somehow made the situation funnier still, and a laugh exploded from Emma despite herself, though she quickly turned it into a series of coughs.

Leeth scowled. "It wasn't just textured vegetable protein – I also found a store cupboard, with some spaghetti in *tubes*." She grimaced, remembering. "It was pretty crunchy, though."

"Crunchy?" Emma whimpered. "What- what did the Doctor think of it?"

"I don't know. He was working while he ate, and didn't pay much attention."

Emma mulled that over, her laughter at last dying, and she decided to ask about the other thing. "Though it isn't just the emergency rations you've been raiding, is it?" At Leeth's blank expression, she added, "You've been eating all the chocolate, haven't you? From the rec room." *Still no reaction.* "From the food dispenser: the 'Black Magic' bars."

"Oh! They're chocolate?" Leeth's expression became dreamy. "They're better than lobster mornay. I could eat them all up."

Emma raised one eyebrow. "I think you mean 'did,' not 'could.' It's been empty almost every time I've looked since you arrived. You'll get fat if you keep that up."

"I don't get-"

"Not to mention pimples."

Leeth's reaction was both instantaneous and out of all proportion. She jumped up, one hand flying to her forehead, probing at first in dismay, then slowing as she found the skin smooth and unblemished.

"It's not ret- I mean, I don't have any pimples." She stared at Emma accusingly. "Why did you say I had pimples?" Her voice held a strangely flat inflexion.

"I didn't say you had pimples. I was just warning you that eating too much chocolate *can* result in pimples."

Leeth slowly relaxed; then seemed to realize she was standing, and sat back down.

"Besides, it's nice to leave some for the rest of us."

But more than Leeth's over-reaction, something about the exchange was worrying Emma. "Leeth, had you ever had chocolate, before the Black Magic bars?"

The girl grimaced. "I don't remember. I don't think so. I sort of thought chocolate was a kind of egg." She rubbed her forehead. "It's all kind of vague. Colored eggs? No, it's gone."

"Easter eggs? Back at the Institute?"

"What's an Easter?"

About to answer, Emma snapped her mouth shut. She remembered the odd list of topics not to be discussed with Leeth, and suddenly saw not a naive young girl, but something *other*: some kind of strange experiment, memories created from nothing; or edited. *The Institute for Paranormal Dysfunction*. Was she even *human*?

With real effort, Emma forced a smile onto her face. "Best ask the Doctor. But I'm tired now, so I think it must be time for you to leave."

"I'll help you clean up."

"Leave it for the cleaning units."

The tone was sharper than Emma had intended, and the girl froze. "No, really, it's all right, leave it for the bots," Emma added softly.

They stared at one another.

Leeth tried to work out what it was she'd done, as she stood unmoving before the blank surface, Emma's door closed gently but firmly in her face. She'd thought they'd been getting on so well.

Eyes prickling, standing like an idiot in the empty corridor, bathed in the faint light of the projection of another random night-time woodland scene, she felt suddenly all alone.

CHAPTER 7

"She needs dancing lessons."

Father looked up, surprised by the sudden outburst. Mother's area of responsibility included training, and he knew she'd been reviewing the new recruits' performance evaluations, but... dancing?

She looked angry. At his unspoken query, she continued. "*If* she passes training, we will often deploy Leeth in the guise of an innocent, harmless young girl, yes?"

"Of course."

"So we can expect she'll visit nightclubs. Go dancing."

"Yes. Undoubtedly. And, ah, other things, afterwards."

"Yes." Mother paused. "Quite."

Father opted to ignore the carefully bitten off words: each time someone referred to the *other* uses planned for the girl, Mother's expression soured as if taking personal affront. Sometimes, Mother was too soft. Any sacrifice was acceptable, for the good of America.

"Watch this footage from the gym."

He accepted the internal link she sent, cueing the VR stream in conference-mode so they could share it.

It was Leeth, dancing in the gym, to a quite foot-tapping tune. *Mmm, very graceful. Very athletic, too.* He was soon engrossed, watching her leap and spin dramatically through the room, her movements perfectly timed to the rhythm of the music.

Mother's voice was an unwelcome interruption. "I *said*, Father, if you can tear your eyes away from her performance, you can see why she needs lessons in formal dance. Ballroom. Rock and roll. Jive. Club."

"Er..."

"Father," she began, in that overly patient tone he so disliked, "that was the most beautifully deadly looking dancing I've ever seen. Half those leaps, sweeps, and arm motions are katas from her martial arts training. Were she completing those moves she'd *slay* her partners, not seduce them. She needs formal dance lessons simply so she'll have something other than her killing arts to draw on to express herself."

He skimmed through the video again, then sighed. "Agreed."

"I'll have Nelson load James and Preacher's chips with dancing skills. Emma's too, when they're all present at the same time. She can practice with them."

"Oh, they'll *love* that."

"Then let them know that should they give less than their full support, I will add interpretive dance and ballet, too."

Surprisingly, over the following weeks, the other agents complained less than either Father or Mother had expected. Indeed, the girl's enthusiasm and enjoyment was so infectious, and the rare four-person-balls so joyous, that even Father joined in once or twice, to Mother's intense annoyance.

CHAPTER 8

No one paid special attention as James and Leeth followed the waiter to their table.

Holding James's arm, Leeth curled into his side, trying her best tonight to be the young ingénue, Samantha Westin. They'd told her it wasn't a mission, but from her suppressed excitement, James suspected she saw this outing differently.

For just a moment, as he pulled out the chair for her, she scowled, but then appeared to remember Mother's lessons and allowed him to seat her.

So far, so good, thought James, glancing from the impeccably set table to the exquisitely dressed young woman. He'd doubted her readiness at first – when he'd had to *insist* she wear a bra with her cocktail dress, for example. He planned to speak to Emma on the subject tomorrow. Leeth had strange gaps in her social skills. He wondered again about her upbringing by the Doctor. Nothing that chap did struck him as accidental: so why did Leeth seem in some ways more like a young savage than a young woman?

Leeth's eyes widened as she took in all the cutlery. Lips moving, she studied the place setting, but at last nodded and relaxed. Then read the menu with equal intensity.

"All right?"

She started to nod. "Oh – wait! Can we order stuff that's not on the menu?"

"Certainly. This *is* a five star restaurant."

She leaned forward, eyes wide. "Then can we get them to barbecue some tarantulas?"

James went still.

"They're s'posed to be delicious."

Still James said nothing.

"Just a few. I've got this old documentary. You pounce them with a forked stick and tie their legs up together. You have to do that carefully, cause they can shoot their hairs-"

"No! No, I'm afraid tarantulas are not currently in season."

"Rats."

"Don't you *dare*. We would both be thrown out!"

"Huh? Don't dare what?"

"Ah. I thought you meant... never mind. Just choose from what's on the menu. Are you ready to order? Do you need any help?"

She shook her head, and he met the Maitre'd's eyes. Derek glided over, summoning one of his waiters with a glance. Sizing 'Samantha' up in a fraction of a second, Derek inclined his head in approval.

"It's been too long, James. What would the young lady-"

"I'd like the seafood pasta. That's a starter. For the main course, I want, I mean, may I please have the seven-hundred gram sirloin steak, rare, with a, a *side* of vegetables. For dessert, I'll-"

"Perhaps," Derek interrupted, "it might be wise to wait until you have finished your main course."

"Why?"

"Ah... pardonne?"

"Why would it be wise?"

James seemed to be signaling her, so she waited for *Derek* to speak. He was the one she had to fool each night, after all.

"In case madame decides she is no longer hungry. When one considers the magnitude of such a cut..." He smiled, tactfully indicating the size with two hands.

She sighed. "Alright. I get it. It's a lot of meat. So give me *two* servings of vegetables to go with it."

Neither man spoke.

"What?"

"If madame is certain...?" At her look, he turned to James. "And for you, my friend?"

After dinner, they strolled together. The air was warm, just a faint breeze, a full moon sailing the gaps between passing clouds. Here, tonight, deep inside the glittering forest of the city, the harsh reality of the real New Francisco seemed far away.

They were returning to the Opera House, still in good time for the performance. Despite some awkward moments, in the end Mother's lessons on table manners had sufficed. 'Samantha' had even approached elegance once or twice.

She looked up at the moon, and he half-turned to her, noticing her cheerfulness had vanished.

"Something the matter?"

"I was just wondering what Faith was doing, tonight."

"Faith?"

She pursed her lips. Finally, nodded. "We used to... do stuff together. Play."

James raised one eyebrow.

"Not that kind of stuff! She's just a friend. A dog, actually: an Asgard Model 3 CK9."

James looked it up, and stopped dead, which forced Leeth to turn toward him. "CK9s were designed to hunt and kill eco-terrorists! It'd be deadly!"

"Well, sure. But fun to play with, and super cuddly."

She slipped her arm around his waist, and snuggled in to his side.

"Much like you," James suggested. The comment appeared to cheer her, though her thoughts appeared to be far away. "Did you have any, ah, adventures, with Faith?"

The look she turned to him held a great depth of feeling, and her mouth opened; but she didn't speak. After a moment, she forced a smile. "I'm Samantha Westin, remember? I don't have cyberdog friends." She looked around. "We need to stay in character."

James checked. The nearest person was well out of earshot, a hundred meters away – well, ninety-four, his optic range-finder showed – but he was happy to play along.

He patted her slender wrist, draped over his arm. "You know, Samantha, this is probably one of the few places in the whole cityplex where people can walk the streets safely, at night. It has the lowest murder rate of anywhere in New Francisco."

Smiling down at her, he saw her expression sour and her lips purse as she pulled her arm free of his. *Defensive,* he wondered? *Why would she-*

"That's not *my* fault. I've only ever even been here once before!"

He blinked. *She thinks I'm* blaming *her for the low death rate!* Suddenly, the doubts were back.

They took their seats near the center of the eighth row comfortably in time for the performance. As the crowd finished filtering into the large, ornately-decorated auditorium, James was all smiles and anticipation. Leeth, however, pushed herself further back into the dark red velvet. Her face had screwed up in disbelief, as if tortured by the orchestral warm-up.

"Stop over-reacting: they're just tuning up," he admonished her.

"Why wait till *now*? Are they running late?"

James blinked. "This is just the final tuning. It's part of the ritual; adds to the ambiance." Her lips compressed into a thin line. "Part of the joy is hearing harmony blossom from cacophony, like magic."

Leeth put a finger to one ear, drawing it back to theatrically examine the tip. "Huh. Well, at least they're not bleeding. *Yet.*"

James frowned, and met her eyes directly. "Come, *Samantha*, try to be open-minded."

Leeth scowled, then forced a happy expression onto her face, telling herself she was supposed to be *enjoying* this, impressed by it all.

"They're of course using *analog* instruments," James added, nodding significantly. Like that made them somehow better than digital.

Leeth was unconvinced. Sure, the instruments sounded richer and *realer* played live – way different to recordings. At the edges of hearing, some of the odd peaks and deep notes even sent shivers through her. But a lot of those bits were also... *off*.

Maybe they *couldn't* tune them? That'd explain why no one ever recorded those parts.

She kept her opinions to herself, but if the painful torture went on much longer, someone was going to be sorry.

James chose that moment to put his mouth to her ear: as if she was deaf or something. "We're very lucky – this is the first part of *Das Rheingold*, the Ring Saga. I think you'll like it."

She quickly forced her grimace back into a smile. Then the lights were dimming, the massive gold curtain rising.

She wondered how long the performance would be.

For five disbelieving minutes Leeth kept silent, before conceding defeat. "James, I can't understand what they're singing."

James didn't seem to hear her, so she whispered it again, louder.

"James!"

Leeth gritted her teeth. Not only was she being tormented by the piercing soprano, the vocals were drowning her out so James couldn't even hear her question! She imagined jumping up on stage to claw the woman's throat out.

"James! I can't understand them!"

The couple in the seats directly in front turned and glared at her. Leeth glared right back, fighting down a sudden urge to thump them.

"Shh." James put his finger to his lips, eyes still on the performers. "Here's the programme."

She took it from him, puzzled. Frowning in the dark, she re-read the pamphlet while the soprano continued her sonic assault.

Looking up from it, and around, everyone else seemed completely absorbed. Even James. She looked back at the programme. It sure *sounded* exciting. But it was like they were all singing in *code!*

"James!"

After the curtain fell, Leeth seemed in no hurry to move. James watched her studying the departing audience with a strange intensity. "Well – what did you think of The Rheingold?"

"There was an awful lot of it."

"Would you like to meet the lead singer? Maria Lempriere?"

Leeth's eyes brightened. "Yeah. Yeah, I would."

After a short flurry of messaging, Maria flung open her dressing room door as they arrived. "James! James Connor!"

She pronounced his name 'Shames Kon-nor,' Leeth noticed.

"How marveilleux to see you. And who is your little friend?"

"This is Samantha Westin. She was dying to meet you."

"'Ow wonderful. What did you think of our performance?"

"I thought you were very brave."

Maria's face stiffened.

"Singing, with your throat hurting like that." She'd been half-guessing, but Maria's reaction confirmed it. Leeth sensed James go still, at her side. "You might have some kind of growth: you should see a doctor."

Maria raised one trembling hand.

"Or maybe a mage? They could-"

Maria pointed. "Get out!" she hissed. "At once! And you, James Connor..."

James dragged Leeth away as the singer's eyes fell on a heavy crystal ashtray.

From there, he took her to a night café. He *had* intended to take her to his club, but common sense prevailed. *Perhaps after she's more... rounded.*

They sat now with their coffees, James watching with quiet disbelief as Leeth wolfed down a generous serve of carrot cake. After every mouthful or two, she stirred more sugar into her mug.

"Ah, that's better!" she said, after the seventh spoonful.

"Milk? Cream?"

"Oh? Uh, yeah. Sure."

He poured. She tasted.

"Mmm, good." She licked her fingers clean of cake, then took a large gulp of her coffee, though her lips twisted immediately after.

"You don't like the Colombian Novo-supremo?"

"No, it's, um, good. Very, you know. *Coffee* flavored. It's one of my favorites." She tilted her head back and drained her mug. "See? It was, yummy."

He sipped at his own espresso. "Would you like another?"

"No! I mean, no, thank you, James." She shivered.

"Cold?"

"No." She shut her eyes, then pushed back from the table, spreading her fingers wide. *Definitely trembling.* "Hey. What should we do next? We don't have to go back yet, do we? We could go dancing. Oh! No, I know: the Tenderloin district's not far from here, is it? Yes! Let's! I'm sure we could Hunt down some fun there. Please, James? Please, please, please..."

He took another cautious sip. "I take it you've something specific in mind?"

She sprang up from her seat, twirling from their table and then dancing back to him, shimmying down to press her front into his side. "*Several* things. *Please*, James? Please, please, please...."

-

Maria Lempriere was still fuming. *Never* had she been so insulted! Her anger made her fumble the key in the lock, and she had to strangle an urge to throw the foolish thing away. A brass key! What was this, the twentieth century? Finally, the mechanical lock clicked. Thrusting the door open, she stalked out into the small courtyard enclosed within the Opera House.

Which was another insult: to be forced into smoking *outside* – putting her delicate throat at further risk from the night air! Almost, she forgot to lock the door behind her.

She lit up her herbal cigarette, calming with the first inhalation. Already, she could feel the rare Amazonian *medicine* relaxing her throat, *improving* her register. How dare that baby-faced-

From behind her, back by the doorway, came a loud and ugly snapping sound. She spun around to see a large figure, a man, step through the door and close it behind him. She moved back as he emerged from the shadows.

"You are agitated tonight."

He was tall, with a heavy build. He wore a very expensive, but also very *tired* suit.

"How did you get in here? This is not open to the public."

Ice blue eyes stared at Maria, unblinking. "You Called. This one came."

He stepped forward.

She stepped further back. "Stop. Do not come one step closer or-"

She rocked back on her heels as a large hand clamped around her throat.

"You are distressed." He nodded. "Yes. And angry. And now, afraid. These are phantoms, clouding your mind." The cold eyes burned into hers as she beat futilely at the arm holding her. "There is no need for fear. You will soon see. Prepare yourself for the gift of clarity...."

CHAPTER 9

"Come *on,* James, stop *dawdling.* Let's race!"

Pulling her hand free of his, Leeth darted ahead, deeper into the quake-twisted streets. From doorways of the buildings on either side, several large figures watched the girl speculatively as she sprinted past them, her high heels clutched in one hand.

Christ! She could move! James charged after her. *And silent, too,* he noticed, realizing if he didn't catch her before he lost sight of her.... «*Faster*» he ordered his bio-chip, and felt power surge to his legs.

Down two, three alleys he chased her, scarcely gaining ground, before she slowed, then stopped, standing with her head tilted to one side.

Thank god, he thought, just as she blurred back into motion, smashing through a barricade to disappear inside what looked like a squatter's den. From within, ply-board crashed to the ground. He heard her scream a challenge, and answering male cries.

When he burst into the squalid, ill-lit room, it was to see one tattooed male falling backwards, blood spurting from his neck. Leeth's foot kicked out into another man now collapsing behind her, while throat-punching a third in front who fell, dropping a knife. To one side, a terrified youth scrambled away from the fight on heels and elbows.

"Stop!" James yelled.

Leeth didn't. Instead, her teeth gleaming in a fierce smile, she hauled upright the gasping man she'd just punched. Behind her, the man she'd kicked rose groggily to his feet.

Knotting her hand in the jacket of the ex knife-wielder, she spun him around and *up,* hoisting him over her head to slam down into the man swaying behind her.

James winced as their skulls cracked together.

The youth, still scrabbling on the ground on hands and knees, grabbed up... a credstick? Then fled.

Hands on hips, Leeth watched him depart. "Huh. He could've at least *thanked* me."

James reached the tattooed ganger bleeding out from... *Good lord!* His eyebrows raised at the sight of Leeth's stiletto heel jutting from the jugular.

As he crouched down, the man's chest stopped rising and falling, her bloody victim falling still.

Placing her feet carefully, he saw, Leeth stepped past him and bent down to wrench her shoe free.

"Are you- what do you think you're doing?"

The face she turned to him was alive with delight. "Hunting for more people to rescue, of course!" She squeezed his arm. "Thanks so much for bringing me here – this is heaps more fun than the opera!" She frowned at her blood-soaked shoe as she turned away. "We *can* do more, right? Just let me finish off these other two, first."

From behind, James tasered her. She staggered. But instead of collapsing, she spun around, jerkily, with an expression of disbelief. Only half-stunned. He followed up with a blow to her temple, a hard tap. *Still* she didn't go down! Instead, eyes glazed, her fist punched out to his belly. Even at full augment, he was only just fast enough to deflect the blow.

A third, harder strike to the side of her head finally rolled her eyes back, and she collapsed, her gaze still accusing.

Holy hell! He looked around, assessing the scene. He had an evidence bag, which should be just large enough for her bloody heel, to keep his suit clean. He tucked that one inside his jacket and the other into a trouser pocket. Then, hauling her up and over one shoulder, he brought up a map to work out the best place to direct his car to, to meet them. Then called up the schematics for this address, and began picking his way out, toward the side exit.

Wincing, he thought ahead to his report on tonight's outing. She'd just taken it from ten minutes work, to two hours.

What the devil had gotten into her?

CHAPTER 10

It was the next day and for once, all three agents were mission-less. Emma and James lounged in the rec room, though with a palpable tension between them.

James had just returned from a short debrief with Father. Who had reacted to his account as he'd half expected: with indifference. "Nelson set a watch – the deaths have passed unreported. Was that by accident, d'you think, or has she been paying attention to her lessons?"

James had been unable to say.

It also appeared that Father had reviewed just the highlighted portions of the optic and auditory downloads, covering the night's dramatic finale.

Father had nodded happily. "Made short work of *them*, didn't she? Good job. She didn't look too pleased with *you* though, at the end. Do you think I need to have a word with her?"

James nearly snapped back that he didn't need protection from an eighteen-year-old girl. Then paused and frowned.

Father smiled. "Exactly. Let's not, then, eh? Be another little test for her."

The debriefing over, James headed to the rec room.

"James!" A complex mix of emotions played across Emma's face, and James forced himself not to wince. "How did your 'date' with Leeth go?"

Preacher watched: scowling.

"So-so. She was... a little wild. We returned to the Department earlier than planned."

"And?"

He just shrugged, refusing to say anything further. With the result that for the last ten minutes, Emma had been very pointedly ignoring him.

Finally, James sighed. "She's going to put on weight if she keeps eating like last night. She ate *a lot*."

"Oh?" Emma asked.

"Yes. A large seafood pasta starter, then a massive steak, with *two* orders of vegetables. For dessert-"

"Dessert!"

"Quite. For dessert, she finished off with their famous waffles and home-made ice cream, drenched in Derek's chocolate sauce. He could scarcely believe it."

"Well, she *is* extremely active. Have you ever seen her idle?"

James thought. Then thought harder. "By god, you're right."

Emma concealed a smile behind her hand. '*By god.*' But from his lips it didn't sound contrived. Just a trifle quaint.

"Oh, and look at this, after she asked if we could request things not on the menu. Give me a channel."

Emma transmitted a link address, then accepted the data feed. Since she was being social, instead of mixing the audio and video over her live senses, she cast the footage from James's eyecam to her newssheet.

In it, Leeth looked excited, leaning forward over the elegantly set table. The view shifted down to the girl's cleavage, and Emma shook her head.

"*Then can we get them to barbecue some tarantulas?*" Leeth asked.

Emma sprayed a fine mist of tea, then cut the link, feeling faintly nauseous. Preacher, looking on, rolled his eyes at her reaction. "The kid's right. They're delish. Amazonian delicacy."

After that, though, James had refused to be drawn further, eagerly accepting Preacher's challenge to a game of poker.

Emma left them to it, sinking herself back into the newsfeed on her tridsheet, the flexible display held up to signal her activity. Fifteen minutes passed before James tensed, so abruptly it made the other two turn to see what had caused the reaction.

Leeth was in the room, halfway to them.

"Hello, Leeth," James said, and Emma noticed he'd put his cards face down on the table, watching the girl with a carefully neutral expression, his arms loose at his sides. Emma had seen that same deceptive readiness from him before. On missions.

"Hi."

Preacher merely grunted.

But Leeth didn't move: just stood staring at James, her eyes narrowed.

James had grown even more tense: and with a sense of shock, Emma saw her augments register that James's had just entered combat mode. Preacher's head went up, and he looked on with interest.

And Leeth....

Leeth *relaxed*. With a private little smile now on her face, she padded silently over to them on bare feet, seating herself cross-legged in one of the large stuffed leather chairs by the card table.

She wore just a thin singlet and a pair of denim shorts, her skin gleaming with a sheen of perspiration.

Emma smiled a tentative greeting and Leeth smiled back, but said nothing. Emma's augments signaled as James powered back down. She glanced back at him as he warily picked up his cards. *«James: what was that all about?»*

But James, with lips pursed, ignored her.

Turning her attention to her 'sheet, Emma began angrily clicking through the articles she'd selected.

Silence fell while James and Preacher studied their cards. Leeth watched them all intently.

At last James looked up. "How are your lessons going today, Leeth?"

Her eyes lit up, and she stretched comprehensively. "Sensei just finished with me for the day. I don't have anything till Emma's free this afternoon."

"Killed anyone today?" Preacher asked sarcastically.

James's head jerked up to stare at Preacher.

"No." Leeth cocked her head to one side, trying to work out the reason for Preacher's strange tone. "I've been too busy, and I'm not allowed out."

Emma laughed at the response, but it caught in her throat at the look James turned on her. She stared from the girl to James, his grim expression telling her more than she wanted to know. Father's injunction about safe topics of conversation made sudden sickening sense.

With a hollow feeling in her stomach Emma cued a search onto her newssheet: 'opera and murder.' *There.* She read it, quickly. The murder of a well-known soprano at the War Memorial Opera House last night. Just like several other murders over the last few months. Gruesome.

Hard to believe the happy young girl before her could be responsible. That she could be the awful killer the newsment shows had started to call 'The Breaker.' Emma looked at Leeth with an equal mix of horror at what she'd done and pity for her future; then bent her head back to her 'sheet.

At least it explained how Leeth had come to Eagle's attention.

"When d'you go out on your next mission?" Leeth asked the group. The three operatives exchanged frowns.

"Why do you want to know?" demanded Preacher.

"I thought maybe you could ask Father if I could come with you, to help?"

Preacher snorted. "Chip out, girl. You've been here what, a few weeks? Ask again in six months."

"Six months? You mean weeks, right?" She looked from one face to another. "Are you *serious*?"

At Preacher's amused nod, she sprang from her chair. "Six *months*?" She prowled around the billiard table, grimacing, then circled the coffee machine. "Six months!"

"You've got a *lot* to learn, yet, Leeth," Emma answered gently. "We all have to teach you as much as we can."

Leeth stood, tense. "Well," she gestured vaguely with one open hand, then frowned. "Preacher! Can you teach me some more shooting? Now?"

"I'm playing poker, Leeth. Maybe if you're nice to me, I'll give you an hour's workout, say at two?"

She scowled, continuing to prowl the room. Emma went back to her news. The silence didn't last long. "Does anyone want to play pool?"

"Billiards," corrected James, automatically.

"All right, billiards." She looked at the table in puzzlement. "Hey, where are all the other balls?" she asked, hunting around the table.

"That's all there are. It's for James' scuzzin' billiards. And we're *trying* to play poker," Preacher answered.

Silence once more descended, Leeth pacing the room until her attention was captured by Emma's absorption in whatever she was reading. The girl came silently over, reading over the older woman's shoulder. It seemed to be just news, but then a heading caught her eye. "What's 'i-rape,' Emma?"

"Identity-rape. Like r-theft." At Leeth's blank look she added, "Reality-theft."

Leeth screwed up her face.

"You know, like someone overlaying you with a naked replacement or a diseased one; or someone hacking your mediated-reality with their own one – like they might re-place the prices on items with higher ones, or otherwise hide parts of reality from you."

"We had some trouble with Nelson, when he was younger," offered James.

"Nelson?" Leeth asked. "I've had some systems, search, and security lessons with him. What'd he do?"

"Well, technically it wasn't i-rape or r-theft," Emma said, "since he was only modifying his own senses, but it was highly unprofessional."

"But what'd he *do*?"

"He was replacing my body's image with a real-time nude simulacrum," Emma said. "It was obvious when he was doing it – he'd have this stupid grin, and his eyes would be practically glued to my breasts. Mother and Father came down on him like a ton of dragon-shit."

"Oh." Leeth considered asking if there was something funny about Emma's breasts, but decided not to. Then she wondered how Nelson *saw* the images... but she just wasn't that interested. She wanted to be *doing* something, not talking!

Emma continued reading her news pad; James took a card from the deck.

Leeth decided to relax, like the agents were. Plopping down in a seat, she stretched out and tried to think calm thoughts. She adjusted her position, trying for a posture that declared 'I'm a professional, relaxing calmly in be-tween missions, and I could stay like this for *hours*.'

Five minutes later she was prowling the room again.

Pausing by the coffee machine, she furtively poured a cup. She knew Uncle said it was a drug, a stimulant, but the others were always drinking it and it didn't seem to af-fect them at all. But she added creamer and plenty of sugar, having learned *that* much last night.

"Oh, no," Emma suddenly announced. "Another copter went down in the Sonoma Valley – twenty three people killed. Private charter company." She held out her 'sheet so they could all see, before continuing, angrily. "When the old US government controlled licenses, these people had to meet proper standards. Twenty three dead. It's horrible."

Leeth trod softly over. A rectangular window showed rescue workers picking through wreckage. A small frown creased her brow. "Who was on the copter?"

"It doesn't say. New Francisco Joyflights Inc haven't released the passenger list yet."

Leeth's crease deepened. "Was somebody important on it?"

"I doubt it. Otherwise they'd have said."

Leeth moved around and sat back in her chair, sipping at the hot liquid with an expression that seemed to say she was trying hard to enjoy it. "Why was it horrible, then?"

Emma frowned. "Because twenty three people died in a copter crash."

Head tilted to one side, Leeth tried to puzzle it out. "I don't get it. Was the *copter* special?"

James's voice on their shared comm-channel interrupted her. «*Emma!*» She looked across, where he was making a face at her, subtly shaking his head. With a chill, she realized this too must be part of Leeth's 'psychological orientation.'

She tried to recover. "Oh. Well, no, not exactly *special*. Just expensive. And the loss will, ah, it'll seriously inconvenience a lot of people."

Leeth put down her now-empty cup, drawing up her knees. Hugging herself, she rocked back and forth, then jumped out of the chair, laughing. All three agents looked at her strangely. Her skin tingled and her thoughts had started buzzing like wasps sucked into a cyclonic vacuum.

"Anyone wanna come for a swim? We could race!"

Preacher snorted, James shook his head, and Emma gently declined. Leeth laughed again, hugging herself. "How about sex? Do any of you feel like sex? Even Preacher."

All three stared at her in astonishment. Preacher glared down at his cards, looking torn.

But Leeth had already bounced to her feet and run from the room. She had to move. Sprinting harder, feet slipping on the corridor as she slammed through the door into the swimming pool, she tore off her clothes and dived into the water.

The agents exchanged looks as Leeth surged down the length of the pool.

"She *on* something?" asked Preacher.

"I don't *think* so," James answered, sounding uncertain.

"Did you notice something, while she was here?" asked Emma.

"Besides the business about the copter crash?"

"Mm-hm."

Both men shook their heads.

"She barely sat still for five minutes."

"So?"

"But she said she'd just come from Dojo." The two men looked suddenly thoughtful. "I'm always wrecked after a session with Dojo. *She* sits down for five, then can't stop flitting about the room."

All three turned to the transparent wall, where Leeth now... *cavorted* in the water.

Half mesmerized, they watched as she dived and swam, her activity becoming steadily *more* frenetic as each minute passed.

"She *must* be on something," muttered Preacher. "Looks like she's going to fragging blow!"

Suddenly she stilled; then a moment later, plunged underwater to the side of the pool. Her tanned shape crouched on the bottom, then shot from the water like a dolphin. Hands slapping the sides for an instant – *she's got that down pat*, Emma thought – she raced from the room, ignoring her clothes.

James turned to face the door nearest the corridor outside. But as seconds passed and she didn't reappear, he let his breath out in a slow hiss of relief.

Emma looked at him. "Does *that*-? How *did* things go last night?"

He grimaced. "I don't like to criticize a lady. Let me put it this way: at least she knew how to use a knife and fork."

"And the opera?"

He groaned. "I didn't truly understand the meaning of the word 'embarrassment' until last night."

"Not an opera fan, then?"

"No. Not. And you may not believe this, but she thought 'German' was a *city* – didn't know there were any languages besides English, Japanese, Street and Mumbles."

The other two looked doubtful.

He stared, eyes unfocused, at the swimming pool. "And *that's* how she started acting last night, after the opera." He frowned. "We, ah, left after I'd introduced her to Maria Lempriere. I took her to a night café." He shook his head. "But she dragged me out before I'd finished. Convinced me to take her into the Tenderloin to show me something."

"Which was where she...?" Preacher made a slashing motion, and James nodded.

"What was Maria doing in *that* part of town?" asked Emma.

The two men stared at her blankly, and she gestured down at her "sheet. "Maria Lempriere was murdered last night. I assumed that was who Leeth killed."

James looked stunned. *"Maria's* dead?"

He sat motionless for so long that Preacher half rose to his feet, mock-helpfully. "Looks like your chip's slipped. Want me to bash it back in for you, 'old man'?"

James snapped out of it, ignoring the jibe. "She did say she wanted to kill Maria. But... she couldn't have. Impossible. We were together the whole time."

"Really?" sneered Preacher. "How was the ladies room?"

James's lips thinned, but he said nothing, merely shook his head again.

In the following silence Emma found herself staring at the empty cup beside Leeth's chair. She looked up at the other two. "You said, she dragged you out of a *café*? What did *she* have?"

"Well, just cake and a cup of-."

"Coffee?" exclaimed Preacher. "You think she goes into orbit over a cup of coffee? Come *on.*"

For a moment, James didn't respond. "You weren't there," he said, quietly.

Preacher rolled his eyes. "Come on, deal up. You've been chipping too much oh-oh-seven, *James*. This is real life, not one of your null spy dramas. Some of us have *real* work to do, not just sleep around with interns while playing pranks on stuck-up nobodies like your fucking pal *Derek* at his five-star restaurant!"

James froze. Then, staring coldly back at Preacher, he rose and tossed the cards down onto the table.

"I believe I've had enough," he said, and stalked from the room.

"Hey, you can't just- I was winning, dammit!" Preacher looked hopefully into the pool, then across at Emma, whose mouth drew tight as she deliberately focused on her news scanner.

With a snarl, Preacher thrust from his chair and stormed off, plowing through the door. *Bastards. Oh-so-pure bastards. Whose operation did they think* funded *their delusional rich-spy lifestyles?*

Emma shut her eyes tightly against the surge of anguish awoken by Preacher's chip-dream taunt. Her right hand involuntarily brushed aside the hair concealing her own headjack, fingers tracing the hard edges of the precious socket. She could go to her rooms right now, chip in and return to Maldemort. The villagers there now recognized her worth, as the plot moved towards its climax. Or continue the Enigma Charade – Charlie was definitely in over his head, if he only had the sense to know it.

She half rose from her chair, but with the door still swinging shut from Preacher's departure, the mental image of his sneering face was too fresh a reminder of her own weakness. Instead, she made herself sit back down and resist the siren call. Blinking away tears, she forced her eyes open and her attention back to the 'scanner.

"Damn him," she whispered.

CHAPTER 11

Some weeks later, Leeth stalked down the corridor, the heels of her stylish faux-combat boots cracking whip-like against the concrete floor. So angry, as she stormed from her meeting with Mother and Father, that she'd forgotten her private vow to always walk silently. She could hardly believe it. She'd been here well over a month now, and they were *still* treating her like a baby!

What's wrong with them? Did they really think she couldn't work out for herself when it was okay to kill someone? What'd they think she was going to do – kill the mayor during a press conference or something?

Unbelievable. Being told that when she was out, she was only allowed to 'retire' the nominated target or targets. She wasn't allowed to do *anyone* else except in emergencies.

'Probability of detection,' 'pervasive surveillance,' 'home and street spirits.' *Funt!* She knew all that stuff! She paid attention in her lessons. And it wasn't like she wasn't careful! The metrocops wouldn't have investigated the deaths of gangers and rapists. No one would: everyone hated the RedSkulls. It wasn't fair.

She'd worked out a whole plan: she was going to make the 'Skulls think some kind of supernatural monster was hunting them, like in *Eyes of Darkness*; with slime and everything. It would've been so cool, too! She'd even studied the old sewer system so she could sneak around their territory more easily.

And now, all that planning was wasted.

I bet the other agents are allowed to kill whenever they like, she grumbled to herself.

But as she stomped past 'soothing' woodland scenes of stupid chipmunks and swallows, a distant sound gradually penetrated her thoughts. She slowed, then stopped, tilting her head to listen. *Machine gun fire!*

The sound had Leeth racing to the rec room, but even as she approached, the clipped frequencies told her it was only a recording, not the real thing. Her eager sprint slumped to a disappointed walk, and she looked in from the doorway. James was grimly watching a large holo-projection occupying fully half the space inside.

She'd had to watch the newsment shows every night for the last month, now. But it wasn't the regular time, and the waif-like newscaster, Nina Summers, was doing the most serious pout Leeth had ever seen her achieve. Leeth, frowning, tried pursing her lips the same way as she crept in, wondering what it was all about.

In the trid, people were running sideways and forwards, shooting as they went. Nina and a gorgeous man with wavy golden hair, who towered over her, strolled through the center of the carnage like two translucent angels. Leeth didn't recognize the man but he, too, was looking real serious. So it had to be a news show.

The gunfire and background sounds damped down as he spoke. "Yes, Nina, a shocking waste of life. Corporate estimates place the death toll between ten and twelve thousand, after only two days of fighting."

"Wow," whispered Leeth, boggling. *What could slay so many people so fast?* A dragon? Would they expect *her* to be able to do that, eventually? Twelve thousand? You'd have to be *super* fit. She stepped further into the room.

"That's terrible, Dan. Is the Vatican planning to send in reinforcements?"

"Hard to say. The Big Guy could choose to send in more troops, although," he replied, his voice sinking to a conspiratorial level, "I've heard rumors he may deploy a crack squad of New Inquisitors. I'd put money on that, Nina. They'll need magical – or holy – assistance to locate these guerrillas."

Huh? wondered Leeth.

A hail of bullets flew through the two commentators, and camera angles shifted to move them out of the line of fire. It was true, what Uncle said: with a nice outfit you really could set a good example, show people how healthy you were. Nina was wearing a cute pink halter and a gray nanoskirt, revealing the sleek dragon-welt coiled round her belly button. Leeth sighed. The Department wouldn't let *her* get any scarwork: 'No permanent distinguishing features allowed.' And Uncle thought scars were ugly.

"Can you tell us anything, Dan, about the reports of the Order of the Knights Templar re-forming?"

"Well, Nina, I can. Reliable sources suggest the Knights are already back in action. Whether they'll be given a role in this conflict, and whether that escalation leads to a full-scale Holy War..." he shrugged. "Right now we can only speculate."

"Well, that sounds pretty important, Dan, but I'm afraid that's all we have time for now."

"No problemo, Nina." He turned to face the unseen audience. "But stay tuned to Kroneco News for further details as the situation heats up, and don't forget *you* can participate in the action. Just access the link below to guess the number of days this conflict will run, *and* the total number of casualties for your chance to win-"

With a vicious gesture, James killed the projection.

"What was *that*?" Leeth asked.

James started in surprise, turning to face the girl. "That was the flare-up of an old, old conflict. Engineered, I would say, because of the recent discovery of deep oil deposits offshore from Istanbul."

"But Dan said it had only been going on for two days."

"Dan Jackson is an idiot, and a corporate puppet. That war has been going, off and on, for centuries."

"Oh." Leeth stood there frowning, digesting the information. "But I thought you only had wars against violence, or skin cancer, or pollution. That looked a lot more exciting than any of *those* wars."

James narrowed his eyes. "That's not funny, Leeth."

She stared at him blankly.

Gradually, it dawned on him – she hadn't been joking. "Surely, you must have seen other wars. God knows, they rate well enough these days."

"No," she said, still puzzled.

"But... there are thousands of sites devoted entirely to war coverage. Not to mention stimsenses, or even old 2D movies. The Battle of Britain!"

Leeth shook her head. "I've never seen anything like *that* on the trid. We didn't use to get many newsments, though, at the- I mean, where we used to live."

James stared at her.

"And I've not done any stimsenses – unless you mean VR simulations? I've done some VR for stuff like martial arts, and athletics. But Uncle doesn't like stims. He says too much secondhand experience makes you soft."

"Your uncle-" suddenly, James had the distinct impression he stood on thin ice. Such a large blank space in her education could not have been accidental. 'They didn't get many newsments?' Ridiculous. But why in god's name would the man conceal from her that wars were a fact of life – still common?

"So what are they like, wars? You're saying they're like a really big fight?"

James realized he was stuck now. "Er, yes. Basically,"

Leeth waited for him to go on.

He didn't.

"Well, juice!" She sprang over the couch to face him. "So, was this a *big* one? Is twelve thousand people a really big war, or what? Is that a record?"

"No. Nowhere near."

Leeth stamped her foot. "Funt, James! *Unload!* Would I *like* it?"

James's emotions ran from shock, to horror, to pity, but he tried to keep that from his expression as he stood to make a tactical withdrawal. "I suggest you ask your uncle," he said, and left the room.

She watched him go. *What just happened?* Puzzled, she decided to do exactly as he'd suggested, and made her way to her uncle's new office.

"Keepie?"

"Mmm? What, Leeth?"

Leeth stepped inside, looking around. Trailing her fingers over the familiar spines of his printed books on their new shelves, she felt a curious pang for the Institute. What would Faith be doing, now? Sighing, she let her fingers fall. She dropped into the comfy visitor's chair in front of his work-desk, folding her bare legs up under her. "What's the record for the most people killed in a war?"

"Mmm, oh... what?" Harmon looked up from his work. Put the stylus down. Picked it up again and began tapping. "What kind of war do you mean?" he asked carefully.

Leeth frowned at him suspiciously. "A proper one. With guns and knives and stuff."

Well, that lets out d'Artelle's engineered apocalypse, Harmon thought. *And the Great Conflict, too.* "In that case, I would say fifty million. Perhaps sixty."

Her jaw dropped. "Sixty *million!*" She looked stricken. Then brightened. "But they would have been killed by lots of different people, wouldn't they? Not just one or two."

He blinked. *Oh.* "Certainly. And they would have been using weapons of large scale destruction, and often against unarmed, helpless victims."

She looked shocked. "So they had no chance at all? That's not fair!"

Harmon nodded.

For a while she was silent, thinking. At last, slowly, she continued. "Who does the actual killing? Soldiers, right? But aren't soldiers... are soldiers Hunters, too?"

"A few are. A very few." For a moment the words "but soldiers follow orders," teetered on his lips. Mother and Father would not thank him for drawing her to *that* conclusion, however: that a Huntress was different, and need not obey orders. Yet how many times had he explained that *sheep* did what they were told?

She still waited, he saw. And the more he thought about it, the more delicate he knew his answer must be.

"For a soldier, fighting and killing is like a *job*, that he does because he *must*. For a Hunter, fighting and killing is a way of *life*. Constantly testing herself against her opponents."

Harmon held his breath, waiting.

And Leeth nodded.

He plunged past the danger point, and explained War.

CHAPTER 12

Leeth was bored. She'd had one session today on the pistol range with a new automated instruction program Nelson had designed. She was certain he'd deliberately made it even more annoying than Preacher. But after that she'd had a super training session with Dojo. The idea of *deliberately* breaking your rhythms to confuse your opponent? Genius! Plus it tied in to the idea of pausing and assessing, moment by moment.

But then she'd had another session on body language with Keepie: who'd looked like he'd wanted to be somewhere else; then a lesson with Mother. She shuddered, remembering. *Ergh!*

She was s'posed to be learning Mumbles now in her room. But *she* wasn't a troll or an ogre, and *they* all understood English anyway. Even if some of them couldn't speak it properly 'cause of their mutations.

She'd had to escape her room or go mad.

Wandering to the rec room, since that's where the agents hung out when they were available, her face lit up to see James there. The 3D projector made the darkened room look like the inside of a derelict spaceship. Whatever he was watching also had lots of subsonics, which she always enjoyed. Right now, a heavily-armored male mercenary with a bandage on his head and an extravagantly-chromed plasma cannon was explaining they had to carry the fight to the creature.

Leeth crept in. Uncle said too much 'canned entertainment' was bad for you, but really, they were great! They also gave her ideas to try out for herself.

In this one, it seemed an alien was hunting a small group of heavily-armed mercenaries on a maze-like spaceship. While the creature hunted them, in turn. Leeth was instantly engrossed.

It's been ages *since I Pounced anyone*, she suddenly realized. Sinking quietly down on all fours she began slowly sneaking into the room towards James.

But the trid's tense hunt down dark passages was actually pretty good. *No sense rushing*, she decided.

Now the creature was opening a cryo-storage unit where the mercenaries had put one of their critically-injured friends. A shiny black limb opened and a purplish organ extruded, covering the dead woman's face. Leeth's mouth fell open as the thing started absorbing the woman into itself.

It was budding another one of itself, she realized. She felt deliciously wicked as she settled down, just to watch for a little bit while she picked the perfect moment. Uncle would grimace if he knew she was watching a 'silly trid.' But she wasn't watching, exactly. She was just creeping up on James real slowly.

By the time the credits started rolling, she was practically burning with excitement. She was also positioned right behind James's chair.

Arching her neck forward, she ca-a-arefully stretched out her tongue like the creature in the final scene, and slid it wetly behind his ear.

James *exploded*. One hand smashed out, and she only just deflected it, taking the impact of his other arm on hers as he spun around.

James has cyberware! she realized, recognizing the familiar burst of ultrasonics from powered muscles and the sudden increase in his speed. But then he froze, recognizing her. She saw him trembling, as if his automatic cybernetic systems fought his natural muscles.

From some of the tricks she'd played on Faith, Leeth recognized the signs, and ducked her head to hide her smile, finally looking up to shrug a half apology.

For his part, muscle and nerve augments online, body still vibrating with adrenaline and threat assessments still crowding his vision, James swore at her. "I could have killed you!" he began, fists clenched, as the crazed animal trying to batter its way free of his chest changed slowly back into a normal human heart.

He could see the impish grin Leeth thought she'd concealed.

He spent several minutes succinctly explaining the error of her actions before seeing it was having as much effect as a literary criticism on an alligator.

The delighted grin still struggled beneath her more serious expression, and her next question only reinforced his assessment. "What *is* the scariest thing you know, James?"

Sighing, he gave up trying to scold her. Then, after a little thought, queried the Bureau's databank. He sent the lights down again as a flat picture appeared on the wall screen. The scene was a little jumpy, and Leeth realized it must have been shot from something like a lapel camera.

"This footage is classified, you understand? It's what happened when seven highly trained men, including two very strong mages and a powerful shaman, attempted to arrest Melisande d'Artelle."

At the hiss of her indrawn breath, he turned to her, pleased he didn't have to explain the identity of the former Enemy of Mankind. Indeed, Leeth's attention had locked on the woman with more focus than he'd ever seen from her. But was there something more, there?

Something about her expression disturbed him. An element of... satisfaction? *Ownership*? Half his attention stayed on Leeth as the playback continued.

In a large office, with a view down onto the Empire State Building, a woman – Melisande d'Artelle – dressed in an elegantly-tailored cream suit and tasteful jade necklace, faced seven dangerous-looking men. All wore Interpol uniforms; all were heavily armed and armored.

Between the men and the woman, a huge simulacrum of an office copier-thing rolled ominously forward, buckling the ceiling as it came. But with a casual brushing motion of one of D'Artelle's hands, the bizarrely-animated device collapsed, shattering into pieces that flew across the room and out of sight, with the sound of a metal river crashing into a bus shelter.

James paused the action. "That was a *very* large office spirit she so casually dismissed. But watch." Leeth didn't look at him; merely nodded as if she'd expected no less. After a moment, frowning, he continued the playback.

The wearer of the camera started to speak, over the sound of still-falling pieces of equipment. Strangely, everyone in the room was acting like nothing at all had just happened. "Madam d'Artelle, I am placing you under arrest-"

Ignoring the speaker, d'Artelle simply looked at the two mages, who exploded back across the room in flames. The other men's guns jumped as if they were about to fire, then suddenly, amazingly, all relaxed back again into simple alertness. The shaman alone looked confused, shaking his head and seemingly trying to focus himself.

James glanced across at Leeth, who sat hunched forward now, her hands like claws, looking like she wanted to throw herself into the scene. Her lips moved, and his analysis software told him what she'd whispered: 'She's tricking them.'

But despite feeling there was something *more* behind Leeth's intensity, he couldn't help but be sucked back to the horrible scene.

Although light from the two burning men reflected off the large picture windows, no one seemed to notice. The woman licked her lips and turned, smiling, to the shaman, while the speaker continued sternly on, apparently unaware of the deaths around him.

"-on the charges of treason, mass murder,-"

A strange light flared around the shaman before it collapsed inside him. An instant later, the man screamed as flesh flowed like syrup down his bones. Once more the weapons twitched, but again only for a moment.

James watched Leeth's lips move, and saw her nod.

"-illegal genetic experiments,-"

Another man silently fell to the floor. No one reacted, unless you counted the small smile that twitched at the corners of d'Artelle's mouth.

"-kidnapping,-"

An instantly-silenced scream sounded from the next man, as his shotgun flew from his hands. Limbs snapping tautly outward as if racked, his spine bent backwards, each jerking movement matched by the sickening sound of tearing gristle. At last, as if released by an invisible force, he slid to the floor.

"-use of mind-altering magic,-"

The irony of that statement was an added cruelty, as the speaker remained oblivious to the slaughter around him.

The last man in camera shot simply vanished.

At that, *finally*, James saw Leeth startle, then pale.

"-and making ecologically damaging bargains with Greater Inorganic beings."

The woman smiled graciously, rising and stepping daintily from behind her large desk. "If I am so dangerous, m'sieu, should you perhaps not have brought some men with you?"

She had a faint French accent.

Several seconds of silence followed, the camera panning from side to side, strongly suggesting confusion. But it didn't linger on any of the corpses around the room; as if the camera-owner couldn't see them.

"I- I am quite prepared to use this weapon, madam."

She smiled and bowed her head, and something red and black flashed out from her a moment before the clip ended.

-

For a while, neither of them moved; then Leeth exhaled deeply and James spoke. "As I said, that was Melisande d'Artelle. The woman who made the World Storms, the Red Plague, and orchestrated the Melt virus. Who caused, indirectly, two *billion* deaths, a hundred million minds ruined, fifty million mutations."

Leeth's eyes met his briefly, then slid away. "Yeah."

Familiarity. That was it. That was what her expression told him. Goosebumps prickled across his skin, but he forged on. "We only have that footage because it was being broadcast. By the time the backup teams got into the office, she was gone." *How could Leeth be familiar with d'Artelle?* There was very little footage of the witch, and she'd been killed fourteen years ago. Leeth would have been scarcely a child.

"She didn't kill them herself though, did she? Not personally. It was the storms and the plague that killed most of them."

James looked at her strangely, realizing she wasn't talking about the grisly magical slaughter she'd just seen, but about the indirect deaths. It wasn't the reaction he'd expected.

"Didn't Lord Lao Pi Shen, um, kill her in the end?" she asked.

"That *is* what he's supposed to have said, just before he closed off China to the rest of the world. Which was six months after his dramatic return and rise to power. Some people think he was hunting her, that entire six months."

"Yeah. Him, and Godsson, and the monk. It must have been some hunt," she sighed, eyes dreamy.

James frowned. *Godsson? I wonder....*

«*Emma?*»

A secure channel opened.

«*She* did *react to the picture of Benson from sixteen years ago, just before his disappearance.*»

«*Dear god: so Benson is at the Institute for Paranormal Dysfunction. Pretending he thinks he's God's Son, or genuinely mad? I'm not sure which possibility is worse. But what about her familiarity with* d'Artelle?» The depth of Emma's horror came clearly down the Link, an overtone of black dread.

For a long time, neither spoke.

«Eagle *had her brought in*» James offered, at last.

In the tones of a prayer.

CHAPTER 13

Leeth sat in the cosmetologist's chair in yet another tucked-away room inside the Department. Watching Emma in the brightly lit mirror with interest.

"Are you sure?" the auburn-haired woman asked, scissors in hand.

Leeth shrugged. "It's too long. Dojo said so."

Emma ran her left hand under the heavy black hair, the silken threads slipping through her fingers. She sighed. "It seems such a shame, that's all. When was the last time you had it cut?"

Leeth shrugged again. "I don't know. When I was little. Uncle cut it for me." She frowned. "He stopped, when I got bigger."

What else changed as you got bigger? Emma wondered. With a grimace, she began cutting. Laying each sheaf of hair along the benchtop before them with care.

As Emma brushed at Leeth's shoulders, the girl giggled at her own reflection. The straight fringe across the top, the simple bowl cut of the rest. She tugged her eyes up at the corners. "I already look a bit Japanese, don't I?"

"No, not yet. Now, *please* sit still for the skin dye."

"Oh. Wait a minute." Leeth unpinned the sheet from around her neck, refastening it around her waist.

"What-" Emma stopped as the girl stripped off her top, smiling, bare breasts now jauntily exposed. Emma swallowed. "What on earth did you do that for?"

Leeth flashed a grin. "I've a *special* dress to wear for James, tonight. So don't stop at the neckline!"

Taking a deep breath, Emma gloved up and dipped the soft sponge into the solution. Leeth, eyes shut, shivered as the first cool touch slid up her neck, her lips parting at the contact.

Emma glanced down despite her resolve not to. Yes, both nipples had hardened and now stood erect. She ignored them with a wry smile. She was supposed to be *teaching* Leeth.

"It's important to apply the solution quickly and evenly. If you leave it too long it can streak."

"Mmm," Leeth purred.

"You have to apply the dye before sculpting on the pseudoflesh, so the colorizing agents properly seed."

"Mmm."

Emma did Leeth's face, ears, and neck, then her back. Once more between her and the mirror, she began working her way down the subtly-muscled shoulders. "This will last about two weeks, if untreated. But you'll be using a bleaching agent before then." Emma frowned at the breasts before her. "You're getting to see more of James than I am, these days." She imagined his hands, stroking those firm breasts. She wasn't jealous. James was just... a convenient friend. Not really a lover.

Leeth opened her eyes, scowling. "Opera! Why does he always take me to the *opera*? I hate it!

"Plus, he starves me!" Leeth recalled the first night, and the wonderful steak. She'd planned to order it again the second time, but James had stopped her. And last night, too, he'd let her eat only a tiny amount of food. Sure, she was practicing her disguises and acting, but who'd recognize someone just by their healthy appetite?

"Two different women with the same enormous appetite, especially if they order the same food, cooked the same way? Derek would realize at once they were the same person."

"Then I'll order something different!"

"Certainly. And only a small portion, too."

"But I'm hungry!"

He shook his head in disbelief. "If you're really still hungry later, eat something when we return home. You don't eat that amount normally, do you?"

"Well, sure. You think I'd eat more just because the food is tastier?"

He looked at her doubtfully, which only intensified her annoyed expression. He shook his head. "If that's true, I really don't know where it all goes."

She preened, then shrugged. "It just does go, that's all. If I don't eat enough, my stomach starts to hurt. And I get all sluggish."

He shook his head again. "Then in future, eat before we leave. So you only pick at your meal here."

"But the food here's better!" At James's expression she'd turned, to see Derek listening: looking intrigued. She lowered her voice. "Plus, that's wasteful."

"Leeth.... Never mind. The Department can afford it. Consider it part of the expenses for your training."

Emma wondered what Leeth was thinking about. *Probably food.* She looked miffed, and Emma decided to direct her mind back to her training. This wasn't a game. "You really don't like the opera?"

Leeth scowled. "No. I really do hate it. I don't know why he has to take me there all the time!"

Emma shrugged, taking a faintly malicious pleasure in her reply. "You know very well why: we're teaching you how to appear to be different people. We have to test each disguise, and the Maitre'd at the opera's restaurant is a trained observer, good at remembering faces. By making a bet with him, James focuses attention on his companion while providing a plausible explanation should anyone realize you're in disguise. Besides, it's hardly 'always.' You've only been doing this the past three nights."

Leeth fell briefly silent. "Do men really have bets like that? I mean, who cares if a guy takes a different woman out each night?"

"A different *gorgeous* woman, Leeth."

"Do you really think I'm gorgeous, Emma?" Leeth opened her eyes wide, batting her lashes as she'd been taught.

Emma laughed. "Don't try to change the subject. You've been attending the Doctor's lessons with us. How does it apply here?"

Leeth grimaced. Practical Psychology – Psychology as a Weapon. It *sounded* good, but having to sit there for an hour... it was more fun trying to distract Uncle than to actually listen to what he was saying.

Leeth realized Emma was watching her, one eyebrow raised. Her expression was a mixture of accusation and amusement as she leaned back, half-sitting on the bench top facing her.

"How are you finding your lessons?" Emma asked.

"Learning how to handle guns is chill, and so is the stuff you and James are showing me. But Nelson and his computers.... I mean, he's shown me simple stuff, and I can see how that'll slot, but-"

"Young ladies don't say 'slot,' Leeth – it has crude connotations." She waved the correction aside, though, when the girl looked ready to argue. "And the Doctor's lessons?"

She rolled her eyes. "Bo-or-ing."

Emma leaned forward, deadly earnest. "It's an *edge*, Leeth, and in our business, whenever anyone offers you an edge, you take it."

"Huh. That's what Father always says."

"Because it's true." Emma looked at her. How to make her see the importance of this? "Think about this: knowing what motivates your enemy, knowing how he'll react – sometimes that's the only way you'll get close enough to... do whatever you have to do."

"Kill him."

Emma tried not to wince. "All right, let's say you have to kill someone. Don't you see the *value* in what he's teaching us? Just learning to use your own body language consciously – that alone is an amazing weapon. But your original question – James's bet with the Maitre'd – apply what the Doctor has been teaching us: identify the active participants."

"Well, James and the other guy."

"And what does each stand to lose and gain in this interaction?"

"Um, a really expensive dinner?"

Emma raised her eyes, then looked back down at the seated girl. For a moment the taut, up-tilted breasts distracted her. She frowned. Was Leeth trying to seduce *her*? "You have to learn to look beneath the surface. You asked 'Who cares if a man takes a different woman out each night?' Obviously the Maitre'd and James do. So, why?"

Leeth thought. "Is it a kind of fight? Like, James is showing he can attract women; more women than the other guy? So he's *better* than him?"

Emma nodded. "You'd be surprised how many of the things men do are just variations of this contest. The male superiority thing. Showing he can attract *beautiful* women just makes the win bigger. Look."

She stepped away from the mirror, dropping the sponge into the bowl and stripping off her gloves. Leeth examined her new reflection, clearly approving.

Emma smiled. "Rather exotic. Just wait till we do your eyes. Even your own uncle won't recognize you."

"Just because I look different?"

Emma looked at her strangely, before understanding. "Oh, well done! You mean, because he's a mage, he could recognize you from your aura?"

"I was actually wondering if there could be an opposite kind of disguise."

Emma frowned. "Opposite?"

"Yeah, like, if someone changed on the inside, so they were a different person. That'd be a *perfect* disguise, wouldn't it?"

Emma went still. Leeth, eyes distant, didn't notice. "But if it was a different person, you'd have that other person's aura, wouldn't you?" Her eyes returned to Emma. "So a mage like Uncle could see through that kind of disguise, too."

She looked relieved.

Emma, on the other hand felt cold. She shook herself. "Now for your eyes."

Leeth shut them, and for long minutes neither spoke, while Emma did things involving protein glues.

"Do you like Jack Shadow?" Leeth suddenly asked, eyes still closed.

"Too anarchic for my taste. Didn't some of his later stuff go weird?" *Disturbing, more like it.*

Leeth shrugged, though keeping her head still.

"Why do you ask? Do you like him?" Emma prodded, worried the question might relate to the earlier topic.

"Ye-e-es. I think. I only really followed *Soul Quest* – each new song, the story got scarier! – but there was this one bit that kind of creeped me out."

"Doesn't surprise me. Which bit?"

Leeth sang, her voice surprisingly light and sweet, a disturbing contrast to the lyrics of the song and its martial rhythm:

> *"In the dust dead beetles breed*
> *Demons old wail to be freed*
> *Black lightning splits the sky above*
> *Now the fog enfolds me –*
> *wo-orld's be-e-lo-oved.*

"That bit, at the end: wo-orld's be-e-lo-oved. It... the way he whispers it, all 'let me in, we love you...' All sneaky and lying, trying to trick him...."

With her eyes shut, Leeth didn't see Emma shudder. Softly, she asked, "That reminds you of something?"

"Yeah. It reminds me too much of, of some- of some-one who tried to trick *me* like that."

This could be it, Emma thought; afraid to ask, but needing to know. "Back at the Institute, yes?" She kept her tone light.

"Yeah."

Emma waited. "Mmm. Who? Not your Uncle. Someone else there. Someone working there?"

Leeth shook her head.

"Ah: an inmate. You were friendly with many of them?"

"No." Leeth shook her head. "Only one." *Poor Godsson. How ever am I going to get him out?* She opened her eyes, her gaze far away. "No, it wasn't him."

"So, not an inmate, and not someone who worked there. Who was it? Or *what* was it?"

Emma saw her last question strike home. Leeth's eyes locked with hers.

"I don't want to talk about Her."

"*Her?*"

"I won't. Talk about. *Her.*"

"But... there was some, ah, powerful mage living there? Imprisoned?"

Leeth shuddered, hunching forward a little, both hands going to her left breast. Or perhaps her heart. Her gaze lost in infinity.

"No. Not after me and Godsson killed Her."

Leeth blinked, then glared at her with such intensity Emma expected her to fling herself from the chair and stalk from the room. The girl's clenched fists pressed into the sides of the chairs armrests, bowing the metal outward.

Emma's eyes widened. Then realized something more: *she has no idea how to retreat.* She'd pushed hard enough: perhaps *too* hard.

Then both Leeth's hands flew to her mouth in horror, her eyes entreating Emma in the mirror.

"I wasn't s'posed to talk about any of that." Shaking her head. "Please don't tell anyone what I said, Emma? Please?"

Oh, no, thought Emma, feeling sick. Forcing a smile, she rested her hands on the girl's bare shoulders. "I promise, Leeth. It will be just our secret. I promise."

She squeezed Leeth's shoulders. Knowing that Eagle would know.

CHAPTER 14

James was quite looking forward to seeing how much trouble Leeth would cause Derek, as the touchy 'Jennifer Dei.' The cover personality had been carefully crafted by the Doctor. And a clever move, highlighting the similarities between verbal and physical sparring.

But the rest of it worried him. Deeply.

Nelson *was* a computer genius, James knew, but how could digital knowledge be dumped into an organic brain, as Nelson had supposedly done tonight? He, Emma, and Preacher were Augmented with the necessary headware to accept data and skill downloads. Leeth was not.

And the look on her face when they'd strapped her head into the device and the finer-than-hair probes had been inserted through her skull? He'd wanted to knock them all aside and drag her free.

Instead, he'd simply waited alongside Father and Mother while Nelson wove his technological spell.

But by god, her expression when the Doctor had stepped forward to do *his* magical part, applying a 'personality overlay' to reinforce it!

And didn't everyone say magic and tech didn't mix? But the Doctor had countered that the magic and technology were affecting *Leeth*, not each other.

"How safe is this?" James had demanded of them. "Have either of you Dr Frankensteins tried this before? Aren't you re-programming a *human being?*"

Both had looked shifty. Only his faith in Nelson had eased his fears, in the end. Mostly.

No wonder Leeth now seemed confused and distracted. Several times already she'd slipped into Japanese without apparently realizing.

Yet despite all that, he suspected she still thought of the whole exercise as a game. Which was not a safe attitude: not one the Department could tolerate.

Perhaps she'd respond to a threat, framed the right way? As a challenge. He mulled the problem over.

Finally he nodded. "Leeth, I want you to identify the active participants in tonight's exercise."

She shook herself. "You and Derek. It's a fight between you and him to prove who's the dominant male, by showing who's most attractive to women."

He blinked, surprised by the answer's promptness. "And? Who else?"

For the first time tonight she really looked at him. Perhaps noticing his scrutiny.

"Me?" she asked, at last. He nodded; and waited. After a while she added, "me and Derek, too." She thought for a while longer, no doubt deciding what each stood to gain or lose. "I guess he could be trying to get me to slot- I mean, to *have sex* with him instead of you? And if I did, he'd owe me."

James winced. "I suppose that's true, in a way. But it's not what I was thinking of. Has anyone told you Derek has looked into each of your cover IDs? He's had people run background checks on all of them."

He spared her a quick glance.

She seemed astonished. "Why would he bother doing that?"

"Because he cares about the bet. He wants to make sure I'm not using paid companions. But that's not what I'm getting at. The other active participants are Derek and you, and through you, the Department. So now, what do *they* stand to win or lose?"

She answered slowly. "If Derek uncovers who I really am, I'd have to kill him. So-"

Good lord. But he simply shook his head. "That's not going to happen. Even if Nelson failed to do his usual impeccable job, there is no way you could be traced to the Department. It's this: we create identities in layers. Which we add to, piece by piece over the years, making them more solid. Occasionally you'll blow one and it'll be scrapped, but that's why a good agent always has a whole set. They're an investment in your future. Each time one undergoes scrutiny, you're risking it. On the other hand, each time one *passes* scrutiny, it becomes a bit more real. A bit more valuable.

"So that's what you stand to lose or gain. Derek has very little at risk, in comparison. Very little. Because these aren't just training exercises, Leeth. They're tests. Of you."

The rest of the walk passed in silence, and she seemed to be thinking. He hoped he'd managed to snap her out of her odd mental state. He also hoped Nelson and the Doctor knew what they were doing with their weird experiments on her tonight. Leeth seemed... *too* unlike herself. It worried him.

They walked on. High above, a band of clouds rolled in to obliterate the moon, and the evening seemed to cool as it darkened. Jennifer shivered and looked around, as if searching for something. But when James raised an eyebrow in query, she merely shook her head. Though her grip on his arm tightened.

James entered the foyer of the Muses restaurant through the lacy forest of green ferns, with his 'new' conquest on his arm. He caught a shimmer of annoyance slide across Derek's features as the Maitre'd prowled elegantly up, sparing a glance for the girl at his side.

The arcs of metallic green and blue in her low-cut evening dress echoed Leeth's own curves. The facial cosmetic alterations gave a definite Asian cast to her features. James wondered whether Derek would identify her as Japanese. Probably: he had a keen eye when it came to people, and Emma had done her usual excellent job.

Elegant black onyx and silver earrings peeked out from the short, feathered bangs exaggerating the roundness of her face. Red, full lips that made you think of succulent plums. The only jarring feature was the twist of a sneer ghosting over those lips.

Derek was bowing, Japanese style, welcoming James's guest. "*Komban wa*, miss" he purred.

Jennifer had been feeling weird, like she was somehow seeing double inside her head, but the man's 'Good evening, miss' seemed to snap everything into focus. With it came intense irritation. *Just because I'm Japanese by birth, why does everyone automatically assume I'm a foreigner?* The stupid bowing and show-off phrases to make her feel 'comfortable.' She was as American as he was. There was something fuzzy and prickly about that idea, but she pushed it down.

Contempt flared. "Yeah, 'Komban wa, *miss*' to you too, grandpa." The sneer vanished as she turned to her companion. "Shunt, James, what's this creep gonna do next, offer me a selection of Jiu Jitsu moves to make me feel 'at home'?" She shuddered extravagantly.

James patted Leeth's arm. "Please, Jennifer, Derek didn't mean anything by it." *Perhaps I'll enjoy this evening after all!*

If Derek had simply cut his losses, he would have been okay – but he wasn't the sort of man to easily accept a rebuff. Withdrawing until their waiter for the evening had bowed and left, he stepped up to their table again. "James, it *is* good to see you. Will you allow me to apologize to your lovely lady friend for my earlier crassness?"

'Jennifer' bristled. "You don't need James's permission to apologize to me – you need mine. And if I want a judgment on my 'lovely' looks, I'll enter a beauty contest."

With an effort, Derek kept the smile on his face. "Again, my apologies, Miss...?"

"Jennifer Dei."

He waited, but she didn't add anything. "Please allow me to introduce myself. I am Derek Tate, the Maitre'd of this fine establishment. I've known your companion, Mr Connor, for some time now. He's quite a regular during the season. I'm very pleased to meet you."

Leeth blinked, feeling oddly dizzy, glad she was sitting down. Coming back to herself, she noticed how his hand rubbed the side of his nose as he said that, and remembered something from her uncle's lectures on body language: that gesture often accompanied a lie! Which would make sense – surely what he really wanted was to punch her? She surreptitiously looked down, and saw with a small stab of pleasure his other hand was closed in a fist. Wow – one of her uncle's lessons had actually been useful! This was actually kinda chill. As Derek continued, she allowed a small disbelieving smile onto her face, knowing he had to pretend to be polite to her.

"Do you also follow the opera? How did the two of you meet?"

Perfect. "*So* glad you brought that up, Derek," she smiled, the Jennifer persona flowing back around her without her even noticing.... If she was going to get blamed for the accident, at least she'd get some pleasure out of it. Her thoughts split, doubling confusingly. She remembered ordering her auto-drive off by accident, and the sudden crunch of impact; but she also remembered someone *hacking* her car... *her* car? She had a car...? But now was no time to show weakness.

She glared at Derek. "We met after I ran into James's sports car."

Derek winced, half-turning to James. "Ah, no! Not your beautiful Windsteed?"

"Yes, his 'beautiful Windsteed.' The same funting beautiful Windsteed we weren't going to mention tonight!" She stood, throwing down her napkin in disgust. "I'm going to the Ladies." She paused, swaying for a moment, then blinking. Remembering a somehow frightening older man, lecturing her about male psychology. She shook herself. "Maybe when I return, you'll both have finished discussing the scratch on James's stand-in dick."

James watched her stalk off, before turning to the Maitre'd with an apologetic shrug.

Derek raised an eyebrow. "Sometimes, James, I confess I've wondered whether you were paying for your escorts to be sure of winning our bet."

"Derek, I assure you I am not paying for-"

The Maitre'd held up a hand to cut off the protest. "Of course not. It's more likely your Ms Dei usually pays for *her* companionship." He smirked. "You do seem to have grabbed a prickly peach this time."

James raised an eyebrow, deciding to rub a little salt into the wound. He stretched comfortably back in his chair. "Well, our bet just specified beautiful *looking* women. Though no doubt Jennifer *would* be a handful for most men."

Derek nodded fractionally and moved away, but considering possibilities. Perhaps a solicitous enquiry as to injuries sustained in the collision?

As he stood, scanning his beloved restaurant, an eye motion all he needed to direct his well-trained staff, he noticed a solidly built man in the foyer. The first point of concern was the privacy makeup. Derek frowned. Celebrities commonly used the bold, distorting patches of color to avoid facial recognition software. But so too did criminals. And as he took in the disturbingly blank expression in the pale eyes, the expensive suit soiled and worn, the untidy light hair uncut for a long time, he keyed for security even as the man approached. Dead eyes panned across the diners in the room beyond, hunting.

The man stopped when Derek stood in his path.

"Do you have a reservation?"

The man didn't answer; didn't even react. Just continued scanning the room and the diners; partly turning away.

"Sir, if you don't have a reservation I'm afraid I'll have to ask you to leave." Derek's nose wrinkled at the smell. When had this... derelict, last washed? "I'm sorry, our dress code, and health and safety regulations-"

The man pulled his eyes away from the restrooms. "A girl. You have interacted with a girl tonight. Where is she?"

Dammit, where was security? "Sir, I think you may be unwell. Do you have a booking? The restaurant is, unfortunately, full at the moment."

"The restaurant is unimportant. Where is the girl that disturbs and unsettles you?"

Some new street drug, Derek decided. He moved, setting himself squarely in front of the larger man, blocking his entry.

Derek yelped as the man *jolted* forwards; felt himself yanked from his feet and towed into the dining area.

But deeper inside the restaurant, James had seen, and now headed calmly to intercept Derek's attacker. A pity the Opera House had a no-handgun policy.

He needed to think fast, though: Leeth would soon return from the Ladies, and if she found a fight in progress, she'd be certain to join in.

He needed to end this quickly and quietly.

As he wove between tables, the man saw him, recognized the threat, and tossed Derek sideways into a table. Wine and food catapulted into the air.

Sparing only a glance at Derek, already struggling to his feet, James went to full augment. Almost toe to toe with Derek's assailant, he spoke calmly and clearly. "You need to leave this restaurant."

Expecting violence, James saw the man instead consider what he'd said. He felt Derek return, to stand at his side.

The room had frozen.

Poised, ready to act, James saw two security personnel approaching.

The man blinked; swallowed; then licked his lips. "Apologies. There is a girl that requires help, from this." The man tapped his chest as his eyes stayed on James.

This, James wondered? The fellow was clearly unhinged.

The man's head tilted. "Requires help from *me*." His face stretched in a robotic smile, uncanny even through the privacy camouflage. "The search... *my* search, has been long. Sleep has been short. The disturbance is unfortunate."

The unsettling individual turned to depart, as the two security personnel moved forward.

"Make sure he leaves the building," Derek instructed them. "But remove that damned anti-face-rec makeup, first, and add his face to the Red list for the scanners. I don't want him in here again. Ever. Run it through the Wanted lists, too."

They grasped the intruder's arms.

And Jennifer returned, eyes alight, slipping up to James's side. Sliding her hands up his arm to his shoulder, she draped herself against him; and the man spun back around.

Jennifer eyed the two bouncers dangling like giant bracelets from the arms of the man her date had been talking to. He looked... interesting. Cold. Threatening. The stranger took a step toward her, and she reached out one hand, trailing it seductively down his front. "James, what's going-"

Ice flared up her arm from the point of contact. She stumbled to a halt, and her mind crashed down around her; visions of her Japanese father thrashing her, splinters of language spearing through her brain, and *cold*. Cold numbing walls that pulled at her, separating her from herself, squashing down around her. Squeezing her down. Sealing her *in*....

As if watching, Leeth felt *Jennifer* sway, saw her clutch weakly at James's arm for support. She tried to straighten, and failed. Tried to scream.

And couldn't.

James swore, grabbing at Leeth as she collapsed against him – apparently hoping to lure the madman closer. He needed his hands free! But now that she'd clearly decided to join in, he couldn't simply hand her off to Derek.

For his part, the large man stood gripping the collars of the two security guards, holding them down at his sides like two struggling suitcases. James had been certain

they'd been about to have their skulls cracked together –
until the moment of Leeth's pretended collapse.

And *still* she clung to his arm without attacking.

Something was wrong.

More strangely, although Leeth's mere arrival had spun
the man around, he now hardly spared her a glance while
she clutched at James's sleeve, barely upright. Indeed, the
man had begun calmly scanning the restaurant again.

And after several long seconds, he simply let the security people back to their feet and allowed them to escort
him away.

James watched them go, turning his attention back to
Leeth. But she, too, had pulled herself together. While
Derek and James paused to recover their equilibrium, Jennifer sneered at the Maitre'd. "The food here attracts a lot
of bums?"

James blinked. *Ouch.* That had been below the belt.
Jennifer disengaged herself from his arms in some annoyance, making her way back to their table. James made an
apologetic face to Derek and followed her. *What the hell
had just happened?*

CHAPTER 15

James was impressed.

In truth, he'd moved beyond impressed and was now into *worried.* Leeth, as Jennifer, had stayed solidly in character throughout dinner.

Too solidly.

Several times she'd asked him a question in Japanese, then chuckled an apology and asked him again in English. Earlier, Leeth in her Jennifer persona had struck him as an intelligent young lady, albeit with a distinctly acid personality. But who was attracted to him, and who had decided to act on that.

But he had seen no signs of Leeth now for the last hour. On one occasion when he'd been watching her pensively, trying to see the young trainee operative he was growing fond of, she'd demanded to know why he was 'looking at her like that.'

He'd laughed it off – but she hadn't laughed along with him. Had instead become suddenly wary of him. As if they really were on a first date, and she was reconsidering her decision to spend the night with him.

He could lose this bet with Derek. Leeth was capable of it. Even if she thought of these exercises as games, she played them deadly seriously.

He shook his head: it made no sense. If she made him lose the bet, she'd be terminating her own exercises. Prematurely. He knew precisely what Mother would say.

Surely Leeth did, too? *Unless... Leeth was gone.* Was Nelson's organic programming playing up? Or the Doctor's spell? Or both?

He *had* to charm her.

Tweaking his MetaLife settings, he prioritized the body language parsers. Then began working – hard – to win the acid-tongued girl back over.

Derek tried one more time, at the end of the meal, as his guests paused at his station on their way out. Having considered her expensive dress and jewelry, he felt he'd thought of some safe ground. After a little small talk he asked, "Tell me, Jennifer, what line of work are you in?"

She stiffened. "You have a real talent, Derek, did you know? As of yesterday I'm in the unemployment line. I've just been replaced by a Tik Tek Mark VII gynoid with the twelve language, executive assistant software pack." She smiled icily, offering her arm to James. "Shall we go?"

Derek watched them disappear through the ferns, then let out a long breath. "I can't *imagine* why they would have replaced you with a gynoid," he muttered quietly, but with considerable satisfaction.

At the whispered words behind her, Jennifer's stride faltered. Anger heating her face, she pictured storming back to stuff Derek's words down his throat. Then sanity reasserted itself, and she put the strange thought aside. Really, it was sort of funny. She *had* enjoyed needling the smarmy maitre'd, after all.

She suppressed a giggle.

She wondered if she'd like the opera? But that innocent thought triggered something deep inside her to lunge violently upwards, struggling. Visions of herself attacking and killing the smiling, well-dressed people people crowded round her in the ornately decorated halls suddenly swam crazily in her head. The strength of the desire to give in to the rage was astonishing.

"Jennifer?" James's deep rich voice was a lifeline. "Are you all right?"

She fought the odd visions down, locking the strange ferocity down and forcing a laugh. "Hai, hai. I'm fine. Fine. Let's get this over with."

In the darkened concert hall, the audience sat in respectful silence. James spared a surreptitious glance at his companion, who sat immobile, staring into space; not fidgeting; barely moving. Just the slight movement of her chest, from strangely rapid breaths.

It worried him.

They were an hour into the performance. By now, Leeth would normally be squirming as if the music caused her physical pain. He looked more closely. Was her jaw clenched tight?

He leaned in to her, placing one hand comfortingly on her knee and smiling at her in the dark. She didn't react.

Actually, he realized in sudden dread, the flesh under his hand felt rigid. His eyes lowered to her lap, and gingerly, he kneaded her thigh.

Feeling muscles locked impossibly tight, the limb like wood.

His hand stilled, and he turned to fully face her. She hadn't reacted to his touch at all: just continued to sit, motionless. *Like a ticking bomb.*

For Jennifer, it had started as a feeling of swelling pressure: an uncomfortable fullness, like she'd eaten too much. The music didn't soothe, it jangled her nerves until they felt like they bled, raw and twitching. And *something* responded to that, struggling like a trapped animal deep inside her.

Endure, she told herself, gripping the seat's armrests as if anchoring herself against a storm. Strange visions flailed and clawed at her. A man with hooded eyes whipped her naked body, trawling serpents of pain along her skin.

Still the pressure swelled, until she knew that if she moved, if she so much as twitched, she'd explode. Her eyes no longer saw the hall; her ears no longer heard *music*: instead, they fed barbed ropes of sound to the furious thing inside, a thing now using those ropes to climb out of her. Or perhaps *into* her.

The music dragged a chaotic, burning landscape behind it. A landscape where a man waited, chains and scalpels in his hands, and a smile that touched his lips but never his eyes.

The Fury inside tore her away in pieces, feeding on them. Confusion swelled, knowledge draining from her as she tried to resist. Thoughts twisted in her grasp, changing, transforming into screams of defiance. Screams that she wasn't real, that *it* was real, that it was a Huntress, that it would Kill-

At that moment on the stage below, the soprano's arms went wide, emptying her lungs as she strained for the note-

And Leeth *erupted*, leaping to her feet. With a scream of animal rage she *killed* Jennifer, jerking cries from the throats of those nearby. Some even jumped from their seats.

A man sat beside her, frozen – staring up at her as if in wait – then flinched back at the primal howl she roared in defiance at him, challenging him. Ready to kill again.

Around her, no one moved. No one spoke. On the stage, the performers stood paralyzed; the orchestra a still life of raised instruments, stopped mid-note.

For long seconds there was absolute silence.

Then, one by one, shock faded from people's expressions. Anger welled in its place as they turned to face her as she stood, panting heavily, her hands clenched like claws.

-

Frosty silence filled the car on the drive home as James remembered his training, and drew down calm. He'd hoped Leeth would enjoy the lighter touch of Saint-Saën's 'Samson et Dalila.'

But her explosion during that unfortunate mangling of *Mon coeur s'ouvre á ta voix;* where she'd looked ready to storm the stage and kill the mezzo-soprano in front of the entire theater....

Just how unbalanced *was* she? *Could* she have been Maria Lempriere's murderer? She did seem to genuinely suffer during the performances. He suspected she wouldn't last the distance.

Would be *retired* from the Department.

Thinking of the report he'd have to file for tonight felt like planning a betrayal. Which was ridiculous: the *Department* had his first loyalty. Had to. *Why did she make everything so hard?*

At least she'd stopped muttering "I killed her!" before they'd been drug tested, and ejected.

She'd been sitting staring fixedly ahead, silent for so long now that he twitched when she finally spoke.

"What happened? Did somebody drug me?"

Sparing her a glance, she seemed back to normal. "Drug you?"

"Yeah. Was it a *test*?" Venom underscored the word. "Or did Nelson try to reprogram me out of existence?"

"What on earth are you talking about?"

In his peripheral vision, she turned fully toward him. "Or did *you* do something to me, James?"

The hairs at the back of his neck prickled upright. Activating his combat augmentation and the car's self-drive, he turned carefully toward her. Saw that she'd gone dangerously still.

Shit. "I have absolutely no idea what you're talking about. But if this is your planned excuse for Mother and Father, rethink it."

"Excuse for what?"

"Oh, I can't imagine. Jumping up? Screaming like a wildcat tearing the throat from a wildebeest?"

The look on her face started out pleased, before draining into open-mouthed shock. "You're kidding. I didn't do *that*." Her eyes lost their focus. "But... people *were* talking to me. Who didn't like me...." Her voice trailed off. "After I killed Jennifer, to escape."

He shook his head, frowning. "What are you talking about?"

Her eyes met his. "James, what happened after we sat down to order dinner? All I remember is killing Jennifer, then kind of waking up as we left the opera house."

James stared at her. She sounded honestly puzzled. The trouble was, she was getting to be such an accomplished actress. "What do you mean, 'killing Jennifer'?" he asked, cautiously.

She stared ahead into the night, hugging herself. "I don't know. It was kind of like climbing out of a dark hole, except there wasn't any *me* climbing out. I think I killed Jennifer, and then I was back."

"What are you talking about? You are Jennifer. Or, you were, for tonight. And clearly, you're still alive."

The look she turned on him was dark, and as close to scared as he'd ever seen from her. She shivered and looked away.

James re-engaged manual drive, needing the distraction. Trying to ignore the thought that she would not survive the night.

-

Nelson's analysis noted a violent erasure of his experimental neural programming. The Doctor reported a similar destruction of his reinforcing magical Suggestions.

Despite this, Mother's opinion remained firm. "The girl is unstable and unsuitable: a danger to everyone around her. She should be Retired."

Father called up a section of James's report, highlighting a sentence. '*My impression is the Jennifer persona had taken a position of complete control.*'

Mother scrolled back, stabbing at the section to highlight it. "*After* returning from the Ladies. Who knows what she was taking in there?"

"Our own tests and those of the opera's security personnel were negative. And the Doctor says he raised her to consider any drug use as an admission of weakness."

In the end, lacking sufficient evidence to convince Eagle, Mother accepted the Doctor's analysis. Although she insisted on noting it was an unproven hypothesis, and that some unreported activity on Leeth's part remained an alternative explanation.

The rest of the exercises, however, were restricted to simply dining out at the opera house restaurant.

The strange intruder was considered irrelevant.

CHAPTER 16

Newly-minted Special Agent Adam Garland of the Bureau for Internal Development dismissed his notes on the mega-corp, Tik Tek. Still uneasy. With their new creepily-lifelike Mark VII androids and gynoids, it made a kind of sense for the Corp to be acquiring bio-med companies. Even moribund ones like CyclonalMT, ruined by the Moratorium of '38. Probably just wanted to clone skin cells for the Mark VIIIs they were no doubt developing....

With an effort, he put the technology giant out of mind and moved to the next item on his 'bud list.' Spending an hour a week on niggling concerns before they could flower into disasters was a large part of the secret behind his 're-markable intuitions.'

Yeah, which had gotten me noticed by Eagle and 'pro-moted' to the BID. He grimaced. That girl, and her guardian, Harmon, were still there on his list, too. They'd pop back onto his radar, he knew, sooner or later.

He shook his head.

Okay: next was 'The Breaker.' He pulled up the map of possible incidents, color-coded by the degree of the match to the perp's pattern.

On a hunch, he switched to a 3D visualization, showing the date of each murder-assault.

Ah, shit. He reviewed a sample of the cases.

Yeah, the torture motif had evolved, crystallizing into its current fixity only in recent months. And the assaults now occurred only in New Francisco, though shifting into the poorer areas. And growing less frequent.

Or less reported, more likely.

Ah, no! He zoomed out, expanding his map. There, tracking the Lincoln Highway across the country: a series of unsolved, pointless murders, a day or two apart, buried in the larger set of homicides. But following that trail backwards became harder and harder, as the earlier pattern of the killer's murders became less unique; less identifiable. Making it impossible to say where the first death had occurred. Especially if it was New York, with *its* homicide rate.

He made a note in the file, but set aside the question of the origin point for now. It'd probably be better to follow up on the disturbing magical angle. Like that first weird experience in the Golden Gate Park – after questioning Sara and her 'uncle' Harmon, come to think of it....

But, yeah, *that* summoning had been just bizarre. His then-partner, Berlusconi, had been as freaked-out as the shaman, Lucas. And Lucas had grown more and more reluctant to assist each time since then.

He'd worried, in fact, that Lucas was losing it. Going off the rails, as so many shamans did, down their traditional *drug* route to altered states of consciousness. Especially when they struck difficulties.

Lucas, last time they'd met, had been distracted and jumpy; paranoid that 'something was after him.' It made him wonder whether there even *was* a weird magical effect, or just Lucas, burning out. But the... dead magic zones, or whatever the fuck they were, and the, *shit*, vaguely *robotic* spirits? They'd freaked out the other shamans he'd called in at *least* as badly as they'd freaked out Lucas and Berlusconi.

Yeah, 'the shaman test' looked like an excellent litmus test for a Breaker murder or torture. Survivors always described the same large man with dead eyes. Half of them thought he was a robot, not human at all: a failed AI experiment running in a military *combot* unit. But that wouldn't explain the magic angle: how it seemed to screw up the shamans. Shit, he hadn't even been able to *find* Lucas, last time he'd needed him. Not even his squat-mates seemed to know where he was.

Yeah, his instincts were screaming at him over this Breaker guy. As if a major calamity was brewing.

CHAPTER 17

Leeth danced into the rec room where some guy on the trid was droning on about something. Her eyes lit up when she saw James, and scampered over. Before she could speak, though, he held up a hand to silence her.

She flounced heavily into the seat by his side and pouted up at him, but he paid no attention. Gradually she noticed the strange expression on his face: blank but tight. He seemed really absorbed by the boring guy, so she reluctantly spun around in her seat to see what was so interesting about whatever he was lecturing on about.

"Then he said if I didn't cut off her finger he'd blind her." The man didn't shrug, but it would have matched his toneless voice.

Leeth frowned, and sat up. *Cut off her finger?*

"I tried to cut him again with the knife but the chain didn't reach that far. Then he pulled her head back and pulled out one eye. My daughter started screaming and so did my wife."

James's face looked pale. And as the monotone description of torture continued, Leeth hunched in on herself. It was far worse than anything Uncle had done to her, she realized, as the recitation went on. Despite herself, she tried to imagine her uncle hurting her without even caring about what he was doing. Just bored. Even at his worst, when he was so mad his face sort of clamped solid and his speech got really precise and cold, he was *there*, thinking about her. But doing it the way this guy had.... She shuddered violently. It'd be so much worse. Like a nightmare.

She came to herself to see Nina Summers now interviewing some expert explaining how sometimes the brutality of the lives of non-CID'd people sank them into the worst kind of primitive savagery. That the 'demon' the murderer had described, who had made him torture his own family to death, was a classic schizophrenic projection.

"But professor, there have been examples of real demons returning-"

"No, Nina, there have been powerful magicians, somehow preserving themselves to reawaken when the magic once more Unfolded. People so corrupted by their own power they thought they were demons-"

The man continued, but Leeth had stopped listening. "I think it *was* a demon!"

James shook his head.

"Why not? It's possible!"

"No, Leeth. *That* kind of horror is something all too human, even if from the very darkest part of ourselves."

"So you're saying this guy was evil and stuff, and did all that to his wife and daughter for no reason?"

James looked tired. "No. And I'm not the only one to think there *was* someone there, just as he said. Some of the media are calling the thing behind these incidents 'The Breaker.' About a week ago someone found a couple in their apartment not too far from here. The 'sheets said they'd tortured each other to death."

Tortured? Leeth's eyes fell to her own arms. But there weren't even any scars: he was always very careful in his healing afterwards. "*I'd* never torture someone to death. I'd just kill him."

James searched her face. "You have someone specific in mind?"

Her mouth opened, and James waited for her to speak, but no words came. "Leeth, are you all right?"

It had happened again. She knew. She recognized the empty confusion. James was looking at her like he thought she was something fragile, or stupid. She shook her head. "What were we talking about?"

He frowned. "The couple who tortured each other to death. Under some sort of twisted duress. Tortured, I suspect, just like this guy tonight. I think someone out there is subjecting people to the most disgusting mental and physical cruelty I've ever heard of."

"We should stop it! I could Hunt him! It'd be awesome: me against The Breaker!"

He shook his head, tiredly. "It's not something for us. It's too small. Not important enough. But we have contacts. I've passed on my thoughts, and some people will look into it."

CHAPTER 18

The interior of the squad car was dark and warm. They'd been here hours, now, and Detective Marta Sanchez's stomach rumbled at the smell of Henderson's cinnamon donuts and espresso.

"Go on, Marta, your body just outvoted you, I heard it. There's still one left." He held it out. "No?"

With difficulty, Sanchez ignored him.

"Best damn money I ever spent, that FatBurner genemorph," he rumbled, as half the remaining donut disappeared into his large mouth. Henderson was large all over – and thanks to the genetic modification and bacterial tuning, very little of it was fat.

"Yeah, dumbass, and escaping all the possible side-effects from your illegal gene work has probably used up your entire life's luck quota."

Henderson just grinned at the dark-haired woman beside him. Draining the last of his coffee, he crushed the rubbish into a ball and tossed it without looking into the cardboard box on the floor behind.

Sanchez raised one heavy eyebrow.

He nodded, and the playfulness fell away. He was ready, now.

The two were pretty much everything cops were always supposed to have been – tough, smart and dedicated. If they'd also cared less about the street people and more about those who 'mattered,' they'd have been stationed somewhere other than the massively sprawling 'Dumpyard Precinct.' The Dumps covered pretty much everything south of Sixteenth Street and east of the inverted wreckage that formed the now-appropriately named heights of the Noe Valley. No valley any more.

The entire precinct consisted of just Sanchez, Henderson, sixteen security bots on automated patrol routes, and two ancient Tik Tek arthrobot cleaners. Plus the all-terrain Asgard CrawlTank – surplus from the Brazilian Eco-wars and lovingly maintained by their permanently-stoned mechanic, Josh Taverner. In Sanchez's opinion the tank was too dangerous to ever deploy. God help the mostly CID-less residents of this human wilderness.

"I just wish I'd picked up on what was happening sooner," Sanchez said for the fourth time that night. They were parked in a side street off the main road, giving them a clear view of the alley. The soup kitchen was seven blocks away.

"Stop hammering yourself, Marta. At least you did spot it."

Sanchez wanted to admit the truth: that it had been a tip-off, but.... She and Henderson were colleagues. Workmates. Sure, she liked him, but that's as far as it went. And if she mentioned her contact, Henderson'd start digging. And for some reason, she didn't want to tell him about the other man.

"And they're not dead. Maybe they'll recover."

"Sh'yeah, right. No one even understands what exactly's wrong with them! These people depend on us, Henderson. You ever think, if we didn't take the time to talk to people like Old Joe, how long this would've kept on before anyone noticed?" *That, and my tip-off,* she thought. "I just wished we'd happened to talk to Joe on Sunday."

"When there was no pattern, just a single chica zombied?"

The discussion died mid-breath as three people headed toward the alley. The woman was wearing old, threadbare clothes, and held the hand of a small, thin boy. The man was solidly built, but his tailored suit had seen better days. When they reached the alleyway where the last girl had been found, the man stopped them.

The two detectives tensed, ready to move.

The man said something and the woman shook her head, pulling the boy tight to her side. The man spoke again, and the woman's shoulders slumped. She looked torn as the man gestured for her to enter the alley; perhaps wondering if it would be kinder to leave the boy briefly alone on the street corner.

Sanchez swore under her breath as all three moved off down the disused alley. Henderson was already on the comm, ordering one of the security bots to meet them here as he and Sanchez exited the car and raced across the street.

At the end of the alley, the three figures disappeared to the left. The two citycops pounded down after them, guns drawn.

Things happened very quickly as they rounded the corner. Their quarry stood waiting, facing them from five meters away, the boy and the woman on either side. The man's face registered nothing as Henderson shouted for him to freeze.

He moved, shockingly fast. Jerking the boy, screaming, into the air. The child arced high before hurtling down towards Henderson.

Cursing, he slammed his weapon into his holster as he raced forward to try to break the child's fall.

With inhuman speed the man bore down on Detective Marta Sanchez, the woman held in front of him, a screaming shield.

Sanchez tried to dodge to the side, tried to risk a shot... then the woman's skull slammed into hers, and blackness claimed her.

CHAPTER 19

For long seconds, Miss Leeth lost herself in admiration of the sky. *So blue.* She'd never seen the sky so blue. So very blue. The warmth of the sun, so *warm*; the wind so breezy. Even their progress along the winding country road: so *speedy.* Everything was just so... *very.* She looked at the man seated beside her as he drove. On her right. It seemed strange, yet so normal. So *very* normal. It made her uneasy. He smiled back at her, his dark eyes sparkling. She did love the way they crinkled up at the corners.

She knew him so well. Her dear colleague.

"Keep an eye peeled, Miss Leeth."

Miss Leeth. It sounded wrong, but somehow comforted her.

"What are we supposed to be looking for?" Her own voice sounded odd: her vowels all... rounded, every syllable perfectly enunciated.

"I'm not entirely sure. Something odd about the people. Anyway, we'll see for ourselves, shortly. The village is just around this bend. We'll stop at a charming little pub for lunch, and then take a stroll and see what we can uncover."

English. He spoke with an English accent.

So did she.

The road dipped down as it curved under a verdant tunnel of interlacing branches.

And then, abruptly, they were passing a field on their left so deeply green it made her heart ache. The smell of the cut grass was intoxicating, overpowering her senses.

The car cruised into a village square. Ancient, low houses enclosed a small pond. Miss Leeth saw white-washed walls and a lot of dark wood. Aged wood. *Teak.* Briefly, she wondered how she knew that.

A sign sticking out from the front of the pub drew her attention: 'The Elephant and Castle.' The flowery script of the lettering was carved deep, and filled with gold paint.

The man steered them past, and parked. Picking up his umbrella and his funny rounded hat with its stiff brim, he strolled round to her side. Smiling, he opened the door for her, holding out the crook of his arm. For a moment she bristled – did he think she couldn't get down from the vehicle by herself? But an odd compliance settled over her, damping her annoyance. Taking his arm, she stepped down onto the... running board. The car looked very old, yet gleamed like something new. Together, they entered the pub.

Her vague unease grew. Apart from the unnaturally pure birdsong, the village was eerily silent. She herself felt strange.

Inside, the room was dark. More of the same black wood. Exposed, roughly hewn beams supported a low ceiling, and the furniture was all dark, heavy wood. She felt a rising panic. Threat seemed to hang like a miasma in the gloomy interior, and *she couldn't hear anything from outside!* She swallowed against a throat suddenly dry. Something else was wrong – the darkness wasn't clearing properly: her eyes weren't working right. What was wrong with her?

A man at the bar stood *silently* polishing glasses and staring at them blankly. With a shock, she realized she couldn't hear *him*, either! Not his breathing, not even the rustle of his clothing – what was *wrong* with her?

Eyes wide, she gripped the arm of the man beside her for reassurance. He watched her in growing concern.

"Miss Leeth? Are you all right? Whatever is the matter?"

And with a shocking chill that started at her scalp and raced down to her feet, she realized she couldn't hear *him* breathing, either. Dropping his arm, she backed away from him, toward the door.

It was like a nightmare. As though this one room was all there was, and everything else no longer existed. Outside would be nothingness, the car and village swallowed up. And she was trapped in here with two robots that looked like human beings.

A nightmare.

The face seemed to swim, the room wavered.

Stimsense.

Abruptly, she remembered the helmet going over her head. Remembered asking Nelson about his 'special' work with Emma. It was like a kind of game, he'd said, and kind of like training, at the same time. She'd done interactive stimsense, right? It was kind of like that.

She never had, but she wasn't going to admit *that*.

He'd asked if she'd like to try one of Emma's recreational scenarios? It *did* sound interesting.

"I dunno. Uncle wouldn't approve."

"Well, I won't tell him if you don't." Nelson had smiled; looking *so* superior. "But I guess you do everything he tells you, don't you?"

That had decided her. "I can get out if I don't like it, right?"

"Sure!" he'd laughed, and rolled his eyes, then sat there, clearly expecting her to ask a bunch of dumb questions. "Are you *scared*, Leeth?"

She *so* wanted to punch him, right then. "No! Of course not."

He waited. Raised his eyebrows.

"Okay, okay! So, how do I do it?"

He'd looked pleased, she remembered. Maybe even more than pleased.

He tricked *me into doing stimsense!*

Snarling, she reached up to her head to tear off the sensory induction helmet... only to feel nothing but her own hair.

Hissing in fury, she shut her eyes, and while still holding her head, forced her other arms – her *real* arms – to reach up again.

Felt plastic.

And wrenched it off.

Blinking in sudden light, the dark inn room vanished in one dizzyingly chaotic moment. Nelson stared at her in shock as she shuddered in her seat, then forced herself to stand, legs wobbling.

"Miss Leeth. Uh, Leeth, what are you doing? How did you know...."

She ignored him, while *Miss Leeth* fell away. She swayed as facts vanished, leaving gaping holes; knowledge draining like a dream and casting her adrift from herself. Blinking at Nelson – who had a strong resemblance to the older man, she saw – she felt herself shedding the strange deference to that older man. Felt the *like*, perhaps even *love*, evaporate. The loss tore at her, like the memory of Faith, of having to leave her behind. Faith, who still waited for her back at the Institute.

Tears sprang to her eyes.

I'm me *again.* The debonair gentleman's pallid young imitation unplugged a hair-thin cable from the back of his own head. And as he watched her, *guiltily*, she understood why.

He just tried to program *me! Again!*

She flushed. *No,* she vowed. *Enough.*

She tried to speak, but her lips had pulled so far back in a snarl, she couldn't. Anger burned in every muscle, flared in every nerve, its intensity momentarily paralyzing her.

Nelson's face whitened, reading his death in every line of her shaking body.

Batting aside his out-flung arm she grabbed his throat and pinned him in his seat. Summoning the razor tingle, fingers poised over his chest, she saw him jolt back as she pricked his flesh. His eyes jerked down, searching for the knives, then back up to meet her gaze, uncomprehending. *Good.* For a moment she paused, surfing the cresting immensity of her anger, picturing her hand plunging-

"LEETH," boomed Uncle's voice like a thunderclap. "LET NELSON GO!"

She stared up at the concealed speaker in shock.

"LET HIM GO!"

The room seemed to shake with the cry.

The desperation in her uncle's voice reached her. Turning back to her prey, she hauled him up from his seat one-handed, by the throat, until their eyes were level.

Their faces only inches apart, she didn't speak. She didn't need to. Tossing him back down hard into his chair she stalked from the room.

-

In another room in the complex, the lights came up as the recently-recorded scene faded. Nelson drew a shaky breath, turning angrily to Mother and Father.

Seated to one side, looking smug, Harmon radiated an air of 'I told you so.'

"Why'd we have to watch that?" asked Nelson. "You were all watching it on the monitors, and I was *there!*"

Mother glanced toward Harmon. "Apparently the Doctor thinks it will help him explain that Leeth is neither unstable nor a personal danger to everyone here."

Harmon looked down his nose at her. "I *did* advise against the experiment. Although I admit she reacted a little sooner, and more strongly than I predicted. You must also admit she would be no use to you unless she *were* dangerous. And she *is* predictable, to me. Therefore, controllable." He spread his hands.

"She didn't have *you* by the throat!" Nelson rasped.

"Exactly," responded Harmon.

"She didn't look controllable to me!"

"Because you don't understand her, Nelson," Harmon replied. "I warned you all against trying to program her as you do your other agents, through their NuLife 'entertainment.' And for Leeth, with no experience of that type of stimsense...." He shook his head.

"Boot up, Doc!" Nelson snorted. "Where'd you think she grew up – a desert island?"

"It was the Doctor who raised her, Nelson," Mother said. "From the age of eight. So he should know."

Nelson snorted. "So what? Even if the Doc didn't allow it, her friends would've let her use theirs."

"She had no friends," Harmon said.

Mother and Father exchanged a look.

"Boo hoo," said Nelson. "Killed them all, did she? Look, the readings showed she was meshed: deeply."

"At first, Nelson, only at first. Within nine minutes your fantasy was falling apart."

"That just means I need to implant my MetaLife chip so she can receive direct neural stimulation instead of a washed out, toned down, analog-"

"No, Nelson." Harmon gave a single emphatic shake of his head. "Adding cyberware subtracts magic. And so much of what Leeth can do lies in her very subtle magic. So it would rather defeat the purpose in this case."

"So you say. We only have your word for it she's magically active," Nelson retorted. "I've never seen her do any magic."

Harmon raised one eyebrow. "It's encouraging that you still think that, despite having just experienced a taste of it. A *tiny* taste, which came near killing you. I believe Dojo will also vouch for her magical abilities." *Though extracting that information from her trainer had been tediously difficult.*

Nelson's hand went to his chest, recently healed by the Doctor.

"She can bench press more than Dojo and James combined, for example," Father offered.

Nelson blinked. "But she's so-" He made a curving hourglass gesture in the air.

"Mmm," Father agreed. "She certainly doesn't appear to carry the necessary musculature. Her reactions are frighteningly fast, too – faster than any but the most extensive neural re-wiring. And all without a single cybernetic implant. On any security scan she appears to be a perfectly normal girl."

"Yeah; a normal girl who might go mad any moment and kill us!"

Mother steepled her fingers. "That *is* the issue, Doctor. We all agree she is deadly. But if we can't control her, she is worse than useless."

Harmon examined his hands, then looked up. "So you authorize me to use extreme measures?"

Mother and Father's eyes narrowed, but they nodded.

He smiled. "Give me one hour."

All three now stared at him.

Inclining his head, he rose to his feet and left the room.

After a moment, Nelson, clearly unhappy, clamped his mouth shut and stomped out.

Mother sighed. "You know, Father – I don't know which of those two I like the least."

Father looked at her, in mild surprise.

CHAPTER 20

Emma sat in the common room reading, trying not to fume. Why were James and Preacher given more missions than her? Especially Preacher – he spent almost all his time on the streets, almost none at the Department. She didn't even know what he really did. Just that it involved Nelson and the Department's accountant – the grayly unnerving and identity-less 'Checkbook' – more than anyone else.

She dragged her attention back to her tridsheet, and once more tried to become interested in the news.

Yamatetsu was announcing a new process for removing heavy metal pollutants from soil. Ah. *That* explained why they'd been buying industrial wasteland at the edge of the southern Dumps. And another one of those awful torture-murders in that same area, weeks-old, by the creature the media were calling 'The Breaker.' She shuddered, determinedly telling herself it wasn't Leeth. *Please.*

She flicked with relief into the social section. There was another vidspread of Happy Joe Holliday, 'Bodyguard to the Stars.' Emma snorted. If he wasn't an out and out merc, she'd retire from this biz. He and his team must be good, though, since none of the Corps or cops had ever laid charges.

Jack Shadow had another anti-Corp anthem catching fire on the P2P infranet. *Expect riots in HK and Wall Street,* she predicted to herself.

Ah, Tik Tek were announcing more funding for their artificial intelligence programme. People wondered why they bothered: AI researchers had been trying to solve the problem now for a hundred years. She smiled. But a public announcement of more AI research made cheap advertising for the Tik Tek androids and gynoids. Probably meant a new model was due for release.

The door at the far side of the room swung open. Emma put down her 'sheet as two small feet swung into view, followed by the rest of Leeth as Dojo carried her into the room. She registered the livid mark over his cheek, already swelling angrily. A head shot! Considering that the rest of them had rarely even landed a *body* blow on Dojo....

Impassively, he carried the unconscious girl to the deep lounge chair opposite Emma's and gently deposited her in it. She was utterly limp, breathing raggedly, but with no mark on her.

Emma stared.

"I could not find the Doctor – he was not in his office, nor his quarters. And Mother and Father are in a meeting, not to be disturbed." He seated himself in the chair midway between Leeth and Emma. "She was highly... agitated. Do you know why that might be, Miss Emma?"

"Me? No. Why?"

Dojo watched her carefully. "She spoke your name. You can think of nothing that may have upset her?"

Emma raised her eyebrows. "No, I haven't spoken to her since yesterday. What happened?"

"I heard someone... damaging the gym. When I asked her to stop, she challenged me to make her. We fought."

"Damaging the gym? What do you mean?"

He frowned slightly. "She had removed the weights from the barbell, and was hurling them into the climbing wall."

Emma shifted her shoulders. "That doesn't sound too terrible. Only the small weights, I imagine?"

He blinked, several times. "The disks are still embedded in the synthrock. She had started with the five kilogram weights, and was working her way up from there."

She stared at him. Looked at the slim form of the unconscious girl. Then back to Dojo. She gestured to his swollen cheek. "But how did she manage to, ah...?"

"Injure me? She was *creative* with one of the exercise mats."

"She hit you with an *exercise mat*? But- those things are heavy!"

"True. Yet Miss Leeth flipped one on top of me then dived over it, landing – silently – behind me as I sought to avoid it."

For a moment, Emma had the feeling Dojo was smiling. "Most ingenious."

"And then?" she prompted, interrupting his reverie.

"Then we fought in earnest. She was most angry, but not so angry her attacks were wild. She is improving.

"I enquired as to the cause of her anger. It was then she spoke your name. And Nelson's. You have no idea what had upset her?"

Emma shook her head. "None at all. Then what happened?"

"We fought. For some time I sparred with her, correcting her mistakes, but she did not speak. At last I realized she did not intend to stop until one of us lay unconscious." They both stared at the girl. "Why would she wish me to do that to her?"

"It's a comfort to her," spoke a voice from the open doorway. Harmon came the rest of the way into the room. "I'm sure it sounds terrible, but this type of thing calms her. No doubt you're aware she considers herself competent. But graphic demonstrations of superiority from people she trusts make her feel secure; reassures her there are higher authorities she can call on when needed. To put it simplistically.

"And of course," he continued, "at your level of skill, you are in no real danger from her."

Dojo eyes narrowed. "She has demonstrated to me her... spirit claws."

Harmon stared at Dojo. "Has she."

Spirit claws? Emma looked from one man to the other, wondering what they were talking about; and why the Doctor looked annoyed.

"Indeed. She said she wished me to be aware of them, should she ever lose her temper." Dojo smiled with a rare tenderness. "She said she did not want to accidentally kill me."

"*Kill you?*" blurted Emma, feeling a prickling down her spine. "What 'spirit claws?' She's never mentioned them to *me*."

Dojo met her eyes. "Maybe she thinks she would never be so angry with you, Miss Emma."

Emma digested that. "But what about James, and Preacher? Don't they need to know? And why keep it secret? Doesn't she trust us? What else can she do that we don't know about?"

And then Harmon saw something move behind Emma's eyes; some deeper awareness that spoke of genuine fear. Her lips clamped shut.

Turning away from her, he formed a Mindmeld. Then casually turned back, delicately draping it over her. At least the infuriating months of cat and mouse with Leeth had yielded one benefit: improving his stealth at spell-casting.

But the thoughts he skimmed from her mind froze him to the spot: *«Melisande d'Artelle... infection... alive...? And The Manipulator...? Infiltration...?»*

Mentally reeling, he had to school himself to give no sign. *How on Earth...? Why did Emma associate Leeth with* d'Artelle? *Had Leeth truly been infected?* His heart pounded in his chest. And how did she know of Leeth's connection to Godsson – David Benson, 'The Manipulator?'

None of that showed, however, as he calmly met her eyes and smiled. "Do you fear her, Emma? She is still a child. Though one who has faced... terrible things. And survived." He didn't try to conceal the pride he still felt; nor the horror at what she had put herself through.

"What things?" Emma whispered, with a shudder. *«D'Artelle! ... Benson!»*

Harmon was aware Dojo had been lost by the conversation's turn. But he needed to know what *else* Emma knew. "I'm afraid Eagle himself has forbidden Leeth or me to share that information. Nor would Leeth disobey those orders, I'm sure." He watched Emma's eyes; and each thought.

"She hasn't," Emma agreed. *«Just a few words.»* But a flood of memories followed: Leeth reacting to horrifying footage of d'Artelle; Leeth recognizing a recent image of Godsson, even whispering his name. And chaining the fear that Leeth had been influenced by d'Artelle or Benson, a single thread of hope: *«Eagle knows. It'll be all right.»*

He almost groaned aloud. The last thing he needed now was for the idea to take root that Leeth had been infected by Melisande d'Artelle or subverted by a madman.

And how had they obtained such a recent image of Godsson? Had one of them *visited* the Institute? Something about *that* thought prickled a faint unease, almost a dream memory.

It faded.

He'd become so lost in his own thoughts he'd dropped the Mindmeld, but Emma's attention, too, seemed turned inward.

Dojo simply watched them both, observing everything. Patient. He inclined his head toward Leeth, lying unconscious and ignored.

Harmon took the hint. Leeth's pulse, lungs, and heart were fine, though he noted that Emma still appeared to find his matter-of-fact style of examination objectionable. He turned to Dojo, and the welt over his cheek. What had they been discussing? Ah, yes....

"I see you didn't demonstrate *complete* superiority, however. Does that hurt?"

Dojo bristled. "No."

"Still, it gives your face a displeasing cast. Don't you agree, Emma?"

Emma felt off-balance. Of course Dojo should have it Healed. But his pride.... "Well, it does look *uncomfortable.*"

Dojo's expression hardened. "We learn from our bruises. They teach us our weaknesses, and our opponent's strength."

Harmon nodded. "True. But I hardly think you will forget Leeth's efforts today." At Dojo's expression, he nodded. "Ah. You fear it will make you *susceptible*? Not so. Each time I heal you, it simply makes it easier for me to do so in the future. Nothing more."

"That's true," Emma nodded. "I've followed the research reports."

"Please; allow me. Since it was my young charge who injured you." He formed the healing patterns, and waited.

Dojo said nothing, which Harmon took as assent.

In twenty seconds, the injury had vanished.

"She attacked Nelson," Harmon continued, "not half an hour ago. "I blame myself, for not providing the discipline she needs."

"She attacked *Nelson?*" exclaimed Emma. She and Dojo exchanged a worried look. "How is he? Does Mother know?"

So I'm not the only one to notice Leeth has failed to charm Mother? Interesting that they assumed Eagle already knew. "Yes. Leeth scarcely injured him, so Mother has given her another chance. But one more lapse like that...."

All three stared in silence at the girl.

She looks so helpless like that, thought Emma. "Aren't you going to heal her too?"

"I have. She is no longer physically injured, merely stunned. We could apply a stimpatch, but I prefer to let her come around naturally. In her quarters. I have some words to say to her." He looked at Dojo. "May I impose on you to help me carry her?"

Emma could tell Dojo was not happy, but he stood and lifted the girl back into his arms. The Doctor inclined his head to Emma, then followed after.

If only James were here, to discuss it all. Too much seemed to be going on; ugly currents under the surface. Was Leeth beginning to crack? The girl *had* basically been cooped up here since her opera house tests. Suddenly Emma herself felt stifled.

At last, unable to resist the temptation, she headed to her own rooms. *Just one MetaLife scene.* She'd visit Steed. Nelson had a new episode prepared.

CHAPTER 21

Sitting on the edge of her bed, marking time until she woke, Harmon looked around her room. A jumble of vid cubes: the energetic music she liked, wildlife documentaries, trashy monster movies jumbled in amongst martial arts training exercises. Some fruit in a bowl.

A few posters on the walls, a mixture of singers he didn't recognize and heroes and heroines from the foolish action vids she seemed to enjoy so much. Mounted on one sliding door of her wardrobe, a full-length mirror; the other door covered with a poster providing assembly and cleaning instructions for a smartgun. Heckler and Koch. A pity she seemed to prefer German engineering to American.

From her almost bare bedside table he picked up the wooden carving of a shark. It was a thing of planes, the edges unsmoothed; he wondered if she was still working on it. Pitiful really. He put the crude carving back. Just as well for her to focus on the things she did well, instead. Beside it rested an old padlock and a worn paper-clip.

He frowned. Little outward expression of the occupant's personality except her deadly-looking matte black slingshot, and those frozen images from her ridiculous movies. Several appeared to be from a single film: three heroines in improbable armor, armed only with swords and bows, facing progressively less likely foes. A final image showed one girl with long blonde plaits and a Nordic helm, descending in an impossible leap to plunge her silver sword through the skull of a horned creature ten times her size. Below that, in lurid red, the film's title: Demonsbane.

He shook his head.

Leeth made a small sound as she regained consciousness. *I must teach her not to do that.* She sat up and their eyes met, her mouth setting in the familiar stubborn pout.

He waited, but soon realized she was not going to break the silence. Of course not. He sighed. "Leeth, what did I tell you about finding ways to defeat someone other than by attacking their strongest point?"

It was the wrong remark to make, he saw, checking her aura. From hostile and defensive it had shifted to disdain. Disdain? How *dare* she? Anger surged, but he forced it down. So. She thought her defeat merely peripheral, and expected him to understand her real motivations. He felt his way forward.

"But then, you weren't really trying to beat Dojo, were you? You just wanted to smash something, but knew we'd both be 'evicted' if you did any real damage." He read the accuracy of his guess from her aura.

He shifted his perception back to the mundane world for a second, and was disconcerted to see she still returned his stare. So, there was more. He continued, slowly. "You chose Dojo because you didn't have to worry about killing him. But just letting off steam wasn't enough, was it?"

She flushed slightly.

"You really did want him to knock you senseless, didn't you? You wanted the pressure to stop. You gave up." *I should have been the one to make you do that.* She was slipping from his control. *She should come to me when it all gets too much.*

"I did not!"

He smiled, one eyebrow notching upward. "Then why did you attack Dojo as you did?"

"Why did you stop me from killing Nelson?"

He stared at her. "You're not stupid, Leeth, even if you act that way sometimes. Kindly explain how slaying one of our host's operatives would improve our acceptance here?"

"He's not an operative. Only Emma, James, and Preacher are operatives. Nelson just does computer stuff." She got up from her bed. An excuse not to meet his gaze. Rolling her shoulders, accepting the healing as a matter of course. "Anyway, you could've healed him. I wouldn't have killed him *properly*. I just wanted to pay him back." She spun around to face him. "Do you know what he did?"

"I have a reasonable idea, yes." Best to leave her unaware that the Department had orchestrated the entire experiment. And, thanks to his own warnings against performing it, had been closely monitoring the situation. "Also, I know from my experience today that healing Nelson is numbingly hard. I am not at all sure I *could* heal him from a truly serious injury."

She stared past him. "It was like I was lost. Like I wasn't *me* anymore. There were all these rules and it was like playing...." She shuddered. "It was terrible. And Nelson, lurking like a poisonous little spider in the middle, so I just wanted to-"

"Leeth! Do you realize both Mother and Father now feel you are too unstable to be useful to them? Feel that at any moment you might take offense and try to kill one of your colleagues?"

Now her eyes met his, as she shook her head in denial.

"No? So you claim now. But can you assure me you won't lose your temper again? Snuff out a life without thinking, destroying a set of irreplaceable skills the Department cannot afford to lose? Can you assure me of that?"

"But- well... I can *try*."

"No, Leeth. That is not enough. It can't be a matter of *trying*, nor even of *trust*. You fail to realize that those little simulations – constructive scenarios like the one Nelson tried to involve you in – are the bread of life to the operatives. They instruct, reinforce, condition. Deeply. So their loyalty is assured."

"I don't understand."

He raised an eyebrow. "I can see I must be blunt. Very well. The kind of computer-generated stimsense Nelson tried to involve you in – watered down, since you aren't augmented – is what is fed to each of the department's operatives. It is similar to the addictive NuLife, Leeth, but taken a step further."

"NuLife – that's some kind of drug, isn't it?"

He frowned. "I am sure I have explained this to you in the past."

"Yeah. It's a drug."

"Not in the traditional sense. It is more like an educational or entertainment stimsense, except used to provide interactive serials that are psychologically addictive; triggering the reward centers of the brain and heavily laden with subliminals. Nelson has produced a more advanced tunable ER variant-". Seeing her incomprehension he started again. He wondered if her ability to ignore information she found boring was uniquely hers, or common to all teenagers. "An Enhanced Reality stimsense is one which is not fully immersive, merely overlaying normal reality. Nelson's 'MetaLife' provides considerable computer and communication assistance to the agents, and is tunable in its degree of immersion and stimulation of certain cortical functions. Unlike NuLife, it is directive and non-harmful, though still addictive. And obviously anathema to you – as it should be. It is, after all, an artificial experience."

She shuddered.

"But it leaves us in a rather awkward position, doesn't it? Because they *also* use it to condition their operatives to guarantee their loyalties. And now, thanks to your outburst, they need the same sort of guarantee of your behavior that they have for James, Emma and Preacher. And yet they dare not use neural augmentation since it would ruin your own special abilities."

She looked down.

A rush of anticipation swept through him. Perhaps now, finally, he could advance his own experiment to a new level. "Do you trust me, Leeth?"

She looked up at him. "I don't know, Keepie. I used to."

He should have expected that; but the answer still hurt.

He let that hurt show, and saw her turn away. Saw the guilt.

"You remember that first day? When you thought you were to be sent away? Do you remember what I promised you, then?"

Her eyes returned to his. "That you'd never abandon me." Her voice a whisper. "That we were a team. That the whole world wouldn't be enough to split us up."

He stared, not expecting such an accurate recall. He felt a pang; perhaps, even, something more.

"Leeth, I know it's hard for you to believe, but you are the focus of my life. Everything I do, I do to make you stronger. Better. More *yourself*. Even Dojo must have told you, there is no gain without pain."

She stared at him, shaken now, he saw.

"So I ask you again: do you trust me?"

She worried her lip. "Yeah, Keepie. I guess I do. Deep down."

Looking into her trusting young face, he felt suddenly cold. Even sick. As if he stood now at a precipice. *It had to be done, though.* Someone *has to have control of her.* And if it weren't him, through magic, Nelson would be certain to come up with something else they could *try*. Even if it magically crippled her in the process, or killed her. No, it had to be him.

A whisper of excitement crept in. "Lie back down on your bed and close your eyes. Listen to my voice, and only my voice. Remember your trust. You will have to help me, Leeth, with all your heart." For long seconds, she studied him, deciding whether or not she could do that.

At last she nodded, and lay down. "You won't do anything... *bad* to me, Keepie, will you?"

The knife twisted in his stomach. "No, Leeth, I will do only what is essential." *Unfortunately, that will be a lot.*

"You promise?"

"I do."

For a second her eyes remained open, wide, staring vulnerably up into his. A strange pain stabbed into his heart, a part of him begging him to find some other way. Begging him to *want* to find another way. He pushed it down.

Eyes still locked on his, Leeth took a breath, then closed hers.

He gazed down at her: the new and still unfamiliar urchin hair-cut; the full lips and snub but faintly too broad nose; the innocent faith. What he was about to do.... He felt loose, adrift. Like he stood at some great height.

From on high, he studied her. He knew her mind so well. Strange, really, how all the minute adjustments he'd already made, over all the years, made such a perfect foundation for the lines of control he *had to* weave through her mind now. As if he had planned it that way from the start.

Absurd. He put the ridiculous notion aside and focused once more on the difficult task at hand.

It had to use her own inner strength, of course.

Like a god he looked down at her, his heart racing so madly that a tide of blackness swept up, almost overwhelming him.

With a deep breath, he began to work the magic.

CHAPTER 22

She sat up slowly, blinking and frowning, rubbing her forehead, unsure how much time had passed. One hour? Two? She felt strange – like someone was standing just behind her. She had to look around to be certain there wasn't.

«Shh.» To her, Harmon's voice was a faint whisper. Which meant, she knew, that no one else would have any chance of hearing him. Which meant he thought someone was listening.

«Think to me clearly and slowly,» he whispered, «and I will be able to read your surface thoughts.»

She blinked, considering the implications of that. She thought she'd stopped him from being able to do that *years* ago. Belatedly she quashed the thought. *«Who's listening?»*

«Several people, I imagine.»

His voice sounded really strange – like his throat was hoarse and he was blowing the words out. And his lips hardly moved. It always made her want to laugh, when he did that.

He frowned. Then in a normal, loud voice, said, "That's done, Leeth. You are now limited in what you can do to your colleagues here. Furthermore, you are unable to discuss the Department, or any of its people, or any of its secrets with anyone you haven't already met here."

She sat still as the meaning sank in. Tears rose to her eyes for no reason she could think of, and she angrily blinked them away. *«What do you mean, 'limited?"»*

«Aloud,» he whispered.

"What do you mean, limited?"

Harmon permitted himself a small smile, and spoke normally. "Well, we don't know who could be listening, so it wouldn't be fair to you if I let everyone know exactly what you are no longer able to do. I *will* inform Eagle of the specifics, naturally." He shrugged. "Perhaps he will see fit to inform Father and Mother." In a whisper he immediately added, «You may not kill any of them, without express orders from Eagle, or from Mother and Father together. Or from me. That is the main limitation.»

"Oh. But how will you prove to them that- that I really am 'limited,' unless I get pushed into- trying to break my limits?"

"A problem, I admit. My assurances will carry little weight, as yet. So I want you to show people that you can behave yourself. That you aren't completely headstrong and self-centered. That you can follow orders, even orders you disagree with." His voice sank – «I have also imposed one other control to help you in this.» – then rose – "To demonstrate that you can be obedient." – and sank again – «Leeth – Mode One.»

A wave of strangeness shivered through her at the whispered words, and her eyes widened involuntarily.

"Stand up."

She stood.

"Take off your clothes."

She blinked, confused. Her blouse had to come off, first.

She began undoing buttons. If Mother and Father really were watching, she wondered if this would be the first time either of them had seen her naked. She was removing her bra when he interrupted her.

"Stop. Put your shirt back on."

For a moment, as she bent to pick up her top, a feeling of doubt flitted through her consciousness. *Why?* She shrugged back into the blouse, did the buttons back up.

"Come with me, Leeth. I want you to apologize to Nelson." And added, just for her: «You will apologize for attacking him. And for frightening him.»

A surge of anger washed through her. She wasn't going to say sorry to that little-. She shook her head as she lost her train of thought, frowning as she followed her uncle out of the room. Determined to apologize.

A few minutes later, they stood by the door to Nelson's apartment. Before Harmon could press the chime in the corridor outside, a voice snapped out over the speaker. "I'm not opening the door while *she's* there!"

Harmon looked up to where he assumed the security camera was concealed. "But Leeth has come to apologize to you."

There was a second's pause before Nelson replied. "What, she doesn't want to kill me anymore?"

Leeth glared at the speaker in the wall. "Yes."

Harmon turned to her, scowling, which only deepened at Nelson's response.

"Yes she does want to kill me or yes she doesn't?"

«Say no,» whispered Harmon urgently, suddenly realizing his orders – to simply apologize – had been too vague. «And you no longer want to kill him.»

"No. No, I don't want to kill him."

Harmon ground his teeth. "Don't tell *me*, Leeth, tell Nelson."

"No, I don't want to kill you, Nelson."

"She doesn't sound too sure about that."

"Nelson, why don't you let us in, and Leeth can reassure you face to face?"

"*Rip* my face off, more likely. Nah, I'm happy for her to apologize to me from there."

"Good," Leeth said, "then I won't have to see your pasty little face," she snapped.

Harmon stared blackly at the girl, before turning back to the door, ignoring Leeth's remark. "I can assure you that Leeth has only come to say she is sorry, and won't hurt you. Wouldn't you rather make her do that personally?"

There was a pause. A long pause. Abruptly, the door clicked and slid open. "All right, then. Come through into my lab."

As they stepped into a harshly white room of stark furniture and trideo machines, and benches of expensive-looking equipment that neither guest could recognize, Harmon sub-vocalized his angry instructions. «You are to convince him you don't want to kill him, and that you're no longer angry. You will pretend you were in the wrong. Dammit, Leeth, if you can't do even this, what sort of spy will you make?» He sensed her still resisting, probing for loopholes in his control. Why couldn't she simply trust him? The wave of sudden anger was overpowering. «You will do whatever it takes to convince him you like him!»

An inner door opened. "Well, don't just stand there like two borked bots."

With a massive effort, Harmon smoothed his expression and turned, following the voice into the adjacent room. "Ah, Nelson, thank you for letting my young ward apologize in person."

Nelson sat behind a long bench covered in electronic components, data jacks and optic cables. The only clear space was directly in front of him. Concealed from the others' view, he quietly slid the safety catch off as he checked the video feed to Father. Even now, Dojo would be on his way, to wait right outside in case he was needed.

Harmon and Nelson faced one another across the workbench. Leeth waited, further back, still in the other room.

"Well? What's she waiting for?"

Leeth stepped hesitantly into the doorway. She'd recognized the quiet sound. She took another tentative step forward, seeing the expected twitch of the arm that must be holding the gun. Looking down, she counted to three to compose her face into an expression of regret, then looked back up and into his eyes.

"I'm sorry, Nelson. I'm sorry I attacked you and frightened you. It was just that I was confused, and angry. It was wrong of me." She stepped further into the lab.

Nelson frowned at her doubtfully.

She hung her head again and continued in a soft voice. "I guess I can't blame you for not trusting me." She moved one hand up, pressing one small fist between her breasts. "And I suppose, in a way, it's a sort of a compliment that you think you have to point a gun at me to feel safe." She looked up to meet his eyes once more, catching the surprised expression that proved her guess. "But really, I think we should try to be friends."

"What makes you think I've got a gun?"

She wasn't going to tell him she'd heard the sound of the safety disengaging.... "Well, you've cleared all your expensive equipment away from in front of you; you haven't got either hand in view; and your right arm twitched when I moved forwards. So I *guessed* you had a gun. You should lift it up, you know – Preacher says you have to shoot at a pretty sharp angle through cover, or the bullet will be deflected really badly."

Nelson stared at her in confusion, then saw the Doctor seemed as surprised as him.

"I don't know how to convince you," she shrugged, "but they say actions speak louder than words." She closed the remaining distance steadily as she moved around the bench toward him. Almost involuntarily, he raised the gun and swiveled to face her. She looked into the ugly muzzle, then back into his eyes. "You don't need it, Nelson. I'm here to say I'm sorry, remember?"

She continued to advance, not avoiding the gun, and bent down, leaning forwards until the barrel touched her breast. Her mouth opened slightly, and, never taking her eyes from his, she slowly parted her lips and lowered her face to his. Her lips opened wider as she tilted her head back, closing her eyes.

Harmon's fists clenched as he watched Nelson lower his head hesitantly, heard Leeth's small "Oh!" as their lips met, then watched as the kiss quickly became avid. Watched as Leeth guided Nelson's hand to a breast.

Abruptly, Harmon exploded. "Leeth! That's enough!"

Immediately, she stood, and Nelson jumped, suddenly recalling the other man's presence.

The tableau held for long seconds – Nelson trying to look unaffected, Leeth holding tight rein on her emotions as her skin crawled from the recent contact, and Harmon trying to calm himself.

"Please excuse us, Nelson. I have something I would like to discuss with my ward."

"Uh. Sure." Nelson looked reluctant to move. "I guess you can find your own way out?"

Father's voice sounded in Nelson's audio implant. «I'm ordering Dojo to stand down, Nelson. Before they leave.»

«Sure», Nelson responded, equally silently. «She really did, uh, apologize. Pity her uncle came with her.»

Leeth smiled at Nelson, then left, not trusting herself to speak. She forced the smile to remain as she sashayed out, unsure how many cams Nelson had scattered through his rooms. Harmon's mood darkened further as he hurried after her, looking as if he was being led by her. Following her down the empty twisting corridors linking the Department's underground apartments.

"Leeth, stop!" She obeyed at once, and he grabbed her by one arm as he caught up to her. "What the devil did you think-"

"Do you really want to talk about it out here?" she hissed at him.

He glared at her, biting down on the things he wanted to say. "Go to your room."

Even braced to resist, this time, and with the flush of anger that his words aroused, a vision of herself going to her room punctured her thoughts and threw her into confusion. As if everything drained out of her head and reformed in a pattern that felt... *different*. She pictured herself marching toward her quarters. *He was doing it again!* A new surge of anger flushed over her, and she grabbed hold of it hungrily. Desperately. *I* won't *do what he says.* Feeling sick that she'd trusted him; had *let* him gain this control of her.

"Go to your room."

No, don't. Hate! she told herself, fists clenched and lips parted in a silent snarl as she faced him. *So* angry with him.

Uh. She shook her head. *Why* am *I so angry with him?*

Harmon watched, his cold fury growing even as her temper slowly dissolved into confusion. *Why does she always challenge me? Always oppose every request?* She really did need to learn obedience. Even if they weren't in such a difficult situation.

Well, he told himself, he now *had* the control he needed.

"Go to your room, Leeth."

The two glared at one another. Until Leeth blinked, confused; then finally lifted her chin, spun around, and stalked off.

He makes me furious *sometimes.* She was going to her room. She had nothing more to say to him.

-

For a while Nelson stayed lost in a pleasant sexual haze, but when he gathered his wits again he knew he had a decision to make. Should he try again to find some choice dirt on her, something to get rid of her – or reboot the game, give her another life? A *Meta*Life, one where she'd be friendly, like just now?

But he'd already used her DNA with Ghost to hunt for matches, in every net-linked holographic data store on the planet, and drawn a complete zero. *Had someone gone through the entire net, wiping any traces of Leeth's parents?*

Eagle had to be behind it. But why on earth do that? Unless it involved the Department's big scary 'bogey man'....

CHAPTER 23

Detective Marta Sanchez awoke cold and nauseous. Something squeezed her head in a vise with each pulse of her heart.

Her hands were bound.

It was quiet, too – the normal city sounds gone. She lifted her head, and a surge of adrenaline cleared the nausea at the sight of her partner, tied upright to a steel rod. Henderson slumped, his face swollen and bleeding, one eye bruised shut.

The man they'd cornered in the alleyway stood to one side. Watching.

Below them, the water of the Bay glittered in the night, and looking around she saw they were perched at the edge of the broken Skyway. She was tied to a lamp-post that leaned to her left, stretching out toward the shattered layers of concrete and the yawning emptiness below. He'd brought them deep into the Dumps.

"He said he's been working in the soup kitchen, Sanchez."

Her eyes swung back to her partner, bound to a twisted steel reinforcing cable curving up from the pre-stressed concrete. He'd been badly beaten.

"He's been turning these people into zombies – he calls it 'perfecting them.' He was doing it in that alley because he'd heard of us, and wanted us out of the picture. He said everyone says we're the only people in all New Francisco who give an ogre's fart about crime in the area.

"I don't know *what* he is, Sanchez. Some sort of cybered merc, maybe. He took me out like I was a kid."

"Where's the boy? And the woman?" Sanchez demanded.

Henderson shook his head. "The woman went down, and stayed down. Last thing I heard was the boy wailing, as *I* went down. You wouldn't believe how strong this guy is."

"What does he want?"

Why are we still alive? she was really asking, reading her partner's expression. Marta knew Henderson well enough to see the fear he tried to hide. It told her more than she wanted to know.

She tried her bonds. Then gritted her teeth. It felt like their kidnapper had used their own rip-cords against them.

She tried to access her commlink, only to realise a moment later that it had been removed. *Of course it had.*

The man stepped over to them, and she braced herself for the gloats and taunts.

"The boy is in the alley with the mother."

The voice was noninflected; uninterested.

"His mother's all right?" She couldn't believe it.

"Unlikely. The woman's body was much frailer than yours. The skull cracked. But that is irrelevant. Now it is time-"

Sanchez's cursing interrupted him. Her temper was legendary, and this time she lost it big time. Henderson struggled against his bonds as the man approached his partner, looming before her then reaching out to grip her head. Sanchez began spitting, thrashing in her bonds, screaming abuse, trying futilely to break free.

"Your anger makes you a stupid animal. You cannot think." The man's hands framed her head, pinning it still despite her fury. "If you let go of your anger perhaps you can win this contest. You cannot escape if you do not think."

Henderson couldn't see what happened, but suddenly Sanchez froze. Long seconds passed, the only sound her panting breaths.

Gradually they slowed.

Then the man rose and turned toward him, and Henderson felt a simultaneous surge of anger and fear as he strained to see his partner, see what had been done to her.

He caught a glimpse of her face while the man walked the few steps separating them. She seemed... stunned. Then the man was crouching down before *him*, the hands reaching out to grip Henderson's own head. The cop fought against the ties binding his arms, feeling the nylon crush flesh against bone.

The hands were chill, and radiated a sense of contamination so strongly that Henderson squirmed against the implacable grip.

"That is not anger. Those ugly shapes are fear. Do not hold out your fear now, it will be needed later. Feel your anger instead."

Henderson cringed away. At last the man stood and stepped away, leaving him shocked at the relief he felt; ashamed by the feeling of escape even while standing bound to the twisted steel rope. This guy scared him; scared him more deeply by the minute. Behind the fear lay a strange emptiness now. He hated being helpless, being made to feel weak; but instead of anger at his situation there was a strange acceptance.

The man walked back to Sanchez. She watched, her hands still bound in the rip-cords, those in turn tied to the broken lamp-post by strands of electrical wire, her fingers told her.

A soft whir and the brief flash of scanning lasers across the scene was the only announcement of the arrival of the security bot Henderson had summoned earlier.

Sanchez saw it first. Somehow it had found them, deep inside the shattered Dumps, and she grabbed her chance. "Take down the hostile."

The squat robot shuttled forward, taser rounds ready and pepper spray armed, and the man turned. Then strode to meet it.

Electroshock projectiles fired. The man jerked as thousand volt pulses shot through him. Freezing, he collapsed – but to Henderson, it looked more like he'd knelt down, rather than fallen down. His eyes widened. *It hadn't worked – it was a con!* "Lethal force! Shoot the fucker!" he screamed.

The bot objected. "No hostile activity detected. Lethal Response authorization required."

"Detective Richard Henderson, badge num-"

But the large man was already standing and lifting the chunky armored robot by one of its four sturdy legs.

The bot responded instantly, fine wires stabbing into its assailant, electricity this time visibly sparking across the man's skin as it tasered him again. But again, the man merely jerked. *What was he?* Gripping the bot tighter, he swung it up, then down, slamming it into the broken roadway with the sound of a pile-driver.

Concrete shattered, the impact cracking the case-hardened steel like a walnut. Electronic guts spilled out. The man walked back to Sanchez and stopped. Her eyes moved in disbelief from the smashed robot to the lunatic before her. Wondering what he'd do now.

For several seconds he said nothing. Then: "You have been distracted by the robot. It is destroyed; irrelevant. Focus on the matter at hand."

Sanchez gaped at him.

"Recall: you had inquired of the mother. This Marc Disten told you she was likely dead. You remember?"

Sanchez stared at him in disbelief, then Henderson saw her shake her head, then her whole body, and then spit at him, cursing.

But the man failed to react, simply reached out to grasp Sanchez's head. "Yes, anger. Bring forth the rest of your anger."

Sanchez struggled and swore. And then she calmed. Too quickly. Henderson saw her expression alter. It was hard to read: confusion, yeah, but she appeared to be in some kind of distress, too. Straining at his bonds, he felt them cutting again into the flesh of his wrists.

"What did you do to me?" Sanchez demanded.

"You are being Perfected. Your anger is gone. Now bring forth your hatred, so it too may be taken. Hatred. Now."

"Are you crazy?" But even as she asked it, Sanchez herself could feel that something had changed. She really didn't feel angry anymore. She'd been knocked unconscious, seen her partner beaten.... Had been kidnapped and was about to be tortured – yet she didn't feel angry. She felt *calm*.

"Hatred. Now."

"Don't be stupid. People don't emote on cue."

"That is true. You will need a focus." He appeared to think. "Consider the people killed. The people you are sworn to serve and protect. Their deaths at these hands. It has been difficult, learning how to bring others to clarity. Perhaps tonight it can be achieved, with your help."

"You *are* mad."

"Pity. Yes, feel pity for the man who stands before you. His successful life in society destroyed. A stockbroker. Now skulking in the wastelands with the human and near-human refuse. Preying on them, trying to bring each one to Perfection; watching each one shatter in these hands instead, as they resist clarity, resisting the truth. Remember the boy, tonight, alone in the alley as his mother moaned in pain, dying. Pity him."

When his hands went to her head again, Henderson saw, Sanchez's face shone with an expression he'd only seen in the trids.

"Sorrow, too. Think of the lives lost. Think of the pain they suffered. Sadness is a pain that can be removed."

Sanchez was crying. Though calming. A cold prickling ran through Henderson at how quickly she calmed. And at the look of shock that dawned on her face.

The man addressed her. "You begin to see, don't you? You know what is being done. Man is a rational creature. That is the ideal. But a rational creature would not engage in war, or destroy and foul its environment.

"Fear, and greed. Desire, arrogance. Man is an angel in a devil's body, ruled by lusts and drives that blind him. With these removed, man can achieve Perfection."

"Monster!"

The man stiffened. "Horror. Good." His hands returned to Sanchez's head despite her efforts to squirm away. With apparent ease he forced her face up, to look into his eyes. "Your body language reveals that you find the touch of these hands repellent, now that you understand. Horror too, shall be taken. Fear will be left till last. Fear is an excellent motivator."

When the man stopped, her eyes no longer sparked with fire.

"Why are you doing this?"

"To improve the world. To save mankind from itself."

"If that's true, why take away pity? That's a good emotion. It makes people help others."

"You are not yet thinking clearly. The emotions are a web. Each is not alone, not an absolute. They form opposing points. Unless all are removed, the web would re-form in time.

"You ask this because you realize love is next. That is perceptive. Already you are improving."

"No! Please, no more."

"It is not time for fear yet. Now is the time for love."

He took her head, angling it toward her partner. "Do you care for him?"

Sanchez only moaned, and Henderson found himself screaming obscenities and thrashing at his bonds as he watched this thing in human form destroy Sanchez piece by piece.

Turning her into a zombie, like all the others!

Then it stood, crossing the short distance to him with the tread of an implacable nightmare. Terror rose up through the fear until Henderson felt he was going mad. Chill hands pressed *cold* into his head, eyes and touch passing secret knowledge as anger and fear drained from him like water through those wintry fingers, in surges like a retreating tide.

Henderson blinked, unsure whether he'd passed out – maybe more than once. He couldn't tell how much time had passed when at last he sagged against the nylon bonds. He felt numb. *Am I in shock?* He felt calm, though. It was a relief. With the fear gone, the heart no longer pumped like it would explode from his chest.

Sanchez watched as her partner slumped. She wished to get to him, to free him. To free them both. This man was breaking the law. She clung to that thought. He had killed people, and that was wrong. *It was against the law.*

He stood before her again. "Your emotions are strong, and come easily to the surface. Unfortunately, your partner could not separate his fear from his anger. It will make it impossible to motivate him for the final steps. He may motivate you, however. You can control how he will die. If you co-operate, he will be killed quickly."

"You don't need to kill him."

"He cannot be Perfected now. And he now knows far too much. He must be killed."

"You could kill him very slowly."

Henderson heard the words with shock. "Sanchez. What has he done to you?"

Sanchez stared back at him, her expression open, wistful. "That way we could be together longer." Her eyes returned to the madman's face. "Or you could cripple him, so he wouldn't be a threat, and I could care for him."

"Sanchez!" Even as Henderson said it, a sick horror threatened to overwhelm him. *Sanchez had already been destroyed.* She turned to look at him.

"I love you, Richard Henderson. I will look after you."

The man looked content. "Very well. If you co-operate, he will be crippled so he is no longer a danger." He stood, turning towards Henderson. Who watched him approach. In terror, he watched the hand grip his throat. "No, Sanchez, he said *all* the emo-"

The grip tightened, strangling the words. Then pain exploded as the hand crushed his larynx, tearing a gurgling scream from him that echoed across the dark waters of the Bay.

Barely conscious, he saw the man cross back to his partner. Barely heard the words past the agony of the raw internal wound.

"Now. You understand what must be done. Let us try jealousy."

Henderson watched Sanchez as she appeared to think, then nodded. "That bitch Hollings. What did she have that I didn't?"

It was like a nightmare Henderson couldn't wake from. And the loving looks she was casting at him only deepened the horror. How could Sanchez have forgotten that this creature said *all* the emotions had to be destroyed? How could she think she'd be left capable of feeling love? He was sinking into shock, he could tell. *Sanchez loves me?* They were partners, that was all. Cops.

He passed out.

CHAPTER 24

Leeth looked around her bedroom, frowning, trying to remember why she'd come here.

Because Keepie told me to.

She hadn't wanted to.

He'd told her to. And somehow, she'd just done it. Just like he'd made her say sorry to Nelson!

She felt the blood rush to her cheeks.

Sure, she could see she had to make everyone realize they could trust her, and maybe that meant she should seem to apologize to Nelson. And convince him she was sincere. But why had he made her think of *seducing* Nelson? He'd even threatened to *make* her do it. She grimaced, remembering Nelson's sour breath.

And then *he'd* been angry with *her!* Ordered her to go to her room! She looked around, fuming.

Well, she *had* gone to her room.

And now I'm leaving!

Still angry, she stalked down the corridor, on her way to the swimming pool, hearing the *click* of the lock on her front door as she moved off. Then heard her uncle's distinctive tread from behind her.

"What do you think you're doing?"

Uh-oh. She froze, then realized he'd surely order her back. She ran, hands over her ears.

"Leeth! Stop!"

He'd hardly raised his voice, and she'd already made it round the corner, but still she heard him clearly.

"Come back here!"

She flushed cold, then hot, in anger. But moments later, she was turning around and walking back toward him, determined to face him. As she rounded the bend of the corridor, she tried to read his expression. Nothing. That was a bad sign. And his fists were clenched.

That was a *worse* sign.

The awful feeling was back. *It wasn't fear.* No. She wasn't afraid of him. She *wasn't.*

She wanted to run.

But it was *his* fault! She'd just explain. "Why did you-?"

"Be quiet!"

The answering flash of anger and defiance drained away into a newly-familiar gray nothingness. She blinked in confusion.

Was he doing it again? She didn't think so, but wasn't sure. She just knew she wasn't going to give him the satisfaction of speaking to him.

"I don't want to hear your excuses. And I've had enough of your willful disobedience. Now come with me." As he turned away, she swayed forwards toward his departing back, the urge to leap and *strike* almost overpowering.

And something in his expression... she didn't want to be alone with him now. She took one step after him, the rage surging higher.

But what would the others think if I attacked my own uncle? They'd both be finished here. And she still had so much she needed to learn.

She blinked. Had he heard that thought? The angry set of his shoulders hadn't changed. She frowned, trying to remember if he'd done that finger-thing he did to cast his mind-reading spell? Then shook her head, confused. *What is* wrong *with me?*

She took another step after him, then another. Feeling like she clung to rationality by the barest thread, as her gaze lashed his oh-so-vulnerable back.

She shook her head again, forcing the confusion aside. *Ignored* it, determined to follow him no matter what, the avid *tingle* burning at her fingertips. Eager.

At his quarters, he placed his hand to the lock, gesturing her inside as the door slid open.

She'd hadn't been in here much. Looking around at all his familiar things, set up in their new positions, a curious sense of dislocated nostalgia drained some of her anger. Some of the fear.

For some reason she felt reluctant to speak. She had to force herself to ask what was upsetting him. "Uncle, why are you-"

"I told you to be silent, Leeth." His voice was dangerously calm.

Her stomach felt hollow. She had to firm her resolve not to speak – not one more word – as she faced him, hands on hips. Hiding the storm of emotions inside.

His eyes narrowed. "I've rarely chastised you physically – I see now that that was a mistake. And since you apparently prefer to behave like a balky child, your punishment will be a child's one."

She lifted her chin defiantly, still refusing to talk to him. Turning away, she deliberately ignored him as he crossed to a desk in the corner and dragged a chair into the center of the room and sat on it.

"I believe a bare-bottom spanking is the traditional punishment for disobedience."

She turned back to him in disbelief. In the following silence, a faint high-pitched chirp sounded several times, puzzling her.

"Come here and lie down across my lap."

Anger and confusion swelled at his words, churning inside, but she fought them down. They cleared, leaving the decision to be punished standing starkly alone in her thoughts. *I'll show him!* She approached him.

She didn't understand. Why was he doing this?

Why was she *letting* him?

Part of her raged helplessly, but her decision to drape herself across his lap was solid as steel. *He* couldn't stop her. Her thoughts strobed between horror and the desire for him to hold her. But not like *this*.

Why couldn't he just hold her like a father held a daughter: the two of them close, and warm, together? Why couldn't he stroke her hair, and tell her if he was proud of her?

Instead, here she was, lying stubbornly across his lap, determined to be spanked. It felt *wrong*.

But the close intimacy of even this contact – how long had it been since he'd really *held* her? – made her yearn for more. At the idea of his arms wrapping around her, water welled up in her eyes.

And suddenly the confusion swirled back in, and through it, she felt something move inside her mind. An oily sliding something, nudging aside thoughts as it delved deeper. Stirring up her deepest, most secret thoughts. Turning them over and probing into them.

Her eyes flooded. *Tears?* She shook them away, confused afresh. If she wasn't going to *speak*, she certainly wouldn't *cry* in front of him!

The confusion cleared. With renewed determination she reached up behind her, awkwardly wriggling till she could unbutton the top of her denim cutoffs.

He drew his breath in harshly.

In the silence that followed, she once again heard the chirp, ever so faintly, this time stretched into a whine like a tiny mosquito. An ultrasonic motor. Like a camera's focusing mechanism. Her eyes widened. *Nelson.* She was sure.

Her uncle pulled down her shorts and underwear.

Her resolve not to speak almost broke, then. She wasn't even sure anymore *why* she'd made the stupid resolution. Reasons to break it swarmed through her mind.

He hadn't moved for the longest time, but suddenly she felt him tense, and a moment later his hand cracked against her bare backside.

Fiercer than the sharp pain was the tide of rage it awoke. Again the tiny noise of the motor, and her face flushed red in embarrassment at the thought of what Nelson must be seeing. She imagined his eager face as he perfected the focus of the hidden security camera.

Almost, it was enough to make her speak, to tell her uncle that Nelson was watching.

Smack!

Her muscles locked taut in fury. Spanked like a child! And it was *his* fault she was on exhibition. Her uncle's.

Smack!

Almost, the pain was enough to make her cry out. But she would never give either of them *that* satisfaction. She clenched her jaws tight-shut.

Smack!

Twenty five. She wanted to cry out, her buttocks a flaming agony, her skin feeling raw. But each blow just locked her jaw tighter, stoked the anger burning inside.

And the anger was *building*, too, deep within her. Unfurling. Feeling strangely like her Unfolding, almost two years ago.

The feeling swelled, pushing against binding walls, straining against them as it grew. The walls responded, pressing harder. But the fire fought back, burning hotter. Each blow feeding it.

Twenty six! Inside, the flames banked higher still. Inner muscles bulged, and finally found purchase on the slick sinews caging them.

Inside, some deeper part of her *dared* him to strike her one more time; *yearned* for it. She felt the power grow, gaining strength by the moment. Knowing the next blow would shatter its chains.

Inside, she smiled, feeling her potency. Sharpness flared at her fingertips, ready. *Almost there.* One more blow.... She tensed. *Throat, or heart? Heart*, she decided, picturing her hand plunging into his chest-

And at that instant, with a gasped inhalation, her uncle froze. Stopped breathing altogether. For a moment, she had the sense he panicked.

Then he shifted – just a subtle movement – and in a shockingly intimate caress, *something* slid invisibly through the behemoth straining inside her. Slithering between the flames, nudging them. *Turning* them.... She sensed it wrap around and through her thoughts. Dredging up images of Jax, of James, naked. Probing and caressing, twisting them up alongside images of her uncle and her in his bed, together... *Huh...?* It all churned around, tumbling over and sinking back down. *What...?*

The hand that had been beating her suddenly moved again. It slipped gently, almost nervously, between her legs, coming to rest there in a startling but compelling touch. *Unh...?*

She felt an echo of his movement through her, as if he'd moved his other hand – or maybe just the fingers – then a horribly confusing *need* curled around her, deep inside. Low down, in her belly. In her groin.

No. I don't want *this. Not now!*

But another voice inside her disagreed. Like a separate, traitorous part. *«Yes, I do»* it said. *«I want him. He's my Keepie. He knows what's best for me. I trust him.»*

So why did she want to *scream*, in fear and rage?

Memories of her first time suddenly swamped her: his sweating body below hers as she crouched hungrily over him, pounding down onto him, taking what she demanded.

Huh? Why *that* memory, *now*? She shook her head, confused. Then felt a key turn in her heart, against her will. Unlocking a warmth that flooded out, staining the rage.

Inside, the giant roared. But its purpose suddenly uncertain.

Her uncle's hand cupped her. Tenderly.

"Get up," he whispered.

Spinning off and up from his lap, she faced him, bursting with power. She felt herself vibrating, the force inside lashing through her, surging now with hungry lust. Confusing her in a different way.

The giant inside clutched the lust. Claimed it and devoured it. Then turned outward; to those walls. One single moment more-

And he whispered: nonsense words that made no sense. She felt mental chains fall away, her mind suddenly clear, truly clear. And the giant inside exploded free.

Free, but cheated. *No-o-o!*

A moment of dismay, then every muscle of her body spasmed as she threw her head back. But *still* with her lips clamped shut; still refusing to make a sound.

The energy smashed and rebounded within, arching her spine backwards – then finally her head snapped forward. Staring at her uncle, she took a step toward him, reveling in the fear and awe she saw. That, and... hope?

But behind her, above, from high in the wall, came a long ultrasonic chirp as the hidden camera focused on her. *On my backside.*

Nelson!

She stopped, swiveling her head slowly to work out exactly where the sound was coming from...? *There!*

Enough! Fury smashed through her. She dropped, twisting, slamming her hand into the chair leg beside her uncle's own. Snapping it with a sharp crack, she saw his eyes widen in shock as he toppled forward from the chair, like he thought she'd just broken *his* leg.

She leaped through the air, the jagged spear of wood grasped in both hands. She felt her lips stretch in a savage grin as she plunged the spear into the spying camera. Like the elven Valkyrie in Demons-bane, slaying the Beast.

For several seconds she just stood, arms still raised over her head, panting, perched somehow on the back of his sofa. Releasing the length of wood that now impaled the belly of her enemy, she twisted her head back to her uncle, and saw him look up from the dismembered chair to stare at her like she'd gone mad.

He opened his mouth. "What-?"

She sprang from the sofa, turning in the air to face him, shaking her head once to order him to silence. Taking the collar of her denim jacket, she ripped outward, the material tearing like it was rotten. With tingling fingertips she sliced her bra free, letting it too fall to the floor.

She took a step toward him, allowing him to see the hunger in her smile.

I'm not too young now!

Desire and power flooded through her. For just a moment, as she saw the answering hunger in his own eyes, she wondered if he'd somehow *made* her feel this way? Was somehow still controlling her? But at that thought, the desire surged higher, and she cast the idea aside.

«*Of course not.*»

Afterward, she lay curled against him, listening to his breathing: now slow and regular, heavy with sleep.

Feeling conflicted.

The faint light creeping under the door gave everything that ghostly gray clarity which she'd worked out, long ago, that others never saw.

As their sweat cooled and dried, as the smells and urgencies faded, and thought returned, she stared at his back, stretched out so vulnerably beside her.

I could kill him so easily now, she mused, gnawing at her bottom lip. But there was... it was just so... the thrill of it, like a fire inside, or a great wave.

What *was* it about him that she found so compelling? His hooded gaze, the way his eyes burned into hers? His unshakable certainty in his own powers? It certainly wasn't his physique! She stifled a giggle, mentally comparing his lean but aged and ordinary build to James's beautifully-muscled, tight body, then to Dojo's hard, toned perfection, and grinned to herself in the dark. *Yeah, it's sure not his* body!

I should just kill him, she thought: for controlling her; for humiliating her. Surely, he must *want* her to kill him? But then, that look he'd given her, just before he'd rolled over, to sleep. Not *trust*, exactly. But like he knew he was putting his life in her hands; offering himself up to her justice. Whatever she decided.

And then, too, there was his promise: *I will never abandon you.*

She stared at his long form, lying quietly beside her in the dark, his side moving slightly as he breathed.

Abruptly, unbidden, she remembered the time she'd shown him what she'd secretly taught herself in the old gymnasium at the Institute, back when she was still a child. Remembered leaping to him from the trampoline, knowing he'd catch her. The feeling of his arms folding around her, holding her close. Remembered him healing Faith, as her friend lay dying.

I should still be angry with him.

But the anger was faint, now. Washed away by the storm that had followed, maybe.

Besides, if she *did* kill him, she'd do it without any co-operation from *him!* What'd be the point if he made it this easy? What'd *that* prove?

No, when she bested him, it'd be in a front-on confrontation.

She watched a vein in his neck pulse with sudden force. She was close enough to hear his steady, strong heartbeat.

Besides, if I do just end *him, everyone'll say I can't be trusted.* And she didn't think she could kill them all before Dojo could get her. Didn't even *want* to.

What she *wanted* was to be here, working with them, helping them. She was learning so much, especially from Dojo – everything she'd ever dreamed of learning. And she liked Emma, and James, so much. And maybe, they liked her a little bit, too.

She felt a smile curve her lips as she slowly nestled her body right up against the length of his, gently winding her arms around him, ever so carefully snuggling close. He didn't like people touching him: if he woke up now, he'd push her away, maybe even send her back to her room.

She closed her eyes.

And Harmon, with even greater care, disengaged his mind-meld.

CHAPTER 25

Old-Nelson had parked the car back under the Elephant and Castle sign, which swayed in a wind that wasn't there. She heard that super angry snarl of Faith's which she'd heard only once before. She knew what that meant! She just had time to dive away from the car before Faith's mini-rocket had blown both him and the car up.

She buried her face in her friend's shaggy coat, inhaling the rich scent of dog and ozone and machine oil, and knew she'd come home. "Good dog!"

But Mother and Father were cross. They said Faith was a very *bad* dog and Leeth should have trained her better. Which was totally unfair. She hadn't *trained* Faith – they were just a team.

They were going to disguise Faith as a Japanese girl so she and Leeth could go on missions together, but Preacher had curled his lip as they passed him on their way to the front lawn. "I wouldn't have needed a *rocket*," he sneered.

Faith rolled her eyes.

Leeth grinned. "I know. He's always grumpy like that. But Emma and James are real nice. You'll love them. And wait till you meet Dojo – he's a-*maz*-ing!"

Faith looked interested, but reminded her she was late. "For pat*roll*ing" she growled, and took off in a loping run, her cyber muscles powering up.

The Jungle had gotten a lot bigger, and as they climbed the last stretch of the mountain, past the laser-blast crater in its side, Leeth saw Faith realize her paws couldn't grip the rocks properly.

Why on Earth *did I choose* this *route?* Grabbing onto the mountain with one arm, and Faith with the other, they dangled high above the buildings of the Institute that sprawled out far below.

"Sara! You should cover yourself!"

Godsson, on the front lawn, eyed her Hunting Outfit as if its bikini top and the fringes of her shorts were making fun of him.

Faith growled at him to shut up or she'd blast him again. The three of them were walking abreast down the road from the Institute's front doors, heading for the front gate so Godsson could escape. Faith said it was a bad idea. Which was true. She'd promised Professor Sanders she wouldn't break him out illegally.

Godsson was waving a finger at Faith. "*You* have to stop blowing people up. I won't warn you a second time.

"And you, Sara, do you remember what I told you? What you decided you had to tell the Bird?"

"Uh...."

"What Melisande told my companions and I? Before we killed her?"

She did. That is, she *could* remember. Almost. She just needed a hint, maybe?

Godsson sighed. "The reason she broke the Net." He stared at her. "It's very important, Sara. You have to tell the Bird about the aliens."

"Oh! I do! I mean, I will. Come on, we can tell him together, right now."

But the elevator kept going down, and down, and down. And when she stepped out alone into Godsson's cell, he looked up like he was shocked to see her.

"Sara? Or should I say, L'ith? How are you here? How *can* you be here? What has Harmon done?"

She felt heavy. *I've gone too deep*. She didn't know what she meant, but she knew it was true.

"Never mind." He smiled, and rose from his cot. "It's good you're here. I thought you'd forgotten your promise to rescue me."

"But I promised Professor Sanders-"

"*And* you promised me. But come now. I have someone for you to meet. He's been searching for you. You two will be Perfect together."

She backed away. Suddenly cold. Like Bad Robo was nearby.

Godsson stopped, looking at her strangely. "Wait! Before you go – there's something you need to know. Something even more important than the message for the Bird."

She hesitated. The Bird was important.

Seeing she wasn't leaving, Godsson seemed to relax. "But how did you get down here, girl? You're not allowed here." He walked around her, studying her.

She turned, but he stayed behind her.

"Yes, how *did* you get here? And... dear me. What *has* Alex done to you now?"

He was in front of her again, smiling. But in a way that made her uncomfortable.

"That *will* come in handy," he said, looking her up and down. "But never mind that now. You need to hear this. You need to remember it, as only I and the Dragons do. Yes. You will *need* to know this. *Remember* it: Aus-"

His lips kept moving, and sounds came out, but mufflers had appeared on her ears. She tried to take them off, but powerful coils wrapped around her wrists. Godsson's eyes bugged out as something majestic, and ancient, of rainbow colors, yanked her into the sky.

And she woke, panting, feeling... exhausted.

Without Faith. In the dark. Beside her uncle. Clutching shreds of fading dream.

Faith had been in it. And something she had to tell Eagle....

In his dark bedroom she stared at her uncle's back. Then up, at the ceiling, and thought of Faith.

Remembering Faith in her arms, she closed her eyes and rolled away from him, curling up around the empty space.

And let the tears fall.

CHAPTER 26

Henderson's waking was a cruelty beyond belief.

He lifted his head, the simple movement skewering his throat, the pain tearing a thick sound from him. Sanchez was free, he saw, and his heart leaped at the sight.

Only to plunge past his boots. The man was still there, too. Both stood a short distance away, watching him.

"He is awake now."

It was Sanchez who had spoken, in the same lifeless tones the man used. *Sanchez.*

Tears welled from his eyes, blinding him. Two pairs of feet approached.

"He will be untied now, as agreed." Sanchez.

"As agreed. But first he must be rendered unable to communicate."

"It is already done. You have crushed his voice-box."

"He can still write. Mages could read his mind. A lobotomy is necessary. It is a simple procedure." He held a cooking skewer in one hand.

Henderson struggled, but once again the implacable grip took him, this time around the back of the neck. He tried to scream.

But Sanchez moved up behind the man. A meaty sound of impact, and the grip was gone, the skewer dropped.

The man turned to face Sanchez.

"Why do you attack? An agreement had been reached."

"The agreement was a lie: a trick to make you release both prisoners."

There on the finger of bridge that pointed brokenly into space, Henderson fought the pain. Blinking tears from his eyes, he struggled to focus on the scene before him.

There was no more conversation. The two simply fought, with a speed and brutality he'd never before seen; could scarcely believe. Sanchez's leg flashed in an arc, the man's arm swung up to block – to the ugly sound of bone breaking.

Sanchez paused, warily.

Though his arm bent unnaturally, the man didn't flinch.

"Why do you attack? You can think clearly."

Sanchez circled closer. "You break the law. You are being arrested. You should allow yourself to be taken into custody before you are severely injured. You cannot defeat someone trained in unarmed combat."

Henderson watched, not breathing, as the man seemed to consider Sanchez's words.

"Perhaps you are correct." With his good arm the man drew a gun – Marta's own gun – turning from her to take a single step towards him.

For Marta Sanchez, thought now flowed crystal-clear and blindingly fast. Perhaps the criminal did not know the gun was keyed to Sanchez alone, that only Sanchez could fire it? She circled in to take advantage of the possibility. When the other transferred it to the left hand – poorly held due to the broken arm – the moment came. As the criminal raised the gun jerkily to Henderson's head, Sanchez darted forward.

The weapon was inches from Henderson's face when it swung away, moving to the oncoming threat. The finger squeezed the trigger before the distance could be closed, but the security lockout prevented the gun from firing in the criminal's hand.

Sanchez's body slammed into the bulkier figure while her hand fastened on the gun, wrenching it from the now-weakened grasp. She saw Henderson staring at the side of the weapon; saw his eyes widen; saw his mouth open to cry out. But the man's arm had reached around the back of Sanchez's head, the heavy hand clawing into Sanchez's face, gripping the chin. But, as planned, too late: the gun was up, pressed now to the criminal's head, the trigger pulling. The hammer of the gun struck.

Sanchez had time to deduce the gun's failure was because it had been unloaded; that the entire maneuver had been a trap.

Despite locking her neck muscles rigid, her head continued in its implacable turn. Sanchez felt spinal disks crack and part; a visceral crunch, shocking in its intimacy. All sensation ceased. Sanchez's head now faced the criminal, his eyes locked on hers, expressionless.

Crystal clarity of thought held that one final image, before thought itself blurred into endless dark.

On the ground at Henderson's feet, the red digits of the ammo-counter on the side of the barrel read 'oo.'

He watched, helpless, as the man dropped his partner's body to the ground, then approached to squat on his heels before him. For several seconds neither spoke.

Strangely, he felt no fear, even as one large hand reached out and gripped the back of his neck. It tightened with dismaying strength.

"This has been very instructive."

Then muscles clenched, and with a gristly crackling sound, Henderson, too, spasmed and fell still.

-

Disten looked down at the broken arm, considering. It was interesting the policewoman had grasped the physical capabilities of Perfection so quickly. It had taken Disten several days to unlock the speed and strength improvements.

This was the first significant injury since attaining Perfection. It was interesting, too, how the normal physiological response to a pain stimulus was entirely absent. Nevertheless, medical attention for the arm should be sought. Then perhaps there should be a period of waiting while it healed.

First, though, these bodies should be removed and hidden. The death of the two officers would inevitably draw police attention, but it would be short-lived. There was no corporate or political advantage to be had from this area.

Moving deeper into the Dumps would further reduce the risk of discovery. More subjects could safely be drawn from that area, too – the human waste that lived there would provide ample practice material. Failures would be removed by the local predators. With the knowledge gained tonight, good progress would follow.

For perhaps another thirty seconds the man stood, calmly thinking. Not disappointed at having come close but failing: simply satisfied that Perfection could indeed be communicated, if the correct techniques were used. At last, with the good arm, Henderson's body was gripped, then hoisted up and off the metal rod it was bound to. Turning, Disten carried it back to the female's corpse, the male's feet dragging across torn concrete slabs of quake-twisted roadway. The body was dropped beside its partner's. Stripping both of their comms harness, each camera was crushed between two pieces of rubble. But after several minutes spent trying to destroy the radio links, the small case-hardened nut shapes remained unharmed.

After a pause for thought, Disten tore off a gobbet of flesh and pushed each device deep inside, one after the other. Walking then to the brink of the jutting roadway, the chunk of meat was hurled far into the night. Disten watched it arc away out of sight. With the extra elevation, the distance achieved would be two, perhaps three hundred meters.

It should suffice. Checking the jammer, the *Active Links* light finally showed red, staying red even back at the bodies. Safe now to switch the jammer off.

Bending, both bodies were grasped by their shirt fronts and lifted.

Pain flared from the broken arm, and Disten paused, frowning, assessing the extent of the damage and the sensation of fresh injury being done. Dropping the female, the damage stopped. The male's body was carried back down the broken highway to the Great Wall Electrikar registered to Marc Disten.

Two hundred and sixty meters away, Sanchez and Henderson's radio links reconnected to the emergency network. Had a display been paired to Sanchez's, it would have shown that her ex-husband, the PASWAT's Detective Diego Berlusconi, had just tried to call.

Disten went back for the second body.

CHAPTER 27

The call tone woke Harmon from a deep sleep, and he rolled over to see Leeth watching him from a chair across the room, her knees tucked under her chin, rocking forward and back as she stared at him. She looked strangely intent. He could imagine why.

The insistent tone continued, and he angrily answered it. "What?" Father's face appeared, looking annoyed. "Please be in my office in five minutes, Doctor. And bring Leeth."

"For what purpose?"

Father's expression hardened. "Five minutes." The image died. Harmon drummed his fingers against the firm mattress, thinking. Father had been angry, at Harmon himself and at Leeth, and did not want to explain or give details. Which suggested he didn't want to allow preparation.

Harmon rose, and as he did, a half-remembered image drew him back into the lounge. For long moments he stared across the room to where the chair leg stuck out into space, speared high in the wall above the sofa.

Spinning around he stalked back into the bedroom. "Come," he snapped as he passed the girl in the chair, and proceeded to the bathroom. He just had time for his ablutions, he decided, eyeing his face in the mirror. Unshaven and pale. How long had it been since he'd seen real sunlight? Would he ever see it again?

Leeth had not appeared. He scowled into his reflection. Stepping back to the bedroom he took control of her once more. «Leeth – Mode One.»

"Come here," he ordered, this time loud enough for microphones to overhear as he returned to the bathroom. Ten seconds later, while he shaved – he disdained depilatory creams – he saw her face appear in the doorway, and cast the Mindmeld.

So. A hidden camera. In his own quarters. Probably related to Father's summons. A muscle ticked in his cheek. If he'd cast the spell last night instead of just Percepting her aura, he would have known, then. Though given the state of her emotions, perhaps it was just as well he'd not attempted it. But why hadn't the foolish girl told him, herself?

As they walked the corridor together, Leeth following obediently behind, Harmon fumed but continued his sub-vocalized instructions. «You will speak only when spoken to. You will agree with any suggestion I make. You will not contradict anything I say. If asked what we were doing, you will merely explain you were being punished. That you deserved it. Understood?» Reading the futilely resisting acceptance in her mind, a brief smile touched his face.

He had half-expected Father to make them wait, when they arrived, but the door whisked open while they were still meters away.

Father spoke as they entered, staring coldly at them both. "At 21:32 last night the audio monitors in the hallway outside your quarters registered a heavy impact on the inner walls, Doctor. This was the same time the emergency cam in your room went off-line. The cleaning bot this morning reports a broken chair and an anomaly in one wall.

"Explain."

Harmon went straight to the attack. "I was told, when my ward and I agreed to join this organization, that it was committed to the ideals of democracy and fairness embodied in the once-extant American Constitution. Was that a lie?"

Father's eyes narrowed. "No, Doctor." For several seconds he was silent. "How is this relevant?"

"Because at nine-thirty last night, the 'emergency' concealed spy camera in my private quarters was activated. A clear betrayal of trust. Is it the practice of the Department to spy on its own people in their private rooms? Because if it is, I dislike the implications. How can you hope to restore America if you resort to methods that betray the very soul of the thing you are trying to heal? What comes next? Secret police? Compulsory lie detector tests?"

Father's eyes narrowed. "The United States is not run like a mega-corporation, Doctor. The room monitors are only for emergency use, and require Eagle's special authorization. These are serious accusations. Can you back them up, or is this merely empty rhetoric to cover some fresh tantrum of Leeth's?" He looked at the girl, but she simply gazed back at him expressionlessly. He turned back to Harmon.

"Leeth believes Nelson hacked the system."

Father stilled, then massaged his temples. "I see. Is this true, Leeth?"

At last, a direct question. Her jaws unlocked. "Yes, Father."

"How do you know?"

There was a hint of reluctance as she answered. "I heard the camera's focusing mechanism."

Father was silent for a long time then, staring at her. Absorbing the new information. For some reason, he looked from her to her uncle; and he didn't seem pleased.

"Just like it was a minute ago, in this room," she added.

Father's head swung up and around, to stare at the wall behind her, where she'd heard the chirping sounds coming from.

In another part of the complex, Nelson swore. *She can hear the cameras? Little bitch!*

Father's hand lifted from his console. Then for perhaps half a minute he watched the security system probes at work. At last he raised his head. "It seems I owe you both an apology."

"More than that. You must re-earn our trust. I demand the 'emergency' monitors be removed from Leeth's quarters and my own. As a sign of good faith."

Father inclined his head. "You are in no position to make demands, Doctor, but I'll pass your request on to Eagle. You realize, though, that in the event of a real emergency-"

"I believe both Leeth and I are prepared to take that risk. Correct, Leeth?"

"Sure," she agreed, bitterly.

CHAPTER 28

Josh Taverner groaned, eyes fluttering open, and moistened his mouth, swallowing something he immediately wished he hadn't. *What time is it?* He tried to access his link, but it futzed out. Sitting up on his bed, the room swam and he hunched forward. Not sure if he was going to pass out or throw up.

In the darkness, he waved his hand, and felt the plastic bottle on his bunk-side table go flying. *Oh, yeah. Electrolytes. I'd been gonna drink that before lying down.*

«Lights» he sent; but nothing happened, and he swore. "Lights!" he croaked.

His bedside lamp burst on, and he slammed his eyes shut against the glare. Then carefully eased them open, and tottered forward to the bottle of orange-colored liquid rolling to a stop on the concrete floor. He downed it in long gulps, and felt the fluid race through him like spring rain.

Beside him, the massive bulk of the Asgard CrawlTank loomed like a friendly warning of Armageddon. He patted it lovingly as he staggered across the floor of the echoing garage-slash-workshop. With a flare of pain, he felt his neural links reconnect, and bit back a curse.

A little after two a.m., he saw. *Tuesday?* And the air was *still* hazy? *Ganja-mana! Just how much did I smoke last... uh,* Sunday *night?* He signaled the door open.

At the end of the short corridor the next door slid open at his silent command. Across the tiny squad-room, from inside the glass-fronted fridge, a liter bottle of orange Nervade called to him like a chorus of angels.

Wonder how Sanchez and Henderson got on with that stakeout, Sunday? I could murder *a meat pie.*

Ten minutes later, pie crumbs dusting his lap, his nausea was gone. Their comm links had been stationary now for over a day. Guilt gave his actions urgency as he piloted the third drone into the Dumps, hoping *this* one wouldn't be shot down before he could locate Marta and Hendo. Wondering if he should've already raised the red flag.

But what'd HQ do, if he did? Just say they were idiots for heading into unsanctioned areas. And probably wind up the precinct.

There! Okay, he had lock. He buzzed the drone lower, wishing he'd thought to install UV cameras in them all. He lit the scene up, sure now he'd see Marta and Hendo, waving up at him.

Instead, he stared, flummoxed, at a stretch of rubble. No one at all in sight.

Phut. The camera died. The signal from the drone lost.

"Shit! *Felshing drekhead nilspecs!*" He continued swearing, jumping up from his seat to pace the room. Now what the fuck could he do?

Berlusconi? Yeah, Berlusconi'd handle it.

-

Two hours later, puffing, sweating, and cursing, PASWAT detective and mage Diego Berlusconi stared in confusion at the direction indicated on his tracker. Why her fuckwit permanently-stoned mechanic couldn't have contacted him during daylight hours.... Marta and her partner had been off-net since the evening of the day before.

This was going to be bad, he knew it.

Studying the tracker, he tried to make sense of what it was telling him. He looked around through UV goggles. The tracker said Marta's comm-node was right here.

Shit. That meant it had been removed from its harness. *Worse and worse.* His powerful UV torch shone over an impossibly fucked-up jumble of rocks, the tumbled slabs of torn-apart highway. Mud-filled crevasses gaped open even now, twenty years after the Big One.

Still no one in sight.

The torch and goggles were precautions. Cutting yourself on a rusted, jutting length of rebar in the darkness was the least of the worries for any fool venturing here. A lone person shining a *visible* light would have attracted predators.

He swung the light down, looking for the almond-shaped radio unit, crouching down with one eye still on the tracker's screen. He should be able to see it by now... unless whoever tore it from Marta's harness had *buried* the fucker?

Between his feet, a strangely smooth piece of stone glowed under the powerful UV beam, fine... *hairs...?* dusting it.

Berlusconi's world fell away. *No.*

Hesitantly, he prodded the lump, and it *gave* as he pushed.

Fuck, no. No!

With the end of the goddamned tracker unit, Berlusconi rolled the 'rock' over.

For several seconds his mind refused to recognize the
raw flesh, exposed striations of fat and muscle in the
crusted, bloody surfaces.

Berlusconi collapsed to his knees, breath rushing from
lungs that somehow couldn't draw air.

It was Marta.

The second last thing Berlusconi had ever expected was
to out-live his fitness-fanatic ex-wife. The *last* thing he'd
expected was to learn that he still loved her; even after
their stupid fucking messy divorce, all those years ago.

Why hadn't her fucking partner, Henderson, protected
her? That was what partners did. That was what *he'd* have
done!

Tears puddling in the fucking UV goggles, he ripped
them off, plunging himself into darkness.

For a long time, then, the hardened cop cried, hunched
forward in the rubble before managing by degrees to drag
himself together.

Forced himself to think. To push aside the pain. *For
now.*

The killers – Marta was tough, it'd need more than one
to take *her* down – *might* still be hiding or disposing of her
body. Even now. Though the... mutilated flesh looked
dried-out, like it had been lying there a whole day.

But why was the signal coming from here?

Shaking, he watched his hands go through the motions
of extracting a plastic evidence bag, pulling on rubber
gloves, and bagging... the remains. Despite his best efforts,
his throat constricted.

Holding it reverently, he unbent stiff knees and labored
upright, fighting his too-generous weight. Fumbling the
UV goggles back in place one-handed, he moved back a few
meters.

The signal stayed with him.

Disbelieving, he stared at the... evidence bag. *The fuckers had jammed her unit* inside *her own flesh.*

It was too much. "*Fuck*tards! You *hear* me, out there?
I'm going to hunt you down, and I'm fucking cutting you
into tiny pieces!" Roaring into the darkness, his voice
rolled over the broken hills and mounds of the Dumps.
"I'll fucking *kill* you! Just like you killed Marta!" And he

meant it. There'd be no jail cell for these scums of bitches.
If the murderers thought they were gonna get away with
this, they hadn't reckoned on a trained police mage discov-
ering the crime within a day of it being committed.

*And they've even thoughtfully left me a fucken' great
piece of Marta I can use for a Sending.* He'd find her;
then hunt down her killers. There was even a slab of concrete close by where he could chalk out a Circle, before as-
trally projecting.

I'm coming for you, you fuckers!

-

It was almost dawn when BID agent Adam Garland took a
call from his former partner, Detective Diego Berlusconi.

Sitting up in bed, noting the time on his internal clock
– 5:12am – he came fully awake. Berlusconi wouldn't be
awake at this hour, let alone calling him, unless it was an
emergency. He signaled the room light on and okayed a
video hook-up.

Berlusconi stood by the shore of the Bay, but at the
look on his face, Garland sat up straighter. He'd only once
seen Berlusconi with tears in his eyes, and that'd been five
years ago, after his divorce. Behind him, two police divers
were hauling a male body, in a cop's uniform, from the waters.

"It's the Golden Gate Park killer again, Garland. And
this time they took out-" Berlusconi stopped, struggling for
composure. "They took out *Marta.* And her partner, Henderson."

Garland checked Berlusconi's signal. "You're at the
Lash Lighter cliffs? That's right on the edge of the
Hunter's Point Dumps. I can be there in twenty."

"Thanks, G. I've got a shaman on his way. But I've got
a feeling it's gonna be a weird null result, just like in the
Park. It was the same killer. I'm sure."

"Twenty."

Garland signed off, threw on clothes, grabbed his gear
and left his new and larger apartment.

He wondered if the girl, Sara, would have an alibi for
tonight? But would he ever know? She'd disappeared off
the radar even before he'd left Eagle's office that day two
months ago. Hell, even the record of her arrest, and her
uncle's, Harmon, had been expunged from the police database.

Damned spooks.
And he was one of them, now.

CHAPTER 29

From their first day in the Department, he and Leeth had hardly been welcomed. Merely accepted – at best. But that gradually changed in the weeks following Leeth's attack on Nelson. For the worse.

Slowly, the agents had become more distant. Less forgiving.

Harmon presumed that, since Nelson programmed the agents' MetaLife, he was subtly adjusting their attitudes. He wondered whether Father and Mother knew that.

All that, however, retreated into the background as he sat in Father's office. Wondering if he had heard correctly, but recognizing how neatly this new initiative fit into the developing pattern. They would blame him for their pain and suffering, naturally. Isolating him further, and by association, Leeth too. Making it far easier for either or both to be discarded.

The question was: was this simply Nelson's revenge, or a more deadly testing of his own skills? To see whether he could escape the trap being built around them?

Or was it something more subtle still? Hurting the agents, then healing them. Over and over again. Such simple stress could be used as the first step toward unlocking magical potential – if there were any. Eagle knew Leeth herself was proof of that: proof of Harmon's theory. But he had seen no sign of such potential within the agents. And even if there were, with all their cyberware....

"Well, Doctor? Do you have a problem?"

Father's body language gave no indication of any qualms at what he'd just suggested. Harmon shifted his senses to the Imaginal, Percepting the man's emotions.

Calm. Perhaps a faint concern, but more directed at how Harmon himself would react. He shifted his perception back to normal sight. "Let me confirm: this new robot gun will shoot and injure your own agents, and you wish me to heal them afterwards?"

"Correct, Doctor."

"You realize an unlucky shot could damage areas of the body I may be unable to heal?"

"The SHUTZ unit can be programmed to avoid designated target areas."

Harmon tapped his fingers against his chair's armrest. Was it possible Father didn't anticipate how the agents would react? "Gunshot wounds must surely be quite painful. You realize they will blame *me* for their suffering? They already do to some extent, due to the new training programme with Dojo – those exercises are only feasible because I bring you magical healing capabilities. Capabilities the Department did not have before."

Father nodded. "You are the psychologist, Doctor. I leave it to you to consider how I should present the exercise to the agents."

"I doubt *any* presentation could entirely eliminate the perceived blame."

Father stared at him coldly. "I see no reason why the agents must *like* you, Doctor, for you to do your duty."

I see, thought Harmon, staring back with equal chill at Father. Abruptly he stopped his tapping as a new thought opened a hollow expanse in his stomach. "Will these exercises involve Leeth, too?"

"Of course."

"That's absurd! She's only just started training with firearms. She can't be ready for something like this!"

"I am the judge of that, Doctor, not you. She has been showing great promise and improvement with Dojo. I plan to accelerate the more physical aspects of her training." Father's face closed in. But after several seconds, he unbent. "For Leeth, we can lower the difficulty of this exercise. Initially. The purpose is to give experience under fire rather than improve marksmanship skills. Or do you have reservations about her courage?"

Harmon's jaw clenched; and with an effort, unclenched. "No. None at all."

"Good. In that case, give some thought as to the areas of the body to rule inadmissible as targets. We can provide you with all the data you require, if you are unfamiliar with such wounds. Up to and including real victims to heal.

"Speak to Nelson when you've decided. I think that's all, for now."

Harmon stood, staring unblinkingly at Father for several seconds. Still hunting for a way out of the corner which Father had painted him into, considering the cold brutality behind it. In the end, shaking his head in disgust, he left the room.

CHAPTER 30

Leeth had been pacing outside the 'Aegean' room since eight forty-five, but even pressing her ear against the door, all she could tell was that Father and Uncle were inside, and not talking much. She thought they sounded cross with each other.

At last, she heard the others approaching – Emma's heels, James's soft but sure tread, and Preacher's quiet, scuffing steps. She waited, alert, as they arrived. James and Emma acknowledged her with small nods.

Not smiles. None of the agents seemed to smile at her like they used to. Only Dojo.

She wasn't sure what she was doing wrong. But just then the door chimed and slid open. So it was probably exactly nine a.m. With a sneer, Preacher waved her in ahead of them.

From their looks, though, they had as little idea as her what this new training was about.

Inside, her uncle sat stiffly by the robo-medical unit from the infirmary, a strange pair of glasses and surgical instruments at hand. Four army cots covered in blue plastic sheets crowded the small room. Leeth caught a look pass between Preacher, James, and Emma when they saw the cots, and it wasn't reassuring. Then James and Emma both looked at *her*, for some reason.

Surgical instruments? Keepie could heal people magically, *why would he need surgical instruments?*

Another door slid open and the three agents filed past her, past him. He looked angry or upset; she couldn't tell which.

But when his eyes met hers... just for a flash, she thought she saw concern. For her. *For her.* Hugging that knowledge to herself, she followed the others into the next room. Behind them, the heavy inner door slid shut.

She stepped into a shooting range. Emma had perched herself on a large bullet-absorbent crate at the near wall. They'd been told to dress in clothes they didn't mind ruining, but Emma still looked elegant in a mustard cardigan over a cream pantsuit. James sported a jacket, shirt and trousers less perfect than normal; Preacher, his usual leathers and T shirt.

Leeth had spent an hour trying to find something she didn't love. In the end, she'd decided to wear her favorite outfit – after all, it'd survived endless patching and mend-ing, from rocket blasts to being stabbed through the heart. What would a few more patches and stitches hurt?

It was only now, standing in the room alongside James and Preacher, that she started to wonder *why* they might ruin their clothes?

At the far end of the room, Father stood with one arm resting on a matte black, deadly-looking machine. A gun barrel poked through a hemispherical shield, held by a robot arm. Mounted on rails, it could move forward, backward, left, right, up and down.

It looked fierce.

She saw James and Emma exchange a short, worried look.

On top of the gun's shield, a small yellow target had been set.

"You're not going to like this," Father warned them, "but keep in mind the purpose of this training is to increase the likelihood of your survival in a gunfight. This device," he said, patting the ugly machine, "is known as a SHUTZ unit. That acronym can be blamed on the sense of humor of some egghead in Nemesys WeaponTech. The SHUTZ is a laser-scanning auto-targeting computer-controlled gun. For these training exercises, we have mounted a low caliber firearm.

"We're not trying to *kill* you, just sharpen your edge." Father smiled, and Leeth found herself smiling back at him. "Now that we have magical healing capabilities, we are able to provide more realistic training exercises. As we are all now aware, from our refresher course with Dojo."

The others groaned, and Leeth eyed them in surprise. *Didn't they* like *training with Dojo?*

At their reaction, he held up a finger. "Think of it this way: every time the Doctor heals you, it makes it easier for him to heal you the next time. In that sense, the more you're injured, the better!"

For some reason, though, the others didn't respond to his encouraging smile.

"Now, although you all have either neural enhancement of your reaction speed, or are..." he glanced at Leeth, "uncommonly fast, I know each of you have experienced situations where you faced someone even faster." He shrugged. "Some people will always overspecialize."

She frowned. *Emma and Preacher had cyberware too? Not just James?*

"And I'm sure I don't need to remind any of you that a firefight is the last refuge of the incompetent."

Yeah, agreed Leeth, nodding. *You should kill people with your bare hands.*

"Still, they are not always avoidable. Of course, the accepted wisdom is that the person who shoots first gains initial control of the situation. Which is true – normally. One's instinctive reaction is to take cover, dodge, at least flinch...."

Father's briefing continued. Leeth looked around, eyeing the target they had to shoot to 'win'. It was pretty small; and she had a hunch the robogun would move fast on its rails.

She chewed her bottom lip.

"The rules are quite simple. When the hologram wall is turned off, your object is to shoot the designated target on the SHUTZ unit, disabling it. However, until you have done so, or are down and no longer firing, it will continue to live up to its name.

"Of course at maximum rating, the unit can target and shoot with inhuman speed and precision."

So saying, he turned sideways to the machine, commanded it back ten meters along its rail, then struck a match in a broad sweeping arc through the air.

It was still flaring alight as its head blew off. The crack of gunfire died quickly against the sound-deadening walls.

Wow! Leeth glanced at the others, but for some reason they looked even *less* happy than before.

Father continued, explaining all about how Nelson had changed the gun's software for this training – including stuff about 'variable enemy skill simulations' – and how the Doctor had helped choose what areas the gun wasn't allowed to shoot.

But the explanations and discussion went on, and on, until she began to wonder if Father would *ever* ask the question she was waiting for.

"If there are no further queries, we can start. Who would like to vol-?"

"Oh! Me! Please, me!"

The other three looked at her. *Hah!* She stuck her tongue out at them. Slowpokes!

They all looked at her strangely.

"I thought you might, Leeth. Good girl. Now, considering your relative inexperience with firearms, we'll be making the target area larger." From inside his jacket, he replaced the small yellow target with a larger flexible disk. "The rest of us will join the Doctor in the outer room."

At some hidden command, the room darkened. A hologram of a brick wall sprang into existence, temporarily hiding the robot gun and its opponent from one another. Leeth heard the heavy whirring as the device moved to a new location.

"We'll watch on camera from the next room, Leeth. Do your best."

"Sure!"

"Father?" Emma asked, "how long will we be doing this?"

"The Doctor has already determined how responsive your bodies are to his healing magic. Depending on the vagaries of each healing – as I understand it, the effort is not entirely predictable – and since we are limited only by his ability to heal your injuries, we estimate you should each be able to have two, three, or perhaps more of these exercises each day."

"For how many days?" demanded Preacher.

Father turned towards the leather-clad agent. "Until I am satisfied by your performance."

A minute later the brick wall winked out, the heavy gun-carriage already hurtling closer along its rail. Something about the sureness of the way the barrel swiveled towards her made Leeth change her mind about standing her ground to take her shot. She dived to the left, firing at the yellow target. Missed! She saw the barrel swing round and down, following her movement. Rolling, she fired again as the robot weapon boomed. Something slammed into her right thigh.

But she'd expected the pain. Pushing it aside, she fired again, even as the gun swooped, tracked a fraction to the left, and shot her left thigh.

This time, she cried out, but snapped off another shot, feeling blood wetting both legs. *It really is targeting kindly,* she thought, as her third shot also missed, the robogun continuing to move and weave. This time the implacable matte-black barrel twitched left and shot her through the kneecap; and at that she screamed and fell. Through red and black waves, she fired again and again from the ground, and finally saw the yellow target flutter.

At once the firing stopped.

Keepie burst through the kevlar curtains looking stricken, while she tried to smile through the honest pain.

James and Preacher followed with a blue stretcher-cot, easing her onto it. Behind them, a calm, synthetic male voiced said "left thigh, round exited; right thigh, round not exited; left knee, round not exited."

Her uncle swore, but even as they carried her into the next room past a shocked Emma, she felt Uncle pour healing into her left thigh.

Father swung the digital X-ray screen out while James and Preacher slid her left knee under it.

With effort, she slowed her panting breaths. Keepie finished his first healing as Emma injected an anesthetic in and around her shattered kneecap.

"Ahhh. *Thank* you!"

The snap of rubber gloves brought her eyes open. Keepie stood over her with a scalpel, the arms of the robot nurse-unit outstretched towards her, ready for his verbal commands.

But at the sight of the familiar scalpel, a wave of panic flooded her and she tried to scrabble backward, off the cot. Emma pressed down firmly on her shoulders, holding her still. "Easy, Leeth, easy."

Leeth's eyes flashed to her uncle's – and for once, just for a moment, saw pain there. His lips parted; and somehow she knew he was about to suggest she look away.

Her panic vanished in a flare of outrage, and she glared back at him, *daring* him to speak his lie.

His expression closed in. For just a moment, then, she thought she saw something else. Then the cool disinterest returned.

Studying the X-ray, he angled his scalpel tip along the entry path of the bullet. Touched her skin with it. "Anesthetic here, here, and along here...."

Using the AR glasses, he set up the robot-held instruments and marked out trajectories. Instructed by voice commands and gestures, the bot began cutting even as he mapped out the next, and the next incision.

Leeth watched as it cut precisely, passionlessly; painlessly. *How different to normal.*

Oh! Maybe I can say that out lou..., out... outlaw, outlived, alive, a-la, a-la-la-la....

When she could think again, she blushed, knowing she'd failed again to break his controls, right in front of them all. Like she'd been flaunting the truth right in front of them. As if she *wanted* it; or didn't even care.

She growled, focusing on the impersonal blades slicing her numbed flesh. Then stared at her uncle, accusingly – until her thoughts started vague-ing out again. Growling louder then, she dropped her gaze back to the surgery. From the corners of her eyes she saw the others shift, and felt her ears burn.

"Uh, Leeth, wouldn't you like a sedative?" Emma offered. "You don't need-"

"I'm not a *baby!*"

Emma flinched back, and her lips pressed shut.

Leeth turned away, to watch the surgery.

Harmon slid the Senjik three-prong claw in to grip and extract the main fragment of the round as soon as the scalpels retracted.

Drawing it out he checked the X-ray and began directing the nurse's next incision. His eyes burned briefly into Father's, who stood coolly watching, before returning to operating on Leeth's leg.

"I take it you would like to include kneecaps as an interdicted target area, Doctor?"

"Yes."

"Very well. I'll have Nelson add it while you work."

"Have him add in *all* the joints. I don't want to be picking shrapnel from inside such delicate parts of anyone's body. Why didn't someone tell me bullets broke up into fragments?"

Father and the three agents looked at Harmon as if he were an idiot.

One minute later he fished out the last round, embedded in her right thigh.

Two minutes later, Leeth carefully paced the room, letting her fresh-healed tissues realize they were fine. James left then to enter the firing range, pushing through the kevlar curtain and taking up his position.

Emma and Preacher stared from Leeth to her uncle, then their attention was grabbed by the screen as James dived, firing, at the SHUTZ's target.

Father nodded approvingly to Leeth. "I'm impressed by how quickly you learned to accept the pain."

Leeth looked at him, stunned by the stupid remark. She opened her mouth; then shut it again and turned back to the screens, the fun suddenly drained away.

Her uncle was watching her, she saw, his expression carefully neutral. For long seconds, they just stared at one another. When she looked away, back to the screen, James stood grinning and uninjured.

"Good work, James," Father said. "We'll shorten the response times for you, next time."

James's grin vanished.

"Who's next?" Father asked. "Emma?"

Leeth tugged at his arm. "Do we have to take turns? I could go again!"

James entered the room to find everyone staring at Leeth as if she'd just declared she was the queen of the zombies or something.

"What's going on? Did I miss something?"

Father ignored him, his eyes on Leeth, measuring her. "I think it best if we follow a strict rotation. Emma: you're next."

By the end of the second week, though, even Leeth was glad when the SHUTZ exercises finished.

CHAPTER 31

"We know almost nothing of your social skills – except that they're woefully inadequate."

Mother and Father had called Leeth to a joint meeting, this time in Mother's office. For once, it looked like maybe Mother had done some actual work, since there was an e-sheet and a small package on her desk. Which otherwise, as usual, was completely empty.

"So. What kind of social interactions did you experience at the Institute for Paranormal Dysfunction?

"Eagle said I'm not allowed to talk about anything that happened there. Maybe you should ask him?"

Mother leaned forward. "Those instructions would not apply to facts already on the public record, such as the Institute's reputation for being cursed or haunted. So you can at least comment on that."

Leeth forced herself not to rush her answer, looking up, and left, then right, before finally looking back down to Mother. Since as usual, they had her standing while they went on at her. She kept her expression innocent, knowing that keeping the secret like she'd been ordered to, would infuriate Mother. "Um: that's interesting?"

Mother's eyes narrowed. "I still fail to see how Eagle expects us to properly structure your training with such a paucity of information. The Doctor's older published research suggests he was hunting the underlying mechanisms for magical Unfolding. And here you stand, with unusual magical abilities."

Again, Mother waited.

"Um... yes?"

"You have no comment?"

She shook her head. "No, Mother."

Mother leaned forward, and for once, didn't look cross with her: she looked *open*, maybe even a little excited. Like if Leeth told her something, she might gain points, or something. Leeth *wanted* to tell her about it, just to see that expression a little longer.

But she *couldn't*. Her shoulders slumped. "Eagle said it's all secret."

Mother glared at her. "Absurd. If the Doctor has learned how to unlock magical potential, we should be using that knowledge for key people in the government, military, business and research communities. It's precisely the sort of breakthrough that would lead to a quantum jump in

US capabilities – which is *precisely* what the Bureau for Internal Development is charged to do! And you have no comment?"

Leeth grimaced, but shook her head.

"Would you like to know what Eagle's briefing material has to say on the subject of your Unfolding?"

Leeth had the feeling that somehow Mother was laying a trap... but even so, she *did* want to know. Very much. *Would it be something cool?* She allowed herself a small nod and shrug, trying not to look too interested.

"It says: 'While perhaps related to Dr Harmon's research, the circumstances of Leeth's Unfolding are quite unique and unreproducible.' Would you care to comment on Eagle's own words?"

"Huh. That's all?" At Mother's microscopic nod, Leeth mulled it over. "Well... yeah, I reckon he's probably right."

Mother waited. At last, she saw Leeth was going to offer nothing more. "You do realize, should anyone uncover a connection between you and your 'uncle,' the inferences drawn will require a much stronger rebuttal than that. Yet Eagle's sole protection is to try to keep that connection hidden. Ridiculous."

"Shouldn't you be having that argument with Eagle, Mother, not with me?"

"I am, Leeth. Our disagreement is ongoing."

Leeth looked at Father, whose expression was carefully neutral.

"But Eagle's a lot smarter than you, Mother."

At the expression on Mother's face, and the way Father's expression froze, Leeth sensed she'd been misunderstood. "I mean, *even* smarter than you."

Strange: Mother seemed still not to get it. "I mean, you're the next smartest one here. Except for Nelson when it comes to computer stuff. Or Uncle."

If anything, Mother became even stiller, her eyes just burning into Leeth's own. *Had that jaw muscle just tightened a notch?* "For *magic*, I mean." She almost added, *duh.* "Except for Uncle when it comes to *magic*, I meant. Oh, and Psychology, of course."

Leeth noticed Father's eyes doing this weird left-right-left flicking thing while he stayed otherwise utterly still. It reminded her of someone shaking their head....

Father jumped into the silence. "I think Leeth is merely revealing her complete confidence in Eagle, Mother."

Mother thinks she's as smart as Eagle? Wow, I didn't think she was that dumb! No wonder her small gibe had struck so hard. And it did feel good to get a little payback for the steady stream of put-downs Mother subjected *her* to.

But Mother's eyes now held a strange satisfaction when she finally responded. "You've been pestering everyone to be allowed to leave these secure premises to do some real world training, yes? Like hunting 'The Breaker'?"

Leeth's eyes lit up, but Mother was shaking her head at that last part. And this *was* Mother. So there was sure to be a catch.

"And I think our little interaction just now highlights Leeth's social incompetence and her need to work on those skills."

Leeth opened her mouth to point out she was very socially competent – then saw the trap, and said nothing.

Mother smiled. "So to that end, you are being sent on an external live training exercise. Your 'mission' is to learn to fit in seamlessly with other children your own age," – Leeth clamped her lips tighter shut – "and your success or failure in this exercise will be determined on the basis of a written analysis, from you, on the group dynamics you will observe, absorb, and participate in; and on your being taken to be nothing more than an ordinary eighteen-year-old girl. Should you make your peers find you exceptional or abnormal, you will fail this part of your training. Which you will repeat at six-monthly intervals until you pass."

Leeth frowned. She had to appear normal? A written report on 'group dynamics?' She didn't even know what that *was*! This had suddenly flipped from sounding like great fun, to maybe-horrible.

"Um, where am I s'posed to learn these 'socialization'," she bunny-eared, "skills?"

"The Lindsay Wagner Memorial Drama School, across the Bay in Oakland. It's a small drama school, well-regarded, for young adults such as yourself. The students are a mix of children from middle class families for whom it is the best they can afford, and the well-to-do, who have chosen it for its reputation. You will have three weeks."

"Ah. Okay?"

"You'll start on Monday."

"But... doesn't it take more than three weeks to learn how to act?"

"That's a good attitude to go into this with, Leeth," Father said. "And in the future, your ability to pass convincingly in a variety of roles may well be a matter of life and death. But your main goal in this exercise is simply to learn how to appear to be a girl who has grown up in the usual way: going to school, having dates with boys, attending dances and parties, gossiping with girlfriends and doing whatever else it is that young girls do."

"But I never did any of those things! What do I say if they ask me about any of that stuff?"

"That's what you'll be there to learn," said Mother. "Perhaps you should watch some contemporary teen movies, to do some homework beforehand?" Mother finally slid the e-sheet and small package across the desk to her.

It contained just a cashstick – or maybe a credstick.

"Your background is in the reader: study it so you can provide any of that information without hesitation or mistake, when asked. Your IDs are in the 'stick."

So it *was* a credstick. Leeth looked for the lens, aimed that end at herself, found the dimple to activate the projector, and shone the image into her eye. Then frowned at the picture of herself. "I don't wear glasses, my eyes aren't green, and my hair isn't.... Oh."

"Try to keep up, Leeth. You may choose some temporary tattoos, too, should you wish. Your budget will be fifty credits per day." Mother narrowed her eyes as she spoke the figure, then waited.

"Um. Okay? A budget is how much I can spend, right? Not how much I have to earn."

"If you don't know the difference between-"

Father interrupted. "Then it demonstrates that this socialization exercise is very much needed. You'll be sharing Emma's city apartment, and commuting to Oakland each day. That is, Monday to Friday, of course."

Of course? thought Leeth.

Father tapped the sheet in front of her, turning it on. "The necessary information for you regarding Emma's identity is in there. Get into the habit of referring to her as Aunt Elizabeth for the duration of this training. Do not do anything to jeopardize Elizabeth Remington's cover identity: Emma has been developing it over the last two years."

"So I've got like five days to learn all this stuff?"

"That's right. Which is a luxury. There may be times in future when you'll be expected to grasp the essentials from such background material in only an hour."

Leeth considered that. "If I've got questions, who do I ask?"

"Emma will be working to prepare you," Mother told her. "Any further questions?"

"No."

"Good. Dismissed."

She considered saluting, but decided against it.

CHAPTER 32

The night before she was to join the drama school, Leeth moved in to Emma's luxury apartment, and was introduced to the security systems.

"I have a surprise for you," Emma said, and passed her a case about the size of her hand.

Excitedly, Leeth examined it. It hinged open, revealing... a pair of glasses, with flip-out thumbscreen.

Emma chuckled at her expression, then took them out, unfolded them, and slid them over Leeth's ears, settling them onto her nose. Which Leeth wrinkled in annoyance.

"Wait, let me explain. You've learned a lot, but there are years of cultural references you've still to catch up on. Okay. So you flip the thumbscreen away to show you're not Linked, right? Do I need to explain attention etiquette?"

At Leeth's head shake, she continued. "So, that's your ostensible private screen. But quite independently of that, the lenses of these glasses provide net access with an AR interface. They use side projection with total internal reflection: only you as the wearer will see the information. Just like having your own implanted iLens.

"Picture a blue question mark, and say 'Solid Seven'."

Leeth frowned, but did as asked, then blinked in surprise. "Huh. Solid Seven was a boy band popular in the '40s. Members Joal, Trey, Raze.... Hey, these things are actually cool!"

"I should hope so – I had Nelson make them up for you. They're cutting edge."

"Oh."

"Oh, Leeth, don't be silly. Nelson's great. And a genius, too, no matter how he behaves."

"Mmm."

"The information projects to a virtual focal distance of the nearest warm body you're facing: so it'll look like your attention is on whoever you might be looking at, not accessing the net. It's the next best thing to being wired."

"Wired?"

Emma just smiled.

The next morning at eight a.m, Leeth emerged from the spare bedroom to pose for Emma, one knee thrust forward. She put her small handbag down on the kitchen benchtop with a suspiciously-heavy clunk. "How do I look?"

She wore a cheetah-patterned unitard with black faux-leather boots up to her knees. A bunch of silver bangles adorned her right wrist. Her credstick was strapped to her left, in a black sheath to make it look like the hilt of a slender knife.

She'd put the unitard on backwards, to show her ivory Michele St. Germain push-up bra and its delicate scrollwork of tiny dragons. A dangling orange crystal drew the eye to her cleavage.

"Well? Say something, Emma! Should I change the boots? I have some strappy black sandals."

Emma had her hand raised, covering her mouth. "Leeth... your mission is to blend in; to be taken for a normal girl. What message do you think your choice of clothing is sending?"

The girl cocked her head to one side, puzzled. "Well, that I'm fit, and healthy. And ready for any hot dance parties after class! I figure I can show the boys I'm ready for sex by doing stuff like this-" She flipped her hair; looked away, then back, and pulled at her bottom lip with her teeth....

She looked prepared to run through the entire 'flirtatious body language' repertoire she'd been taught. Emma held up one hand. "Leeth! Your choice of dress alone will do that!" She stopped, wanting to grind her teeth in frustration. Being instructed to teach Leeth how to fit in, while not 'narrowing her moral flexibility.' Was that even possible? All week she and Leeth had been having variants of the same argument. Just getting the girl to agree to wear a swimsuit going to, from and *in* the apartment building's pool had been a major victory. And something about those arguments – about her inability to get through to Leeth – had felt *wrong*. Emma suspected the hand of the Doctor.

Well, bugger instructions, she decided. Surely Mother didn't want Leeth to fail? *Ah – wait!* "Everyone likes a challenge. You value something more when you struggle to earn it."

Leeth blinked. "Are you saying... even the *sheep* like a challenge?"

"What sheep?" Studying Leeth's expression, many things became suddenly clear, and Emma's heart sank. "Oh, *Leeth*. No...." She felt like punching the Doctor in the face. How could the girl survive, long term, if she disdained normal people? Worse, she'd been forbidden to correct that misunderstanding. "Leeth, you must never... never...."

Leeth waited. "What? Never what? Emma?" But Emma had shut her eyes.

The agent opened them again, huffing out her breath like she was angry. "Never let them know you think of them as sheep. Anyone you said that to would hate you forever. And they'd also tell all their friends what you'd said."

Emma watched the girl absorb that.

"So... you're saying I've gotta make them *earn* sex with me?"

Emma winced but nodded.

Leeth frowned. "How much should I... But if I charge them money, that'd make me a whore, and that's bad. So... you mean they've gotta earn sex by doing other jobs for me?"

Emma grimaced. "Not 'jobs,' Leeth. Don't frame sex as a transaction. Anything that looks like that, would have the same stigma as a monetary transaction."

"Um. Stigma is bad?"

"Yes, Leeth. Sex.... Sex should be earned through personal acts – things that make you like them better. Things that show you what kind of person they are."

"Well... okay. I guess that makes sense. But what about when you just want some sex, and don't *want* to know them as a person?"

"Leeth...." Emma shut her eyes, wincing as if she was in pain, before opening them again. "That's an advanced topic. You'll need to ask the Doctor. For this mission, just follow my advice, okay?"

"Okay." Leeth looked down at her clothes, then back up to Emma's eyes. "I need to change, don't I? Make it secret that I want sex?"

Emma nodded. "Yes, Leeth. Very secret. It will help you fit in with the girls much better, I promise you. And it's the girls you'll have to worry about."

"I know, I studied some films."

"Um, you do have a contraceptive implant, don't you?"

"Of course."

Of course you do.

By the time Leeth had re-emerged, Emma had already re-planned her morning. And the heavy brass padlock sat on the benchtop beside the girl's purse.

"Leeth. Why did you have this in your bag?"

"It's my lucky padlock."

Emma just quirked an eyebrow up, and waited.

"And I thought if I *did* have to hit someone, it'd help explain... stuff."

"You shouldn't be planning how to explain how you can hit someone so hard, Leeth. Let's leave the padlock behind, hmm?"

Leeth had seemed to agree, and shyly welcomed the offer to make sure she knew how to navigate the rapid transit system to Oakland. But as Emma closed the door behind them, she saw the padlock was gone from the benchtop. She sighed.

At the Montgomery St BART station, not far from Emma's apartment, she showed Leeth how to choose the right train, the right line, the different platforms; where to wave her credstick to pay the fare. She even offered to escort Leeth to the school – feeling strangely like a mother planning to take her daughter to kindergarten for the first time.

But Leeth had said she'd be fine.

Emma had one final piece of advice. "Remember: you need everyone to see you as just an ordinary girl. So please, keep in mind that much of what you've seen in movies about teenagers is exaggerated or even just made up. Don't do something you haven't seen someone else do first, okay?"

So now Leeth approached the warm-colored brick building, enclosed behind its yellow stone fence on the leafy suburban street. Adjusting her glasses, she remembered she hadn't set the frame color. Focusing on her emerald-green skirt, she thought of a blue question mark. "Okay glasses, action: set frame color." She took them off and held them against her over-long skirt. Perfect! Maybe Nelson wasn't so bad after all?

She slid them back on, passing a smiling young mother pushing her young son in a stroller. *I'm outside! And alone!* The sun shining through the tree branches made her smile. Three boys, arguing about how to encourage more immigration from Mexico, glanced approvingly at her as they walked by. Though as soon as she was out of earshot – they *thought* – they started talking about how they wouldn't mind 'doing her.'

Maybe her skirt wasn't too long after all? Despite the fact you couldn't see even her knees.

She came to the gate, a set of grilled bars that kind of reminded her of the Institute, except this entrance-way had a camera and intercom set into the wall. After a moment, introducing herself as Jane Baker, the lock clicked and she pushed through, and inside.

The grounds were green and lush, a well-kept lawn. It was dotted with trees standing about like dignified old gentlemen posing casually while knowing perfectly well how impressive they looked. *Probably a hundred years old, at least.* The building looked even nicer up close with the sunlight shining on it, and all at once she was sure this was going to be a great adventure. She leaped up the front steps to the main doors.

"Whoah, d'ya see that, bro!"

Funt! Hunching her shoulders, she darted inside without looking back, but still listening....

"That chick, I swear, she just *flew* up the front steps..."

Damn it! That'd been really stupid. She imagined Mother's sneer. 'Really, Leeth; less than ten seconds? You did even worse than I expected. I had bet Father you'd at least make it through the front door.' Inside, a few people strode briskly about, but she could still hear the man outside telling his friends about 'the flying chick.' And their voices were getting closer!

She needed to change her appearance so they wouldn't recognize her. She looked around, desperate.

There: restroom.

Ripping off the brown shoulder-length wig – *yeeow!* – she slammed through the door, throwing the hair into a bin under a sink. Eyes watering – 'I've woven it in so it won't come loose,' Emma had explained – she shimmied out of her skirt. Thank goodness it was so long! Turning it inside out so the charcoal gray lining was now on the outside, she slashed with her fingertips, then ripped it across its entire width, halving the length. She quickly reset the color of her glasses. The bottom half of her now ragged-edge mini-skirt followed the wig into the bin.

She had one leg lifted to step into her newly-adjusted clothing when a toilet flushed, and a man banged out from behind a row of doors just behind her.

Standing on one leg, her bum outlined by her ivory lace knickers, her eyes met his in the mirror. For a second, neither spoke, then Leeth unfroze and finished stepping into her skirt, wriggling it up to sit on her hips.

"Are you, like, transgender?"

"What!"

He raised his hands defensively, while his eyes checked out her behind and legs. "Just sayin' – this is the Gents, after all."

Gents? That was for men; but shouldn't it have *said* that? All there'd been was some stupid stick figure. Something *else* everyone knew about?

She smiled at him: maybe that'd be enough? "Sorry. My mistake. Bye!"

Pulling open the door leading back out into the corridor, she almost barreled into a boy reaching for the handle. She pushed past him, and between the two immediately behind him.

He gaped at her. "What the *fuck?*"

Great. Just... great. Amused calls followed her as she hurried along to the Admin Office, ears burning at the joking of the male, behind her – especially when the guy who'd been in the toilet stall emerged and joined them.

Ears aflame, Leeth pushed open the Admin door. *Well, I guess things can't get any worse,* she reassured herself. As for her ID photos – she'd just say she'd had her hair cut since then, if they asked.

CHAPTER 33

"Class, I'd like to introduce Jane Baker. She grew up on a farm, across the Bay over in Sonoma. Jane, why don't you tell us something about yourself?"

Leeth tore her eyes from the crowd of over ten people in the room and glanced at the tall Nordic drama teacher. Ms Sorensen smiled and nodded at her. She turned back to the students. Two of the men... boys were whispering: "I don't know, man, she's the right height and build."

She tried to ignore what they were saying, for the first time ever wishing she could shut off her super hearing. "Hi, I'm Jane. Mother and Father thought I might be good at acting, so here I am!"

In the third curving row of seats in the auditorium-slash-performance space, a regal, tall black woman leaned to the equally gorgeous blonde girl on her left. She, too, Leeth heard clearly. "Mommy and Daddy sent lil Bobbi-Jane to learn how not to be a farm girl."

The blonde giggled. "And sum her slut-skirt – like some cheap knock-off Ferez faux-shred, only *crooked*. I mean: what – she make it *herself*?"

Leeth resisted the urge to try to tug her ragged hem straighter, feeling her smile kind of curl up and die inside, even as she kept her expression happy. "Uh, I haven't been off the farm much, so I hope you'll understand if I ask a lot of dumb questions." Thank goodness she and Emma had practiced a few possible conversations!

"Ooh! Ding! Bonus points: she's dumb, too!" This time the queenly girl had spoken out of the side of her mouth to the – *eww!* – Altered girl on her right. Who *was* stunning, though – if you could ignore the pointed ears, too-narrow chin and absurd cheekbones. But she had *amazing* eyes.

All three girls giggled.

Leeth clenched her fists. Knowing she wasn't allowed to kill them.

"Thank you, Jane. Take a seat. Perhaps next to Beth, Tara, and Ava there in the third row. Tara, please make an effort to make Jane feel welcome."

The three girls who'd just been making fun of her scowled. The Altered girl, whose dramatic makeup made her enormous dark eyes look even larger, and who was dressed in black leathers like a heroine from Dark Slayers, flicked her fingers in a 'come' gesture. She didn't smile.

Leeth felt a bit uncomfortable at the idea of sitting next to an Altered. Uncle always said how awful the genetically-altered were, calling them mutants – at best. But Emma had been surprisingly positive about them. *Either way, she sure is pretty.*

Leeth moved quickly from the stage area, trying to catch the girl's eye as she slid into the seat beside her. But the girl didn't even glance her way.

She sneaked an envious peek at the girl's bust, which had to be something like a D cup. Weird: the Altered were usually slender, trying for that whole 'elven aesthetic.' At that moment the busty girl flicked her head to the side, catching Leeth checking her out, and turned up her nose and looked away.

Great.

Bottling up a sigh, Leeth turned to the front, where Ms Sorensen cast an outline of the day's lesson plan onto the large projection surface.

"This morning we'll be doing some basic expressive movement exercises, imagination exercises – acting colors, strength, secrets – then some improv. Then..."

Did she just say we were going to act colors? Leeth looked around while the teacher continued. No one else looked confused. *Great.* She wanted to put her head in her hands, but instead sat up straighter, concentrating like her life depended on it. And thought the blue question mark. A lot.

Along from her, she heard the gorgeous black woman snicker. "Looks like Mousey's got competition for teacher's pet!"

Leeth just ignored her. *Them*, rather, as the other two joined in.

"Okay, Jane, your turn."

Leeth felt her insides squirm. How had she been supposed to know that red was all about energy and explosions, and green was just growing things and stuff? Shouldn't someone have written all that down somewhere? She'd used her glasses to access wikipedia, but it'd been no help.

"-are you listening, Jane?"

"Uh, sorry Ms Sorensen."

"I said, I want you to imagine you're hunting a creature."

Leeth froze. Tilting her head she examined the teacher's expression; then the class, who sat watching the exchange without much interest. "Me?"

The woman nodded.

"Why me? Why'd you pick *me* to hunt something invisible?"

"Imaginary, Jane. Because you're new, and it's an easy exercise. Easier than acting out raw concepts."

Leeth shook her head. And Ms Sorensen rolled her eyes. "Come, Jane, stop behaving like a prima donna. Get out here and act!"

Leeth reluctantly left her seat, stepping out into the huge, empty space to face all those people now staring at her. Tara and her nasty friends studied her with amusement; a few with curiosity; but most of them just looked bored. She pinned the teacher with a fierce stare. "Not all invisible creatures are imaginary," she hissed.

A stir went through the audience.

"Good! Great start, Jane. But I want you to do it without words, okay?"

Leeth closed her eyes, reached up behind her to shrug her bow from her shoulder, and passed it to her left hand. With her right, she reached up and drew an arrow from her quiver. Nocking it to the bowstring she angled the bow to keep it in place.

With one foot feeling the ground ahead of her, placing it to avoid tree roots, she inched silently forward. Opening her eyes then, but keeping them unfocused, she scanned up and around, and began stalking through the Jungle: head turning slowly from side to side, ears pricked, alert for Her.

And the Hunt began.

Leeth lost herself in memory. Re-imagining Mean Robo, and Her... but this time *both* attacked her, wrapping around her. She exploded, dropping the useless bow and arrows to tear and claw deep into her invisible attackers, remembering the insubstantial wisps trying to slither from her grip as she screamed her hatred and defiance-

Panting, blinking, she slowly collected herself. Remembered where she was. And turned slightly, to face a room full of stunned faces and open mouths.

Tara dropped a mascara brush, the clatter loud in the ringing silence.

Ms Sorensen collected her wits first, and clapped. "Bravo, Jane! Very good indeed! Though perhaps a little less histrionics there at the end."

The door to the class crashed open, one of the other teachers striding in, the members of his class piling in behind. "What's the matter – we heard screams!"

"Mr Beckman, this *is* a drama school. Jane simply provided a little more drama than requested."

Everyone was staring at her. She felt herself flush. *Good work, Leeth. Fitting right in, behaving just like everyone else.* Surely the day *had* to start getting better soon? Plus she was starving now, too.

On cue, her stomach growled, loud enough for everyone to hear, which caused some laughter.

Leeth wanted to sink through the floor.

Ms Sorensen clapped her hands. "I think this is a convenient point to break for lunch. We'll do a little revision of the basics when we return, then try some intensity exercises, then some subtlety." She eyed Jane as the girl returned to her seat. "Sometimes less is more: it's the tiny hints, barely detected, which make a performance most powerful."

Oh, and my acting is unsubtle, too, she's saying. Leeth sighed. The three girls she'd been sitting beside now stood up, and Leeth had to admire the black girl's face, and figure. A full head taller than her, and every movement so elegant. *She's almost as tall as James*, Leeth thought. *It's because her legs are so long. Her skin's perfect, too. I wish my breasts were that size...*

"Put your eyes back in their sockets, girl, this lady is reserved for the men only!"

"Huh? I wasn't... I was just admiring you. You're very beautiful. Why are you being- I mean, I was hoping we could be friends?"

"Oh yeah, girl, 'friends.' I bet. I can just imagine the kind of thoughts rolling around in that lezz-ly little head o' yours."

"Lezz-? I'm not a lesbian! And what would it matter if I was, anyway? I was just wishing my breasts were a bit bigger, more like yours. And your skin is so lovely. And you're so tall!"

The statuesque girl's perfect arches rose. "Any other not-Lezzly thoughts you wanna share with us, freak? Cause you're totally hammering that hetero shade, Lezzlie."

"My name's not Leslie, it's *Jane*. Jane *Baker*."

"Uh-uh, no, don't think so." Tara made a show of looking around. "I don't see no Tarzan swinging in from the trees. Reckon you's confused, Lezlie."

With a contemptuous toss of her head and her long, curly black locks, the tall girl and her entourage pushed past her.

"See ya, *Lezlie*," the two shorter but equally beautiful girls chorused, finger waving as they sashayed out.

Leeth followed the other students to a large room, its wood-paneled walls crowded with posters from movies and various movie stars – all autographed. Natural sunlight flooded through the large windows in the far wall, the air rich with aromas that made her stomach clench in anticipation, grumbling again.

Tara, Ava, and Beth, carrying food-laden trays – how'd they gotten their meals so fast? – strutted across the room to a table in the center and stared down at a neatly-dressed girl there with short brown curly hair. The other sounds flooding the room faded out as Leeth *focused* on the group of girls and moved closer.

"There's a mouse at our table. Scurry away, Mousie, before the cats unsheathe their claws. Mreow!" Tara made a silly gesture with her curled fingers, and Leeth felt her own fingertips tingle in response.

The smaller girl's lips set, but she just picked up her things and moved away.

"Good Mousie. Scamper, scamper, off you go!"

"It's Marcie," the girl said, but so quietly, only Leeth heard it. *Coward*, she thought.

But as the girl passed by and their eyes met, Leeth saw the anger simmering there. The girl's eyes swept from her face, to her chest, to her skirt and legs, then back up to her face. Marcie's eyes narrowed and she moved on, disappearing into a corner.

Tara, Ava, and Beth were chattering brightly away, a fourth place at their table vacant. Leeth clenched her jaw and went over there. As she put one hand on the back of the seat, conversation in the room seemed to drop.

"What are you doing, Lezlie?" asked Tara.

"It's Jane, and I'm sitting down for lunch. Look, I thought-"

"That seat's taken."

"No it's not, it's right here."

"No, retard, it's taken. It's reserved."

"For who?"

"For anyone except you, Thunder-thighs," Tara snapped.

"What do- huh? Thunder thighs? What's that supposed to mean?"

"You crack walnuts with those thighs? I guess you need them well-muscled so you can trap your lez-victims."

"What-? I've only ever had sex with men."

Tara rolled her eyes in disbelief.

"And there's nothing wrong with my thighs!"

"Yeah. Thass true. Nothing wrong – for a Tyrannosaurus."

The other two girls snickered, as did some of the people at nearby tables.

One strike into the larynx... but apparently, normal girls didn't fight to the death. For some dumb reason.

"What's with the death-stare, Lezlie? Imagining crushing me between those thighs? Bet you be dreaming about me tonight, yeah? Or, you roam the night with your invisible bow and arrows, having psychotic episodes?"

Leeth pulled out the chair and sat down, beside the buxom blonde girl, Beth, then smiled directly across the table at her tormentor. "I know there's nothing wrong with my legs, since I had a car full of soldiers drive off the road once 'coz they were looking at them."

"Or they was drunk."

Leeth wanted to snap a reply, but she'd possibly already said too much.

Tara sniffed the air. "Ava, where is that stench of cheap perfume coming from? Beth, *please* tell me you haven't slipped in a puddle of Walmart Jasmine Star."

Could Tara *really* recognize the smell, just like that? Leeth *was* wearing Jasmine Star, and Emma *had* wrinkled her nose...

Beth sniffed. "Why, Tara, I think it's coming from my right."

All three girls looked at Leeth.

"We'd better leave – the stink of eau de cheap's gonna ruin my mango salsa salmon." Picking up their trays, noses twitching, the three girls stood, swaying across the room to a table by the large windows. Then glared down at the two girls already seated there.

"Move, peasants," Tara ordered, and for some reason the two hunched their shoulders, picked up their own trays of food, and quietly left.

Tara and her two minions were already chattering as they seated themselves. Once again, the fourth seat at their table was vacant. Leeth clenched her jaw, stood up, and took a step that way.

Across the room, Tara watched her, a smile tugging at her lips.

She wants me to try again. So she can do it all over again? *She's probably even thought up some more insults.*

Instead, Leeth stopped, met Tara's eyes, and pictured herself sliding her hand into that imposing chest, slicing her heart free and pulling it back out. She'd put it down on the table right in front of the three of them, then just walk away.

Smiling with lazy pleasure at the image, she turned away. And saw everyone was – once again – looking at her. *Just great.* Except, in a darker corner, face lit faintly by a screen's flow, the cowardly girl shifted her things. For a moment, Leeth saw a familiar cartoon face in the montage of images on the girl's handbag. *That was Sleena!*

She watched as the girl looked back to her backlit paper screen and resume reading

She'd looked angry, before. *And* there were three empty seats at her table. Still smiling, still ignoring Tara and her shadows, Leeth wove a path between the tables and headed for the darker corner. Yeah, that was definitely Sleena, the pixie warrior! The cartoon heroine was part of a whole collection of images of lots of her favorite characters... *Oh! She's got HyperGirl, too!*

Her thighs bumped the girl's table, and she stopped as the girl looked up.

"What."

It wasn't a question.

"I was just noticing the pictures on your bag, and saw Sleena the dark pix-"

"And you thought 'I'll go and diss Marcie: that'll show the Power Princesses I'm one of them,' right?" Marcie leaned back, the anger once again clear in her eyes, but with a beaten-down look riding alongside it. "Do your worst, but something tells me you're not in Terrible Tara's league."

Leeth blinked. "Uh, no. I was actually gonna say I loved Sleena. I mean, when I was little."

"Really."

Leeth looked up and away, smiling. "You remember that time the giant slug thing was about to chew through the Flower Palace, and Sleena fanged him right in his eyeball-on-a-stalk? That was so cool."

Marcie's lips twitched. "Yeah, it was kinda 'cool.' But gross." She paused, waiting for the hidden knife to come stabbing out. Tentatively she added, "I liked Hyper Girl and Argon best." She twitched her bag so the blonde superheroine's face was uppermost, then touched it to zoom it larger, revealing Argon by her side. Ever-faithful. "I used to imagine what it'd be like to have adventures with my own cyborg wardog, patrolling our neighborhood lasering all the bullies." She smiled, looking back up and across into the new student's eyes. "Jane? What's the matter?"

Her possible-new-friend's lips were pressed firmly together, and she was blinking rapidly. She shook her head. "Nothing. I was just remembering *my* dog. Faith." Her blinking sped up. "I had to leave her, back at the, back on the farm."

Marcie reached out a hand and took Leeth's. "That's rough, kiddo. And all this – it must be like starting high school all over again, yeah? And with Terrible Tara wielding her magical mind-controlling charisma over males and females alike. That and her lips that lash, and wit that wounds. I swear, it's like she has a sixth sense for your Kryptonite zones."

"Uh, yeah. Crypt tonight zones."

Marcie looked at her oddly. "You *do* know who I'm talking about, right?"

"Uh, sure. That girl who, you know, with the vampires...."

Marcie shook her head. "Hey! You wanna see the very first superhero ever?" At Jane's eager nod, she accessed her Link, projecting an image onto the table after placing her bag to hide the picture from the people nearby.

"Mmm. Niiice. I like the little curl of hair." Leeth admired the muscles. "But why are his underpants on the outside? Does the big 'S' stand for Stupid?"

"It stands for hope."

"Hope?"

"Yeah, he kinda, well... I guess he kinda gave people hope that no matter how much evil there was in the world, no matter how powerful it seemed, it could never destroy hope. Hope is indestructible – just like Superman." She shrugged. "But yeah, maybe people were kinda lame back then."

The moment was interrupted by Jane's stomach, and both girls giggled, while Marcie withdrew her hand.

Leeth looked around. "Where's the food dispenser?"

Marcie smiled. "The school has a reputation to maintain. We have a chef." A small chime sounded from her hand. "That'll be my order." She slipped off the chunky ring on her right hand, now projecting a multi-colored rectangle onto the table. "Scan that QR code for the link, and you'll see the menu. The 'bol is nice." Marcie stood up.

Boll? QR code? What the...? Why didn't Uncle or Emma teach me any of this stuff?

The blue question mark, though, answered all her questions – 'Do you mean, spaghetti bolognese?' – and her stomach growled again as she skimmed the menu. But it was only as Marcie returned from the counter across the room with her tray, that Leeth realized she'd better keep her special Nelson-glasses secret. Hurriedly, she scanned the square pattern of colored dots with her wristlink, and activated its projector.

Marcie set down her tray, bumping the sauce bottle she'd set near the edge of the table. It had hardly started to topple before Leeth was across the table, her hand around its neck and righting it.

"Whoah! Nice reflexes, Jane!"

Leeth froze, mortified. *Not special, dope!* She wanted to bang her head against the table. *Think before you act!*

"That was a compliment, babe." Marcie shook her head. "You are one weird chica, you know."

Leeth felt her eyes widen.

"*Now* what'd I say? Come on, all of us are weird, right?"

Leeth blinked. "We are?"

"Sure," Marcie grinned. "Some people don't like Sleena!"

Jane smiled back, weakly, as Marcie picked her ring up from the table and slid it back on, tapping its projection off. Her meal did look good... and smelled better. The aroma decided Leeth: the 'bol' and a nice rare steak. Selecting both with her fingertip, she tapped the Pay button and heard her credstick chime.

"Uh, Jane, I think you just ordered two lunches by mistake."

Not this again! Briefly, Leeth considered agreeing.... *No! I'm* not *going to spend weeks here, starving to death every day!* "Uh, I have a metabolic condition. I have to eat bigger meals. At lunchtime."

Marcie looked doubtful, but said nothing. Instead, she picked up a shaker and sprinkled a pale yellow powder all over her food. When the smell hit her, Leeth reeled back in her chair in disgust as Marcie began some complicated twirling motion with her fork and the spaghetti. *Soft spaghetti?* Maybe she *should* read that cookery book Emma had given her?

Leeth watched, open-mouthed, as Marcie put it into her mouth.

"Mmm!"

O-kay. Maybe I do *need this 'socialization training!'* "What's that, um, strong-smelling powder?"

When Leeth returned with her lunch, sliding her bag to the side, Marcie looked puzzled by the sound the heavy brass padlock made when it fell over inside. A little sheepishly, Leeth drew it out and passed it to her.

"Oh, wow, that must be, what, fifty years old?" Marcie turned it over. "I think this kind of lock was the first I ever learned to pick. Dad used to use it to lock the shed where he kept his power tools!"

Leeth wanted to ask about the power tools, but... "What do you mean, the *first* kind of lock you learned to pick? D'you mean you can pick this?"

"Sure!" Marcie took a hairpin from her hair.

"Could you teach *me* how to pick it?"

"Sure."

Leeth jumped up, spun around the table, and trapped Marcie in her chair with the hugest hug. "You are the best!"

When they returned to the auditorium, Leeth sat with Marcie instead of the Princesses of Power. The two of them were getting on so well, it wasn't until Ms Sorensen cleared her throat they realized the lesson had started. Leeth heard Tara, across the room, make a stupid joke about the new Loser Club that had started.

"Now, since we have a new student in the class today, it's a welcome excuse to review the basics."

Groans from some of the students quickly died under Ms Sorensen's laser-sharp gaze.

"Your craft as an actor is to *feel* the emotions and motives that lie beneath; and then to let just enough shine through for the audience to see inside.

"Less is more. Don't drench the audience in colors – sketch the outlines; let their own imaginations paint in the details. You don't want your audience thinking 'What a marvelous actress Sorensen is;' they must be thinking 'Can't Eliza see she's being manipulated?'"

By the end of the day Leeth felt more exhausted than after a long session with Dojo. Marcie, it turned out, lived in Oakland – and seemed impressed by the address of Jane's Aunt Elizabeth in New Francisco. Tara and her friends were picked up by limousines with drivers and security – "Beth's mother is some exec at Omnicomm," Marcie explained, "and both Tara's parents are bigwigs at SegaFox. Ava's grandfather was a founder of Softgene."

With Tara and friends gone, at least the taunts ended.

"What about *your* parents?"

Marcie looked sad. "It's just me and my dad, and my little sister. Amanda. She's a real cutie, you'd like her. Mum died when I was only little. Dad's doing well: he runs an auto-trucking biz. He's got like a fleet of fifty, now," she said proudly.

At that moment, an attractive boy huffed up to offer Jane a lift home in his sports car – in tones that suggested she should know what a Konnigs-egg G12, or something like that, was. But Leeth wanted to walk with Marcie to the MacArthur station instead.

A bunch of other students were headed in the same direction, and even through her tiredness Leeth heard some of the boys *still* talking about the 'Green Ghost Girl' that had flown into the school in the morning and then disappeared.

Meeting Marcie had made up for all the rest of it, though. But she was surprised and thrilled when the other girl later hugged her goodbye before stepping onto her train. Leeth waved to her, too, then summoned her energies to sprint for her platform, on the green line. She made it onto the carriage with seconds to spare.

But as she got on, looking around for a clear space to play 'train surfing,' a really weird feeling reached up her spine. Her mind flooded with images, so disorienting that she wobbled and almost fell. A Japanese girl, with James, in a restaurant. *Trapped!* For a moment, she felt panic, and spun around.

In the crowd waiting for the next train on the platform now disappearing from sight, she glimpsed a large man, staring at her.

Expressionless. Patient. *Waiting*.

She shuddered.

CHAPTER 34

At Emma's insistence, Leeth had spent an hour that night talking to her uncle, getting advice about ways to handle Tara, Ava and Beth – that didn't involve exposing their internal organs. Not that he'd been all that helpful: other than suggesting Leeth picture doing something gruesome to them, and then smiling boldly and ignoring them. Which had actually been exactly what she'd already done, in the cafeteria.

Which just showed she wasn't as badly socialized as they all thought.

She also asked him about the 'advanced' topic Emma hadn't wanted to discuss the previous morning – what to do when she just wanted sex from a boy, not to know him as a person.

He had *not* been pleased with the question. Which she'd found *very* satisfying. *He* does *care about me.*

But he hadn't answered the question, either. Instead, he'd warned her about all sorts of diseases she could catch. How curing diseases magically wasn't like healing injuries, and *blahing* on about immune systems.

Which told her he really didn't want her having sex with other people. Talking to him by secure video was weird. It felt... safer. Yet kind of exciting, maybe because of that.

It'd left her feeling quite churned up, inside. She wasn't sure how she felt about him, any more.

She'd tried to talk about it with Emma, somehow forgetting about his mental controls. Which made her look like an idiot, of course, when her brain froze up. So instead – after she'd recovered – they'd talked more about what she'd learned, and about the girls, and boys. Actually, it was funny how the boys, who'd seemed like men to her in the morning, had by the end of the day somehow magically morphed into boys.

But that had led Emma to strongly encourage her to start making notes for the report she had to write at the end of it all. Dutifully, Leeth created a file called 'Normal girls and sheep dynamic groups,' then lay on her bed admiring the impressively scientific title. Then, remembering Emma's words, she deleted the word 'sheep,' frowning as she did. *Why hadn't Uncle ever told me people would hate me if I called them that? Was* Marcie *a sheep?* Obviously not – but why not?

Oh, and it was actually supposed to be 'group dynamics.' She fixed that, too. And then realized she didn't know what it meant, and started reading the wikipedia entry. Somehow, she got distracted by thoughts of Superman; especially his outside-underpants. That led to hunting down a chill-sounding collection – from a few years ago, since that way, Marcie might have read them too. Besides, some of the older ones cost less. She tapped the credstick to the Buy button on her e-sheet, pleased at successfully executing her first ever on-screen purchase. Checking her balance, she saw she still had almost thirty creds to spend today. She bit at her fingernails. Why had Mother given her such a big budget?

Who knows? She settled down to Superman... and woke the next morning with her e-sheet on the floor by her bed, and nothing in her report except the title.

Anyway, she was kind of looking forward to this second day of lessons – despite the Power Princesses – and was messaging Marcie before she even headed down in the lift.

That strange feeling came over her again, though, while talking to her new friend as she walked to the Montgomery St station. She stopped, looking around, feeling cold. She found she'd let her eyes unfocus to look for Her, or Robo, here in the middle of all the people bustling about on their own busy missions.

A chill rippled through her. She wondered: had her vivid recall, acting out the Hunting of Her and Robo in the class yesterday, somehow summoned one of them?

She shook her head, as people bumped past her, some muttering insults under their breath. She ignored them. It couldn't be Her: she and Godsson had killed Her, together. Properly, and once and for all.

And it felt... more like Robo.

She gazed around, eyes still unfocused, but there was no sense of the straight line movements of that invisible thing. Or *curving* ones. She shuddered, remembering *Her*. She didn't know what she'd do, if She returned.

"-Jane! What's the matter? Jane, are you there, I can hear-"

"Sorry, Marcie, I, uh, thought an old, um, friend called out to me, and I was just looking." She started walking again. "So, you're getting the 8:42am from 'Fruitvale.' Is that even a real place? It sounds like a cartoon suburb for happy munchkins...."

It was weird, yet at the same time perfectly natural, meeting up with Marcie on the crowded platform. It was nice, walking together to the drama school. The day was overcast, a bit cool. Probably that was the reason Leeth kept feeling uncomfortable, like she could sense Mean Robo around.

But chatting with Marcie was strangely easy, especially since the first topic of conversation was Tara.

"I talked to my uncle last night, and he said they're mean because they see I'm different to them, maybe better, and that makes them feel smaller. So by trying to make me feel small, they can feel big."

"Yeah, that sounds about right," Marcie agreed.

The walk to the school seemed to take no time at all.

That day at morning break, most of the class headed again to the cafeteria. Marcie explained that people usually put in their orders in advance, arriving as their order neared the top of the queue. She also explained how you could bid to pay more, to get your order 'bumped up' in priority, and how a bunch of them always put their orders in before Tara, knowing the rich girl would always outbid them so she'd be first.

"So what's the point?" Leeth asked.

Marcie giggled. "I just find it funny that the Power Princesses have to pay fifty creds for a coffee, and anywhere from two hundred to five hundred for lunch! And the funniest part is, the higher the price we bid them up to, the more pleasure they seem to take from 'winning!' They have no idea."

They were joined by two other girls, who Leeth thought maybe were the two Tara had called 'peasants' the day before. Delta, and Sam, they'd introduced themselves.

"Anyway, what'll you have?" asked Marcie. "We have to be back in class in fifteen. The mocha latte with hazelnut's good."

"Uh, yeah, sure, that's a fav- ohh! What's *hot* chocolate?" Leeth asked, the drinks menu projected on the shiny tabletop from her 'link.

When no one answered after a few seconds, she looked up to see them all blinking at her. "I meant, uh, they have hot chocolate!"

"Amazing," Marcie dead-panned.

One of the other girls – Sam – giggled. "Are you about to go beddy-byes, Jane?"

Leeth pictured the big blue question mark. "Um. Beddybuys. Uh... What? No! I just like chocolate. I'm... I'll have two!"

Tara and her cohort chose that moment to pass their table. "Good idea, Thunder-thighs," Tara sniped as she passed by, eyeing their small group with disdain. And went straight to the serving counter at the exact moment their orders arrived. Leeth and Marcie exchanged a look, hiding their smiles.

But after about ten minutes, something weird started happening. Jane and Marcie's little group seemed to be attracting looks from the other students, and people began snickering. Leeth concentrated, and heard several people talking about 'the Losers Club.' And then noticed a small pink icon flashing over Marcie's head.

The fourth girl in their group, Delta, was looking abstractedly into space, then swore. "That bitch! You should see what she and her followers are saying about us on her feed!"

"Her feed?" Leeth asked. "What's that?"

This time, all three looked at her like she'd just grown a third eye. Delta shook her head, tapping the wrist where Leeth wore her link. "Project a keyboard for me," she ordered.

Leeth obliged, and the girl began rapidly typing. A moment later Leeth was signed up for 'SoBo' – a 'social feed' – and creating her own 'Profile' and subscribing to 'feeds' from Tara and a bunch of other students. She felt simultaneously dazed, and pleased by how much she was learning.

But she couldn't give it her full attention. Delta had a small pink icon now, too – a chubby, cartoonish penis, Leeth realized – flashing above her head, positioned within easy reach to 'touch.'

"Is that a fruit fly?" she asked, casually pointing so her fingertip seemed to her to touch the icon. The moment she did, a maroon 'L' appeared, tattooed on Delta's forehead.

What the-? Leeth took off her glasses, and of course it vanished. But more people were giggling, now, and a few others pointing. Leeth put her glasses back on, and the maroon 'L' tattoo reappeared.

Sam burst out. "Oh, that..." her lips pursed. "Witch!" They all turned to her, and she blushed. Marcie frowned, then swore and projected Tara's feed onto the tabletop.

At first, Leeth thought they'd all seen the penis icons, too, and their virtual tattoos. But none of the other girls mentioned them, and as she read the upside-down text, her heart sank. "What? So she's calling us 'Lezzlie's Loser Club.' Just ignore her. That's what my uncle said we should do."

"No, it's not that." Marcie grimaced, projecting her own keyboard and typing madly. "I don't know how she's doing it, but she's put up a vid stream of... four girls, um, having sex, and she's 'shopped our faces onto them." She swore. "And I can't forward it, capture it, or project it! How is she doing that?"

"Um, why do you want to forward it, or whatever?" Leeth asked.

"So we can report it, Jane!"

"*Report* it?"

"Yeah, report it. To the School. Maybe even to the police."

"*We* should report it to the *police?*"

Was this what it was like to be a sheep? What would happen if she *began thinking like that?* She shuddered, then saw Marcie, Delta and Sam were looking at her. Again.

"Yeah," said Sam, "shocking idea. Why, you have some other idea how to stop them?"

Leeth glared across the room at Evil Tara and Co. Then carefully, unclenched her fists.

Delta laughed. "You *totally* looked like you wanted to stomp over there and slap her face!"

Marcie reached out her hand, placing it over Leeth's wrist. "Jane. Don't even think about it. She'd slap *you* with a lawsuit that'd ruin you *and* your parents. Hitting her isn't going to stop her."

That depends on how hard I hit. With an effort, Leeth forced the thought aside, then met Marcie's eyes. *What might a normal girl say?* "Maybe, but it'd sure feel good, don't you think?"

Marcie grinned. "Hell, yeah!"

At that moment, Leeth's Link chimed her order's readiness, and she excused herself. But from the whispers following her as she crossed the room – 'yeah, whip that tail, babe!' – she knew something more was going on.

On her way back, muttering "Darn fruit flies" to cover her mid-air gestures, she clicked on each of her friends' pink icons.

And almost dropped her two chocolates, as penis-tipped tails unfurled from her friends' rears, waving about behind them while they huddled together in conference.

Juggling her chocolates to take off her special AR glasses, of course the ugly 'tails' all vanished.

Back at the table, Leeth tried to access the pink icons using her wristlink alone, so she could warn the others about the worse stuff Tara was doing. But the icons only appeared using Nelson's glasses: nothing she could do on her Link would bring them up. They didn't even appear in the glasses' flip-out thumbscreen. And the super secret spy-wear didn't have a projector, of course.

She sat, fuming, trying to work out a way to let her friends know about the doctored and humiliating 'additions' virtually dubbed onto them. And onto her, no doubt.

Kind of like what Nelson had done to Emma: what had she called it? Identity-rape.

The hot chocolate drink was wonderful, but she just couldn't enjoy it.

Across the room, Tara and her evil friends were watching, trying hard not to crack up; and the amusement seemed to be spreading.

But why wasn't anyone *telling* any of them what Tara was doing? She looked around. A lot of people seemed to be enjoying what was going on, although some seemed really uncomfortable. When she raised her eyebrows, though – *what's so funny?* – each one just looked away.

Oh. They must be afraid of what Tara would do to *them* if they reported what was going on.

Well; what she or her *hacker* would do: no doubt Tara had paid some expert.

Nelson could sort it out in seconds, she knew; hungering to let him loose on them. He'd *destroy* Tara's hacker!

But if he did, Tara would be sure to spend a lot of money finding out how her nasty little attack had been ruined. Which might lead to an even bigger mystery. *And bring exactly the sort of attention that'd score me a big fat Fail; with an extra serving of disaster sauce on top!*

The return-to-class chime sounded. And huge wobbly penises sprang from each of her friends' foreheads. Leeth almost choked on her chocolate, as quickly-stifled laughter exploded around them.

I could just kill them all...

Marcie patted her on the back. "Jane? Are you all right? Come'n, we gotta get back to class."

Tara, smirking and superior, watched them leave.

The worst part, though, was that thanks to Nelson's glasses, Leeth saw the horrid virtual tarring and feathering of her friends; and couldn't find a way to *un*-click the horrid little penis icons.

I bet if I looked in a mirror, I'd see an icon for me, too, and I could click on it and see what Tara's done to mess up Jane's *appearance.* But she could imagine losing her temper, if she did.

What to do about Tara? Maybe Nelson could at least offer her some advice. Probably. Or was this a normal sort of thing, which they'd expect her to solve on her own? She'd ask Emma, tonight.

At least she was learning a lot.

Lessons for the rest of that day were horrible. Except when they worked with each other, none of the exercises the four girls took part in went smoothly; and Leeth could see why. It was hard enough for *her* to follow the instructions, with all the silly and embarrassing visual graffiti. And she couldn't just take her glasses off since she was supposed to need them to see; and she couldn't tell the others what was going on since she had to keep her glasses secret.

By the end of the day she was seriously plotting ways to kill Tara that'd look like an accident.

Marcie noticed something was wrong, too; and seemed hurt when Jane wouldn't explain what that was. And that just made the whole thing an even taller pile of horrible.

And in the background, reveling in it all, were the smirking trio of Tara, Ava, and Beth.

Like the previous night, Marcie and Leeth walked together to the station, but this time they didn't talk much. Nor did Marcie hug her goodbye, which made Leeth feel like she'd done something awful.

And to rub salt in the wounds, she kept feeling an uncomfortable sensation like Mean Robo was lurking around. On the train ride back into the city, there *was* a heavyset man who made her think of Robo. He kept staring at her, but not like he was interested in her, exactly. More like he thought she was a fascinating bug or something. He could even have been the same man who'd stared at her from the platform, yesterday.

She had the weird feeling she'd seen him before, somewhere. Why did he make her think of an angry Japanese girl she'd... met? It made no sense. She didn't know any Japanese girls.

He creeped her out. He even followed her to Emma's apartment building. She'd hoped he'd be a mugger, sure that there'd be a chance to beat him up without letting anyone find out that 'Jane Baker' had done it. But he didn't make any moves. All he did was follow her home.

When she got up to the apartment, she crossed to the window and looked out and down, but he wasn't around. By the time Emma came home, though, she'd forgotten all about it: she had so much to tell her about what Tara had done.

Emma was outraged, but couldn't see an obvious solution. She also agreed that Nelson's hands were almost certainly tied. They contacted the Department, just in case, but Mother and Father seemed to consider it simply a worthwhile if somewhat extreme test for Leeth. They reiterated she was not to resort to physical violence, nor to stand out. But something about the look in Nelson's eyes when they called him into the vidchat made Leeth suspect he'd somehow already seen the augmented reality defacement of herself and her friends. Knowing Nelson, he'd probably been *recording* it to enjoy again later.

Leeth hated being in his debt in any way. "How come I can see it through your glasses?" she asked, pursing her lips. "Which are pretty useful, actually. Thank you."

Nelson smiled, then shrugged. "You wouldn't understand. The specs scan network traffic, and present options to tap into whatever AR feeds are active for your immediate location. You'll see little flashing pink icons-"

"I already worked that out. But how do I tell Marcie and the others we're all being... 'augmented' with mean 3D images?"

There was just a trace of smirk. "I doubt you could. I checked out the streams: they're only available to students at the school, excepting you and your three Loser Club friends, of course."

Father, sharing the vidchat with them and Mother, growled. "Nelson."

Nelson grinned openly. "Sorry. Excepting you and your three new girlfriends. So even if you told them, and they had AR, they still wouldn't be able to see that the feeds exist. Oh, and the feeds are proximity-keyed to you."

Leeth's mouth fell open. "What – you mean, Marcie and Delta and Sam only get graffiti-ed if I'm near them? So I could protect them by staying away from them.... But to explain doing *that,* I'd need to tell them I have special AR glasses. And then they'd want to know why; and why I kept them secret... aagh!"

"Leeth, you are to keep the glasses secret," Mother jumped in. "The network penetration algorithms are better than military grade."

"Well, *duh,*" said Nelson.

"So Tara's trying to make me split up with Marcie and the others? But... how does she know I can see her images?"

"I doubt she can," Mother said. "I expect the proximity feature is just to warn everyone else not to make friends with you."

"Yeah. That Tara chick must really hate you, eh?" added Nelson unnecessarily.

"This sucks! Can't I *please* just kill Tara, at least? Please, Father?"

"No." Mother answered before Father could. "The whole purpose of this exercise is to teach you non-combat skills, including how to socialize with other girls. This is an excellent test for you. I look forward to seeing how you resolve the matter without 'blowing your cover' or resorting to violence. Now if you don't mind, we have far more pressing matters than holding your hand while you deal with a mean bully."

Mother's face vanished from the vidcall. Nelson gave a little finger wave and a phony smile, and also disappeared.

Father frowned, looking sympathetic. "The best solution, Leeth, would be to bring the matter to the attention of someone in authority there – although that sounds technically difficult, given the protections Tara's hacker has set up around the various offensive social feeds. But if you think of a way I can help, I will try to do so.

"All right, girl?"

Leeth found herself blinking suddenly, her eyes watering. "Thanks, Father."

He signed off.

"Oh, Leeth, I'm so sorry," Emma said.

Leeth gratefully accepted the offered hug. It was nice to know that *some* people cared. She melted into the older woman's arms.

CHAPTER 35

Discussing it again the next morning, Leeth had a good idea.

"If I see someone with an AR device behaving weird when he or she's looking at any of us, I could just snatch it off and demand to know what they're looking at!"

Emma nodded. "I'd been thinking the same thing. That could work. Do many of the other students have AR glasses or viewers, or are they all using optic implants?"

"No one else wears glasses like me."

"Oh. Well, never mind. Good luck today."

"Thanks, Emma, bye." They hugged farewell.

Leeth was so deep in thought as she mulled over what to do with Marcie that she didn't notice the large man step out from his car, following her to the BART station.

She was still deep in thought as she forced her way onto the crowded platform, craning in the crowds of taller people for her friend.

"Hi! Marcie! Over here!" She jumped, waving her arms as commuters streamed off and then on the carriage. Marcie looked... cautious as she snaked her way through the thinning crowd. The maroon 'L' appeared on her forehead as she got closer, and Leeth winced.

Marcie saw, and stopped an arm's length away, with arms crossed. "Goodbye, right? You want out of the Losers Club."

"Huh? In case you hadn't noticed, in Tara's eyes I *am* the Losers Club. I couldn't leave it. Even if I wanted to."

Marcie blinked. Then the corners of her mouth quivered upward. "You mean that?"

"Yeah, of course." She took Marcie's arm in hers and began walking. "But I think there's something else going on. I heard some weird whispers, about a red 'L.' Any idea what that might be? And I thought I caught some strange looks from a few of the other students, so I've been trying to work out why. I mean, why *those* students in particular? You've been here longer than me, maybe you know...."

Heads together, they walked to school.

Once again, the day was overcast and cold. Behind them, the man followed.

By five pm, after a day watching vile appendages dangle from her friend's bodies, Leeth wanted to rip out Tara's poisonous heart and stuff it into her smirking mouth.

More and more, she took her glasses off: they were making her too angry. But at least she wasn't letting her mood rub off on Marcie or the others today.

They all now agreed *something* was going on, though Marcie, Delta and Sam couldn't work out *what*. And Leeth did learn some good stuff in the drama exercises. She'd particularly enjoyed one 'improv' with Tara, where they had to explore anger. Leeth had found that the quieter she spoke, the more restrained she behaved, the more worried Tara grew.

Like Tara could see that what Leeth really wanted to do to her was something quite permanent.

The strange guy was on the train again that night too, she noticed. But though he got off when she did, and followed her, he stopped at the end of the block. When Leeth paused at the entrance to the apartment block and looked back, she saw him turn and walk away.

She wished he'd *do* something. If he attacked her, obviously she'd have to defend herself. And if he happened to attack her when she was alone, with no witnesses, no cameras.... Well, a girl could dream, right?

But inside, waiting for the lift, her thoughts circled back to Tara the Terrible and what to do about her. Scarcely aware of others stepping in before her when the doors opened – "Oh, sorry," one murmured – she punched the button for Emma's floor, then slumped back against the wall.

The lift dinged, doors opening. "Sorry," the woman who'd spoken earlier said again, startling Leeth from her thoughts. Which gave her just enough time to slip out before the doors shut.

It was only as the lift continued on its way up that she realized she'd gotten out two floors too soon. Stalking to the adjacent stairs, she paused as heavy breathing and a heavier tread from above announced the arrival of a man, in good clothes but all slightly askew. On his wrist he wore a chunky gold band with a clock built into it.

The timepiece was making a faint *tick-tick-tick* sound and she hesitated, wondering what it was; what *he* was. The sound seemed familiar, too: she was sure she'd heard it before.

Stepping down from the stairs, he stood head and shoulders taller than her, making her feel small. He stopped, swaying, eyeing her up and down.

His breath smelled strange.

"Jane, yeah, in 7D?"

Which was true. She frowned. She didn't know him.

"Eliz'beth's niece. Swee' li'l niece."

He stepped closer, and for a moment she thought he was going to fall, and moved to support him.

"'Lizbeth's hot!"

He leaned on her, looming over her, draping one hand on her shoulder to steady himself.

"You mean she's got a fever? Why'd she send *you* to tell me? Why wouldn't she just call me herself?"

The man hunched over, seeming to find that hilarious. "*You* gi' me a fever, Janey," he got out, at last.

She pushed his hand off her shoulder. He wobbled, but didn't fall down.

Was he ill? Maybe that was why his breath smelled so strange? His clothes, too, smelled weird: smoky, but not wood smoke. Something more acrid.

"I didn't give you a fever. I'm perfectly well."

He laid his hand back on her shoulder, and his other arm snaked around her waist, pulling her close. "Yeah, you perfec'." He bent his head down, moving his lips towards hers.

She pushed his head away. "Stop that! I don't want to kiss you."

The hand on her shoulder slid down her front, over her left breast, and gripped it, while his other arm tightened, pulling her closer.

No fighting, Mother had said. But what was she supposed to do? Just let him slobber all over her? Surely even a normal girl would fight? *Surely?*

She trapped the fingers of his right hand and twisted, moving in against his arm. Bending it out and down, she forced him to follow it, finally locking his elbow at her waist.

First Tara, now this.

No fights.

She let go of his finger and stepped past him, fists clenched in frustration.

"Ow! That real' hurt, li'l bitch!"

"Touch me again and I'll do more than *hurt* you."

The stupid grin was back. "Tough sliv, eh? I c'n show you some better moves." He thrust his hips forwards, then stepped in close.

Leeth snapped.

Her palm struck the jutting jaw, twisting his head with a sharp crack. He collapsed, boneless, to the floor.

To lie very, very still.

Uh oh. She froze, hand covering her mouth, hoping he'd move. But even when she held her breath, she couldn't hear his breathing. Shutting her eyes she listened harder.

She couldn't hear his heartbeat, either.

Oh, no! Mother'll kill *me for this! And it was all* his *stupid fault, too!* She was going to be in so much trouble. They'd probably cancel the whole rest of her training exercise just 'cause of this. Even though she'd *warned* the idiot, despite Dojo saying you should never give your enemies an advantage.

And the police would need to try to find out who killed him, and everyone'd be cross, and going all, 'a normal girl wouldn't kill anyone,' and 'we told you specially, not to kill anybody!'

Her teeth ground at the unfairness. This dummy had ruined everything! *And I won't get another chance to do this training for six whole months!*

Unless...?

She tilted her head.

Unless they thought he'd died by *accident?* He *had* been swaying, looking unbalanced. Maybe....

She looked at his shoes; at the stairs.

Bending down, then, she loosened the fastenings and slid one foot most of the way out of its shoe before hoisting him up by his armpits as high as she could, carrying him to the stairwell, his toes dragging the floor.

She was still studying the angles – judging how his head would have to strike the ground – when behind her, the lift dinged its arrival. Quickly throwing him shoulders-first down the flight of stairs, she darted silently up to Emma's apartment.

She was *so* not gonna tell anyone about this! It might even mess up her plans to sneak out and hunt The Breaker, instead of 'socializing' with the other drama students at night.

Breakfast the next morning was French omelets, with orange juice for Leeth and for Emma, some blend of tea Leeth couldn't even pronounce.

"We had some excitement here last night."

"We did?" Leeth asked. "I don't remember it."

"Not us. The building."

Leeth looked more puzzled. "How does a building get excited?"

Emma rolled her eyes, then saw the girl wasn't joking. "It's a turn of phrase, Leeth, meaning there was some excitement in the building last night. You remember Mr Hengist, apartment 5A?" Leeth looked blank. "He insisted on helping carry some of your bags for you, when we were moving you in here."

A great light seemed to dawn on Leeth. "The ticking man! Now I remember!"

It was Emma's turn to look puzzled. "The ticking man? As in, ticking bomb?"

"Why would a bomb *tick*?"

"Never mind. He's not ticking any more. Last night, he fell down the stairs and broke his neck."

While Leeth tried to work out the correct response to that – pretty sure 'good' was not a normal answer – Emma continued. "It turns out, he'd been partying with Mrs Li, in 6B. Quite hard."

"Huh. Hard partying. How'd they find that out?"

"Cam footage from the foyer; access codes. Not drunk when he entered the building, but high blood alcohol levels in his blood, even though he hadn't entered his apartment last night. Turned out Mrs Li had keyed for his prints to have access to the apartment she and her husband shared."

"Is three people having sex together, normal?" Leeth asked, interested.

"What? What three people?"

"Mr and Mrs Li, and Mr Hengist."

Emma stared at her. "Mr Li wasn't there. Mrs Li was having an affair with Mr Hengist."

"Oh." She nodded. "So, three people having sex *isn't* normal?"

CHAPTER 36

In the morning a few days later, at the station, Marcie was acting strange. She kept looking sideways at her and grinning.

Leeth surreptitiously checked herself out, wondering if she'd broken some new dress or makeup code she was unaware of. But that didn't seem to be it – Marcie seemed more like she was kind of excited.

And once they were a little way from the station, she took her arm and tugged Jane to a stop, unslinging her backpack from her shoulders. "Wait a min, I got you something."

Not quite understanding, Leeth just waited, as Marcie drew out a cardboard tube and presented it to her, practically bouncing.

"Uh, gee, um, thanks. This'll come in real handy when I, um...?"

Marcie giggled. "Very funny! Open it up!"

Oh. She smiled, and saw there were caps at each end. At first, after removing them, it seemed empty, but then she saw there was something lining the tube. Carefully, she extracted the rolled up sheet....

At the flash of red and yellow on the blue background, the 'S' in its unique sort of diamond-triangle shape, she realized what it was. Unfurling Superman's logo, she stared in shock from Marcie back to the poster. It felt old, too, printed on actual paper. It had to be valuable. "What- I don't...?"

"It's a gift, dummy. Do you like it?"

For some reason, tears were welling up in her eyes. Marcie had bought her a *present?*

Marcie beamed at her reaction, and then they were hugging, the poster held awkwardly out so she didn't crush it.

"I love it! Thank you!"

They separated, Leeth holding it up so they could both admire it. They shared a grin, and Leeth carefully rolled it back up and put it back in the tube. Where it rested, like a secret code just between the two of them.

Wow. A present. She'd had exactly two presents in her life, before. Both from Keepie. Her bow and arrows, and her PowerShot slingshot. Which'd be a totally simple way to deal with Tara, come to think of it, so long as no one ever found out....

Later, in the cafeteria with her friends at morning 'coffee' – which for Leeth, meant two hot chocolates – she overheard some of the other students talking about her.

"*Miki* said the weirdo stared at Jane the whole time. She said he even got onto the BART with them."

So, others had noticed the strange guy who'd been following her the last few days?

"Lezlie, you mean. Figures: weirdos attract weirdos."

"He was out there again today."

"Jake said he was waiting there all day yesterday, until classes were over. Just watching the School...."

When they returned to class, Ms Sorensen was late – and Ms Sorensen was *never* late. The room was buzzing with speculation by the time she strode in.

"Ladies, gentlemen, I would like to introduce another new student. He'll be joining us shortly, but I need to speak to you all first. He is a trauma survivor who has been severely emotionally damaged. He's joining us in an effort to reconnect with his inner self.

"Of course it's with his permission I'm sharing this personal information with you, since you will need to be especially understanding. Mr Dennis is suffering from an *affect* disorder. He is quite out of touch with his emotions. This will make him seem cold and distant. Even robotic."

At those words, a strange chill went through Leeth. And settled there.

"I want no jokes made about his disability. He tells me he will only need a week or two with us to learn what he needs to know."

"So, what, we're like his therapists?" Tara scowled. "How is that fair on *us*? We're s'posed to be learning drama, not nurse-maiding nutbags."

"Tara, I want no jokes or insults. For each week here with us, Mark Dennis is donating enough to the school to upgrade our audio-visual-cranial systems to cinema-submersive standards. So: deal."

Leeth heard a heavy tread, and then the creepy guy who'd been following her stepped into the room. His eyes scanned across the space from left to right, stopping the moment they landed on her. For several seconds he simply stood, then his eyes continued. And came back to rest on Jane.

From the whispers that started up, Leeth was not the only student to notice.

He stepped forward and the room fell silent.

"It is very good to be here amongst you all. Much will be learned."

Leeth's chill deepened, and she shuddered. His eyes once more slid to her. Beside her, Marcie noticed and moved closer, protectively, and Leeth felt her heart swell, warmed.

The man lifted his hand, gesturing as if touching buttons in the air in front of him as he faced Leeth. Across the room, she heard Tara suck in a breath.

The man tilted his head. "Why do these four girls," he said, pointing to Leeth's group, "have 'L' symbols on their foreheads, and tails with penises?"

Leeth heard Tara swearing under her breath. Turning that way, Leeth saw her squint her eyes as if concentrating, then suddenly all the 'uglifications' vanished. Tara glared daggers at the newcomer.

Beside her, Marcie gasped. "Tails? With *penises?*"

Their teacher looked stunned. "What on earth do you-?"

"They are now gone. The augmentation streams have closed down."

Ms Sorensen looked from Mark Dennis, to Leeth and her friends, and finally to Tara. Who was now pretending to look as surprised as Ms Sorensen. Leeth heard Marcie growl, and put a hand on her thigh. "Don't," she whispered. "Knowing Miss Wealthy, she'll have done it so we won't be able to prove anything."

"Yeah," agreed Sam. "And she'd probably sue *you* for accusing her, Marcie!"

But how had Mark Dennis seen the pink icons? *Oh! He must be augmented.* And as of this morning, he'd become a student... and Tara hadn't had time to get her hacker to exclude him!

"Does anyone wish to explain Mr Dennis's remarks?" Ms Sorensen asked the class.

"Those four girls," Mark Dennis pointed once again, "were augmented with images of pe-"

"I understood what you said, thank you, Mr Dennis. My question was directed toward the other students. Tara, do you know anything about these obscene augmentation feeds?"

"No idea, Ms Sorensen. Is Mr Dennis augmented himself? Could his augments be damaged? Maybe it was a cross-feed from a porn site he'd forgotten to turn off?"

The class laughed, but quietened immediately at the drama teacher's stare.

"That's enough, Tara. Any of you, feel free to come and talk to me about this later. In private. With confidentiality."

"If someone has been messing with any students here, Ms Sorensen, I'm sure Daddy and his lawyers will be only too happy to help," volunteered Tara.

"Fuuuck," said Sam, under her breath. "That bitch."

"I see," said Ms Sorensen, in response to Tara's smile. She visibly controlled herself. "I think it's long past time to begin our lesson. Mr Dennis, please take a seat. Let's begin by considering how the body's posture can reinforce and even *trigger* emotional states..."

Mark Dennis chose the seat behind Leeth, which made her skin crawl. He seemed awfully familiar, somehow. More than just the fact that he'd been following her around the last couple of days. Something beyond that. Something about the dead look in those dull blue eyes. For some reason, he kept making her think of a Japanese girl, who seemed real familiar, but who she couldn't remember ever meeting. Jennifer someone? It was driving her nuts, like an itch in her brain!

Mark Dennis watched her, the whole day. He seemed to sense whenever she looked at him; his head swiveling around to her. And each time, he did this thing with his lips that she suspected was supposed to be a smile.

It just made her feel cold.

-

When the Call had returned, three days earlier, Marc Disten had followed. First to the luxurious, secured apartment building. Then to the Drama School. Then back to the apartment. Back to the School.

The girl was not the Japanese girl from the restaurant. Although she did have a strong resemblance to the girl who had died in the alley.

It was curious.

Disten had decided to get close. To study his prey and learn more. Access had simply required sufficient funds, criminal contacts for papers, and finally, a plausible story.

To match and reinforce the false identity, a residence had been leased for some months. Close by the luxury apartment; ready to take her at once if the girl prepared to leave the area. And a second lease, for the same period, for a mansion near the school, that would be more suited to what was planned.

The final piece of disguise had arrived this morning – collected from the car dealer after seeing the girl enter the school. In the wealthy area, the poorly-maintained Ferrari Quattropotenza would have drawn attention by its state of ill-repair, not for its once-considerable value. Nor would discovery of the Ferrari's ownership by Marc Disten be wise, given what was to come.

-

Leeth wished the school hadn't let Mark Dennis join, even if he *had* ruined Tara's penis plan. With him there, the day passed weirdly. Lessons went poorly – Mr Dennis's detached presence siphoned all the energy from the room. He said little, but was as distracting as a sucking black hole. Today's improv session was a dismal failure: several times, people had just stood, silent; imaginations run dry.

Worse, at lunch, he'd sat with them at Jane's table. Remembering the pain of being told she couldn't join Tara – though that seemed now more like a stroke of luck than a punishment – Leeth felt obliged to smile and welcome him. He'd drawn up an extra chair and squeezed in, not appearing to notice how Delta and Sam shrank away.

No one sat at the tables nearby their now-overcrowded table for four.

Leeth eyed his suit, his silk tie, his neatly-groomed hair and smoothly-shaven face. He might even be handsome, if he ever cracked an expression. Like a real smile, for example. He was certainly sharply dressed. Much more so than the first time she'd seen him, the other day.

"So, uh, thanks for, uh..."

"Yeah, so, like what the fuck?" demanded Marcie. "Penis tails? Seriously?"

"Yes. Jane also had a penis instead of a nose, and se-men dribbling-" Mark Dennis began.

"Stop! Stop!" Delta waved her hand in his face. "Shut up! Really? Did I...? No, don't tell me, I don't wanna know."

"So, uh, what was the awful trauma you suffered, Mr Dennis?" asked Leeth.

"Jane," hissed Marcie, "you can't just ask something like that!"

Mark Dennis tilted his head. "It is no matter. But therapists have said it is best not to dwell on it. And if your friend... Delta? here is disturbed by a description of computer-generated penises and semen, perhaps it is better if a description is not provided.

"You are all friends?"

The four girls looked at one another, smiled, and nodded. Like they'd only just noticed it.

"Good. That is good. Friends provide connection."

Again, Leeth felt that chill.

In the afternoon, everyone's performances became more and more dull and lifeless. Even Tara hadn't peppered Leeth and her friends with her usual verbal darts. At the end of a day of very long, somehow draining classes, people spilled out with a sense of numb relief.

Wow, that had been awful.

Near the gates, Leeth heard a deep, rumbling growl behind her, then exclamations of shock. Dropping her bag, she spun around-

To see a gleaming white abstraction of swooping, vaguely-muscular curves of speed *grumble* down the driveway that curled around from behind the school. Gaping students stepped aside as it swept past, with Mark Dennis in the driver's seat, eyes shut but flicking back and forth as if he were reading. The somehow-sexual sculpture prowled past them, the gates swung open, and then the astonishing car paused, purring to itself before sweeping out smoothly into a gap in the traffic.

"Holy stinking money piles, that was a fucken Bugatti Mach 1.2! That's like, two fucken million creds. There're only like twenty in the country...!" The speaker, one of the boys, was staring at the pictures he'd snapped as if he'd just seen a dragon or something.

Marcie nudged Leeth. "Guess Mr Dennis really is rich, then. Oh, Jane, *look!* Check out Tara's face!"

Leeth had to smile. Tara looked like she'd just swallowed something nasty.

Score two for Mark Dennis, Leeth thought.

CHAPTER 37

Leeth felt she'd started to really 'find her feet.' It was actually nice, mixing with normal people. Especially Marcie. She wondered if she could find some gift *Marcie* would like. Something really special.

At Emma's urging, she wrote up an interim report. Even though it took the whole weekend. Which maybe backfired – since after only seven days into her training exercise, Mother decided Leeth had learned enough and would finish the following week.

But she didn't really care anymore if she failed this exercise: not if failing meant she could stop Tara from arranging some even worse assault on her friends.

She dreaded having to tell them she was leaving, though. Just the thought made her feel weird in her stomach. She couldn't even finish her breakfast. *Maybe I'm getting sick?*

"What! Finishing? Why?" wailed Marcie at the news on Monday morning. Sam and Delta looked almost as upset.

Mark Dennis just tilted his head. For him, though, that was a major reaction.

Leeth shrugged. "Things aren't so good on the farm. And this place is pretty expensive."

"No!" Sam cried. "You can't just quit! People are still talking about that Hunt!" Sam narrowed her eyes at Delta and leaned forward to hiss, "Not all invisible creatures are imaginary."

Leeth groaned inwardly. She was so screwed: Eagle had said she was never to talk about any of that stuff; yet she'd acted it out *right in front of her whole class!* Oh, but wait – Mother and Father didn't know about what happened at the Institute! Oh: but Eagle did-

"-calling Jane. Earth calling Jane. Can you hear me, over? Khhkk." Marcie's hand on her shoulder snapped her attention back.

"Sorry, Marcie, what'd you say?"

Delta and Sam looked excited, watching Jane for her reaction.

"I said, my Dad is pretty well off. Maybe I could persuade him to pay your tuition fees too?"

"Wow. That's- I don't... I don't think so. Mother and Father need me to start contributing. I mean, earning. To help out."

"The fees can be paid for," Mark Dennis said. "A donation can be made to your parents. How much is required? It can be done now."

Leeth gaped at Mark Dennis. "That's very kind, Mr Dennis, but the situation is... complicated. I know they wouldn't accept."

Marcie and the others moaned, and Leeth felt horrible. Partly at having to lie to them, but also because she herself didn't want to leave. This had been the most fun period of her life! Except for Tara. And the feeling like maybe she might actually be *turning into* a normal girl. Sometimes, though, when she thought of people hurting her friends, it made her wish they were right: that making rules was enough to keep you safe.

Does that mean I'm turning into a sheep?

"Then there will be a farewell party for you. The mansion has ample room for such an affair. And it is close by." Mr Dennis shut his eyes.

Marcie and the others conferred by facial expressions and hand gestures.

Delta pointed at Mr Dennis, quirking her eyebrows up and making a gagging motion. Marcie nodded. But Sam made a house gesture, that grew big, then mimicked driving a car. *His mansion; and the Bugatti.* But Delta shook her head. Indicated Mr Dennis with her thumb, then curled her fingers to include the four of them with him, and shuddered.

He opened his eyes, while the three girls tried to look innocent.

"The net says the most popular party organizer is C Sky Sparks. He has confirmed he can arrange a suitable affair this Friday, for forty four people."

Leeth stared at him blankly while the other three squeaked and exclaimed, drawing glances their way.

"Why forty four people?"

"That is the number of people in this school."

"Yes!" cried Delta, punching the air then projecting a keyboard and screen onto the tabletop to begin typing. "I am SoBo-ing this right now!" She dragged a query code from the projected display toward Mark Dennis. "Can you send me an url for your mansion, Mr Dennis? Even just a streetview would do."

The man looked down at the 2D code, and moments later it was replaced by a video tour of a very plush house and grounds.

"Thanks!" Delta dragged it into her message, and Sent. Around the room, a chorus of chimes blossomed.

"Wait, what-" But Leeth was left blinking in the dust, her three friends already planning the party.

"Oh! Can you *believe* it? I'm *chatting* with C Sky Sparks!" squeaked Delta, her fingers moving even faster across the bright keyboard.

Slowly, Leeth started to smile. It wouldn't be normal for a girl to refuse a party which her friends were organizing, surely?

The most intense debate had been about whether to invite the Power Princesses or not. In the end, Marcie's argument that it'd be fun watching them eat crow while Jane was the center of attention swayed their better judgment. Four days, apparently, was just enough time to find the right outfits to wear.

If Leeth thought she'd learned a lot in the previous seven days, it was nothing compared to what she learned in the run-up to her farewell party.

The girls had been blown away by the 'DJ' hired, by the catering the party planner outlined, by the videos of Mr Dennis's mansion... by everything.

Mother, however, had been unimpressed – 'We don't wish your image on the net' – and for a while it had looked like the party would die a death before the second day of planning. 'No problem,' had been the response from C Sky Sparks – apparently the objection was common – and the event simply turned into a masked ball. Mother's next objection had been to Mark Dennis himself – but his background appeared solid, if predictably dull. Nelson assured them the man's wealth was real, most of it in secure overseas crypto accounts that no one except Dennis himself – or Nelson – could access. 'You want me to take some or all of it?'

Mother had said that would not be necessary.

Marcie came with Jane to her 'Aunt Elizabeth's' apartment one night, to help choose an outfit. Though Marcie's eyebrows spent a lot of the time elevated, at the things she found in her friend's closet.

"Guess the farm-boys must've got quite a show. You really wear this stuff? *Girl!*"

The next night, Leeth visited Marcie's house – the suburb really was called Fruitvale, she discovered. Marcie's father and little sister both seemed sweet. Except maybe at the very beginning....

Marcie's sister Amanda wasn't what Leeth had expected: she wasn't a younger, smaller version of Marcie.

She'd squealed. "Ooh, you're the Invisible-Hunter? Will you hunt a monster for *me?*"

The innocent words sent Leeth flashing back to another time; standing beside Commander Amanda Stone while everyone waited for *Her* to attack. She wondered what the older woman was doing; wondered what she herself might be doing now if she'd joined the FBI instead of the Department? The *Commander* wouldn't've let Uncle....

She shook her head. Focused on *this* Amanda.

"Please, *please* do a Hunt?" the younger girl begged, tugging Leeth's hands.

"Trust me," she told Marcie's sister, meeting her eyes, "you don't want me to *need* to hunt something invisible for you."

Amanda shivered, clapping her hands as she turned to her sister. "Oh, M, she's *good!* The way she said that, it made me feel all squiggly inside!"

This young Amanda was sweet, and bubbly; and Leeth found herself feeling oddly protective of Marcie's sister.

And maybe just a touch envious of her friend.

It was a strangely-fun evening, the three of them helping work out what to utilize from Marcie's closet, and shopping online for the required extras.

The day of the party, Mark Dennis hired a bus to take the entire school to his mansion – which was hardly necessary, as it would have taken scarcely more time to walk than to wait while everyone boarded it, to go there, and then disembarked at the other end.

Several of the boys were dismayed to find the rich man let his Bugatti drive itself home, so he could join them on the party bus. 'If I owned a car like that, I'd *live* in it!' had been the general male opinion.

The house was enormous. Set amidst sweeping grounds, the multi-wing mansion sat on a gentle rise, a small forest of impressively old and tall trees screening it from the rest of Oakland. It boasted tennis courts at the rear, several putting greens, an Olympic-sized swimming pool, an orchid house, and extensive gardens which unrolled down the gentle slope behind the twelve bedroom, thirty-five room villa. At the foot of the hill sat a very large and very new shed.

Even the weather was kind to them.

Tara and friends, of course, insisted on making their own way there – which no doubt meant their outfits would be designed to shock and awe when they made their entrance. But Marcie and the others didn't care.

Leeth wore black: high heels, a sparkling feathered owl mask, and a jewel-cut dress with ruffled sleeves and zigzagging angled hem. "Very retro-20s," Marcie had said. With an emerald-colored pendant and bracelets to bring out the color of her eyes.

Marcie wore an extravagant peacock mask, her outfit an off-the-shoulder number with swirls of turquoise sliding like the Aurora Borealis through the shimmering navy material. A dusting of lace at the neckline drew the eye to Marcie's pale skin and modest bust.

She looked stunning, and Leeth told her so.

Mr Dennis's mansion glowed, every window lit. The music could be heard even before the bus stopped in the wide, curving driveway beside the elaborate granite fountain. Age-greened bronze nymphs and a half-man, half-bull relaxed in a wide expanse of water, dancing streams lit by green and blue lights giving it a mystical appearance.

The music pulled them, feet tapping, from the bus, and Leeth, Marcie and the rest of the school danced, laughing, up the stairs and inside.

Which did credit to the images they'd already seen. Suited caterers ushered them in across the parquet flooring. A *secondary* ballroom had been set aside as a quieter area, with a selection of exotic but delicious finger foods and a wide range of drinks, and couches and rosewood coffee tables for relaxing and talking.

This was going to be a magical night!

Even Tara's triumphant arrival failed to ruin it – her dress a waterfall of shimmering and glowing clouds, her hair a complex up-do that alternately sparkled or burned in fiery veins. The masks she and her friends wore consisted just of glowing hologram 'eyes of magical power.'

Tara, Beth, and Ava reminded Leeth of three slightly-scary Faery princesses. But they looked good.

And as the night progressed, it seemed even Tara had buried the hatchet.

A few times, Leeth had felt a little dizzy, and flushed, but figured it was just from all the dancing. The music was *ultra*, everyone agreed. Even Mr Beckman and Ms Sorensen were dancing. Both had some pretty amazing moves, especially for old people in their thirties.

Their famous and expensive *DJ* wound up at ten pm, but left his specially-curated track selection running. But soon after that, Leeth began to worry. She felt... strange. The music started kind of zooming in and out of focus, and she swayed on her feet. *Dehydrated?* She looked around, but saw everyone else had the same kind of, kind of....

She fell, to her knees. Blinking.

What?

Everyone... everyone else was... sleeping. On the floor.

Mark Dennis, his body wavering like a candle flame, walked towards her....

Her eyelids crashed down.

CHAPTER 38

She woke to a hard floor in a dimly-lit space, her body bumping and swaying, and her arms stretched above her head by... chains. Heavy chains. She blinked. At her feet, a plastic bucket. Across from her lay Ms Sorensen and Mr Beckman, heads lolling, arms chained to a railing above them.

She was in a long, narrow rectangular room that jolted and shook. A moving vehicle? Yeah: outside, she could hear the steady burr of tires on a road. From the sound, it was a pretty heavy truck, too; maybe a cattle car? Looking around, it seemed like the whole school was here.

Where was Marcie? Oh: by her right side, pressed up against the rear wall. Which consisted of two doors running the entire width and height. The subtle washes of colors through Marcie's dress provided plenty of light in the darkness – for her. Delta and Sam, she saw, lay slumped to her left.

Tara and her companions rested like drunken dolls halfway down the 'room,' their faery-light dresses glowing with enough softly-shifting illumination for her to see the whole space.

Mr Dennis was also present, chained at the far end of the room in the middle of that front wall. The caterers, too, were unconscious, at his side.

Everyone was here. The whole school! All asleep: drugged. Then she noticed her wristlink was gone. And her glasses! She looked around, but didn't see *any* 'links: not on any wrists, or fingers, or dangling as necklaces.

Something brushed her face, and she flinched back before seeing it was just a length of clear plastic tubing, swaying with the motion of the truck. A drop of clear liquid dripped from the end. She ignored it for now; ignored the fact that a bucket had been carefully placed between each pair of people, even though that sent a chill through her for some reason. She kept looking for anyone with any kind of commlink. Didn't one of the kids have an antique Nexus 16 'smartphone'?

Oh! Some of the students had communication augments. As soon as one of them woke up, they could call for help.

But what was going on? And how had they gotten here? And why would someone kidnap a whole school? It made no sense.

Mother and Father'd be pissed off, too. *I bet this doesn't happen to normal girls.*

At least her legs weren't bound. She pulled them under her, and stood up – only for the room to spin as dizziness struck. Gray swam through her vision, and she would have fallen if not for the chains looped around the cuffs between her wrists. She swallowed, feeling sick in her stomach. Propped against the wall, she pressed her back into a handrail, gripping it while drawing in deep breaths. Gradually the nausea passed and she tried straightening up again, more slowly.

This time she managed it, and twisted around to examine her bonds. She'd become something of an expert in bondage.

Her fists clenched.

The chains were strong, looped around her cuffs and then the thick metal bar bolted at regular intervals to the wall of the truck. She rapped the wall with a knuckle. Metal, she judged, and quite solid, too. Pressing her head against it, she shut her eyes and listened, focusing on the sounds from outside; the *putt* of the tires crossing the gaps between the road's concrete slabs.

She concentrated; picturing it all.... She could hear the front pair of wheels, and the rear pair, just below her; but also two more pairs, close together and close behind. Was the truck towing a small trailer? Yeah: a metallic squeaking, with a slightly rattling jumble and rumble, came from behind. And something else, too: a low hum... like a refrigerator?

She heard another set of wheels, a lighter vehicle, move up swiftly on their left, overtaking and moving steadily past them: the faint high-pitched whine of powerful electrical motors. Some kind of car.

She kept listening, and slowly the mental picture came clear. They were in a large truck, moving at a steady, high speed, towing some kind of smaller – refrigerated? – trailer behind them.

Why would there be a refrigerated trailer? Food supplies? She opened her eyes, studying the situation in the bright starlight from the Terrible Trio's dresses.

There was no food she could see. But tubing ran along the metal bars, a length forking off between every second pair of... captives. The tubes ran from two large plastic jerry-cans set on elevated shelves on the same wall Mr Dennis was chained to.

She felt a chill settle in the pit of her stomach. She eyed the tubes. Drugs? Somehow, she felt not. She took hold of the end of the tube dangling between her and Marcie, and crouching, put her lips to it. Tentatively sucked, ready to spit it out at the taste.

She realized she was thirsty: very thirsty.

She sucked.

Not much taste: a bit plastic-y. Faintly chlorine. It seemed like water. Her body cried out for her to swallow it. But she could imagine what Mother and Father would say if it *was* drugged and she slipped back under its influence. Stretching out one leg, she swept the bucket closer and spat the liquid into it.

At least her mouth felt better.

She examined the restraints. Metal handcuffs, and a heavy gray iron chain looping between each person's cuffs, chaining them all to the long metal bar running down the length of the truck. The same on both sides; the same for everyone.

The end of the chain? In the corner by the rear doors, above Marcie's head, a massive bolt ran through a shackle. She bent closer: something clear and hard shone in the seam where the nut screwed up against it. Screwed so hard against it the metal had buckled. She tried to loosen it with her fingers anyway, but failed.

The truck swayed, and she bumped Marcie.

Who groaned.

Leeth sank to her knees beside her friend, yanking at her own cuffs as she tried to pat her, comfort her. But she couldn't reach.

"Wha-...?" Marcie's eyes fluttered open, and she blinked, peering around as if struggling to see. "Jane?"

"I'm here. With you. I'll protect you. We'll be all right. I promise."

"Wha-..." Marcie licked parched-looking lips. "Thirsty." She tugged at her wrists. The heavy chain rattled, and she seemed to come fully awake, her head turning this way and that in the darkness. "What the fuck? Jane! I'm- I think I'm chained up!" Her voice rose higher. "Jane? What's going on? Why am I chained up? Where are we? What's going on?"

"I don't know." She knelt down beside her friend, pressing against her as best she could, trying to hug her without arms. "I think we were all drugged, at the party. The whole school. We're all chained up, in the back of a truck I think."

"What the fuck is going on? Who did it?"

"I don't know. I think you and I are the first two to wake up, so far."

For some reason, that seemed to help calm Marcie. Who peered at her in the near-dark, squinting like she was struggling to see her. Leeth turned, sinking back down to the floor, and scooched over until they were pressed side by side, her arms once more tugged up above her head.

"Is everyone all right?" Marcie asked. "Where's Sam and Delta? Is Tara here too? I bet that bitch is behind-"

"Tara's here too. And Ava, and Beth. They're the faery-lights you can see over there. And Mr Dennis. Sam and Delta are just to my left. Hey, you said your father runs a trucking fleet. Do you know anything that might help us get out? Can we open the back doors from the inside? When someone with a comm augment wakes up, they can just call for rescue, right? They could triangulate the signal source, yeah?"

"I am *so* thirsty. But... no, the doors are electronically keyed. And..." she rapped her knuckles on the floor, then the walls. "You ever hear of a Faraday cage?" In a wash of emerald light from her dress, she saw Leeth shake her head. "It blocks signals. They could even have a jammer, too, if they've gone to all this trouble."

"Rats."

Across the floor, she heard a male groan. Mr Beckman was coming around. Suddenly he doubled over, and heaved.

A strong smell of vomit washed out in a cloud, and beside her, Marcie groaned.

It had been better, in many ways, before everyone woke up.

The air now was heavy with the smell of vomit and the sounds of sobs, crying, moans, and angry complaints. Tara was screaming out, demanding their captors make themselves known; demanding to be released right now or her Daddy would have an army of security down on 'your sorry coward's ass.'

Several conversations were running in parallel, too; speculations about who was behind this; the hapless caterers demanding to know what was going on, and how if this was a prank they'd be suing Dennis, or the School, or both.

Mr Dennis, when he woke, had of course been completely calm. Leeth had kind of hoped that maybe the shock might be what he needed to cure him of his emotional paralysis or whatever it was. But he'd just asked a few questions: did anyone know who had done this? Had there been any communication, any contact? Could anyone get a signal out, call for help? Did anyone know why this was happening?"

That had taken a long time, since each question was met by a chorus of confusion, anger, wild guesses and wilder accusations. His final words had quieted things down, briefly.

"The most logical target would be the wealthiest person, for kidnapping."

"You?" Tara had hissed. "But why kidnap all of *us*, in that case?"

"The kidnappers may assume that bonds of friendship had formed. They may assume that by torture, they can extract the pass-codes to secured accounts."

After his words, there was just the faint sound of the whooshing of the tires against the road surface, outside.

"Which would work, right?" asked Tara, sounding suddenly much younger.

Long seconds passed.

"No. Friendship is illogical. Nor have any mutually beneficial arrangements been formed."

The silence echoed with dismay.

"But we could form one right now, yeah? My father's wealthy. If you give them a pass-code to buy me free, Daddy'll give you a million creds."

Outraged shouts met those words. 'Coward.' 'Bitch.' 'What about the rest of us?'

"The smallest account holds eighteen point three million. Such an arrangement would not make financial sense."

"Then he'll give you nineteen million," Tara bluffed.

"Eighteen point three million is only the smallest account." After a few seconds, he continued; still sounding as disinterested as ever. "Does anyone have a plan for escape?"

His question spurred a session of wild scheming; including everyone pulling together on the chain, trying to wrench it free of the wall. But it appeared the structure had been designed to cope with fastening enormously heavy containers, and their efforts were fruitless. A susurrus of moans, curses, and insults settled in.

And no one had been able to get a signal out.

At least the tubes appeared to deliver water. Few of the others had resisted drinking, and they all still seemed fine. Leeth thought she could wait a little longer, though, before she'd have to give in, too.

Marcie had been very quiet through the whole thing. Like she knew something the others didn't: something bad. Which, given their current circumstances, was pretty worrying.

"What can you tell about the truck?" Leeth whispered. "Any ideas for escape?" She sank back beside her friend, trying to ignore the stomach-wrenching smell of puke, as the two pressed up side by side, talking quietly.

"Truck-driving got completely automated before it was even halfway popular with cars, Jane. Almost every truck these days is auto-drive. It's cheaper and safer. See that red glow up there? That marks a camera, watching. Whoever took us are probably watching and listening. They could be anywhere on the planet. It could be anyone. And if they wanted, and if they've hacked the auto-drive, they can just drive us off a cliff or into the ocean if they want to."

"Oh. That'd suck."

"You're taking this pretty calmly."

"We'll get out of this."

"I'm not so sure. But I...." Marcie stopped, lips pursed.

"You what?"

"Nothing. No point worrying you."

"Marcie. Anything you know, could be important. I already think-" This time *Leeth* stopped. How much food was in the refrigerated trailer behind them? How long might they be held captive? But she didn't want to frighten Marcie.

"What?"

"Doesn't matter. It's just a... worry."

"Now who's not sharing? Jane, look... you tell me your worry and I'll tell you mine."

"You first."

"Oh, alright. These buckets; the water supply; and... the way the rear of the truck moves on some of the potholes: the way it jerks back, like something's kind of whiplashing it?"

Leeth nodded. Then said "Uh-huh," when Marcie failed to see.

"My sister and I sometimes nicked one of my dad's remotes, to order one of his trucks to take us on rides. Sometimes it'd have a trailer behind it. That's what this feels like. But not a heavy one, I'd say; not one full of stuff." She paused, giving Leeth time to digest that. "Why would you tow an empty trailer behind a truck full of kidnapped people? I think whoever has us is planning to keep us for a long time; and the trailer is so they can take people out, and... do something to them without the rest of us seeing, and panicking."

Leeth went cold. *She'd* thought the refrigerated trailer was carrying food supplies. But if Marcie could tell it was *empty*... that made the possible use much, much scarier: it wasn't to take stuff *out* of; it was to put stuff *in*; stuff that had to be cooled.

"So, go on Jane, your turn: what's *your* worry?"

There was no way she could admit she could hear the compressor running, on the trailer which she could *hear* moving, behind them.

"Uh..." *what could she say*...? "I was just thinking... that if they've kidnapped Mr Dennis, and us just to make him give us the codes, that isn't going to work."

Marcie stared at her. "No you weren't. That wasn't what you were thinking. Now, give."

Instead, Leeth hugged her, their chains making that difficult even while standing. "Look, Marcie, can you just trust me that it's only an idea, a scary idea, and I don't think it'd help you concentrate on rescuing us all to share it right now? And it's just an *idea*."

Marcie pulled away. "I guess so. Yeah, okay. But whatdya mean, me rescuing us all?"

Leeth saw the idea of Marcie being the hero, saving them all, take root. *Yeah, if* Marcie *was the one who was special; who rescued everyone....* "Picking the locks on these cuffs."

"Police cuffs? Are you kidding? I'm good, yeah, but not that good. They're impossible."

Leeth grinned. "But these aren't police cuffs. They're for... bondage."

"*Bondage*? Like... B&D? S&M? *That* kind of bondage?"

Leeth nodded.

"I'm not gonna ask how you know that. But if you know the trick, why don't you just open them?"

"Trick? There's no trick escape mechanism. They're not toys, Marcie. But my guess is they'll be easier to open than my padlock."

In the dim light, she saw the smile blossom on Marcie's face. "O-*kay!* Let's get started. I'll race you!"

It wasn't too hard to get at Marcie's hairpins, and soon both were standing, backs braced against the long metal rail as the truck bumped along, working at their own cuffs.

Sam and Delta were the first to notice what they were doing, whispering excitedly, and the news spread up and then down the truck. By the time Marcie's lock clicked open, ten minutes later, the whole truck was silent – until a cheer went up as she unlocked the cuff and stepped away from the rail, with a small bow.

Her success spurred Leeth on, and she focused even more sharply on the tiny sounds from the pins inside the locking mechanism, through the cries of 'Now me, unlock me!' Then Leeth grinned at Marcie, the cuff dangling from her left wrist, her own loop of chain rattling against the metal wall of the swaying truck.

A smaller cheer went up.

Things got a little sticky after that, though, as everyone started demanding to be unlocked, right now!

Marcie stamped her foot. "Shut up! At ten minutes per lock, it'd take hours to get everyone free, and we don't know how long we've got till we arrive wherever we're going."

"Okay, but that doesn't mean you can't free a few more," Tara said. "We may need numbers on our side when they open the doors. The more people you free, the better!"

"Really? You're gonna rush them, are you, Tara? What if they have guns? What we *need* is to find a way to open the doors, or signal for help, or stop the truck. So unless you've got ideas for how to do that, just shut up, everyone, okay?"

Tara didn't shut up, but Marcie and Leeth just ignored her as they began examining the rear doors. Marcie explained where the electronic lock would be, and how opening it required a special remote control, or else the truck's ID and authorization codes.

Leeth eyed the camera. She could just leap up and smash it, but that might seem... a bit special.

Behind them, she heard the clatter of a pair of handcuffs dropping to the floor and multiple shocked intakes of breath. Heavy footsteps trod towards them. Spinning round, she saw Mark Dennis walking the length of the truck in the gloom.

A few people cheered, but others hushed them: "He wasn't locked in. He was faking!"

Silence spread.

"Move away from the doors. You must be restrained."

CHAPTER 39

"Shitme! It was him all along!" hissed Marcie. "But that means..."

Leeth felt cold. She moved a little away from Marcie, towards the man relentlessly approaching. Something about his lack of expression, his implacable walk....

She'd learned heaps from Dojo. She was strong, and fast, and deadly. She summoned the peculiar tingle to her fingertips, ready to cut and slice.

So why am I afraid? Why did he make her body scream at her to *run!*

Mr Dennis said nothing further, neither slowing nor speeding up, noting her stance but otherwise ignoring it. As if nothing she could do worried him.

Then Marcie whispered, "Yes!" and darted forward.

Dennis's arm shot out as Marcie's hand stabbed into a pocket of his trousers. One large hand around her throat, he lifted her, studying her briefly as her eyes bugged out. In the darkness, Leeth saw Marcie's thumb scrabbling frantically at a small device she now held in her hand. Behind her, something heavy *clicked*, and then cold night winds tore at her as road noises flooded in.

Dennis shifted his weight, throwing Marcie to the side as if she weighed nothing, a sickening crack as she slammed into the wall and cried out, to slide bonelessly to the metal floor.

"*Marcie! No!*" Her friend's eyes met hers, smiling even as her body lay still from the neck down. "I rescued you," Marcie whispered – Leeth seeing the words as much as hearing them. *"Get away! Run!"*

But Mark Dennis loomed over her now, one heavy arm flashing towards her even as the other reached for the swinging door, to pull it shut.

Leeth dropped, diving between his legs and springing straight up again to shove backwards. Dennis overbalanced and flew from the truck, hands flailing. Grabbing at the small semi-trailer behind them, he landed instead on the connecting bar. One hand reached back towards them, large fingers locking solidly on the edge of the doorway.

Leeth stepped forward and kicked the fingers free, hard, hearing bones break. Amazingly, with just two fingers and his thumb, he held on.

She kicked again, even harder, breaking two more fingers.

Off-balance, Mark Dennis slid from the trailer bar, to hit the road at a hundred kilometers an hour. The entire time, his expression didn't change: his eyes stayed fixed on Leeth's, with no indication of surprise, or shock, or anger. Just watching, recording each moment, as he vanished into the night.

She heard the impact of his body on the road, and heard more bones break, hoping he'd fallen under the trailer's wheels. But it hadn't bounced. She listened for the sound of squealing brakes, or car horns... but again, there was just the rush of the wind and the thrum of the truck's tires on the road.

Spinning around, she raced to Marcie, who was lying still and broken on the bed of the truck. Her eyes were open, though her head was at an awful angle.

And she smiled at Leeth. "I did good, didn't I?"

Tears flooded Leeth's eyes. She tried to speak but couldn't; just couldn't. She nodded, taking Marcie's hand, squeezing it tight.

Marcie didn't squeeze back.

This is my fault. I should've realized he had the remote control. I should have been the one to see it, to grab it from him. Not Marcie. Not Marcie! I could have grabbed her, stopped her. Instead, I just froze. Like a total coward.

"Don't cry, Jane." Marcie's voice was just a whisper. "It doesn't hurt."

Leeth wanted to scream. Then went rigid. *Keepie! Keepie can Heal her!*

Ms Sorensen called out. "Does anyone have linkage? Anyone? We need an ambulance!"

One of the boys answered. "I got signal, but it's scrambled. There must be a jammer in here."

"If you get... up on roof... Jane, there'll be ID... painted on top," Marcie whispered. "Give that to the... authorities, they'll... take control... of truck. Drive it to... hospital. Wherever... you want."

Leeth nodded, through falling tears. "Oh, Marcie. You're *still* saving us all!"

Moving to the rear of the truck, with its doors still banging between half-open and shut, she grabbed the edge of one door as it swung nearer. Then kicked off her high heels and found a tiny toe-hold. *Mother and Father are going to just love this. Someone's sure to record it. At least it's dark.* For a second she paused. The climb looked... a little tricky. And if she slipped? Everyone else was still chained up.

Or paralyzed.

If she fell, they'd have to wait for some passing driver to report a truck with its doors banging open. It might take hours before anyone stopped them. It might not happen till after dawn. And above, the red light of the watching camera stared down at her.

I'll just have to be careful.

"What are you doing, you idiot?" shrieked Tara. "Unlock one of us, first, in case you fall!"

Leeth spun back around, gesturing at the small red LED above the rear doors. "See up there? That's a camera, watching. And we don't know if Mr Dennis was acting alone. They could be driving us towards a cliff, to dump us in the ocean. So just shut up, Tara. I won't fall."

She spun back around.

I hope.

Balancing on top, bracing herself against the buffeting wind, she read the ID and memorized it. Then stood blinking in the rushing night wind like a complete idiot.

Now what? What had she just achieved?

If she had her glasses, or her Link...

Jaw clenched, she very carefully moved to the back of the truck, crouching down to ride out the bumps and jolts. *No more mistakes, Leeth.*

She swung inside. Ignoring all the demands, she checked on Marcie. "Don't talk. I got the ID." She patted Marcie's hand and looked up. "Can anyone get a signal? I've memorized the truck's ID."

No one could.

"Okay. I'll have to climb back, and pull up someone who's got an implanted commlink."

Beth looked to be the lightest of all the people who raised their hands. But Tara was the loudest.

Leeth turned to her. "I guess I could *try*, Tara," she shrugged. "But you're not as small as Beth. So long as you know there's a good chance I might drop you, I'm happy to *try*."

But then it took minutes just to re-find the hairpin before she could even start picking Beth's lock.

At one a.m, escorted by police cars and eager news vehicles, the truck coasted to a stop outside the emergency bay of Saint Mary's Hospital, Reno. Men and women raced in, carefully easing Marcie onto a stretcher and into the hospital, while the Reno PD began unlocking people.

With no money, no link, and no idea how to contact the Department, the best Leeth could manage was to get one of the commlinked kids to call her Aunt Elizabeth, and then watch the shit fly.

The worst, though, was not being allowed in to see or speak to Marcie. All they said was 'her condition was stable.'

The *hardest* thing had been avoiding the media. Apparently the networks had been running a story, 'Dramatic End To Acting School,' about how everyone had burned to death in a millionaire's mansion. The blaze had started at eleven pm, the heat so intense that firefighters were only now entering the burned-out wreckage. Alert for more news, some clever soul, hearing of the mass kidnap, had done a little digging and put two and two together.

So at five a.m 'Aunt Elizabeth' arrived to collect Leeth, spiriting away the sought-after 'Plucky Teen in Rooftop Rescue.'

In the car, Leeth watched the headlights picking out cats-eyes on the highway as the vehicle drove itself. Emma leaned back in the driver's seat, eyes shut, like she was tired.

"Oh, Leeth," she said, finally.

Leeth snapped out of her daze. "Have you got a link I could use? I need Uncle to heal Marcie. You should've seen her, she was *so* brave-"

"Leeth, the Doctor will not be allowed to Heal Marcie."

"What? But he's gotta! She's lying there-"

"He will not be allowed to because it would be very newsworthy. Because people are suspicious of magical healing. Because he would need Marcie's father's consent. Because it would link Dr Harmon to you. Because it would start a cascading chain of events all leading toward disaster." She opened her eyes, and turned to the girl beside her. "Trust me on this, Leeth. You're in enough hot water as it is. The last thing you need right now is to be demon-strating you're so naive that you can't see you're proposing a course of action likely to expose Departmental secrets, *and* with as little chance of achieving what you want as winning the lottery."

"But Uncle *could* heal Marcie!"

"He is unlikely to be permitted to try. By the Depart-ment; by Marcie's family."

"But we could disguise him so no one knew who he was; and I'm sure I could convince Marcie's dad to let him heal her."

"And the news media coverage?" Emma shook her head. "It's simply too risky, Leeth. And how does it help the Department?"

"It helps *Marcie*. It's the right thing to do. And we're the good guys, so that's what we should do!"

Dear god, thought Emma. "Leeth... look, my advice is not to push for this. It's extremely unlikely to be approved, and probably unnecessary, too: vertebral nerve bundle re-connection is expensive, not difficult."

"You said 'extremely unlikely.' So it *might* be approved if I ask?"

Emma closed her eyes. "Leeth, at the very worst, she'll need a cyber spinal unit. They're effective in almost all cases. Not everything has to be solved with magic."

"Really? So you *promise* Marcie'll be alright?"

Emma nodded; praying she was right, but sure that she hadn't convinced Leeth.

CHAPTER 40

At eight a.m, Leeth stood wearily before Mother's desk.

"Well? How do you explain this?"

"Why do *I* have to explain it? *I* didn't kidnap the school!"

Mother raised her eyebrows. "You expect me to believe this *didn't* happen as a result of some action on your part? That you had nothing to do with it? You yourself told Emma that this Mark Dennis had been following *you*."

"Yeah, but I don't know *why*. How does that make it *my* fault?"

"Because you must have done something outlandish to attract his attention. Nor did you consider that he might be dangerous. Instead, you allowed yourself to be fooled by him. Checkbook estimates Mark Dennis spent two point eight million credits on this – not to mention the charges for destroying a ten million dollar mansion, when he's found. In my experience, when someone spends that amount of money to kidnap someone, there's usually a reason. A reason which the victim is well aware of." She waited.

Leeth shrugged. "Well, I got nothin'."

"Well, *I* have a hunch that somehow, you caused all this."

For a moment, Leeth had to fight the urge to tell Mother to go... *shunt* herself. *But I still have to ask them to get Uncle to heal Marcie.*

After a moment, she just nodded. "*Really*, Mother? *You* have a hunch?" She shrugged. "Well, it's important to pay attention to hunches. In that case, you're probably right."

Mother stared at her, and Leeth nodded again, encouragingly.

"Well?"

"Well what, Mother?"

"How do you think you set all this off?"

"I dunno."

"But you just agreed that my hunch was probably correct."

"Yeah. It probably is. I just don't know *how*."

Leeth heard Mother's teeth click against one another, then the faint sound of them grinding.

Sweet. She kept her expression innocent, though. She knew she shouldn't bait Mother, but she also knew, by now, they were never gonna be friends.

"So, anyway, you know how we've been making false IDs for me, for when I go on missions? Well, I was thinking, sometimes Uncle will need to go out too, right? So he should get a chance to build a proper cover-"

"The Doctor will *not* be permitted to attempt to Heal your friend. The Department is not a charitable organization. Our existence must be kept secret. We-"

"That's why we disguise him and make up a false identity. We can-"

"Do *not* interrupt!" Mother looked angry: angrier even than normal. "Do you have any idea of the level of media interest in this story? *Disguise* your Uncle?" She laughed. "Your Uncle is a recognized and respected researcher, not an obscure nobody. And the area of his research – unlocking magical potential – is an extremely active one, of enormously high value. If anyone ever links you and your unique abilities to *him*, every interested watching Power will assume he managed to make you Unfold – regardless of any *protestations* to the contrary."

"That's why we disguise him so no one recognizes him. And I go in as Jane, who has no magical-"

"No. It's out of the question. Can you not understand the Department must come first? Do you have *no* understanding of the stakes we play for? I begin to question your suitability."

"*Begin* to? You've *always* questioned it!"

"You always give me reasons to."

Do not punch Mother. Do not. "Look, if we disguise-"

"No. The subject is closed."

"Closed? How come *you* get to say the subject is closed? I'm going to ask Father!" Leeth spun on her heel.

"Leeth! I have not finished your debriefing! Leeth! Come back here! *Leeth!*"

Leeth couldn't quite believe it, when Father *agreed* with Mother.

"But it'd probably only take him a few minutes!"

"That's not the issue, Leeth. I understand: you want to help your friend. Commendable. But the chance for the operation going wrong is not low enough, and the risk-return is far too high. No."

When she managed to see Eagle, and put her case, he studied her in silence for perhaps a minute. She fought not to fidget.

"Did you *understand* what Mother and Father told you?" he asked, finally. "Even if you didn't agree with their logic?"

"Yes. But if we don't do what's *right*, what's the point in *anything* we do? Even if it does have a risk, or a big cost?"

He didn't say anything, but she thought he seemed pleased, and her hopes rocketed.

"Your logic is sound, Leeth. But in this case, I must agree with Mother and Father, and deny your request."

But the look he gave her, as her heart plunged and then hardened, was... odd. Like he wasn't just studying her. She had the feeling he was expecting her to *do* something, or say something.

Only she didn't know what.

For a while, neither spoke. He waited, patiently. In the end, she nodded, frowning, and left his room.

She met his eyes again, as the door slid shut. And tried again to read the message in them. Feeling her lips set in a grim line. Not quite believing that even *Eagle* now had let her down.

And strangely, in her final glimpse of his face, something in his expression solidified. Like he'd seen her reaction and was satisfied by it.

She stared, hard, at the closed door, her shoulders hunched and fists clenched. *Well, I'll show you! I'll show you all.*

Somehow.

Leeth's glasses were recovered, smashed alongside all the other communications devices in the boiled-dry fountain of the burned-out mansion. They were quietly switched with a simple audio-link pair, in case anyone ever performed a detailed forensic analysis.

Mark Dennis was not found, though a dead body was found later in a car parked near a clinic; where a man matching Dennis's description had paid an exorbitant sum for medical treatment for broken bones and other severe injuries on that same night.

And Nelson found that the Mark Dennis ID had been a very expensive, very good fake.

His motives for kidnapping the entire drama school, however, remained unclear. Photo-matching from his fake ID revealed him to be Marc Disten, a very wealthy stockbroker from New York, who had simply walked off the job the previous year. Some kind of nervous breakdown had been assumed. But no criminal record. Nor had Disten resurfaced, as yet. His assets were frozen and wanted notices placed, of course.

Even after the week of mental torture that was the writing of her report, in the end no one actually said whether she'd passed the exercise, or failed! But then, no one said anything about having to repeat it, either.

They let Leeth, with a faked farmhouse bedroom computer-rendered behind her, chat by vidlink to Marcie in her hospital bed.

Things were not going well. Apparently, the injury was more extensive, and more severe, than they'd expected, and Marcie for some reason was not responding properly to the treatments.

Marcie tried to smile. "Dad's arranging a cyber-specialist to come in and check me out for a bunch of nerve shunts. Maybe I'll end up being turned into robo girl. Maybe I'll get super powers? I'll ask Dad to get me some muscle augments at the same time. Then maybe I could throw men out of trucks like you did."

Leeth tried to smile. Knowing all too well that it had been *Marcie* who'd shown true bravery.

CHAPTER 41

Things settled back into their old routine. But the delight was gone: she wasn't even sure if she wanted to be here anymore. Wasn't sure the Department was what she'd thought it was. Wasn't even sure they were really the good guys.

The excitement, the *joy* she'd discovered in mixing with ordinary people, people her own age, seemed just an impossibly-bright dream.

And on top of the Marcie disaster, things were getting much, much worse.

This time it started in her uncle's class. Leeth was sure he was deliberately dragging the lesson out, just so she couldn't go to the pool before dinner. She could tell the other agents were only pretending to be interested. Who cared if the Japanese gesture of a hooked forefinger meant 'thief': someone hooking away your possessions? She didn't know any Japanese people, and at the rate things were going, she probably never would. They'd probably keep her locked up in this underground maze forever. Sterile rooms linked by sterile corridors, with fake 'daylight' lighting, and phony windows onto the real world.

Like the walls of this cramped training room, for example: virtual windows looking out across a darkly sparkling bay to Alcatraz. She wondered what it'd be like to swim those deep waters to the old prison. Cold, probably. Maybe a shark would attack her, and she could-

"Am I boring you, Leeth?"

She jumped, met her uncle's eyes: noted the superior smile. How she hated that smile.

"Not just me, Uncle."

His face went blank, as Preacher sniggered.

Her stomach roiled in instinctive dread – followed by anger at that cowardly reaction. The anger burned away the fear. *I'm not scared of you.*

His head slumped and one hand lifted to cover his mouth. From his own lessons on body language, she knew that meant he was struggling to bite back a response. She had to fight to keep her small surge of satisfaction from showing.

«Leeth: mode one.»

No! Hot glee chilled to ice at the scarcely-vocalized words. For several seconds she couldn't believe he'd done *that* to her right in front of the other agents.

She wanted to shout, to scream: tell them what he'd done. But just the *idea* of trying to do so sent her thoughts flying in all directions, dizzying her. She flailed in the mental trap, thoughts bouncing off walls she scarcely sensed. *Leeth, mode one.* Just words. Barely whispered words. Now he even had a way to use her special hearing against her. She latched onto the thought, chased it: would he one day find a way to use her sight against her, too? Hold up a sign in the dark for her alone to read: 'Leeth, mode one'?

Slowly, she climbed from the spinning mental pit, her reason steadying. *Could* written words do it? Maybe she should test that herself? No, that'd be stupid, since she could never remember the words he spoke to end it and return her to herself. She might wind up stuck.

She realized no one had spoken for a long time, and twisted around to James, then Emma. They looked uncomfortable, avoiding her eyes. What was the matter with them? Couldn't they *see* what he'd just done?

Oh. Remembering, she realized why her uncle had covered his mouth. It hadn't been to hold in words. He'd done it so his lips couldn't be read. Just in case they were being vidded.

Bastard.

Turning back round she froze as she caught his stare. A predator's gaze, now: sure of its prey. She braced herself, determined to resist, but knowing she couldn't. Surely, in front of the others, he wouldn't make her do things?

Please, not in front of the others.

"Leeth, Leeth, Leeth. What are we to do with you? Still treating all this," he gestured vaguely, "like a child's game. Still imagining we're all here just to entertain you."

He sighed. "Well, perhaps a child's punishment will drive the message home. Go and stand quietly in the corner."

Her thoughts churned into a gray muddle. When at last the confusion ebbed, she got determinedly to her feet and stalked to the corner.

"Face the wall."

Again the gray churning of her thoughts, but she fought it down and turned away from her uncle, away from James's and Emma's embarrassed faces, from Preacher's grin. She'd show them. She stared into the pixels of the dark waters rippling on the wall. Silent, resolved to stand there till they all died of old age.

That was how it had *started*: but it had been only the first act.

An hour later, the class on body language finished. With her face still turned stubbornly to the wall, Leeth heard Preacher leave and, more slowly, James. Finally Emma's footsteps moved hesitantly to the doorway, then stopped. "Doctor, shouldn't Leeth-?"

"There is no need to concern yourself, Agent Emma. We both know we can't have Leeth miss out on her training because of a childish outburst. Although listening to a lecture is not her preferred learning method, as she herself demonstrated. Best if I turn the lesson into a game – if she and I act out the gestures. Use role playing techniques."

Leeth's skin prickled. *Roleplay*. Alone, in his rooms. No!

Her determination to stand quietly facing the corner almost failed her, then. But The Rule kept her silent. *Never reveal what we do together, alone.* Frantically, she tried to find a way free. Maybe Emma would insist on staying, would sense-

Footsteps, leaving.

She squeezed her eyes shut, hard.

Behind her, she heard the faint rustle of her uncle's clothes as he turned. Facing her. Watching her. She could imagine the expression on his face: the coldly certain smile.

Slow, heavy seconds slunk past.

"Come, Leeth. We will continue the lesson in private. So you won't feel embarrassed should someone enter the classroom. Come."

Helplessly obedient, she spun and followed him from the room.

-

Six hours later: Leeth skipped happily, as instructed, down empty corridors, a smile which she couldn't seem to alter pasted to her face, and her hair tied up in two short pigtails.

Pigtails. They looked silly, childish. Yet somehow, she wanted them. And each time she considered removing them, or the ribbons, a gray fog swamped her thoughts.

It was after two in the morning, the recessed lights in the ceiling now off, only the glow from night-dimmed scenes lighting the walls. She paused to stare 'out' at a distant farmhouse nestling darkly at the foot of a hill, wishing she could escape through the wall and into that scene.

Escape, and rescue Marcie: save her. Save them both.

She was trying to draw the journey out, hoping someone might still be up, might wander by and ask questions; might be able to read something in her eyes or see through the false smile. But empty corridors swallowed each solitary silent step.

Perhaps she could simply call on James, or Emma. Emma was a woman, and smart. If Leeth woke her in the middle of the night and then couldn't answer the questions she'd be sure to ask-

Thoughts splintered, vanishing into the fog. She almost stumbled as her feet turned her from the wall, heading her back toward her quarters. She puzzled as she continued on. Hadn't she just been thinking... something? But skipping back to her rooms now singing a silly rhyme, the memory continued to elude her.

Reaching her door, she palmed it open. The instant she crossed the threshold the joyful mask vanished. Safe: here she was safe. It was only in *his* rooms that he-

She cut the thought off and leaned back against the protective barrier as it slid snugly shut behind her, plunging the interior into darkness. But all too soon the room reappeared in monochrome tones as her eyes adapted.

She sagged back against the door, her expression blank. Numb.

Her breasts still ached: the *cells* remembering. Even after the healing, the shocking pain lingered as an echo in the flesh.

One arm holding her own shoulder, her other arm clasping her waist, she hugged herself, imagining the arms around her were James's, or Emma's.

For long seconds she stared blankly across the room. Gradually, the accusing glares of the heroes in the *Demons-bane* image penetrated her awareness. The elven valkyrie Hildr stared at her accusingly.

She tried to stare back, but her lower lip trembled, and she had to drop her head in shame.

At least tonight he hadn't made her dress up in some humiliating child's costume. Or, as he sometimes preferred, half of one. Usually just the top half. So she couldn't pretend she'd simply opted for the freedom of going bare chested.

Dully, she unwrapped her arms from herself, lifting them before her, marveling at the once-more seamless skin. Still faintly damp from the shower he'd made her take to wash away the evidence: the blood.

Eyes unfocused, she remembered her own hand descending slowly toward her arm under his command; his words like dripping acid, scouring her soul. 'Self-mutilation is a terrible thing, Leeth. A clear sign of sick self-hatred. I had hoped you would be strong enough to resist....'

The words had drizzled on, and on: a cold leaching rain as the silken bite of her own fingertips carved-

Desperately, jaw clenching, she smashed down that memory, too.

Vision blurred as water welled in her lower eyelids, sinuses thickening. *Tears were for weaklings.* She fought them down. Water brimmed, blurring everything. She wouldn't blink. If she didn't blink, there'd be no tears.

She stood in the dark, fighting the flood, fighting her own body-

He'd caged her in her own body! Made her his puppet, his toy.

But one that fought every step of the way. Never co-operated. He'd had to command every act, every word. Every gesture.

Oh Keepie, every gesture! It made her realize: *Keepie* was dead. Gone. Instead, this monster had replaced him, swallowed him whole. And she didn't think there was anything she could do to get him back.

Sunk to her knees, he'd made her spread-

"No!" But then the breath she didn't know she'd been holding cracked her lips, escaping in one deep moan that drained the strength from her stomach, and legs, and she slid down the door to the carpet. In her mind, he stood over her still, staring at her. *Weak*, he sneered.

"No!" She screwed her eyes shut trying to block the memory, tears flinging from her shaking head. And then her nose joined the treacherous flood as her body flew from her command, again, only this time *he* hadn't ordered it, it was she herself, failing, *weakening-*

She tried to breathe, but her chest shuddered and spasmed, the breath juddering in as her own lungs now fought against her.

But even in this new betrayal by her body, a betrayal that shattered her control, *still* she struggled. She wanted to smash the floor, but didn't; wanted to collapse into a boneless puddle, but wouldn't.

She clamped her jaws to silence the *weak* little girl shrieking inside. She'd *never* give in, *never* give him the satisfaction of truly controlling her, controlling her true self.

Piece by piece, she locked away that small girl; sealed her up inside and turned away from her, to claw her way back toward normality. Her hands were shaking, she saw. She clenched her fists, but that only made it worse. Now all the muscles in her forearms stood out like they'd been carved.

Carved.... No! *Don't remember!*

Now her arms shook, too. But the harder she fought, the further it spread, until her whole body locked rigid.

Sometimes, Miss Leeth, the body knows better than the mind. Sometimes, you must let your body lead. Sometimes, one must let go. Dojo's cool words. But still she resisted, even as that control coiled the knots of agony tighter.

She didn't know what was happening: it felt like her own body was killing her. She fought even harder to stop it: and felt the agony twist still tighter.

Dojo's face glowed in her mind. Could she trust Sensei's advice? Trust her body? *Stop* fighting?

She had to.

She let go, as scared and exhilarated as if jumping from a high cliff.

The spasm of release brought an agony so terrible she thought she'd made a fatal mistake, even as she clung desperately to Dojo's words; a talisman of hope.

Panting, curled on her side, she only slowly realized it had ended. The pounding in her head, easing.

One arm was flung out over her head, her hand stabbed through the carpet, clutching it tight. Mourning the man who'd raised her? He *had* loved her, once, she knew. Had held her after she'd Pounced him, that night in his rooms. Caught her when she leapt from the trampoline. Let her snuggle up to him, after the first time they'd made love.

Or... *had* that been love-making, really?

Either way, that man was dead. And she had had enough.

CHAPTER 42

Emma stood outside the doors to the dojo, looking in through the perspex windows, frowning.

Inside, Dojo and Leeth faced one another. Neither moved. *What are they doing?*

Then Leeth's weight shifted. Something about Dojo's stance changed, and Leeth immediately froze. Then her shoulders moved fractionally, and Emma sensed the tension drain from Dojo.

He slid his left foot forward, Leeth accelerated into motion.... But Dojo swayed minutely and Leeth slowed, and stopped; hissing in frustration. Then turned, slightly.

An opening! Except Dojo apparently didn't agree. After a second Leeth smiled, her shoulders moving in the faintest shrug. As if to say, 'well, it was worth a try.' Emma frowned. *Had there been a trap there?*

Then Leeth began circling, her bare feet sliding lightly over the mats, a curious fluidity to the movement of her body as Dojo turned, and turned, facing her.

Emma had lost count of the number of times Dojo had given her his back yet *still* somehow sensed and dismantled her attacks, even when launched from behind him.

Apparently he no longer granted Leeth that same privilege. She wondered when *that* had changed.

Something about Leeth's movements seemed strangely familiar, too, and it was eating at her. Did she move like Dojo himself? A little... but there was an energetically springy bounce to it, a playful zest that didn't belong to Dojo. The sense that she danced on the balls of her feet. The sense of a coiled spring, eager to-

Holy mother!

Leeth blurred in, triggering Emma's own combat augmentations. With their assistance she half-comprehended the three way- no, four way- *five!* fold attack. Leeth spun in, left leg kicking out from the knee while her left *arm* struck high; right fist punching forward, her left arm tangling with Dojo's right, deflected but sliding back in again in a vicious elbow strike. Their bodies slammed together. Dojo's slightly-angled thigh turned aside Leeth's kick even as she pivoted, her right leg leaving the ground as she spun in the air, folding her knee forward to *slam* into Dojo's side.

But Dojo's forearms had slipped in as if to embrace her even as his forehead hammered into her nose.

The painfully loud crack echoed through the room and Leeth's body crashed bonelessly to the mat. Dojo staggered back, swaying slightly on his feet.

"Request Doctor to the dojo for Healing, please," Emma heard him say as she burst through the doors, forgetting for a moment she was still in combat mode. With a mental command, she eased down.

On the ground at their feet, Leeth lay unconscious. Dojo fell to his knees, took her pulse, and nodded.

He looked up into Emma's shocked face. And *grinned*.

"Miss Leeth is learning well," he nodded down at the girl once more, his expression shifting to a contented smile. Then he winced, and very gently probed his ribs, pulling up his gi to inspect it. The area was already purpling. Gracefully unfolding to his feet, he padded across the room to the cold chest for a chill-pad.

The Doctor's voice sounded from a speaker in the wall. "I'm on my way. How urgent?"

"Just the normal. She will live." The smile was still there as he pressed the cold compress against his side and added, "I too need a cracked rib healed."

"One minute."

From the satisfaction in those two words, it sounded Dojo wasn't the only one pleased by Leeth's progress.

Emma replayed her video capture of the attack, seeing little nuances in the slow motion exchange she'd missed the first time. *My god, I wouldn't want to go up against her anymore, hand to hand.*

The girl was deadly.

Some days there were small military training exercises. Mini war-games, commando-style training, mock hostage scenarios or security penetrations. They were exhausting, stressful, and punishing. Leeth relished them. Relished the relief; and the *pretense* of freedom.

Again and again she tried to convince Father or Mother to allow the Doctor to go and heal Marcie. The cybernetic implants were a little bit more painful than everyone had told her, Marcie had admitted to her by vidlink. *A lot more painful*, Leeth read.

Marcie had looked guilty, like she was letting *Jane* down through her inability to give good news. Trying to look like she wasn't being destroyed by the fear of the future that loomed for her.

Her uncle was willing to try, he said, but could do nothing without approval. *Of course.*

And she *still* hadn't found a way to convince Mother, or even Father.

She decided to concentrate on Father, asking him for extra training, hoping that by showing interest in his area of special expertise – modern hand-held heavy weaponry – she might shift him to her side.

She tried and tried. Even after the first, shocking time, when she'd spent most of the day half-deaf, certain she'd ruined herself. But her hearing *did* come back to normal.

Or after the second time, which had been *worse*: all sound had vanished at the first vibration from the explosion. Utterly deaf. She thought she'd gone truly, permanently deaf, and had fled the session in tears. Had even gone to her uncle's door, to stand panting – in eerie silence – poised to beg for healing.

And at that moment, with her hand raised to knock as she braced herself to go in, sound had finally returned. The shock of relief had been so intense she'd slid to the floor, and found herself crying. *Again.*

It had taken everything she'd had, to go back to Father and continue the training session. Afraid she was being stupid: that her recovery had been a one-off piece of luck. That she shouldn't push it.

But she *had* gone back. *Had* pushed through it. Even though the world had gone silent, again, at the first rocket burst. And stayed silent through the whole rest of the exercise. Even though she'd worn earplugs as well, underneath the muffling headphones that seemed to be enough for Father.

She'd broken down, again, alone in her rooms, when her hearing had returned a few minutes after the lesson had ended.

Amazed and glad; wondering if her ears somehow *learned. Clever old ears.*

But even after all that, Father *still* wouldn't listen to reason.

The fun was long gone. She could enjoy none of it, knowing Marcie was wasting away in her hospital bed. Knowing her uncle could heal her, if they'd just *let* him.

She *had* to find a way to make that happen.

So she suffered through Nelson's attempts to teach her computers – at least, until his patience snapped, each time. Which she kind of enjoyed, actually. It was nice to get some of her own back, since as far as she could see, he'd had no punishment at all for the time he'd spied on her and Uncle. So he hadn't been allowed to access the net for a day – so what? How was that even a punishment? But from the way he *still* moaned about it, you'd think he'd been tortured.

Though now, she wished she *hadn't* exposed him. At least then someone would know that... her thoughts began fogging out. Gritting her teeth, she forced the truth away.

But she *was* still learning a lot, here; useful skills she'd need. And she was doing well. Everyone seemed surprised by how hard she was trying, now, and how quickly she was learning. Though she'd overheard James tell Emma how her sessions with Mother on trend analysis, and with Checkbook on accounting, had been 'impressive failures.'

Huh. She'd thought they'd just been being kind, in stopping those lessons. She'd really, *really* tried hard to stay awake in them.

Her workouts continued unabated with Dojo, though she was now coming away from the sessions with worsening injuries. But the Doctor was always ready to heal her.

He'd then look at her, as if expecting her to smile and be grateful. But it was hard enough just to say 'please,' or 'thank you'.

A lot of their conversations now were in one word sentences. She was pleased that that seemed to bother him.

Something was definitely wrong with him, though. He looked tormented, more often than not.

Good.

Though maybe he still cared about her – *a little* – since it had been him who'd pointed out she was getting injured more often by Dojo *because* she was improving; pushing him beyond his comfort zone. *That* had been a huge relief.

But the rest of it....

'This is for your own good, Leeth,' he'd say.

She shook her head. She didn't understand how it could be. Or how he could even do it. She didn't know how she managed to keep quiet. But she'd vowed to herself she wouldn't let him make her cry out. Even if all the suites were so well sound-proofed that even *she* could only hear through them if she put her ear to the doors.

She'd given up trying to tell anyone what was happening. Every time she tried, she just looked like a broken thing. She flushed, remembering her first attempt.

She'd been in the Rec room, trying to *write* it down but only managing to scratch a few spearing lines into the paper. She'd just snapped the pen, and was still struggling back from the confused chaos in her head when Emma came in, and frowned down at her.

"Leeth? What's the matter?" Emma had sat beside her on the couch, putting one hand on her thigh, the other across her forehead.

Trying not to panic, not to rush, despite the humiliation of Emma finding her like that, she'd *eased* her thoughts free from the gray confusion. When she could think again, she found herself leaning in to Emma, and pulled away.

At first she'd said nothing; just remembered, cautiously, what she'd been trying to do... trying to write; to sneak up on the thoughts. She wet her lips. *Surely*, she could break his control?

She'd stared down at her hands. Her fingertips. "It's at night, he- I have...."

She shook her head, confused, and turned to meet Emma's concerned eyes. She saw Emma turning her words over, recognizing her anguish... beginning to put the pieces together! Excitement seared through her. But then she was pulling Emma's face to hers, plunging her tongue inside; a compulsion to interrupt and distract suddenly overpowering that excitement, twisting it instead into a fever of desperate need.

For a moment Emma froze, then pushed away, even as Leeth herself fought to remember why she found Emma so urgently desirable. Why she wanted to tear away their clothes.

Emma fled.

It wasn't until her pulse had returned to normal, till the strange scratches on the paper and the broken pen reminded her she'd been trying to write it down, that she'd remembered. And then worked out the Doctor had programmed in *yet another* layer of fail-safe. She'd almost cried, then.

She seemed to be crying a lot, these days.

With James, she'd tried more carefully, and just ended up making strange gubbling noises, her mouth opening and closing as she fought the fog.

Fighting it head on was not going to get her anywhere, she'd decided.

And if disturbing sounds sometimes whispered out into the corridor outside her uncle's suite, from the 'treatments' and 'exercises' in his rooms – well, she never showed any sign of ill use, did she? And she certainly couldn't voice any complaint.

She spent long hours jogging, once she'd discovered the programmable running surface in the small room annexed to the main gym. With VR goggles she could go almost anywhere in the world.

She'd danced through Piccadilly Circus at three am in the morning – the small room's air conditioners blasting her with chill gusts to match the real location's conditions – and run lonely through the bustling street markets of Marrakesh, ghost-like in the cheerful crowds. She'd slogged up high cold trails through tough-looking low scrub with tiny purple flowers in a place called Scotland, and anonymously joined a virtual marathon in the French Alps. That had been wonderful – the scenery and sound along the route recorded in high fidelity. Leeth lost herself in the illusion of mountain vistas and the leafy beauty of the sinuous alpine road.

That had gone badly wrong though, when suspicious calls from the other contestants for 'Runner Grrl's' equipment to be re-certified led to a backtrace intrusion attempt. Nelson's firewalls had stopped it, but drawn the Department's attention to her activity.

Mother had called her irresponsible; but why did the equipment have net access if it wasn't supposed to be used? That question led to a refresher course with Nelson on network and security basics. In the end though, she talked Father into upgrading the running surface to the same model the SAS used. And even got Nelson to upgrade it with an interactive multimedia feed, by innocently asking if that was beyond his abilities. So she was soon 'familiarizing herself with the local area' through live data from New Francisco's streets. Neutral buoyancy drones, still used in the apparently-unkillable reality TV shows, were still common enough to be a nuisance rather than an oddity.

Running through live streets, though, became strangely depressing. The combination of the Department's security requirements and privacy legislation meant she couldn't talk to anyone, couldn't jog her little drone into interesting shops or offices. She was like some spirit condemned to run the streets.

She liked the deserted places best. When she was alone, she could pretend she was real.

On her way to rescue Marcie.

And then she remembered that the Department had drone-mapped records of all the storm-water channels and sewer and train tunnels that had been ruined and fractured – or not – by The Big One. And begun studying in earnest.

Carefully noting closed-off entrances to underground tunnels. Especially, those near the Department.

CHAPTER 43

Emma and Preacher, once more between missions, were relaxing in the rec room. Emma in one of the soft, high-backed leather lounge chairs, had her attention focused on a newssheet – her 'Do not disturb' sign.

Preacher went to the wall behind her, switching it from opaque to check the deserted pool area. Keying it off again he slouched over to the billiard table, set up a few balls and played for a while. He soon abandoned that and began roaming the room, examining each of the oil paintings hung on the three wood-paneled walls.

He tossed himself down into one of the chairs opposite Emma and stared at her – which she also ignored. Finally, with a disgusted growl, he broke the silence.

"So how're things here now?"

Emma looked up, coolly polite. "Mother and Father are well. Eagle, as usual, isn't around. I only got back the day before yesterday myself."

"What about the others?"

She shrugged. "Dojo seems happy. I handed in my expense accounts to Checkbook, and he nodded and ignored me. So he's obviously happy, too.

"Little Brother's taught himself welding."

Preacher glared at her, but Emma just looked coolly back. They both knew who he was really asking about.

"So all right. How's our mage – and the girl?"

"Well, I don't see the Doctor very much, but I had Leeth for a session this evening. She seemed a bit frustrated, I thought."

"Lucky you," leered Preacher.

Emma blushed. "She kept asking what she had to do to show she was ready for a mission. I told her, just work hard."

Preacher snorted. "She's too young. I reckon they'll wait another year."

"She'd burst." *And sooner, rather than later.* Leeth had changed, since her friend Marcie had gone into hospital. Since things had not gone at all as Emma had promised her.

"So?"

She stared at the man, hard. "I really don't understand you, Preacher. Just what would it take for you to admit she's doing well? That she could be a real asset?"

"Prove it. On a real mission."

"Which you think is still a year away."

"Yah."

"But I just told you, I don't think she could bear to wait that long."

He sneered. "Gee. Too bad."

"I wish I knew what you've been working on for so long. It must really be very unpleasant." She lowered her reader to her lap and ordered the visual feed to route directly to her optic interface, leaning back and shutting her eyes to make it obvious she was virtually leaving the room.

Preacher threw himself down full-length on the leather sofa. He'd just gotten himself settled when a faint scuffing noise made him tense up.

"Preacher, have *you* seen Uncle?"

Raising his head he saw Leeth in the doorway, and relaxed again, stretching back out. "Nope."

She sighed tiredly, limping as she crossed the room to ease herself down opposite him in the seat along from Emma. *Even her drama school lessons were proving useful.* But she hid that thought.

She was dripping with sweat, and breathing hard. She also had a spectacular welt running from just above one knee to disappear beneath her faded denim shorts.

"Whoa – vish! How the chit'd you do that?"

"Oh, I've just been training, with Dojo. Uncle will fix it – only I can't find him."

"You *still* training with Dojo?" He looked across at Emma, and her closed eyes. "We'd all finished our course in six weeks."

Leeth shrugged. "I'm still learning stuff."

Preacher smiled. "I guess we can't all learn at the same pace." He didn't add that Nelson had also encoded much of Dojo's training into their chips.

"Anyway, Dojo said we couldn't continue till I was mended. So now I'm gonna have to wait." She eyed Preacher speculatively. "Unless *you'd* train with me, instead? Maybe you could teach me some stuff Dojo doesn't know? He said you know... *dirty* fighting?"

Preacher looked across at Emma, who must have shut her ears off too, since she'd ignored the entire exchange. A slow smile spread across his face as he looked back at the girl. "Well, maybe I could, maybe I could. Some tricks I've picked up on the streets, yeah. In real fights. I'm pretty busy, but I guess I could spare you fifteen." His eyes glittered.

"Really? Gee, thanks, Preacher, that's really nice of you!"

"Hey, it's just the kind of bod I am."

Five minutes later, Emma turned from the coffee machine at a groan from the doorway. "Good lord! What happened to you?"

Preacher ignored her. Limping painfully across the room to the small bar, holding his jaw and walking very carefully, he began scooping out crushed ice onto the towel over the bar top.

Leeth bounced in.

"Emma! Would *you* like to spar with me?"

Emma looked from her, to Preacher, then back to Leeth. Her eyes widened.

"Oh, Leeth-"

"Little *bitch*," muttered Preacher.

Leeth looked down at her feet to conceal her grin.

Emma was surprised by her own reaction to that. It seemed a long time since she'd last seen Leeth smile.

"Hey, I'll see if I can find Uncle. Okay? I still need him to fix this," she said, indicating the huge bruise on her upper thigh, "and he could do you, too." Then she was gone.

Preacher gathered up the corners of the towel and held it to his face. The breath hissed between his teeth. "Little bitch," he muttered, again.

As Harmon completed the healing, Preacher cleared his throat. "Mind if I ask you a quick question, Doc?"

"Of course."

"It's about your Practical Psychology course. Leeth seems to be finally starting to get into it at last, yeah?"

Harmon thought there *had* been an improvement in recent weeks – apparently Emma had spoken to her – but he simply nodded, wondering where Preacher was heading.

"Teaching her how to make other people like her, how to persuade people to do things she wants – she's picking it up really well, isn't she?"

Harmon allowed himself a small smile. "Beginning to, yes."

Preacher leaned forward. "Is there anything stopping her from using it here, on people inside the Department?"

Harmon looked as if he'd just been struck. "On *me*, you mean?" Suddenly, his expression was cold, even dangerous.

Preacher gestured airily. "No, not you, of course. Why would she try it on you? I meant us – the agents."

Harmon stared off into space. "Of course. How could it not be so? I should have seen this some time ago."

With a quiet smile, Preacher let himself out.

With the man gone, Harmon sighed, his expression abruptly changing. Was *that* supposed to be an example of subtle manipulation? He wondered what Leeth had done to Preacher to inspire the indirect attack. He *could* ask, but she'd probably have not the slightest clue.

Harmon closed his eyes, one hand massaging his forehead. How his horizons had shrunk! Dealing with mental pygmies – with one or two notable exceptions – trapped in a sterile, airless prison buried under living earth and Warded at the few exit points as strongly as the Institute had been; his research project almost halted, and his own talents wasted on healing brainwashed mercenaries or providing simplistic psychological analyses of uninteresting business leaders.

And all while the magical elephants in the room loomed over everything: the impossible creature that d'Artelle's death had spawned, and which had hunted Godsson for fourteen years. Until Leeth's intervention.

And that *other* creature, that Godsson had summoned? Or *created?* 'Robo,' Leeth had called it.

The existence of those things had implications for the entire theory of magic. Yet here he sat.

And Eagle's *other* peculiar demand, regarding the long-dead trillionaire, Feyborn, and what the Dragon Lord Emperor of China had said of her.

Yes, he and Eagle needed to speak. But not now; not while he and Leeth were still so very much on probation. No sense in rocking the boat just yet.

The *only* interesting work he had at present was that with Nelson on his brain modeling, and on Leeth herself.

With an effort he raised his head, opening his eyes to stare at the deceptive and distracting rural scene on the wall before him.... It would take him years to free the two of them from this trap.

They hadn't even allowed him to *try* to heal her young friend, who had risked everything for Leeth! He may well have failed, but they could at least have let him make the attempt.

It was far too late now, though. The human body's own inadequate systems would have healed over the injury, making the loss of function permanent.

As for the claim that he would have been recognized – he was hardly a high-profile researcher. The chance of him being identified even if *undisguised* was minute, and if disguised, with the Department's capabilities, no doubt impossible. He could have simply pretended to be a doctor. A Suggestion or two, the right air of arrogance and authority, and he would have been in. Or possibly just his hard-won Invisibility spell. No need to request permission, either. With Leeth to deal with any physical obstacles, they could have been in, and out, in ten minutes.

Will they ever let me outside? They assume I would flee: take Leeth and disappear. He and she together. And *what* a team they would make.

At least, since her friend Marcie's crippling, it was obvious that Leeth's rosy view of the Department had been destroyed. Even *she* now saw the trap they were in. Did they not see how they were eroding her trust?

Or was this some subtle ploy of Eagle's? A test of her loyalty, or perhaps of Leeth herself?

Knowing her as he did, however, her disenchantment was as much a cause for concern as celebration. But he would not warn them. Let them discover for themselves just what she was capable of.

His greatest fear, however, was that Leeth herself did not realize just how expendable she was, to the Department. Or perhaps she did, but simply accepted it as a fair price to pay.

But should she die – or, perhaps worse, be permanently maimed or crippled – Eagle would find the misuse of his ward came with the steepest price which could be paid.

Harmon would ensure that, even if it took the rest of his life.

CHAPTER 44

After his manipulative visit to the Doctor, Preacher moved on to Father.

"Hmph. Do you really think she's ready for this?" he asked.

Preacher lounged against the door, hands thrust into the pockets of his habitual black leather jeans, before slouching in to sit down. He shrugged.

"Sure. It's not like it's a mission. And I'll be there to take care of her. Dojo agreed it'd be a good test. Hell, he said to try her against two at once."

Father frowned. "Dojo said that?"

"Well, he agreed she's never had practical experience at fighting anyone other than him."

"And you, I believe?"

"Sure, sure," Preacher smiled. "That's how I know she's good enough to go up against a street scum or two in a FistFest. Chit, it'll be good background for her, too – meeting real street people, picking up some of the vocab. Should be a real lens-opener."

"And if you happen to make a little money on the side...."

"Hey, I'll be the one risking a loss if she loses, won't I? "Sides, it'd help my rep as a good judge of character – if she wins. 'Dad can scan "em,' they'll say."

Father sighed. "She has been somewhat, ah, distracting, lately. Using up enormous amounts of Dojo's time. And still coming up with new schemes that would allow the Doctor to attempt to Heal her friend Marcie – when she's not declaring her mission-readiness. She's almost as disruptive as when we tried training her to be alert for random attacks at all times."

"Funt! Heard about that: glad I missed most of it."

Though he wished he *had* been there when Mother had pulled the tissue from her jacket pocket during a briefing session. Apparently, Mother still had twinges from the pulled shoulder; and he sure would've enjoyed seeing Leeth injure herself while leaving the trail of wrecked desks in her wake. Emma said Leeth had been like a grenade with a five-millisecond fuse.

"It may interest you to know that Dojo suggested it was perhaps the sterile environment here that was the reason for her failure in the surprise-attacks exercise. That perhaps in a more natural setting, she would not be so over-sensitive."

Preacher stared at him. "More natural? Like, outside? Is he *nuts*? Drop her outside and tell her someone's hunting her? What size death toll are you planning on?"

Father nodded. "That was roughly my own assessment of the idea. So I take it, you think Leeth will perform adequately at this gladiatorial event?"

"Sure. Besides, it's not for six weeks, yet. She'll have plenty of time to study up for it, learn how to fit in. Might even be a good idea to toss her into the area before then, let her wander around a bit. Become known. You know."

Father watched him, but Preacher simply looked innocently back.

"Very well. But let us be quite clear on one point, Preacher: when the contest rolls around, I want you to back *only* Leeth in any betting."

Preacher's mouth opened, but Father's expression made him close it again. "Sure."

"One last thing. If she can convince your gang she'd be an asset, let her join. It would be excellent training for her."

"Doubt she's ready for that," Preacher shrugged, "but she can join if she impresses the crew." *Over my dead body*, he thought.

"Dismissed, then."

The man nodded, elbowed the touch panel, and sauntered out as the door slid open. As it shut behind him, Father negotiated a link-up to Mother, choosing 'visitor' mode to superimpose the vid feed from her office over the image of the just-vacated chair across his desk. Apart from the thin frame that labeled it a virtual scene, it looked just as if Mother were physically sitting there.

"Yes?"

"She's done it."

Mother's eyebrows raised. "Already? So it's now unanimous? *Preacher* has reversed his position?"

"Correct. Suggested he should slip her into an upcoming FistFest in his turf. Says she's ready, good experience, et cetera."

"Revenge?"

"Hrmph. Something shifty about the proposal, yes. Yes."

"He'll be trying to retire her."

"Expect so. Expect so. Still, can't make an omelet. Proper test."

"Don't let the Doctor attend."

"Wouldn't fit. Might dump Preacher's cover. Agreed."

"If *she's* retired, the Doctor will have to follow her into retirement."

"Hmph. Check with Eagle, but likely. Makes it a test for both, really."

"A little more final than Eagle had planned, when he told her that only Preacher's assessment was holding her from active assignment, don't you think?" Mother's smile held a vicious edge.

Father shook his head. "If you think that, Mother, then you still don't know Eagle."

They decided to change her hair color to blonde for the upcoming exercise, and her eyes to a vivid blue. Staring into the mirror at them made her feel odd. Like in losing her amber coloring, she'd lost part of herself.

Not that the Department cared.

It was the initial briefing for the upcoming Fist Fest exercise. Even though it was, like, six weeks away. More like six *years. Surely there couldn't be that much to learn about living in the Dumps?*

But she didn't say any of that aloud. Just stood, watching Father, and Mother as she *finally* got to the last item on the agenda. "Have you given any thought to the name for the 'young runaway' you'll be portraying, Leeth?"

Leeth brightened at the question: she'd put a lot of thought into it. "Yeah! I've been studying some of those real old 2D training movies for spying, and I thought of a perfect one: Honey Lick."

Mother and Father said nothing.

They simply sat, blinking.

It wasn't the reaction Leeth had expected.

«I'm not touching that,» Father messaged.

Mother, however, was made of sterner stuff. "Honey. Lick."

"Yeah, as in I'm sweet, and I'm good at licking *and* can also mean I'm good *to* lick!"

Mother stared at her, hard. Several times her lips moved. "No. Too obvious."

Leeth looked surprised, then pleased. "Thank you, Mother. I do *try* to dress well." She stood even straighter, which helped make her chest stick out.

Father messaged again. «Carry on, Mother: you're doing so well. Besides, cultural modalities are your area.»

«Is the girl *deliberately* trying to wind me up?»

"How about 'Kitty-'?"

"No, Leeth, I'll think we'll adopt the Doctor's suggestion, and let *them* name you. It will also help us garner their impression of you. Hopefully, indicating something more related to combat than to sexual skills."

"Oh." She frowned. "Yeah, good point. Oh – that reminds me: when do I get *my* license to kill? Are there some special tests I have to take?"

Leeth thought Mother's upper arms moved, slightly, like she was doing something with her hands, out of sight below the lustrous black desk.

«I think I've worked out what she meant by 'old training movies,'» Father offered.

«This is not funny, Father. The girl-»

«Sink or swim, Mother.»

Mother ground her teeth. "There is no such license, Leeth. You did understand those 'movies' were fiction, yes? Good. Any killing has consequences: it is why we have specifically instructed you, that unless-"

Leeth tuned her out. It was bad enough being treated like a baby. They didn't have to treat her like she couldn't remember, as well.

She'd learned, though, it was best just to nod and say "Yes, Mother."

Six weeks, though? Marcie couldn't wait six more weeks.

And she still hadn't come up with a way to save her. Her own gift, for Marcie.

Maybe it was time to just *do* something?

Anything.

CHAPTER 45

She hadn't even had to sneak out, in the end. She'd just asked if it might be a good idea for her to scout the areas around the fringes of the Dumps to get a feel for the place.

"Will you take the opportunity to go into the area?" Mother had asked, casually.

"No, Mother," she replied, honestly: seeing the trap. She glanced for a moment to Father. "I don't think that would be wise at this stage."

Mother had looked at her suspiciously, but after several more cautions, they'd given their permission.

She'd even done what she'd said she would, traveling along the fringes for an hour or two. Until she couldn't stand it any longer, and gone straight to Marcie's hospital.

"Everyone says you can regrow nerves. Why aren't *Marcie's* regrowing?"

Dr Ranatunga frowned. "How are you related to Miss Dunkirk?"

"Dunkirk? Oh. Marcie. She's my best friend. She was the one who saved us, on the truck. It should've been me, not Marcie, who got the controller from Mark Dennis. But I... froze. It should have been me." *If it had been me, Uncle would have already Healed me.*

When she looked up again, the doctor's expression had softened. "Well, I can't share details of Miss Dunkirk's case. But I can describe a hypothetical case, if you understand?"

It took her a second to work out what he was really saying, but when she did, she nodded eagerly.

"In general, the spinal nerve regeneration problem has been solved: we can reset the damaged cells to a juvenile state so they regrow instead of scar over. But in about three percent of cases, for reasons we don't fully understand yet, the cells refuse the instruction to reset."

He waited for her to absorb that.

"So... okay. But... I heard that even when *that* doesn't work, you can implant cyberware to, you know, connect stuff together. If you can't heal her, why can't you do that? Her Dad's pretty rich, right?"

The doctor sighed. "Money is not the issue. Now – again speaking hypothetically – for digital neural connections, the procedure is more successful the simpler the injury. In cases where the root injury is at the brain-stem itself, the success rate is lower; as is the degree of function that's restored. And in a few, rare cases, the patient's body reacts badly to the implant materials."

Leeth went very still. "And that's it. That's the best you can do."

For some reason, Dr Ranatunga took a step back.

"What about magic? If a mage who was good at Healing came?"

"*Magic?*" He shook his head, his expression disdainful. "This is very delicate neural surgery. It's not like healing cuts or broken bones, Miss Baker."

"Oh?" She stepped forward, and poked him in the chest. "What about if the mage was someone who could mend a heart that'd been cut in two, at the same time as healing a sliced-up lung? Someone who could heal a cyborg dog who'd been blown up by her own rockets? How about *then?* Are you saying even a mage like *that* couldn't heal Marcie?"

The doctor no longer looked either disdainful, or so sure of himself. He looked shocked, if anything. "Even if we could entice one of the so-called 'elite healers' to-"

But she'd heard enough to recognize a 'No' now when she heard it. With a last glare, she spun on her heels and ran from the room.

It was lucky that Marcie's father had been in her room. It had given Leeth time to stop, and remember her eye color had been changed, for the stupid FistFest. She didn't want to explain how they'd changed from green to blue. Or her newly-blonde hair, either.

Stupid blue eyes. Stupid blonde hair.

Sunglasses!

Returning from the hospital gift shop with cap and sunglasses, she slumped in a chair at the end of the hallway, listening until Mr Dunkirk left, and then slipped in.

"Jane!" Marcie's eyes turned toward her, and her eyes lit up. "Why the sunglasses? And have you dyed your hair *blonde?*"

"Uh. My eyes are, they're sore. The light hurts them. And the glasses remind me not to rub them, too."

For a while they chatted, while Leeth noted Marcie's unmoving arms. The weight she had already lost. The sadness she tried to hide.

And Marcie noticed her noticing, and tried to cheer *her* up!

"Jane, don't worry. Remember Hope. There's always hope, right? Hope's indestructible."

But at the tears that welled up in Marcie's eyes when she spoke the lie, it all got too much. She had to do *something!* Not just sit here, holding Marcie's limp hand. Useless.

She patted Marcie's. "It'll be alright. I'll think of something."

Marcie looked at her kindly. "It's okay, Jane. They have rigs you can operate just with brainwaves. A few months of training, and I'll be walking around in a powered exo-" she hiccuped, a drowning look entering her eyes; but she forced the words out anyway. "Exo-skeleton. Like a r- real robo-girl." She even smiled.

Leeth didn't understand how she could be so brave. If it was her, paralyzed from the neck down.... She shook her head.

But even so, Leeth could see in Marcie's eyes the words unsaid. The knowledge of the life lost: dresses, dancing; boys. The understanding that she would truly become an object of curiosity. A freak.

And Marcie saw how it tore at *her*, and tried again to muster the energy to cheer *her* up!

Begging excuses, once again a coward, she fled.

Back in her room, she paced. What was the point of anything? Marcie was never going to walk again, and it was all her fault. Nobody listened to her, nobody wanted to help Marcie. *Which made no sense. Aren't we supposed to be the good guys?* She wasn't so sure anymore.

And how could they not know what her uncle was doing to *her*? Weren't they supposed to be, like, super-observant? Some spies *they* were!

She was never going to be able to get away from her uncle, from his torture and control.

And she was trying so hard, doing her best, but getting nowhere, achieving exactly nothing. *What's the point in even trying anymore? I can't do anything for Marcie. I can't even do anything for myself! I'll never be my own person again. Just Uncle's slave. And there's nothing I can do about it.*

There's no hope.

And then she saw it, there in pride of place among all the others on her wall: the red and yellow on blue poster practically glowing at her.

That Marcie had given her. It was like she was speaking to her, right now. 'The "S" stands for "Hope",' Marcie had said. 'Hope is indestructible.'

And it really was that simple, she realized. There *was* hope. There was *always* hope, just like Marcie said. Just like Dojo said.

I can *do something.*

I have *to.*

Unseeing, Leeth was scarcely aware of the door opening – seeing only Marcie's tear-filled eyes as she'd explained how her body was rejecting the cyber implants.

She blinked. Her uncle was looking at her from behind his desk. "Well? What is it now, Leeth?"

"I need you to heal Marcie."

"Again with this? I assure you, Marcie is in the best-"

"They can't fix her."

"What?"

"I spoke to her doctor."

"Leeth, I am sure you thought you spoke to *a* doctor-"

"I went to the hospital and spoke face to face with Dr Ranatunga."

She explained what he'd said, and watched her uncle's expression shift from disbelief to surprise; before finally going blank.

"I see. And I am sorry to hear that. But Leeth, if you think I can Heal her – it's... not possible. The nerve tissue will already have scarred over – as far as her body is concerned, the healing has finished."

Leeth stared at him. "You're saying if you could've Healed her in the first few days, while the injury was fresh, she'd be okay? You could've done it?"

He didn't answer her right away. She watched him consider her question.

At last he met her eyes. "Yes. I'm sorry to admit it, but given the... extensive opportunities you have provided for me to sharpen my understanding of healing the human body, I probably could have. But it has simply been too long, now.

"I *did* try to get-"

"What if her injury got fresh again?"

"Eh? How...?"

She saw his eyes widen in disbelief as he stared at her. Saw his hand begin that twitching motion – and she threw herself across his desk and pinned his hand to the table.

Her other hand, poised over his heart.

"Don't you dare. Don't. You. Dare."

He opened his mouth.

Her fingers twitched, and he froze at the prick of invisible blades. "No! Not that either."

He stopped. And then, smiled. But it wasn't a nice smile. More like *he* was the one in control. His lips parted, and shock shot through her. He was about to say it. Did he think she wouldn't kill him?

Time slowed down. This was Keepie.

No. Keepie was gone.

"Leeth-"

If she killed him, she'd never save Marcie.

If she didn't stop him *speaking*, she'd be lost, and so would Marcie.

Kill him. Work something out later. She thrust-

"-Mo-"

Her arm didn't move. She tried again. It was like she was paralyzed. What was *wrong* with her?

You may not kill any of them.

No! She tried *again* to stab her hand down into her uncle's heart; but again, her arm locked rigid.

"-ode-"

No!

"-w-"

Her fist slammed into the side of his head. She clung to the edge of sanity as the word 'one' died on his lips, and he fell forward onto his desk.

She stood, heart racing, breathing hard, like she'd run a race. Gradually, the panic faded. *I can't kill* any *of them – including Uncle.* She stared in dismay from her hand, to her uncle.

Now what do I do? When he wakes up....

But slowly, a smiled formed. *He made the Department turn off the cameras in our rooms!* She looked around, her eyes lighting up as she considered the situation.

And payback.

He groaned as he came round, and she saw him stiffen, the moment before he cried out: "Eeh! Oh uhn. Ohh! Uhn!"

She couldn't keep the delight from her face. "Sorry, Uncle, I can't understand a word you're saying. Not with that gag in your mouth."

His arms jerked, and the fury in his face deepened. His arms banged tight in the cuffs binding his arms to the chair.

But very quickly, that anger washed from his expression and he relaxed, looking quite calm. Though his eyes *burned* into hers. Promising her she would regret this.

Despite herself, a shiver of dread ran through her. But she kept the smile on her face.

"That's better. I just want to ask a few questions, Uncle. Okay? Just 'yes-no' questions."

His eyes narrowed.

"Okay. First: you can't help. Right?"

He nodded. Once.

"And the Department won't *ever* agree to let you try, will they?"

She could see him thinking; could see him resolving to 'teach' her a lesson for all this; but in the end he answered: he shook his head.

"You think you're safe, Uncle, even now, don't you? Because you 'programmed' me so I can't kill anyone here – including you."

She saw she was right.

"But look at your left wrist."

She saw understanding dawn in his face even before he rotated his arm and look down. It must have been stinging.

Down his wrist, four very shallow, very sharp lines scored his skin. He looked up into her eyes.

"That's right, Doctor. I can't kill you, but I *can* hurt you." Using his official 'name' felt horrid, yet at the same time somehow satisfying. And she saw something change in him, too, at her use of it.

For a moment, then, she wanted to cry. Like she'd just killed a part of him. A part of *them*.

She pushed the feeling down. She *had* planned to threaten him some more: something like 'not wanting to find out just how much she could hurt him.' But suddenly, she couldn't bring herself to even *pretend* she was happy about any of this any more.

Instead, she just said "Sorry, Uncle," and carefully slammed her fist into the side of his head again. He fell forward once more onto his desk. But instead of the satisfaction she'd expected to feel, she felt even worse.

It took a while before she realized she was hunching forward, clenching her hands together, wringing them. Like a baby.

She forced them apart, and straightened.

Pressing her lips close-shut, she considered her next steps. Now, she had to get them both out of the Department.

Maybe I should have planned this out, first. She shrugged. No time like the present. For a while she stood, chewing her lip, thinking.

Then nodded. Determined. She'd only need a few things.

Just so long as they were still allowing her to come and go as part of her studies into the Hunters Point Dumps....

CHAPTER 46

Dojo was in his room when the channel to Father opened.

"Dojo. We have a problem with Leeth. Take care of it. Nelson is currently tracking her – she's en route to the level seven exit, with the Doctor in a wheelchair. From the medical bay logs, we believe she has administered a sedative to him, and is attempting to flee."

"Why?"

"Unclear. No doubt the Doctor will be able to tell us when he revives."

"I am on my way."

Dojo jogged to the lifts; then frowned, and took the stairs down to sub-basement seven. "Can she exit the complex?" he asked Father.

"No. We assume she is unaware her permission has just been rescinded. Bring her to lock-down two. Avoid killing her."

"Are you sure she cannot exit?"

"Quite sure. We'll be observing, on camera. Do you need assistance? Only Little Brother is available, but I can send him along with tasers or tranqs."

"That will not be necessary."

-

Leeth skidded around the last corner, almost tipping her uncle from the chair. She had to act fast – speed was her only chance, since she still hadn't worked out any way to bypass the Department's security. She just had to hope they hadn't noticed anything yet.

The exit raced toward them; at the last moment, she clamped hard on the wheelchair's brakes, bracing her uncle as the wheels locked, leaving two trails of rubber on the polished concrete floor.

Hauling him up from the chair, she shrugged him over one shoulder, put her eye to the scanner, and pressed the Open button.

She heard the ultrasonics of a camera focusing.

And the exit did not open.

No!

She eyed the door. The hinges. Solid. Strong. Steel.

In the distance, the sound of sure footfalls, rapidly approaching.

Dojo.

Briefly, she closed her eyes. Then dumped her uncle back in the chair and turned to face the end of the corridor. The camera chirped again, and she looked up, straight at where it lay concealed in the ceiling. At Nelson, no doubt, watching.

She smiled. One leap, one vicious stab of slicing fingers, and she punched through the covering, felt the crunch and crackle of the spycam's death, and landed lightly, anger rising.

Waiting.

"Miss Leeth."

"Sensei." She bowed.

"I have been instructed to bring you back."

She shook her head. "I need you to let me and the Doctor out."

"Miss Leeth. Leeth. There is no need for you to escape. You are doing well. Return with me and explain your actions." He stopped; puzzled by the surprised smile that had blossomed as he spoke.

"No."

He inclined his head. "Then I will bring you back."

"No, sensei. You won't."

If Dojo had found Leeth focused during training, today she had stepped beyond herself. And he saw: in her face, in every sure movement – not fear or desperation driving her, but certainty and determination. *She does not* escape, he realized. *She runs* toward *something*.

Then Dojo stepped forward and stopped thinking; forced, as a few times before by Leeth, to enter that state in which the fighter ceases to exist, and becomes the fight.

And as they *flowed* together, he realized his student had entered the same state, already.

He struck for her head: a hard, fast palm strike to end her challenge before it started. But her neck rolled to one side, her body sliding to his left, and a powerful tap to his elbow smoothly deflected the blow. She twisted in closer, avoiding his following knee strike while a slender arm blocked the elbow that would have broken her collarbone.

A series of one-two shots slammed in return at his chest, impossibly fast, but he'd read the tension in her arms and managed to interpose his own, though shocked anew by the forces he parried.

In staccato succession then, knee, elbow, palm, and wrist strikes followed, on both sides; the exchange of attacks and counters rising in a crescendo of violence. Each onslaught met in turn by impeccable defense.

Leeth fought with controlled ferocity, her lips peeled back in joy, delighting in the symphony they wove with their limbs. Close together now, bodies touching, each read the other's intent as it formed; each shifted instinctively to fit the answering move into their deadly contest.

Together, they soared. Spinning and striking in a duet danced on a cliff's edge, where one misstep spelled doom.

Leeth fought with a hunger for this confrontation that bordered on the psychotic. Time and again he hammered blows into her that rocked her. They pounded into one another, every time they dared trade defense for offense. But each blow only steeled her; intensified her answering blow.

Thirty seconds. And Paul Kawatsu sensed Leeth lose herself utterly as she soared higher, unleashing a whirlwind of attacks inhuman in their speed and force. From all directions, unrelenting. *Accelerating.*

He blocked, and blocked, and blocked, but the tornado rose higher; and his stamina, unlike hers, had its limits.

Seeing his vulnerability, she *exploded* in a torrent of attacks impossible to withstand.

His head rocked back and he stilled. Leeth paused, alert.

Slowly, like the collapse of a mighty tower, Dojo folded to his knees, somehow holding her eyes as he fell. His own rolled back in his head, and he slumped to the ground, unconscious.

But with a smile on his lips.

Chest heaving, Leeth collapsed forward, hands braced on knees, gulping air. *Yes!*

She heard lighter footsteps approaching – *Little Brother*. But already, she was hauling her teacher to the scanner to peel back one eyelid.

CHAPTER 47

"What do you mean, Dojo is *down?*" Father demanded. "Where is Leeth?"

Little Brother looked helplessly around the empty corridor, his weapons re-holstered, checking Dojo's pulse. "Well... gone."

Nelson interrupted. «I've got her, she's out on the street- *Shit!* The little bitch just prised open a drain cover. She's folding up the wheelchair... dropping it in. Huh! She just grabbed the Doc and jumped down with him. Hang on, let me shift to another cam....» There was a silence, then a breath that sounded somehow disbelieving. «She just frickin' reached up and dragged the steel grate back into place, one-handed! I've lost her.»

«Then get a drone down there stat, Nelson! She won't be able to travel fast, hauling the Doctor and that chair.»

Three minutes later, Mother, Father, and Nelson were treated to the sight of Leeth plucking the small drone from the air to glare directly at them, before stabbing it with her fingers.

Father swore.

-

Of course, travel through the underground by-ways held its own risks. But nothing was going to stop her now.

Nothing.

Half the time, she had to fold up the wheelchair and lug it as well as her uncle through the difficult sections. That was annoying enough.

But then there were the *other* risks: the people who lived down here. Of course with her senses, none of them could sneak up on her. They *were* slowing her down, though.

"*You* don't want to hurt *us?*"

In the dimly-lit tunnel, the man turned to his grubby cohorts, harsh laughter rolling and echoing around her. As if she'd said something *hilarious*.

"Think you got that backwards, sliv."

She frowned, studying the rag-tag crew blocking her route. Thinking. *I still have to get into the hospital. I should've brought a change of clothes....*

Jugular, she decided, *for the one in front. Spin him down to set me up to gut the ogre....*

Yeah.

"Reckon me and-"

Blood arced as her fingers swept his throat. Her other hand grabbed his shoulder, shoving him aside, directing the arterial spray. But the ogre was already moving, faster than she'd expected. She had to angle her next strike diagonally up across his belly as she dived past, and barely avoided the spray of gore.

Crashing into the two drug-ruined human rats behind him, she broke the arm of one who was drawing a gun she hadn't seen. Plucking it from his hand, she hammered it into the head of the other.

She stepped delicately back over the corpses to her uncle's body and the folded up wheelchair.

"Sorry," she said, waving the gun at the remaining group. "Look, maybe we should start again. Like I said, I don't *want* to hurt any of you, but we *need* to get past. It's real important."

Properly introduced, they were much more polite.

-

Inside the hospital, floppy hats pulled down over their heads, Leeth spent a frustrating ten minutes tracking down Dr Ranatunga, wheeling her still-unconscious uncle up and down corridors and in and out of lifts, tracking him on his rounds.

When she finally heard his voice, she pulled the stocking down over her head, tugged the broad-brimmed floppy hat down to cover it, and wheeled her uncle over to the bedside.

"Sorry. This man needs your help, Doctor. It's a matter of life and death."

She got him halfway to Marcie's room before people started being *really* difficult.

Right.

Tossing away the stupid hat, then, she got serious. From that point, a trail of unconscious orderlies and security guards marked her path to her friend's room.

Marcie was deep asleep. Exhausted, or maybe unconscious. She looked *awful.*

Still dragging Dr Ranatunga with her by one hand, with her other she administered the antidote to her uncle. Then slapped him awake and pushed his chair to the side of the bed.

Leeth felt terrified. *What if this didn't work?*

"Where's her injury? Show me! Where's the scar tissue? *Exactly.*"

"Who are you? This girl is sick, she needs-"

Ranatunga stared at her. The girl ignored him, looking up and past him as if she'd heard something from the corridor. She strode to the door just as it slammed open and two guards with tasers appeared. The girl whirled between them, fists and feet flying, bouncing slightly as she turned.

He blinked. Somehow, both guards were falling to the ground behind her.

She continued speaking as if nothing had happened. "I need you to cut the scar tissue, so she can be magically healed."

"You're insane." He glanced at the older white male, struggling with wrists bound to the wheelchair he'd been tied into. The man's face was obscured by a large floppy hat. "Insane."

A small hand like a vise took Ranatunga by the chin, and he found himself dragged over to the girl in the bed. "The spine goes up in the back of the head, right?" She released him, gently easing the girl onto her side, exposing the back of her neck.

Ranatunga was nearly to the door when something like steel grabbed him by the wrist, almost dislocating his shoulder as he was hauled back to the bed. She bent to the wheelchair, removing a case from a side pocket, and opened it one-handed to reveal a set of surgical implements. "I need you to cut the scar tissue. I don't have much time!"

"No."

The man in the wheelchair still struggled, dislodging the floppy hat that had been pulled down over his face. Ice ran down the surgeon's spine. The man was gagged with some kind of red ball. Some kind of fetish device. His face was painted in crazy camouflage patterns, and his features too were compressed by a nylon stocking.

"Quite, quite, insane," he breathed.

Stunned, he watched the girl take a scalpel, squirt disinfectant on it, and thrust it at him. Behind her, the man made wild eyes at him.

"Cut. The scar. Tissue." Her voice cracked, and he saw she was crying.

"No. Never. That would cripple her. Probably kill her."

"She's *already* crippled!"

"No."

"All right. Just show me. Point to the area where you'd have to make a cut, to re-injure her in the same place."

"No."

The scalpel pressed directly, *exactly*, over his heart.

"If you don't point for me, you're no use to me." She thrust one hand out towards the wild-eyed bound man. "*That* is an expert healer. And if you tell us where the withered nerve endings are, and if the injury is fresh, he can heal them." *I hope!* "We are going to do this, now. With or without your help. If you care about Marcie, you'll tell us where to cut. And if you *don't* care about Marcie, then you don't deserve to live. I'm doing this, one way or the other. So: *where do I cut!*"

She's terrified too, he saw. But utterly determined. And the expression on the man in the chair? Shocked, but resigned. *Not denying her claims.* Perhaps he *was* a mage?

Shakily, Ranatunga indicated the location, even as he shook his head. "The area is small: a centimeter across, twenty-three millimeters in. But you can't. You mustn't. You'll cripple her; more likely, kill her!"

A horrified expression on her face, she touched the spot he'd indicated and a tiny slice appeared, as if by magic. A faint red seam.

"Down exactly there, right?" she asked, turning to him. Indicated a distance with her finger and thumb. "About so deep?"

He nodded, jerkily.

Ranatunga watched her spin to the man in the wheel-chair. The scalpel flashed four times, freeing his arms and legs. She hauled him onto his feet by his shirt-front and growled up at him. "This is Marcie Dunkirk. Guess what's going to happen to *you* if she doesn't walk out of here in the next few minutes?"

His hand moved, but she locked his wrist before it had risen halfway to the gag.

"Don't bother. It's one of yours. And I have the key."

Releasing him to dart to the bed, she slowed, and carefully rolled the girl over. Then propped the pillow under Marcie's chest, arching the back of her exposed neck.

Leeth looked down at her best friend in the world, calling the tingle into her hands, terrified yet certain. And stabbed down with one fingertip, projecting the force down through the tiny surface incision she'd used to mark the spot. Held her finger dead still. Then twitched it, once.

Blood flowed, Marcie jerked, and Leeth heard Dr Ranatunga gasp. She spun to her uncle, quailing at the horror she saw in his face even through the distortion of the stocking.

"Now heal her."

"You're insane," whispered Ranatunga.

The gagged man's eyes never left the young woman – who had to be the same intense young woman from this morning. The man gestured to his mouth; to the gag. His hooded eyes burning.

"Oh, no. I know you don't need to speak to do this spell. Now heal her. *Heal her!*"

Suddenly, with a stricken expression, she spun to the door to the room.

Which thrust open, seconds later.

And Marcie's father stormed into the room. With her younger sister, Amanda, behind him.

CHAPTER 48

The bunch of flowers fell from Graham Dunkirk's hands, slapping down on the floor in a sudden silence.

"What the *fook* is going on here?" he growled, the dusting of pie crumbs on his shirt an incongruous detail as he stood, fists clenched. He took a step forward, trying to understand what he was seeing.

"I leave me daughter for *ten fookin' minutes* and the whole hospital goes mad? What's going on here?"

"*Jane?*" whispered Amanda. "What are you *doing?*"

"I'm not Jane. But I *am* a friend. And we're healing her. Right now. Marcie will walk out of this hospital today, or we'll die, trying."

"*Jane?*" Amanda still stared at her.

Marcie's father took another step forward, but his youngest daughter locked her two hands on his. "Da, no. *Wait.*"

He stilled.

Harmon met the man's eyes; then his daughter's; then moved to Leeth's friend and cast the spell.

The room fell silent as he let the magic and his Imaginal sight study the damage. Both the extensive scar tissue left by the body's correct but wholly inadequate response to that damage, and Leeth's fresh injury.

He shook his head. Shifting his sight back to the physical world, he met Leeth's eyes, and indicated another place, higher on the neck. Made a cutting gesture. Held up two fingers. Then took Leeth's hand, holding her forefinger like a pen – or a scalpel blade. And his eyes burned into hers.

Her own eyes widened as she understood what he meant, and summoned her *sharpness* again. Then held up her other hand, thumb and finger moving together, then apart: *how deep?*

He indicated the required distance, and saw her nod her understanding. Shifting his senses back to the Imaginal, now *seeing* the invisible blade for the first time, he was stunned for a moment by its deadly beauty.

Then, guiding her unresisting finger, he began to cut.

Three more times he sliced; tiny incisions. Marveling each time at the perfection of the cuts. Finally, he pulled her hand back and released it, ignoring her as he sank his spell into the paralyzed girl on the bed.

He began coaxing the nerves to grow, to seek out their matching ends, and reconnect.

Dr Ranatunga watched, half in disbelief, half in awe. Wanting to flee, as he so easily could, but determined to stay. To do what he could for his patient after these mad two ruined her.

Beside him, hope *shone* from the meaty, sandy-haired man, and the girl's younger sister; in the way the father's hands clutched tenderly at his daughter's slender shoulders; in the way her own small hands lifted in return to press against her father's, reassuring him.

Trusting the mad girl.

Jane, she'd called her. So it *was* Jane Baker, the intense friend who'd demanded to speak to him earlier today, before storming out.

On the bed, he saw Marcie Dunkirk's left finger twitch.

Good god! Was it actually working?

The father and sister tensed, seeing the movement at the same instant as him. Both of them drawing in their breath, and holding it. He went to a cupboard. If it *did* somehow work, he should be ready with an antagonist to reverse his patient's sedation. *How lucky she'd had a night of pain, and had needed it.*

Even through the mage's nylon-distorted and camouflaged features, he sensed the man's expression take on a kind of avid fire, an intensity of purpose, exultant. He could imagine arcane potencies *demanding* the regenerative responses lost within the cells' genetic codes.

More fingers twitched. Marcie Dunkirk's legs spasmed.

And with a cry of satisfaction clear even through the gag, the man stood up and stepped away.

"You *did* it, Keepie! *You did it!*"

She flung herself onto the man while Ranatunga hurried forward before Graham or Amanda Dunkirk could move his patient, possibly undoing the miraculous feat. "Wait." He hurried forward, and applied the patch.

Around the room, everyone stood, watching, waiting for it to take effect. Jane Baker suddenly released the mage and stepped away.

In her bed, Marcie Dunkirk groaned and rolled over. Her eyes met Leeth's, through the distorting nylon gauze. "Jane?"

She sat up, while her family and Dr Ranatunga watched in disbelief. As Marcie herself froze in amazement at what she'd just done. Then moved one arm, weakly, dragging the bed-sheet off with effort.

Tears of joy streaming down her face, her eyes locked back on those of her friend, Jane, not understanding her strange disguise, but not really questioning it, either. Taking in the tears running down Jane's face, the *delight*.

Though behind that, a dawning fear?

It wasn't until her shaky legs touched the floor that her family dared to move, her father swooping in to engulf her in a bear hug and Amanda slamming into the two like a small rocket of love.

"You were right, Marcie," Leeth whispered. "Hope *is* indestructible."

And loudspeakers blared from outside the building. "Attention! The hospital is surrounded! To the woman who has abducted Dr Ranatunga, release him and come out peacefully, hands in plain view."

CHAPTER 49

"I don't believe this." Mother glared at Eagle, who sat, quite relaxed, attentive to the confusion of news reports projected into the air.

The entire Department had gathered in the little-used boardroom, and Nelson now selected one floating news-frame, sweeping it larger and increasing its volume.

"This is Nina Summers, Kroneco News, outside New Francisco's Sisters of Mercy hospital, where a drug-crazed young woman has taken control of an entire wing. Sources inside the hospital report that she has abducted the hospital's leading cerebra-spinal surgeon, Dr Jay Ranatunga. We understand the woman has forced Dr Ranatunga to take her to the suite where young Marcie Dunkirk, innocent victim of last month's dramatic mass abduction, now lies helpless and paralyzed. The fear is that this madwoman plans to force Dr Ranatunga to operate..."

At that moment, a man, face covered by a large floppy hat and strapped into a wheelchair, was pushed out the side entrance by a young woman, her own face covered in camo-makeup and a stocking. Two police moved to intercept – and collapsed as the woman leapt the chair to slam their heads together with a *crack* that drew the attention of the news cams.

Emma groaned.

Leeth wrenched open the back door of a waiting ambulance and threw the man and chair into the back. Thrusting the door shut, she slapped a sheet of paper to the back window and disappeared around the vehicle to slip inside. Moments later, the ambulance started, then the driver's door flew open and a man flew out.

Nina zoomed the drone news camera in on the hand-lettered sign.

'Take him if you want him,' it read.

"I think we will," Eagle said. He thought for a moment. "Nelson: replay for the ambulance plate and take control of it. Father: the Stockton Tunnel?"

Father considered, then nodded and turned to Emma and James, urgently recalled from their missions. "I want you two to intercept in the tunnel. Go. Now.

"Nelson. We'll use the old shell game. Sequester another ambulance or two. Here's what we'll do...."

-

The de-briefing was an unusually heated affair. Mother was livid: not the least, at their failure to recapture Leeth. "But she couldn't have known Nelson could hack in and take control of the ambulance!"

"I agree," Eagle said. "I'm quite sure she merely *guessed*."

"No doubt," said Father, "but I agree with Mother. The girl is wild, and dangerous. She does not obey orders, and knows far too much about us."

"She is also quite clearly unstable," Mother added, "and is now loose. We need to Retire her: she risked exposing the Department. Termination is the only option."

"Really, Mother?" Eagle asked. "Dr Harmon's face was never seen, on camera. Leeth herself did an excellent job of avoiding her own – distorted – image being captured on her way in, and she had added the camouflage makeup before her exit. Thanks to his gag, the Doctor's voice was never heard. Never recorded. Nelson and Little Brother's shell game retrieval of the Doctor in the Stockton tunnel went smoothly, and Leeth herself appears in no database. Except our own."

He held up a finger. "It is also quite clear, is it not, that Leeth did not plan this in advance? The events unfolded immediately after her unauthorized visit this morning to her friend's doctor, at the hospital."

Mother stared at him. "Are you *pleased* by this outcome, Eagle?" she demanded.

Eagle smiled. "Consider: as a first step, she defeated Dojo, in hand-to-hand combat."

All eyes turned to Dojo, as if not quite believing the statement. But instead of anger or humiliation, Paul Kawatsu's face held a curiously-satisfied smile. "Indeed. Our bout was quite... instructive. I look forward to our next encounter."

Off to one side sat the Doctor, bitter and silent, saying nothing.

Eagle continued, ticking off points on his fingers. "She escaped this secure facility. She abducted her uncle and brought him to the hospital, without either of them being surveilled until their emergence there. She successfully orchestrated her friend's healing – which required a ruthless determination that should impress even *you*, Mother. She then set up her uncle's return to us. And finally, her own disappearance. And she killed no one, while doing any of it.

"If this were a mission, with those as the objectives, how would you rate her performance?"

Father looked thoughtful; even impressed.

Mother, on the other hand, looked as if something unpleasant had nested in her mouth. "None of that changes the fact that she disobeyed orders, and is now on the loose."

"A fair point. But I *will* have her back, Mother: she is proving to be everything I hoped for.

"You will work with the Doctor to devise a plan to bring her back to us. A little test: she will no doubt be seeking to avoid us; *you* will be seeking to restore her to us."

Mother looked even more displeased, if that were possible.

Eagle leaned forward. "A contest, Mother: you versus Leeth. She will be attempting to stay off our radar. Let's see if you can do as well at recovering her and *restoring her faith in us*, as you did in driving her away."

Mother stilled.

Eagle stared hard at Mother for long seconds, letting her read the message in his eyes. There was utter silence. Mother said nothing; only her eyes narrowed, fractionally.

But when Eagle next spoke, the lightness had returned to his tone. "Let us see how long it takes you to recover her, shall we? Would you care to wager how long she will remain at large?"

Mother thought. The girl had stolen a mere hundred-cred cashstick, and Nelson could breach any security system in the country. Well, with one exception.

Two days, she decided. "Give me four weeks."

"Agreed. And if you win, I will place Leeth's training directly in your hands."

Eagle smiled.

CHAPTER 50

Free!

Leeth hugged herself, looking out over the broken grounds and tumbled buildings of the Hunters Point Dumps.

Over there, and up into the heights, the Blackberry tribe. Down along the water's edge, the Fisher clan. She turned, slowly, identifying landmarks she'd studied, and the peoples who lived and thrived in the quake-ravaged landscape.

Listening for another drone, she felt the slingshot tucked snugly in the rear pocket of her shorts. Her Power-Shot. Ready to smash any sneaking spy-drones from the sky. That was another good thing about her weapon: there was no shortage of ammo!

Free!

Like Marcie.

She teared up – happy tears – remembering her friend's hesitant, disbelieving joy as she'd moved her legs; swayed weakly on shaky limbs, and then been enfolded by her family.

Yeah, it'd been great – until Marcie's dad had turned to her, joy and horror mixed in equal measures in his face.

Until the fear she'd seen, in Marcie's eyes.

Had Marcie woken early, from her sedation? *Had she been* conscious *when I re-severed her spinal cord?*

The fear in her expression, just for a moment, when she'd taken a step toward her, wanting to join the group hug. Her father had seen it, too, and stepped between them.

She'd slammed her uncle back into the wheelchair and barreled from the room.

"Jane, no, I didn't mean it, come back!"

But Marcie *had* meant it. And she was right, too. It could have all gone so horribly wrong.

But now, she was free.

So the Department thought her a child? Foolish? Well, she'd show them.

She felt a smile spread across her face. She had time, now, for the RedSkulls gang.

She could even collect the whole set.

And of course, The Breaker was out here too, somewhere.

He'd be a worthy opponent.

AFTERWORD

And there we'll once more leave our characters.

I hope you enjoyed this second episode of Leeth's story. If so, you may be pleased to know the sequel, titled *Shadow Hunt*, should be released early 2017. And if you did enjoy this, there *is* one simple thing you could do which may make a real difference for authors like myself: publish a review. I believe that if readers like you tell others about books you enjoyed, each book can earn exactly the success it deserves.

So, to the first 50 people who publish a substantive (say, 50 words or more) and honest review of *Harsh Lessons* – good or bad, I read them all – and the first 20 people to find a previously-undetected error in this book: email me at my address below to receive a free electronic copy of any of my books. I keep email addresses strictly private, and only use them to send the free ebook. As ever, though, I reserve the right to decide if something is a genuine error or my peculiar style.

https://www.goodreads.com/review/new/30845516-harsh-lessons is the link you'd use (after first logging in), on Goodreads:

If you have questions or suggestions, check out my web site https://www.AToeInTheOceanOfBooks.com, where I discuss this series, writing, and self-publishing.

Finally, if you'd like a sneak peek of what's in store for Leeth, I've included the draft of an early chapter of Vol. 3 of The Leeth Dossier: *Shadow Hunt*. (Though it needs re-writing, since Leeth took me by surprise. Again.)

luke.kendall@gmail.com, Jul 2016. @LukeJKendall

SHADOW HUNT, SAMPLE CH.

From the new heights of Bayview, she followed Preacher by the sound of his soft footsteps, with their characteristic twisting upward scuff from his right foot. Down they headed, into the wrecked streets of the Hunters Point Dumps, skirting black puddles of ash-laced rainwater. Far below, a fog rolled in off the Bay, partly cloaking the smashed and charred houses. She kept to the middle of the old main road. Here, the rusted and burnt out wrecks were fewest, although it made her more visible, backlit by the night-glow of New Francisco. To either side, shops and offices stared slack-jawed into the desolation.

The Big One of '44 had thrust this whole region up, making a terraced ruin cut off from the city proper. Still following Preacher, she paused for a moment to look back and up at the first escarpment now massing above her. Six more of the cliffs stretched out below her, a giant's steps. Far in the distance on the bottom-most terrace, a few dotted orange fire-lights glowed.

A fair way down and a little to the left sat what had been her home for the last four weeks. She wasn't sure how she felt about that. It had been a good time. Mostly. She sighed, picturing her abandoned nest, empty now on the edge of the RedSkulls territory. Had anyone found it? Dared to move in?

A long way to the right, south of her, the creepy Candlestick Tower loomed darkly out toward the water of San Francisco Bay. She frowned, wondering why they hadn't renamed the Bay when they renamed the city.

She stretched her arms wide, wishing she could grab the ruins and the darkness, the *reality* of the broken landscape, and just hug it. She fitted, here. It was a place she could belong. She shivered in delight. Far ahead, the sound of Preacher's soft steps faded. *Stop being silly*, she scolded herself. *This isn't a game!* But she couldn't keep the grin off her face as she trotted on again.

By the fourth tier, a rusted wreck told her she'd crossed into the inhabited part of the Dumps. It was the first one she'd seen tonight that'd been reduced to a skeleton. Tires crudely hacked away for shoe-soles, every part that could take an edge or serve a purpose, unscrewed or prised off. A carcass stripped to the bone.

She looked around. There was little rubbish – only the burned, the ruined, or the absolutely worthless. She shook

her head in admiration. The people here didn't waste anything.

Below her, Preacher called a distant greeting, and she
heard his pace speed up. She couldn't make much sense of
the words, but thought they meant 'hello.' She quietly in-
creased her pace, frowning. She hadn't realized Preacher
spoke *Street* so fluently. She stopped, head tilted to one
side, and concentrated. Sounded like she now followed a
group of four people.

Continuing on, she began hearing other movements.
Sometimes far behind, sometimes off to the sides. But just
the regular sounds she'd come to expect – vermin burrow-
ing and foraging, insect buzzes, the night wings of bats,
and birds too, adapted to the light from the nearby city.
And people, locals, nesting down for the night – or traveling to the Fest!

By the time she'd descended to the seventh and final
terrace, she was into the clammy fog, and visibility had
dropped to thirty meters. Off to her right and up on a
higher terrace she heard a distant rumble, growing quickly
to a thunder of internal combustion bikes. They skidded,
careening into sight down an impossibly steep rut of dirt
between tumbled concrete blocks, then along a rusted
metal girder before dropping to the merely rough ground.
Juice, they could ride!

She leapt to the roof of a van, flattening herself out on
the rusted surface, watching the outlandishly dressed figures sweep past. She'd thought she'd hidden, but one
hooked his fist up into the air in greeting as he sped past.

She frowned at the disappearing forms, then hurried to
stay within earshot of Preacher and his friends. Who
headed left now, northwards along the Bay.

Fifteen minutes later, the trickle of people scrambling
through the rubble had swelled to a stream, a carnival
fever lacing the air. It'd got so crowded she'd had stay
within ten meters of Preacher to keep him in earshot, easily close enough for him to see her and win the bet – if
she'd been taller.

From up ahead came the smell of smoke from a massive building where orange red firelight flickered from the
lower floors. Music beat out in waves, with a heavy, driving rhythm, speeding her pulse. Warmth radiated from it,
pushing back the fog.

She paused by a darkened side passage, hearing something large and heavy move, growling. The rules of the Truce only applied to the lit areas. She paused, tempted to investigate. Down there, in the private places of the people and things who lived here, she might find a better test than the 'Fest itself.

But imagining Mother sneering at her for getting distracted, she continued on.

The main passage opened out into a bustling area. On tiptoe, craning her head, she sifted the crowds for 'Dad.' *Funt! He was gone!* But did it matter? They'd arrived, so surely their bet was over, and she'd won? Food stalls to her right; past them, even denser crowds. Further ahead.... Ah! She caught a glimpse of him and his companions. One of them, a tall, weedy guy, was nodding earnestly as Dad said something to him with hand gestures that made her think Preacher was describing some woman. She met his eyes and cocked a finger and thumb – got you! He stopped, then spoke a few words under his hand. The thin guy went to turn toward her but she'd swear Dad stopped him. Like he was protecting her identity. *Huh.* That was more than she'd expected; but all the same, she wasn't going to let her guard down. She'd won their bet, but suddenly doubted the wisdom of it. Would it really be better to have him *pretending* to be her friend?

The weedy guy moved off and she nodded a reluctant 'thanks' to Dad before sinking back down off tiptoe. Dad and his other companions continued on ahead. It wasn't too hard, now, to follow them along the fire-lit walkways, through the lingering wisps of fog. She even started to relax a little.

She'd deliberately stayed on the fringes while she'd been living here. She'd had no idea there were so many types of people all crammed into the area. Did they all live here, or had some come from other places, just for the Fest? It really was like she'd stepped into a bizarre dreamworld. At least half the people were mutants. Trolls, ogres – all victims of the terrible Melt retrovirus, in all their strange combinations. But lots more of the Altered, too, than she'd seen before. There were Furries of all sorts: *Bastean*, Dogmen, Wolven, and others she couldn't name.

People strode or sneaked or staggered around, singly or in groups, dressed in leathers or chromes, kevlar or rags. Smoking, drinking, popping or chipping. Dancing, talking, buying, selling. She passed a juggler of blue-flamed acetylene burners, whose audience half-blocked the passage-way; and a male and female artistically coupling further on. A smaller crowd watched, throwing tokens and suggestions in equal numbers.

Leeth smiled and moved on. Yeah, Dumps people weren't sheep!

The central atrium of the plaza had long been open to the sky, and four bonfires threw flames and sparks up soot-stained walls. A portable phasion furnace mounted higher up poured a more powerful wall of heat into the open central area. It'd probably been pumped by an energy raid sometime recently. A band of Dumpers would've tapped the nearby city's power grid for tonight's event, hauling energy cells back before the citycops or one of Phasion Corp's tactical response groups located them.

She looked around. Streams of people continued to swell the crowds seated on the wide steps surrounding the entertainment dais, food sellers and intoxers squeezing through the area screeching their sales.

On all four sides, six floors rose up, each balcony crammed with people, all overlooking the same courtyard. Here, the jungle beat pounded, strong and insistent. At the edges of the plaza, former shop fronts had been barricaded or just hung with curtains, turning them into homes. The small shapes of almost-feral children darted through the crowd, playing. She watched them disappear, with envious eyes.

Across the way, she spied Pr- *Dad* seated in a good position, arms draped across two young but dirty-looking women. He was laughing and grinning with the people around him. She looked around, deciding her next step.

A puff of smoky wind brought scents of fat, spices, gamy meats, and fish. A roasting beef smell wafted from one of several food stalls pressed against one wall. A lean male turned from the counter, passing her with a grilled gerbil, maybe, jammed on a stick. Biting into the crisp skin, he tore off a succulent hunk. Licking her lips, she forced her way over to join the small crowd.

Smoke from grease-caked stainless steel vats of simmering fatty oil warmed trays of fried insects and spiders racked above. A small girl exchanged a token for a scoop full, dumped rattling into a dirty styrofoam cup. *Eww.* Leeth saw a tab for a cashstick and tapped hers to it, catching the cook's eye and pointing to one of the slowly turning vermin.

A minute later she bit into it, and a smoky, gamy flavor flooded her mouth. She paused, fatty juices running down her chin. *Wow! Better than the Landwave!* She began moving again, teasing flesh from the small bones. A whine and a wet nudge against her bare shin made her look down into the furry muzzle and pleading brown eyes of a rangy, thin dog.

"No way," she told it, trying hard to ignore its hopeful, begging expression. It whined again as she forced her way back into the main press of people.

I wonder what Faith's doing tonight? But Faith *really* wouldn't fit her cover: a weaponized security dog would probably make a lot of people uncomfortable. She smiled though, remembering last night, the two of them racing together through the fir trees, explosions and fire at their back.

She'd have to make sure they got to do more missions like that together.

Meeting the sad eyes of her hopeful four-legged shadow, she felt her shoulders slump. "Fine. You look like you need it more than I do." She tossed the small carcass reluctantly down, where it disappeared in a single snap. She was still licking her fingers clean when a throaty voice spoke at her side.

"Cool skins."

"What?" She looked up, and up, into a high-cheek-boned face half-hidden by a cascade of auburn hair. Dark eyes and red, red lips.

"'Miring your covers," the woman explained, sliding her fingertips under the edges of Leeth's tight-fitting shorts, feeling the soft leather. She looked deeply into Leeth's eyes. "So young. So diff. Where you from, special-girl?"

"Nowhere you'd know," Leeth retorted, forcing down a shiver of attraction. She shoved past. When she looked back, the tall woman was gone.

The crowd had thinned as Leeth moved away from the food stalls.

She was standing there, absorbing it all – the confusion of sounds and smells, shadows and movements – when she felt a man staring at her. For just a moment, she thought his expression looked calculating, but then he smiled in approval and pushed his way closer.

She checked him as he approached. No markings of Dad's gang, so he probably wasn't working against her. Stockily built, his head was just a fuzz of brown hair, except for a long braided rats-tail draped over one shoulder. His clothes looked several steps up from the locals' usual scavenged and pieced-together coverings. His teeth, as he smiled, were filed to points.

They looked chill.

"You're new here, aren't ya?" he said. "I would'a marked ya fore now, else." She thought he was going to ask how she'd come here, but instead he said, "Name's Crack. Show ya round?"

"I guess," she agreed, not letting him see how grateful she felt. This was nothing like the sober and serious Dumps she'd come to know.

"C'mon. Follow close 'hind me. Show ya best roost in house." He forged a way through the still-increasing crowds. Leeth looked around at 'Dad.' He'd just accepted a hunk of food, and looked solidly in place.

She followed Crack's compact, well-muscled body as he cleaved a path up densely packed stairs, barging and forcing his way up several flights and then over to a balcony. He hopped up into what had once been a corner rockery, now a miniature wasteland of rubble, dirt and smashed pottery. Jammed into one corner, a sloping cement slab made an awkward perch for one person right at the edge. Further back, people crowded together on once-decorative boulders. "Yo, Tapper," Crack called to one of these, getting a friendly wave in return. He threaded a path over to another guy, whose feet rested casually on the handrail, preventing him from slipping over the edge.

"Ya, Bandersnatch. Couldn' find Luce, but hey – no Luce's good nooz, I'm thinkin' right nano."

Bandersnatch snorted. "Less she spot ya."

Crack bent forward. "Lissen, compadre. I scan it's really sproutin', down-b'low, but..."

His friend rolled his eyes.

"But c'n ya slot me a big one? Let me'n m' little caro here some room to *move*, you scan?"

At the word *move,* Crack's large hand gripped her buttock and tugged her against him possessively. She wasn't sure how she felt about that.

Bandersnatch screwed up his face, looking from Crack to the girl, and stopped. He eyed her carefully up, then down, then up again. "Y'owe me huge, Crack," he muttered, but got up and left. He thumped Crack's shoulder as he moved past, looking down the gap in the front of Leeth's jacket.

Crack gestured for her to slide into the vacated space, then crammed in alongside as she sat. Leeth leaned out and over, looking down three floors to the plaza below while Crack draped a meaty arm across her shoulders. She leaned into him, enjoying the contact. Bonfires burned fiercely at the four corners of the raised dais, the music now settled into something raw, unpolished, but compelling.

"Hard or soft?"

"What?" She turned to face Crack.

"You want hard chem, or just alc?"

"No drugs *or* alcohol."

Her companion laughed, rolling his eyes to heaven. "Flick, chick, loosen up."

She just stared back at him.

He sighed. "I'll get you a sweetwater'n buzz, then. Straight enough?"

She chewed her bottom lip. Her eyes narrowed. "What is-"

More rolling of eyes. "Kaff, chick. Kaff'n sacch. Coffee. Sweet, like you," he carefully enunciated. "Or it zone you out you'll be eyes till late?"

"Uh...."

The last eyes-roll did it.

"Sure. Thanks."

Crack bellowed, making her wince. "Toxer!"

Across the long-ago cafeteria, an arm raised, waving acknowledgment. Crack turned to her. "Where ya from?"

"Here in New Francisco. I made myself a little nest a bit north of here; just been scoping things out, you know? But I haven't been on the streets long-"

He snorted. "Knew that."

"I left Mother and Father. Proving I can make it on my own."

He stared at her. "You sayin' ya *chose* ta come here?"

She lifted her chin. "Yeah. Why shouldn't I?"

At that moment, the toxer arrived, bottles, canisters, tubing and dispenser nozzles looping and bulging under his coat. He was an ogre, with the usual leathery, hairless skin and rough features, and large frame. *I wonder if Teef came, tonight?* She'd have to keep an eye open for him and Barney – it'd be nice to have friends watching her fight.

"What'll it be, frens?" the toxer rumbled.

"Black Velvet, 'n a sugarwater Buzz. 'N two cups."

"Five ten."

Crack held out another cashstick, set the amount, and the man tapped his own against it. He reached under his long jacket, passing them each a thin and crude plastic cup. He dropped pellets – saccharin, he explained, at her sharp look – into a metal shaker, then a couple of black cubes. Tugging down a tube, he pressed a faucet at the end. "Agua," he said, as the water flowed. He capped it, shook it, and with a final disdainful air poured it into the cup Leeth held. Crack's drink came from a bottle; black as ink.

Leeth sniffed her cup suspiciously as the toxer strode off. At least it *smelled* like coffee. She looked at her companion, who slitted his eyes in pleasure as he eased down a single mouthful of his brew.

"I want you to drink half of mine," she demanded.

Crack laughed. "Ah, caro! Wisdom?" He wrinkled his nose, but drank deeply from her cup. Swallowing, he made a face, then handed it back.

"Safe now!" he said, then started laughing.

Leeth blushed, and took a drink. It was bitter and sweet. But okay. Definitely coffee.

"So, tell me about all this," she demanded, putting her thin cup down carefully.

Crack beamed, leaned back further against their boulder, sweeping one arm in an expansive arc. "This-" he began, then abruptly stopped. Slowly, his head turned further to the right, the arrogant smile sliding from his face as all his attention seemed to focus there. Leeth craned around, and saw the tall red-headed woman who'd spoken to her earlier. Who just stood there, watching.

"Crack. Whose seat, dealer?" the woman called.

His voice was shaky when he spoke. "*Tash?*" He shuddered. "Yours. All yours. C'mon bim, let's rat off." He urged Leeth up, grabbing her arm and sliding off the rock then down onto the ground.

Tash stepped forward. She raised one hand and the man stopped dead, flinching away from it.

Leeth scowled at Crack. "What's the matter with you? Why are you running away? We were here first."

Tash raised an eyebrow. "Well, Crack?"

"*C'mon*, ya little sluk!" he swore, pulling at Leeth.

She tugged her arm out of his grasp.

"You scan what she *is*?" He seemed frantic.

"Oh? What am I, Crack?"

Tash's tone had been mild, but Crack backtracked, avoiding the question as he focused on the girl, grabbing at her. "Come *on!*"

She fended off his grasp again. "*I'm* not scared."

"Well, frag you, halfdeck!" he said – and ran off!

Leeth looked around. No one else seemed to have reacted – though they wouldn't have been able to hear much of the exchange over the sound of the music. She looked back at the woman, who studied her with a lazy smile. Predatory.

Leeth bristled. "So what are you? Why was Crack so scared?"

"I... watch the little people. The kinda people Crack slices." She smiled, wolfishly. "And it's been awhile since I been here. Seein' me must've 'freshed some old tales."

"You slice guys like Crack?"

Tash just smiled.

Leeth sized her up. Tash looked strong, capable, and moved with an easy grace. "Well, since you just scared off Crack, if you want to *share* my seat you have to tell me about all this, first," she demanded.

Tash's elegant eyebrow arched again. "That'll take awhile."

Leeth considered, but finally nodded. The woman looked like she might be... interesting.